BELLARION

Other books by Rafael Sabatini in
COMMON READER EDITIONS:

Captain Blood
Scaramouche

BELLARION
The Fortunate

A Romance

by
RAFAEL SABATINI

A COMMON READER EDITION
The Akadine Press

Bellarion the Fortunate

A COMMON READER EDITION published 2000
by The Akadine Press, Inc., by arrangement with Houghton Mifflin Company.

A COMMON READER EDITION and fountain colophon are trademarks
of The Akadine Press, Inc.

ISBN 1-58579-002-8

10 9 8 7 6 5 4 3 2 1

CONTENTS

BOOK I

I. THE THRESHOLD	3
II. THE GREY FRIAR	16
III. THE DOOR AJAR	29
IV. SANCTUARY	44
V. THE PRINCESS	55
VI. THE WINDS OF FATE	68
VII. SERVICE	81
VIII. STALEMATE	94
IX. THE MARQUIS THEODORE	102
X. THE WARNING	109
XI. UNDER SUSPICION	120
XII. COUNT SPIGNO	129
XIII. THE TRIAL	137
XIV. EVASION	150

BOOK II

I. THE MIRACLE OF THE DOGS	159
II. FACINO CANE	175
III. THE COUNTESS OF BIANDRATE	188
IV. THE CHAMPION	200
V. THE COMMUNE OF MILAN	210
VI. THE FRUITLESS WOOING	222
VII. MANŒUVRES	231

Contents

VIII. The Battle of Travo   247

IX. De Mortuis   256

X. The Knight Bellarion   265

XI. The Siege of Alessandria   280

XII. Visconti Faith   296

XIII. The Victuallers   302

XIV. The Muleteer   313

XV. The Camisade   325

XVI. Severance   332

XVII. The Return   345

XVIII. The Hostage   353

BOOK III

I. The Lord Bellarion   371

II. The Battle of Novi   383

III. Facino's Return   396

IV. The Count of Pavia   405

V. Justice   418

VI. The Inheritance   436

VII. Prince of Valsassina   448

VIII. Carmagnola's Bridges   463

IX. Vercelli   478

X. The Arrest   488

XI. The Pledge   502

XII. Carmagnola's Duty   514

XIII. The Occupation of Casale   529

XIV. The Vanquished   538

XV. The Last Fight   547

Book I

Chapter I

The Threshold

"Half god, half beast," the Princess Valeria once described him, without suspecting that the phrase describes not merely Bellarion, but Man.

Aware of this, the anonymous chronicler who has preserved it for us goes on to comment that the Princess said at once too much and too little. He makes phrases in his turn—which I will spare you—and seeks to prove, that, if the moieties of divinity and beastliness are equally balanced in a man, that man will be neither good nor bad. Then he passes on to show us a certain poor swineherd, who rose to ultimate eminence, in whom the godly part so far predominated that naught else was humanly discernible, and a great prince—of whom more will be heard in the course of this narrative—who was just as the beasts that perish, without any spark of divinity to exalt him. These are the

extremes. For each of the dozen or so intermediate stages which he discerns, our chronicler has a portrait out of history, of which his learning appears to be considerable.

From this, from his general manner, from the fact that most of his illustrations are supplied by Florentine sources, and from the austerely elegant Tuscan language in which he writes, a fairly definite conclusion is possible on the score of his identity. It is more than probable that this study of Bellarion the Fortunate (Bellarione Fortunato) belongs to that series of historical portraits from the pen of Niccolò Macchiavelli, of which *The Life of Castruccio Castracane* is perhaps the most widely known. Research, however, fails to discover the source from which he draws. Whilst many of his facts agree completely with those contained in the voluminous, monkish *Vita et Gesta Bellarionis*, left us by Fra Serafino of Imola, whoever he may have been, yet discrepancies are frequent and irreconcilable.

Thus, at the very outset, on the score of his name, Macchiavelli (to cling to my assumption) tells us that he was called Bellarion not merely because he was a man of war, but because he was the very child of War, born as it were out of the very womb of conflict—*e di guerra propriamente partorito.* The use of this metaphor reveals a full acquaintance with the tale of the child's being plucked from the midst of strife and alarums. But Fra Serafino's account of the name is the only one that fits into the known facts. That this name should have been so descriptive of Bellarion's afterlife merely provides one of those curious instances of homonymy in which history abounds.

Continuing his comments upon the Princess Valeria's phrase, Macchiavelli states that Bellarion's is not a nature thus to be packed

into a sentence. Because of his perception of this fact, he wrote his biographical sketch. Because of my perception of it, I have embarked upon this fuller narrative.

I choose to begin at a point where Bellarion himself may be said to make a certain beginning. I select the moment when he is to be seen standing upon the threshold of the secular world, known to him until that moment only from the writings of other men, yet better known to him thus than it is to many who have lived a lifetime among their fellows. After all, to view a scene from a distance is to enjoy advantages of perspective denied to the actors in that scene.

Bellarion's reading had been prodigious. There was no branch of learning—from the Theological Fathers to Vegetius Hyginus on *The Art of War*—to which he had not addressed his eager spirit. And his exhaustion of all immediately available material for study was one of the causes of his going forth from the peace of the convent of which he was a nursling, in quest of deeper wells of learning, to slake his hot intellectual thirst. Another cause was a certain heretical doctrine of which it was hoped that further study would cure him; a doctrine so subversive of theological teaching that a hundred years later it must have made him closely acquainted with the operations of the Holy Office and probably—in Spain certainly—have brought him to the fire. This abominable heresy, fruit of much brooding, was that in the world there is not, nor can be, such a thing as sin. And it was in vain that the Abbot, who loved him very dearly, sought by argument to convert him.

"It is your innocence that speaks. Alas, my child, in the world, from which hitherto you have been mercifully sheltered, you will find that sin is not only real but terribly abundant."

Bellarion answered with a syllogism, the logical formula to which he had reduced his doctrine. He presented it in the Socratic manner of inquiry, which was the method of argument he ever preferred.

"Are not all things in the world from God? Is not God the fount of all goodness? Can, therefore, any created thing be other than good?"

"And the devil, then?" quoth the Abbot.

Bellarion smiled, a singularly sweet smile that had power to draw men's love and lead them into agreement with him.

"Is it not possible that those who invented the devil may have studied divinity in Persia, where the creed obtains that powers of light and darkness, Ormuzd and Ahriman, strive perpetually for mastery of the world? Surely, otherwise, they would have remembered that if the devil exists, God must have created him, which in itself is blasphemy, for God can create no evil."

Aghast, the Abbot descended at a stride from the theological to the practical.

"Is it not evil to steal, to kill, to commit adultery?"

"Ah, yes. But these are evils between men, disruptive of society, and therefore to be suppressed lest man become as the beasts. But that is all."

"All? All!" The Abbot's deep-set eyes surveyed the youth with sorrow. "My son, the devil lends you a false subtlety to destroy your soul."

And gently, now, that benign and fatherly man preached him a sermon of the faith. It was followed by others in the days that ensued. But to all the weapons of his saintly rhetoric Bellarion continued to oppose the impenetrable shield of that syllogism of his, which the Abbot knew at heart to be fallacious, yet whose fallacy he laboured in vain to expose. But when the good man began to fear lest this heresy should come to trouble and corrupt the peace and faith of his convent, he consented to speed its author to Pavia and to those further studies which he hoped would cure him of his heretical pravity. And that is how, on a day of August of the year of grace 1407, Bellarion departed from the convent of Our Lady of Grace of Cigliano.

He went on foot. He was to be dependent for food and shelter mainly upon the charity of the religious houses that lay on his way to Pavia, and as a passport to these he bore in his scrip a letter from the Abbot of the Grazie. Beside it lay a purse, containing for emergencies five ducats, a princely sum not only in his own eyes, but in those of the Abbot who at parting had bestowed it upon him. The tale of his worldly possessions is completed by the suit of coarse green cloth he wore and the knife at his girdle, which was to serve all purposes from the carving of his meat to affording him a means of defence from predatory beasts and men. To fortify him spiritually in his adventurous pilgrimage through Lombardy he had the Abbot's blessing and a memory of the fond tears in the eyes of that old man who had reared him from the age of six. At the last the Abbot had again reminded him of the peace of the convent and of the strife and unhappiness that distract the world.

"Pax multa in cella, foris autem plurima bella."

The mischief began—and you may account it symbolical—by his losing his way. This happened a mile or two beyond the township of Livorno. Because the peace of the riverside allured a

mind that for seventeen years had been schooled in peace, because the emerald meadows promised to be soft and yielding to his feet, he left the dusty highway for the grassy banks of Po. Beside its broad waters winding here about the shallow, pleasant hills of Montferrat, Bellarion trudged, staff in hand, the green hood of his cape thrown back, the long liripipe trailing like a tail behind him, a tall, lithe stripling of obvious vigour, olive-skinned, black-haired, and with dark eyes that surveyed the world bold and fearlessly.

The day was hot. The air was laden with the heavy perfumes of late summer, and the river swollen and clouded by the melting snows on distant Monte Rosa.

He wandered on, lost in daydreams, until the sunlight passed with the sinking of the sun behind the wooded heights across the river and a breeze came whispering through the trees on his own bank. He checked, his dark eyes alert, a frown of thought rumpling the fair smoothness of his lofty brow. He looked about, became aware of a deep forest on his left, bethought him of the road, remembered where the sun had set, and realised hence that for some time he had been travelling south, and consequently in the wrong direction. In following the allurements offered to his senses he had gone astray. He made some homely philosophy upon that, to his infinite satisfaction, for he loved parallels and antitheses and all such intellectual toys. For the rest, there was about him no doubt or hesitation. He computed, from the time he had taken and the pace at which he had come, the extent to which he had wandered from the road. It must run too far beyond this forest to leave him any hope of lying that night, as he had intended, with the Augustinian fathers at their house on the

Sesia, on the frontiers of the State of Milan.

Save for the hunger that beset him, he was undismayed. And what after all is a little hunger to one schooled to the most rigid lenten fasts in season?

He entered the wood, and resolutely went forward in the direction in which he knew the road to lie. For a half-mile or more he penetrated by a path growing less visible at every step, until darkness and the forest swallowed him. To go on would certainly be to lose himself completely in this maze. Better far to lie down and sleep where he was, and wait for the morning sun to give him his orientation.

So he spread his cloak upon the ground, and this proving no harder as a couch than the pallet to which he was accustomed, he slept soundly and peacefully.

When he awakened he found the sunlight in the forest and something else of almost more immediate interest; a man in the grey habit of a minor friar. This man, tall and lean, was standing beside him, yet half turned from him in a curious attitude of arrested movement, almost as if the abrupt suddenness with which Bellarion had sat up—a single heartbeat after his eyes had opened—had checked his intention to depart.

Thus an instant, then the friar was facing him again, his hands folded within the loose sleeves of his robe, a smile distending his countenance. He uttered a benedictory greeting.

"*Pax tecum.*"

"*Et tecum, frater, pax,*" was Bellarion's mechanical answer, what time he studied this stranger's villainous, patibulary countenance, marking the animal looseness of mouth, and the craft peering from the little eyes that were as black beads thrust into a face of clay. A closer scrutiny softened his judgment. The man's face was disfigured; ridged, scarred, and pitted from the smallpox. These scars had contracted the skin about the eyes, thus altering their expression, and to the ravages of the disease was also due the sickly pallor overspreading cheek and brow.

Considering this and the habit which the man wore—a habit which Bellarion had no cause to associate with anything that was not sweet and good—he disposed himself to make amends for the hastiness of his first assumptions.

"*Benedictus sis,*" he murmured, and with that abandoned Latin for the vulgar tongue. "I bless the Providence that sends you to a poor traveller who has lost his way."

The friar laughed aloud at that, and the lingering apprehension left his eyes, which thus relieved grew pleasanter to look upon.

"Lord! Lord! And I like a fool and coward, having almost trod upon you, was for creeping off in haste, supposing you a sleeping robber. This forest is a very sanctuary of thieves. They infest it, thick as rabbits in a warren."

"Why, then, do you adventure in it?"

"Why? Ohé! And what shall they steal from a poor friar-mendicant? My beads? My girdle?" He laughed again. A humorous fellow, clearly, taking a proper saintly joy in his indigent condition. "No, no, my brother. I have no cause to go in fear of thieves."

"Yet supposing me a thief, you were in fear of me?"

The man's smile froze. This stripling's simple logic was disconcerting.

"I feared," he said at last, slowly and solemnly, "your fear of me. A hideous passion, fear, in man or beast. It makes men murderers at times. Had you been the robber I supposed you, and, waking suddenly, found me beside you, you might have suspected some intent to harm you. It is easily guessed what would have followed then."

Bellarion nodded thoughtfully. No explanation could have been more complete. The man was not only virtuous, but wise.

"Whither do you journey, brother?"

"To Pavia," Bellarion answered him, "by way of Santa Tenda."

"Santa Tenda! Why, that is my way too; at least as far as the Augustinian Monastery on the Sesia. Wait here, my son, and we will go together. It is good to have a comrade on a journey. Wait but some few moments, to give me time to bathe, which is the purpose for which I came. I will not keep you long."

He went striding off through the grass. Bellarion called after him:

"Where do you bathe?"

Over his shoulder the friar answered him: "There is a rivulet down yonder. But a little way. Do not stray from that spot, so that I may find you again, my son."

Bellarion thought the form of address an odd one. A minorite is brother, not father, to all humanity. But it was no suspicion based on this that brought him to his feet. He was a youth of cleanly habits, and if there was water at hand, he too would profit by it. So he rose, picked up his cloak, and went off in the wake of the swiftly moving friar.

When, presently, he overtook him, Bellarion made him a present of a proverb.

"Who goes slowly, goes soundly."

"But never gets there," was the slightly breathless answer. "And it's still some way to the water."

"Some way? But you said . . ."

"Aye, aye. I was mistaken. One place is like another in this labyrinth. I am none so sure that I am not as lost as you are."

It must have been so, for they trudged a full mile before they came to a brook that flowed westward towards the river. It lay in a dell amid mossy boulders and spreading fronds of ferns all dappled now with the golden light that came splashing through the trees. They found a pool of moderate dimensions in a bowl of grey stone fashioned by the ceaseless sculpture of the water. It was too shallow to afford a bath. But the friar's ablutionary dispositions scarce seemed to demand so much. He rinsed face and hands perfunctorily, whilst Bellarion stripped to the waist, and displaying a white torso of much beauty and more vigour, did what was possible in that cramped space.

After that the friar produced from one of the sack-like pockets of his habit an enormous piece of sausage and a loaf of rye bread.

To Bellarion who had gone supperless to bed this was as the sight of manna in the desert.

"Little brother!" he cooed in sheer delight. "Little brother!"

"Aye, aye. We have our uses, we little brothers of Saint Francis." The minorite sliced the sausage in two equal halves. "We know how to provide ourselves upon a journey."

They fell to eating, and with the stilling of his hunger Bellarion experienced an increasing kindliness to this Good Samaritan. At the friar's suggestion that they should be moving so as to cover the greater part of the road to Casale before the noontide heat, Bellarion stood up, brushing the crumbs from his lap. In doing so his hand came in contact with the scrip that dangled from his girdle.

"Saints of God!" he ejaculated, as he tightened his clutch upon that bag of green cloth.

The beady eyes of the minorite were upon him, and there was blank inquiry in that ashen, corrugated face.

"What is it, brother?"

Bellarion's fingers groped within the bag a moment, then turned it inside out, to reveal its utter emptiness. He showed his companion a face which blended suspicion with dismay.

"I have been robbed!" he said.

"Robbed?" the other echoed, then smiled a pitying concern. "My surprise is less than yours, my son. Did I not say these woods are infested by thieves and robbers? Had you slept less soundly you might have been robbed of life as well. Render thanks to God, whose grace is discernible even in misfortune. For no evil befalls us that will not serve to show how much greater that evil might have been. Take that for comfort ever in adversity, my child."

"Aye, aye!" Bellarion displayed ill-humour, whilst his eyes abated nothing of their suspicious glance. "It is easy to make philosophy upon the woes of others."

"Child, child! What is your woe? What is the full sum of it? What have you lost, when all is said?"

"Five ducats and a letter." Bellarion flung the answer fiercely.

"Five ducats!" The friar spread his hands in pious remonstrance. "And will you blaspheme God for five ducats?"

"Blaspheme?"

"Is not your furious frame of mind a blasphemy, your anger at your loss where there should be a devout thankfulness for all that you retain? And you should be thankful, too, for the Providence that guided my steps towards you in the hour of your need."

"I should be thankful for that?" Bellarion stressed the question with mistrust.

The friar's countenance changed. A gentle melancholy invested it.

"I read your thoughts, child, and they harbour suspicion of me. Of me!" he smiled. "Why, what a madness! Should I turn thief? Should I imperil my immortal soul for five paltry ducats? Do you not know that we little brothers of Saint Francis live as the birds of the air, without thought for material things, our trust entirely in God's providence? What should I do with five ducats, or five hundred? Without a single minted coin, with no more than my gown and my staff I might journey from here to Jerusalem, living upon the alms that never fail us. But assurances are not enough for minds poisoned by suspicion." He flung wide his arms, and stood cruciform before the youth. "Come, child, make search upon me for your ducats, and so assure yourself. Come!"

Bellarion flushed, and lowered his head in shame.

"There . . . there is not the need," he answered lamely. "The gown you wear is a full assurance. You could not be what you are and yet the thing that for a moment I . . ." He broke off. "I beg that you'll forgive my unworthiness, my brother."

Slowly the friar lowered his arms. His eyes were smiling again.

"I will be merciful by not insisting." He laid a hand, lean and long in the fingers as an eagle's claw upon the young man's shoulder. "Think no more of your loss. I am here to repair it. Together we will journey. The habit of Saint Francis is wide enough to cover both of us, and you shall not want for anything until you reach Pavia."

Bellarion looked at him in gratitude. "It was Providence, indeed, that sent you."

"Did I not say so? And now you see it for yourself. *Benedicamus Domino.*"

To which Bellarion sincerely made the prescribed answer: "*Deo gratias!*"

Chapter II

The Grey Friar

They made their way towards the road, not directly, but by a course with which Fra Sulpizio—as the friar announced himself named—seemed singularly well acquainted. It led transversely across the forest. And as they went, Fra Sulpizio plied Bellarion with questions.

"There was a letter, you said, that was stolen with your gold?"

"Aye," Bellarion's tone was bitter. "A letter worth many times five ducats."

"Worth many times. . . ? A letter?" The incredulity on the friar's face was ludicrous. "Why, what manner of letter was that?"

Bellarion, who knew the contents by heart, recited them word for word.

Fra Sulpizio scratched his head in perplexity. "I have Latin enough for my office; but not for this," he confessed, and finding

Bellarion's searching glance upon him, he softened his voice to add, truly enough: "We little brothers of Saint Francis are not famed for learning. Learning disturbs humility."

Bellarion sighed. "So I know to my cost," said he, and thereafter translated the lost letter: "This is our dearly beloved son Bellarion, a nutritus of this house, who goes hence to Pavia to increase his knowledge of the humanities. We commend him first to God and then to the houses of our own and other brethren orders for shelter and assistance on his journey, invoking upon all who may befriend him the blessing of Our Lord."

The friar nodded his understanding. "It might have been a grievous loss, indeed. But as it is, I will do the office of your letter whilst I am with you, and when we part I will see you armed with the like from the Prior of the Augustinians on the Sesia. He will do this at my word."

The young man thanked him with a fervour dictated by shame of certain unworthy suspicions which had recurred. Thereafter they trudged on a while in silence, broken by the friar at last.

"And is your name Belisario, then? An odd name, that!"

"Not Belisario. Bellario, or rather, Bellarione."

"Bellarione? Why, it is even less Christian than the other. Where got you such a name?"

"Not at the font, you may be sure. There I was christened Ilario, after the good Saint Hilary, who is still my patron saint."

"Then why. . .?"

"There's a story to it; my story," Bellarion answered him, and upon slight encouragement proceeded to relate it.

He was born, he told the friar, as nearly as he could guess, some six years after the outbreak of the Great Schism, that is to say, somewhere about the year 1384, in a village of whose name, like that of his own family, he had no knowledge.

"Of my father and my mother," he continued, "I can evoke no mental picture. Of my father my only positive knowledge is that he existed. Of my mother I know that she was a termagant of whom the family, my father included, stood in awe. Amongst my earliest impressions is the sense of fear that invaded us at the sound of her scolding voice. It was querulous and strident; and I can hear it to this day harshly raised to call my sister. Leocadia was that sister's name, the only name of all my family that I remember, and this because I must often have heard it called in that dread voice. There were several of us. I have one vivid memory of perhaps a half-dozen tumbling urchins, playing at some game in a bare chill room, that was yellow washed, lighted by an unglazed window beyond which the rain was streaming down upon a narrow dismal street. There was a clang of metal in the air, as if armourers were at work in the neighbourhood. And we were in the charge, I remember, of that same Leocadia, who must have been the eldest of us. I have an impression, vague and misty, of a lanky girl whose lean bare legs showed through a rent in her tattered petticoat. Faintly I discern a thin, pinched face set in a mane of untidy yellow hair, and then I hear a heavy step and the creak of a stair and a shrill, discordant voice calling 'Leocadia!' and then a scuttle amongst us to shelter from some unremembered peril.

"Of my family, that is all that I can tell you, brother. You'll agree, perhaps, that since my memory can hold so little it is a pity that it should hold so much. But for these slight impressions of my infancy I might weave a pleasant romance about it, conceive

18

myself born in a palace and heir to an illustrious name.

"That these memories of mine concern the year 1389 or 1390 I know from what the Abbot tells me, and also from later studies and deductions of my own. As you may know, there was at that time a bitter war being waged hereabouts between Ghibelline Montferrat and Guelphic Morea. It may have ravaged these very lands by which we travel now. One evening at the hour of dusk a foraging troop of Montferrat horse swept into my native place. There was pillage and brutality of every kind, as you can imagine. There was terror and confusion in every household, no doubt, and even in our own, although Heaven knows we had little cause to stand in dread of pillage. I remember that as night descended we huddled in the dark listening to the sounds of violence in the distance, coming from what I now imagine to have been the more opulent quarter of that township. I can hear my mother's heavy breathing. For once she inspired no terror in us, being herself stricken with terror and cowed into silence. But this greater terror was upon us all, a sense of impending evil, of some horror advancing presently to overwhelm us. There were snivelling, whimpering sounds in the gloom about me from Leocadia and the other children. It is odd, how things heard have remained stamped upon my mind so much more vividly than things seen, which usually are more easily remembered. But from that moment my memory begins to grow clear and consecutive, perhaps from the sudden sharpening of my wits by this crisis.

"It was probably the instinct to withdraw myself beyond the reach of that approaching evil which drew me furtively from the room. I remember groping my way in the dark down a steep crazy staircase, and tumbling down three stone steps at the door of that hovel into the mud of the street.

"I picked myself up, bruised and covered with filth. At another time this might have set me howling. Just then my mind was filled with graver concerns. In the open the noises were more distinct. I could hear shouts, and once a piercing scream that made my young blood run cold. Away on my right there was a red glow in the sky, and associating it with the evil that was to be escaped, I turned down the alley and made off, whimpering as I ran. Soon there was an end to the houses, and I was out of their shadow in the light of a rising moon on a road that led away through the open country into eternity as it must have seemed to me. From this I have since argued either that the township had neither gates nor walls, or else that the mean quarter we inhabited was outside and beyond them.

"I cannot have been above five years of age, and I must have been singularly sturdy, for my little legs bore me several miles that night, driven by unreasoning fear. At last I must have sunk down exhausted by the roadside, and there fallen asleep, for my next memory is of my awakening. It was broad daylight, and I was in the grasp of a big, bearded man who from his cap to his spurs was all steel and leather. Beside him stood the great bay horse from which he had just leaped, and behind him, filling the road in a staring, grinning, noisy cluster, was ranged a troop of fully fifty men with lances reared above them.

"He soothed my terrors with a voice incredibly gentle in one so big and fierce, and asked me who I was and whence I came, questions to which I could return no proper answers. To increase my confidence, perhaps, he gave me food, some fruit and bread—such bread as I had never tasted.

" 'We cannot leave you here, baby,' he said. 'And since you don't know where you belong, I will take charge of you.'

"I no longer feared him or those with him. What cause had I to fear them? This man had stroked and petted and fed me. He had used me more kindly than I could remember ever to have been used before. So when presently I was perched in front of him on the withers of his great horse, I knew no sense but one of entire satisfaction.

"Later that day we came to a town, whose inhabitants regarded us in cringing awe. But, perhaps, because its numbers were small, the troop bore itself with circumspection, careful to give no provocation.

"The man-at-arms who had befriended me kept me in his train for a month or more. Then, the exigencies of the campaign against Morea demanding it, he placed me with the Augustinian fathers at the Grazie near Cigliano. They cared for me as if I had been a prince's child instead of a stray waif picked up by the roadside. Thereafter at intervals he would come to visit me, and these visits, although the intervals between them grew ever longer, continued for some three or four years, after which we never saw or heard of him again. Either he died or else lost interest in the child he had saved and protected. Thereafter the Augustinians were my only friends. They reared me, and educated me, hoping that I would one day enter the order. They made endeavours to trace my birthplace and my family. But without success. And that," he ended, "is all my story."

"Ah, not quite all," the friar reminded him. "There is this matter of your name."

"Ah, yes. On that first day when I rode with my man-at-arms

we went to a tavern in the town I mentioned, and there he delivered me into the hands of the taverner's wife, to wash and clothe me. It was an odd fancy in such a man, as I now realise; but I am persuaded that whilst he rode that morning with my little body resting in the crook of his great arm, he conceived the notion to adopt me for his own. Men are like that, their natures made up of contradictory elements; and a rough, even brutal, soldier of fortune, not normally pitiful, may freakishly be moved to pity by the sight and touch of a poor waif astray by the roadside." And on that he fell to musing.

"But the name?" the friar reminded him again.

He laughed. "Why, when the taverner's wife set me before him, scoured clean and dressed in a comely suit of green cloth, not unlike the suit I am wearing now—for I have affected green ever since in memory of him and of the first fair raiment I ever wore, which was of his providing—it may be that I presented a comely appearance. He stared at me in sheer surprise. I can see him now, seated on a three-legged stool in a patch of sunlight that came through the blurred glass of the window, one hand on the knee of his booted leg, the other stroking his crisp black beard, his grey eyes conning me with an increasing kindliness.

" 'Come hither, boy,' he bade me, and held out his hand.

"I went without fear or hesitation. He rested me against his knee, and set a hand upon my head still tingling from its recent combing.

" 'What did you tell me is your name?' he asked.

" 'Ilario,' I answered him.

"He stared a moment, then a smile half scornful broke upon his rugged, weather-beaten face. 'Ilario, thou? With that solemn

countenance and those big melancholy eyes?' He ran on in words which I remember, though I barely caught their meaning then. 'Was there ever an Ilario less hilarious? There's no hilarity about you, child, nor ever has been, I should judge. Ilario! Faugh! Bellario, rather, with such a face. Is he not a lovely lad?' He turned me about for the approval of the taverner's wife, who stood behind me, and she, poor woman, made haste to agree, with fawning smiles, as she would have agreed with anything uttered by this dread man who must be conciliated. 'Bellario!' he repeated, savouring the word of his invention with an inventor's pride. 'That were a better name for him, indeed. And by the Host, Bellario he shall be renamed. Do you hear me, boy? Henceforth you are Bellario.' "

Thus, he explained, the name so lightly bestowed became his own; and later because of his rapid and rather excessive growth, the monks at the Grazie fell into the habit of calling him Bellarione, or big Bellario.

It still wanted an hour or so to noon when the twain emerged from the forest onto the open road. A little way along this they came upon a homestead set amid rice-fields, now denuded, and vineyards where men and women were at the labours of the vintage, singing as they harvested the grape. And here Bellarion had an instance of how the little brothers of Saint Francis receive alms without being so much as put to the trouble of asking for them. For at sight of the friar's grey frock, one of the labourers, who presently announced himself the master of the homestead, came hurrying to bid them stay and rest and join the household at dinner, of which the hour was at hand.

They sat down to rough, abundant fare in the roomy kitchen,

amid the members of that considerable family, sharing with them the benches set against a trestle table of well-scoured deal.

There was a cereal porridge, spread, like mortar, upon a board into which each dipped a wooden spoon, and, after this, came strips of roast kid with boiled figs and bread moist and solid as cheese. To wash all down there was a rough red wine, sharp on the palate, but wholesome and cool from the cellar, of which the friar drank over-copiously.

They numbered a round dozen at table; the old peasant and his wife, a nephew and seven children of full age, three of whom were young women, red-lipped, dark-skinned, deep-bosomed wenches with lusty brown arms and bright eyes which were over-busy about Bellarion for his ease.

Once, across the board, he caught the eye of the friar, and about these and the fellow's loose lips there played a smile of sly and unpleasant amusement at Bellarion's uneasiness under these feminine attentions. Later, when Fra Sulpizio's excessive consumption of wine had brought a flush to the cheekbones of that pallid face and set a glitter in the beady eyes, Bellarion caught him pondering the girls with such a wolfish leer that all his first instincts against the man were roused again, and not the thought of his office or the contemplation of his habit could efface them.

After dinner the friar must rest awhile, and Bellarion beguiled the time of waiting, which was also the time of siesta in which all labour is suspended, by wandering in the vineyard whither the peasant's daughters led him, and where they engaged him in chatter that he found monstrous tedious and silly.

Yet but for this and the fact that the vineyard bordered on the road, Bellarion's association with the friar would have ended there, and all his subsequent history must have been different indeed. The minorite's siesta was shorter than might have been expected, and when something less than an hour later he resumed his journey, so confused was he by sleep and wine that he appeared to have forgotten his companion quite. Had not Bellarion seen him striding away along the road to Casale, it is certain the young man would have been left behind.

Nor did he manifest much satisfaction when Bellarion came running after him. The scowl on his face argued displeasure. But his excuses and his explanations that he was but half awake permitted the assumption that it was himself with whom he was displeased.

He moved briskly now, swinging his long legs in great strides, and casting ever and anon a glance behind him.

Bellarion offered a remonstrance at the pace, a reminder that Casale was but some two leagues away and they had the afternoon in which to reach it.

"If I go too fast for you, you may follow at your leisure," the friar grumbled.

It was for an instant in Bellarion's mind to take him at his word, then, partly perversity, and partly a suspicion which he strove in vain to stifle, overcame his natural pride.

"No, no, little brother. I'll accommodate my pace to yours, as befits."

A grunt was the only answer; nor, indeed, although Bellarion made several attempts to resume conversation, was there much said between them thereafter as they trudged on in the heat of the afternoon along the road that crosses the fertile plains from Trino to Casale.

They did not, however, proceed very far on foot. For, being presently overtaken by a string of six or seven mules with capacious panniers slung on either flank, the leading beast bestridden by the muleteer, Bellarion received another demonstration of how a little brother of Saint Francis may travel upon charity. As the column advanced upon them at a brisk trot, Fra Sulpizio stepped to the middle of the road, with arms held wide as if to offer a barrier.

The muleteer, a brawny, black-bearded fellow, drew rein within a yard of him.

"What now, little brother? How can I serve you?"

"The blessing of God upon you, brother! Will you earn it by a little charity besought in the name of the Blessed Francis? If your beasts are not overladen, will you suffer them to carry a poor footsore Franciscan and this gentle lad into Casale?"

The muleteer swung one cross-gartered leg over to the side of the other and slipped to the ground, that he might assist them to mount, each on one of the more lightly laden mules. Thereupon, having begged and received Fra Sulpizio's blessing, he climbed back into his own saddle and they were off at a sharp trot.

To Bellarion the experience of a saddle, or of what did duty for a saddle, was as novel as it was painful, and so kept his thoughts most fully engaged. It was his first essay in equitation, and the speed they made shook and tossed and bruised him until there was not a bone or muscle in his body that did not ache. His humour, too, was a little bruised by the hilarity which his efforts to maintain his seat excited in his two companions.

Thankful was he when they came in sight of the brown walls of Casale. These surged before them almost suddenly in the plain as they took a bend of the road; for the city's level position was

such as to render it inconspicuous from afar. The road led straight on to the San Stefano Gate, towards which they clattered over the drawbridge spanning the wide moat. There was a guardhouse in the deep archway, and the door of this stood open revealing some three or four soldiers lounging within. But they kept a loose and careless guard, for these were peaceful times. One of them, a young man in a leather haqueton, but bare of head, sauntered forward as far as the doorway to fling a greeting at the muleteer, which was taken by the fellow as permission to pass on.

From that gateway, cool and cavernous, they emerged into one of the streets of the busy capital of the warlike State of Montferrat, which at one time, none so far distant, had bidden fair to assume the lordship of Northern Italy.

They proceeded slowly now, perforce. The crooked street, across which the crazy houses seemed to lean towards each other so as to exclude the sunlight from all but a narrow middle line, was thronged with people of all degrees. It was ever a busy thoroughfare, this street of San Stefano, leading from the gate of that name to the Cathedral Square, and from his post of vantage on the back of the now ambling mule, Bellarion, able at last to sit unshaken, looked about him with deep interest upon manifestations of life known to him hitherto through little more than the imagination which had informed his extensive reading.

It was market-day in Casale, and before the shops the way was blocked by trestle tables, on which the merchants displayed their wares, shouting their virtues to lure the attention of the wayfarers.

Through this they came, by low and narrow archways, to an even greater bustle in the open space before the cathedral, founded, as Bellarion knew, some seven hundred years before by Liutprand, King of the Lombards. He turned to stare at the Roman architecture of the red and white façade, flanked by slender square towers, each surmounted by an hexagonal extinguisher roof. He was still considering the cruciform windows when the mule halted and recalled his attention.

Ahead of him Fra Sulpizio was slipping to the ground, bestowing thanks and invoking the blessings of God upon the muleteer. Bellarion dismounted, a little stiff from his ride and very thankful to be at the end of it. The muleteer flung them a "God guard you," over his shoulder, and the string of mules passed on.

"And now, brother, we'll seek a supper, if you please," the friar announced.

To seek it was natural enough, but hardly, thought Bellarion, in the tavern across the square, whither he was led.

On the threshold, under the withered bough that was hung as a sign above the portal, the young man demurred, protesting that one of the religious houses of the town were a fitter resort, and its charitable shelter more suitable to a friar-mendicant.

"Why, as to charity," quoth Fra Sulpizio, "it is on charity I depend. Old Benvenuto here, the taverner, is my cousin. He will make us free of his table, and give me news of my own folk at the same time. Is it not natural and proper that I seek him?"

Reluctantly Bellarion was forced to agree. And he reminded himself, to buttress a waning faith in his companion, that not once had he voiced a suspicion of the friar's actions to which the friar's answer had not been ready and complete.

Chapter III

The Door Ajar

The event which was to deviate Bellarion so abruptly and brutally from the peaceful ways of a student and a scholar, and to extinguish his cherished hopes of learning Greek at Pavia under the far-famed Messer Chrysolaras, was upon him so suddenly and so unheralded that he scarcely realised it until it was overpast.

He and the friar had supped in the unclean and crowded common room of the hostelry of the Stag—so called, it is presumed, in honour of the Lords of Montferrat, who had adopted the stag as their device—and it is to be confessed that they had supped abundantly and well under the particular auspices of Ser Benvenuto, the host, who used his cousin Fra Sulpizio with almost more than cousinly affection. He had placed them a little apart from the noisy occupants of that low-ceilinged, grimy chamber, in a recess under a tall, narrow window, standing open, so that the stench, compounded of garlic, burnt meats, rancid oil, and other things, which pervaded the apartment was here diluted for them by the pure evening air. And he waited upon them himself, after a protracted entertainment with the friar, conducted in a mutter of which nothing reached Bellarion. He brought them of his best, of which the most conspicuous item was a lean and stringy fowl, and he produced for them from his cellar a flask of Valtelline which at least was worthy of a better table.

Bellarion, tired and hungry, did justice to the viands, without permitting himself more than a passing irritation at his companion's whining expositions of the signal advantages of travelling under the ægis of the blessed Francis. The truth is that he did not hear more than the half of all that Fra Sulpizio found occasion to urge. For one thing, in his greed, the friar spoke indistinctly, slobbering the while at his food; for another, the many tenants of the inn were very noisy. They made up a motley crowd, but had this in common, that all belonged to the lower walks of life, as their loud, coarse speech, freely interlarded with blasphemy and obscenity, abundantly bore witness. There were some peasants from Romaglia or Torcella, or perhaps from Terranova beyond the Po, who had come there to market—rude, brawny men for the most part, accompanied by their equally brawny, barelegged women. There were a few labourers of the town and others who may have been artisans, one or two of them, indeed, so proclaimed by their leather aprons; and at one table a group of four men and a woman were very boisterous over their wine. The men were soldiers, so to be judged at a glance from their leather haquetons and studded girdles with heavy daggers slung behind.

The woman with them was a gaudy, sinuous creature with haggard, painted cheeks, whose mirth, now shrill, now raucous, was too easily moved. When first he heard it Bellarion had shuddered.

"She laughs," he had told the friar, "as one might laugh in hell."

For only answer Fra Sulpizio had looked at him and then veiled his eyes, almost as if, himself, he were suppressing laughter.

Soon, however, Bellarion grew accustomed to the ever-recurring sound and to the rest of the din, the rattle of platters and drinking-cans, the growling of a dog over a bone it had discovered among the foul rushes rotting on the bare earthen floor.

Having eaten, he sat back in his chair, a little torpid now, and drowsy. Last night he had lain in the open, and he had been afoot almost since dawn. It is little wonder that presently, whilst again the taverner was muttering with his cousin the friar, he should have fallen into a doze.

He must have slept some little while, a half-hour, perhaps, for when he awakened the patch of sunlight had faded from the wall across the alley, visible from the window under which they sat. This he did not notice at the time, but remembered afterwards. In the moment of awakening, his attention was drawn by the friar, who had risen, and instantly afterwards by something else, beyond the friar. At the open window behind and above Fra Sulpizio there was the face of a man. Upon the edge of the sill, beneath his face, were visible the fingers by which he had hoisted himself thither. The questing eyes met Bellarion's, and seemed to dilate a little; the mouth gaped suddenly. But before Bellarion could cry out or speak, or even form the intention of doing either, the face had vanished. And it was the face of the peasant

with whom they had dined that day.

The friar, warned by Bellarion's quickening stare, had swung round to look behind him. But he was too late; the window space was already empty.

"What is it?" he asked, suddenly apprehensive. "What did you see?"

Bellarion told him, and was answered by an obscenely morphological oath, which left him staring. The friar's countenance was suddenly transfigured. A spasm of mingled fear and anger bared his fangs; his beady eyes grew cruel and sinister. He swung aside as if to depart abruptly, then as abruptly halted where he stood.

On the threshold surged the peasant, others following him.

The friar sank again to his stool at the table, and composed his features.

"Yonder he sits, that friar rogue! That thief!" Thus the peasant as he advanced.

The cry, and, more than all, the sight of the peasant's companions, imposed a sudden silence upon the babel of that room. First came a young man, stalwart and upright, in steel cap and gorget, booted and spurred, a sword swinging from his girdle, a dagger hanging on his hip behind; a little crimson feather adorning his steel cap proclaiming him an officer of the Captain of Justice of Casale. After him came two of his men armed with short pikes.

Straight to that table in the window recess the peasant led the way. "There he is! This is he!" Belligerently he thrust his face into the friar's, leaning his knuckles on the table's edge. "Now, rogue . . ." he was beginning furiously, when Fra Sulpizio, rais-

ing eyes of mild astonishment to meet his anger, gently interrupted him.

"Little brother, do you speak so to me? Do you call me rogue? Me?" He smiled sadly, and so calm and gently wistful was his manner that it clearly gave the peasant pause. "A sinner I confess myself, for sinners are we all. But I am conscious of no sin against you, brother, whose charity was so freely given me only today."

That saintly demeanour threw the peasant's simple wits into confusion. He was thrust aside by the officer.

"What is your name?"

Fra Sulpizio looked at him, and his look was laden with reproach.

"My brother!" he cried.

"Attend to me!" the officer barked at him. "This man charges you with theft."

"With theft!" Fra Sulpizio paused and sighed. "It shall not move me to the sin of anger, brother. It is too foolish: a thing for laughter. What need have I to steal, when under the protection of Saint Francis I have but to ask for the little that I need? What use to me is worldly gear? But what does he say I stole?"

It was the peasant who answered him.

"Thirty florins, a gold chain, and a silver cross from a chest in the room where you rested."

Bellarion remembered how the friar had sought to go slinking off alone from the peasant homestead, and how fearfully he had looked behind him as they trudged along the road until overtaken by the muleteer. And by the muleteer it would be, he thought, that they had now been tracked. The officer at the gate would have told the peasant of how the friar and his young com-

panion in greed had ridden in; then the peasant would have sought the muleteer, and the rest was clear: as clear as it was to him that his companion was a thieving rogue, and that his own five ducats were somewhere about that scoundrel's person.

In future, he swore, he would be guided by his own keen instincts and the evidence of his senses only, and never again allow a preconception to befool him. Meanwhile, the friar was answering:

"So that not only am I charged with stealing, but I have returned evil for good; I have abused charity. It is a heavy charge, my brother, and very rashly brought."

There was a murmur of sympathy from the staring, listening company, amongst whom many lawless ones were, by the very instinct of their kind, ready to range themselves against any who stood for law.

The friar opened his arms, wide and invitingly:

"Let me not depart from my vows of humility in the heat of my own defence. I will say nothing. Do you, sir, make search upon me for the gear which this man says I have stolen, though all his evidence is that it chanced to be in a room in which for a little while I rested."

"To accuse a priest!" said someone in a tone of indignation, and a murmur arose at once in sympathy.

It moved the young officer to mirth. He half swung on his heel so as to confront those mutterers.

"A priest!" he jeered. Then, his keen eyes flashed once more upon the friar. "When did you last say Mass?"

Before that simple question Fra Sulpizio seemed to lose some of his assurance. Without even giving him time to answer, the

officer fired another question. "What is your name?"

"My name?" The friar was looking at him from eyes that seemed to have grown beadier than ever in that white, pitted face. "I'll not expose myself to ribald unbelief. You shall have written proof of my name. Behold." And from his gown he fetched a parchment, which he thrust under the soldier's nose.

The officer conned it a moment, then his eyes went over the edge of it back to the face of the man that held it.

"How can I read it upside down?"

The friar's hands, which shook a little, made haste to turn the sheet. As he did so Bellarion perceived two things: that the sheet had been correctly held at first; and that it was his own lost letter. He had a glimpse of the Abbot's seal as the parchment was turned.

He was momentarily bewildered by a discovery that was really threefold: first, the friar was indeed the thief who had rifled his scrip; second, he must be in a more desperate case than Bellarion suspected, to seek to cloak himself under a false identity; and, third, the pretence that the document proffered upside down was a test to discover whether the fellow could read, a trap into which the knave had tumbled headlong.

The officer laughed aloud, well pleased with his own cleverness. "I knew you were no clerk," he mocked him. "I have more than a suspicion who you really are. Though you may have stolen a friar's habit, it would need more than that to cover your ugly, pock-marked face and that scar on your neck. You are Lorenzaccio da Trino, my friend; and there's a halter waiting for you."

The mention of that name made a stir in the tavern, and

brought its tenants a step nearer to the group about that table in the window recess. It was a name known probably to every man present with the single exception of Bellarion, the name of a bandit of evil fame throughout Montferrat and Savoy. Something of the kind Bellarion may have guessed. But at that moment the recovery of the Abbot's letter was his chief concern.

"That parchment's mine!" he cried. "It was stolen from me this morning by this false friar."

The interpolation diverted attention to himself. After a moment's blank stare the officer laughed again. Bellarion began actively to dislike that laugh of his. He was too readily moved to it.

"Why, here's Paul disowning Peter. Oh, to be sure, the associate becomes the victim when the master rogue is taken. It's a stale trick, young cockerel. It won't serve in Casale."

Bellarion bristled. He assumed a great dignity. "Young sir, you may come to regret your words. I am the man named in that parchment, as the Abbot of the Grazie of Cigliano can testify."

"No need to plague Messer the Abbot," the officer mocked him. "A taste of the cord, my lad, a hoist or two, and you'll vomit all the truth."

"The hoist!" Bellarion felt the skin roughening along his spine.

Was it to be taken for granted that he was a rogue, simply from his association with this spurious friar; and were his bones to be broken by the torturers to make him accuse himself? Was this how justice was dispensed?

He was bewildered, and, as he afterwards confessed, he grew suddenly afraid. And then there was a cry from the peasant, and things happened quickly and unexpectedly.

Whilst the officer's attention had been on Bellarion, the false

friar had moved very soft and stealthily nearer to the window. The peasant it was who detected the movement and realised its import.

"Lay hands on him!" he cried, in sudden alarm lest his florins and the rest should take flight again, and, that alarm spurring him, himself he leapt to seize Lorenzaccio by arm and shoulder. Fury blazed from the bandit's beady eyes; his yellow fangs were bared in a grin of rage; something flashed in his right hand, and then his knife sank into the stomach of his assailant. It was a wicked, vicious, upward, ripping thrust, like the stroke of a boar's tusk, and the very movement that delivered it flung the peasant off, so that he hurtled into the arms of the two soldiers, and momentarily hampered their advance. That moment was all that Lorenzaccio needed. He swung aside, and with a vigour and agility to execute, as remarkable as the rapidity of the conception itself, he hoisted himself to the sill of the narrow, open window, crouched there a second, measuring his outward leap, and was gone.

He left a raging confusion behind him, and an exclamatory din above which rang fierce and futile commands from the Podestà's young officer. One of the men-at-arms supported the swooning body of the peasant, whilst his fellow vainly and stupidly sought to follow by the way Lorenzaccio had gone, but failed because he lacked the bandit's vigour.

Bellarion, horror-stricken and half stupefied, stood staring at the wretched peasant whose hurt he judged to be mortal. He was roused by a gentle tugging at his sleeve. He half turned to find himself looking into the painted face of the woman whose laughter earlier had jarred his sensibilities. It was a handsome face, despite the tawdriness it derived from the raddled cheeks and too vividly reddened lips. The girl—she was little more—looked kindly concern upon him out of dark, slanting eyes that were preternaturally bright.

"Away, away!" she muttered feverishly. "This is your chance. Bestir!"

"My chance?" he echoed, and was conscious of the colour mounting to his cheeks.

His first emotion was resentment of this misjudgment; his next a foolish determination to stand firm and advance his explanations, insisting upon justice being done him. All this whilst he had flung his question "My chance?" With the next heartbeat he perceived the strength of the appearances against him. This poor drab, these evil ones about her and him, offering him their sympathy only because they believed him made kin with them by evil, advised the only course a sane man in his case must follow.

"Make haste, child!" the woman urged him breathlessly. "Quick, or it will be too late."

He looked beyond her at the others crowding there, to meet glances that seemed to invite, to urge, and from one bloated face, which he recognized for Benvenuto's, came an eloquent wink, whilst the fellow jerked a dirty thumb backwards towards the door in a gesture there was no misunderstanding. Then, as if Bellarion's sudden resolve had been reflected in his face, the press before him parted, men and women shouldered and elbowed a way for him. He plunged forward. The company closed behind him, opening farther ahead, closed again as he advanced and again opened before him, until his way to the door was clear. And behind him he could hear the young officer's voice raised above the din in oaths and imprecations, urging his men-at-arms to clear a way with their pikes, calling upon those other soldiers lounging there to lend a hand, so as to make sure, at least, of one of these two rogues.

But that rascally company, it seemed, was skilled in the tactics the occasion needed. Honest men there may have been, and no doubt there were amongst them. But they were outnumbered; and, moreover, honest though they might be, they were poor folk, and therefore so far in sympathy perhaps with an unfortunate lad as not to hinder him even if they would not actively help. And meanwhile the others, making pretence of being no more than spectators, solicitous for the condition of the peasant who had been stabbed, pressed so closely about the officer and his men that the latter had no room in which to swing their pikes.

All this Bellarion guessed, by the sounds behind him, rather than saw. For he gave no more than a single backward glance at that seething group as he flung across the threshold, out of that evil-smelling chamber into the clean air of the square. He turned to the left, and made off towards the cathedral, his first thought being to seek sanctuary there. Then, realising that thus he would but walk into a trap, he dived down an alley just as the officer gained the tavern door, and with a view halloo started after him, his two pikemen and the other soldiers clattering at his heels.

As Bellarion raced like a stag before hounds down that narrow street of mean houses in the shadow of Liutprand's great church, it may well be that he recalled the Abbot's parting words, *"Pax multa in cella, foris autem plurima bella,"* and wished himself back in the tranquillity of the cloisters, secure from the perils and vexations of secular existence.

This breathless flight of his seemed to him singularly futile and purposeless. He knew what he was running from; but not what he might be running to, nor indeed whither to run at all. And for escape, knowledge of the latter is as important as of the former. Had not instinct—the animal instinct of self-preservation—been stronger than his reason, he would have halted, saved his breath, and waited for his pursuers to overtake him. For he was too intelligent to wear himself in attempting to escape the inescapable. Fortunately for him, the instinct of the hunted animal sent him headlong forward in despite of reason. And presently there was reason, too, to urge him. This, when he realized that, after all, his pursuers were not as fleet of foot as himself. Be it from their heavy boots and other accoutrements, be it from his greater youth and more Spartan habits of life, he was rapidly outdistancing them, and thus might yet succeed in shaking them off altogether. Then, too, he reflected that if he kept a straight course in his flight, he must end by reaching the wall of this accursed city, and by following this must gain one of the gates into the open country. It was close on sunset. But there would be at least a full hour yet before the gates were closed.

Heartened, he sped on, and only once was he in any danger. That was when the straight course he laid himself brought him out upon an open square, along one side of which ran a long grey building with a noble arcade on the ground level. There was a considerable concourse of people moving here both in the open and under the arches, and several turned to stare at that lithe green figure as it sped past. Caring nothing what any might think, and concerned only to cross that open space as quickly as possible, Bellarion gained the narrow streets beyond. Still intent upon keeping a straight line, he turned neither to right nor to left. And presently he found himself moving no longer between houses, but along a grass-grown lane, between high brown walls where the ground underfoot was soft and moist. He eased the pace a little, to give his aching lungs relief; nor knew how nearly spent he was until the peace of his surroundings induced that lessening of effort. It lessened further, until he was merely walking, panting now, and gasping, and mopping the sweat from his brow with the back of his hand. He had been too reckless, he now told himself. The pace had been too hot. He should have known that it must defeat him. Unless by now he had shaken off those pursuers, or others they might have enlisted—and that was his great fear—he was a lost man.

He came to a standstill, listening. He could hear, he fancied, sounds in the distance which warned him that the pursuit still held. Panic spurred his flanks again. But though it might be urgent to resume his flight, it was more urgent still to pause first to recover breath.

He had come to a halt beside a stout oaken door which was studded with great nails and set in a deep archway in that high wall. To take his moment's rest he leaned against these solid timbers. And then, to his amazement, under the weight of his body, the ponderous door swung inwards, so that he almost fell through it into a space of lawn and rosebeds narrowly enclosed within tall boxwood hedges which were very dense and trimly cut.

It was as if a miracle had happened, as if that door had been unlocked for his salvation by supernatural agency. Thus thought he in that moment of exaggerated reaction from his panic, nor stayed to reflect that in entering and in closing and bolting that door, he was as likely to entrap as to deliver himself. There was a deep sill, some two feet above the ground, on the inner side. On this Bellarion sat down to indulge the luxury of a sense of security. But not for very long. Presently steps, quick and numerous, came pattering down that lane, to an accompaniment of breathless voices.

Bellarion listened, and smiled a little. They would never guess that he had found this door ajar. They would pass on, continuing their now fruitless quest, whilst he could linger until night descended. Perhaps he would spend the night there, and be off in the morning by the time the gates of the city should have been reopened.

Thus he proposed. And then the steps outside came to a sudden halt, and his heart almost halted with them.

"He paused hereabouts," said a gruff voice. "Look at the trodden ground."

That was a shrew-eyed sleuth, thought Bellarion as he listened fearfully.

"Does it matter?" quoth another. "Will you stand pausing too whilst he makes off? Come on. He went this way, we know."

"Hold, numskull!" It was the gruff voice again. "He came this way, but he went no farther. Bah! Peace, don't argue with me, man. Use your eyes. It's plain to see. No one has gone past this door today. He's here." And on the word a heavy blow, as from a pike butt, smote the timbers, and brought Bellarion to his feet as if he, himself, had been struck.

"But this door is always locked, and he could scarcely have climbed the wall."

"He's here, I say. Don't argue. Two men to guard the door,

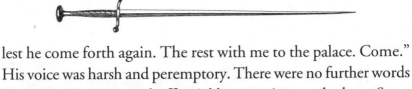

lest he come forth again. The rest with me to the palace. Come."
His voice was harsh and peremptory. There were no further words
in answer. Steps moved off quickly returning up the lane. Steps
paced outside the door, and there was a mutter of voices of the
men placed on guard.

Bellarion wondered if prayer would help him. He could think
of nothing else that would.

Chapter IV

Sanctuary

These grounds into which he had stepped through that doorway in the red wall seemed, so far as the tall hedges of his *hortus inclusus* would permit him to discover, to be very spacious. Somewhere in their considerable extent there would surely be a hiding place into which he could creep until the hunt was over.

He went forward to investigate, stepping cautiously towards a deep archway cut in the dense boxwood. In this archway he paused to survey a prospect that evoked thoughts of Paradise. Beyond a wide sweep of lawn, whereon two peacocks strutted, sparkled the waters of a miniature lake, where a pavilion of white marble, whose smooth dome and graceful pillars suggested a diminutive Roman temple, appeared to float. Access to this was gained from the shore by an arched marble bridge over whose white parapet trailing geraniums flamed.

From this high place the ground fell away in a flight of two terraces, and the overflow from the lake went cascading over granite boulders into tanks of granite set in each of them, with shading vine trellises above that were heavy now with purple fruit. Below, another emerald lawn was spread, sheltered on three sides within high walls of yew, fantastically cut at the summit into the machicolations of an embattled parapet and bearing at intervals deep arched niches in which marble statues gleamed white against the dusky green. Here figures sauntered, courtly figures of men and women more gaudy and glittering in their gay raiment than the peacocks nearer at hand; and faintly on the still warm air of evening came the throbbing of a lute which one of them was idly thrumming.

Beyond, on the one open side, another shallow terrace rose and upon this a great red house that was half palace, half fortress, flanked at each side by a massive round tower with covered battlements.

So much Bellarion's questing eyes beheld, and then he checked his breath, for his sharp ears had caught the sound of a stealthy step just beyond the hedge that screened him. An instant later he was confronted by a woman, who with something furtive and cautious in her movements appeared suddenly before him in the archway.

For a half-dozen heartbeats they stood thus, each regarding the other; and the vision of her in that breathless moment was destined never to fade from Bellarion's mind. She was of middle height, and her close-fitting gown of sapphire blue laced in gold from neck to waist revealed her to be slender. There was about her an air of delicate dignity, of command tempered by gracious-

ness. For the rest, her hair was of a tawny golden, a shade deeper
than the golden threads of the jewelled caul in which it was confined; her face was small and pale, too long in the nose, perhaps,
for perfect symmetry, yet for that very reason the more challeng-
ing in its singular, elusive beauty. Great wistful eyes of brown,
wide-set and thoughtful, were charged with questions as they
conned Bellarion. They were singularly searching, singularly
compelling eyes, and they drew from him forthwith a frank
confession.

"Lady!" he faltered. "Of your charity! I am pursued."

"Pursued!" She moved a step, and her expression changed.
The wistfulness was replaced by concern in those great sombre
eyes.

"I am likely to be hanged if taken," he added to quicken the
excellent emotions he detected.

"By whom are you pursued?"

"An officer of the Captain of Justice and his men."

He would have added more. He would have said something
to assure her that in seeking her pity he sought it for an innocent
man betrayed by appearances. But she gave signs that her pity
needed no such stimulant. She made a little gesture of distraction, clasping her long, tapering hands over which the tight, blue
sleeves descended to the knuckles. She flung a swift, searching
glance behind her, from the green archway to the open spaces.

"Come," she said, and beckoned him forward. "I will hide
you." And then on a note of deeper anxiety, for which he blessed
her tender, charitable heart, she added: "If you are found here, all
is lost. Crouch low and follow me."

Obediently he followed, almost on all fours, creeping beside

a balustrade of mellow brick that stood breast high to make a parapet for the edge of that very spacious terrace.

Ahead of him the lady moved sedately and unhurried, thereby discovering to Bellarion virtues of mental calm and calculating wit. A fool, he told himself, would have gone in haste, and thus provoked attention and inquiry.

They came in safety to the foot of the arched marble bridge, which Bellarion now perceived to be crossed by broad steps, ascending to a platform at the summit, and descending thence again to the level of the temple on the water.

"Wait. Here we must go with care." She turned to survey the gardens below, and as she looked he saw her blench, saw the golden-brown eyes dilate as if in fear. He could not see what she saw— the glint of arms upon hurrying men emerging from the palace. But the guess he made went near enough to the fact before she cried out: "Too late! If you ascend now you will be seen." And she told him of the soldiers. Again she gave evidence of her shrewd sense. "Do you go first," she bade him, "and on hands and knees. If I follow I may serve as a screen for you, and we must hope they will not see you."

"The hope," said Bellarion, "is slender as the screen your slenderness would afford me, lady." He was lying now flat on the ground at her feet. "If only it had pleased Heaven to make you as fat as you are charitable, I'd not hesitate. As it is, I think I see a better way."

She stared down at him, a little frown puckering her white brow. But for the third time in that brief space she proved herself a woman whose mind seized upon essentials and disregarded lesser things.

"A better way? What way, then?"

He had been using his eyes. Beyond the domed pavilion a tongue of land thrust out into the lake, from which three cypresses rose in black silhouette against the afterglow of sunset, whilst a little alder-bush, its branches trailing in the water, blunted the island's point.

"This way," said Bellarion, and went writhing like an eel in the direction of the water.

"Where will you go?" she cried; and added sharply as he reached the edge: "It is very deep; two fathoms at the shallowest."

"So much the better," said Bellarion. "They'll be the less likely to seek me in it."

He took a succession of deep breaths to prepare himself for the long submersion.

"Ah, but wait!" she cried on a strained note. "Tell me, at least . . ."

She broke off with a catch in her breath. He was gone. He had slipped in, taking the water quietly as an otter, and save for the wave that sped across the lake no sign of him remained.

The lady stood breathlessly at gaze waiting to see the surface broken by his emerging head. But she waited vainly and in growing alarm. The moments passed. Voices behind her became audible and grew in volume. The men-at-arms were advancing swiftly, the courtiers following to see the sport their captain promised.

Suddenly from the alder-bush on the island's point a startled water-hen broke forth in squawking terror, and went scudding across the lake, its feet trailing along the water into which it finally splashed again within a yard of the farther shore. From within the bush itself some slight momentary disturbance sent a succession of ripples across the lesser ripples whipped up by the evening

breeze. Then all grew still again, including the alarms of the watching lady who had perceived and read these signs.

She drew closer about her white, slender shoulders a little mantle edged with miniver, and moved like one impelled by natural curiosity to meet the soldiers who came surging up the terrace steps. There were four of them, led by that same young officer who had invaded the hostelry of the Stag in quest of Lorenzaccio.

"What is this?" the lady greeted him, her tone a little hard as if his abrupt invasion of her garden were in itself an offence. "What are you seeking here?"

"A man, madonna," the captain answered her shortly, having at the moment no breath for more.

Her sombre eyes went past him to dwell upon the three glittering gallants in the courtly group of five that followed at the soldier's heels.

"A man?" she echoed. "I do not remember to have seen such a portent hereabouts in days."

Of the three at whom the shaft of her irony was directed two laughed outright in shameless sycophancy; the third flushed scarlet, his glance resentful. He was the youngest by some years, and still a boy. He had her own brown eyes and tawny hair, and otherwise resembled her, save that his countenance lacked the firm strength that might be read in hers. His slim, graceful, stripling figure was gorgeously arrayed in a kilted tunic of gold brocade with long, green, deeply foliated sleeves, the ends of which reached almost to his toes. His girdle was of hammered gold whence hung a poniard with a jewelled hilt, and a ruby glowed in his bulging cap of green silk. One of his legs was cased in green, the other in yellow, and he wore a green shoe on the yellow foot, and a yellow on the green. This, in the sixteenth year of his age, was the Lord Gian Giacomo Paleologo, sovereign Marquis of Montferrat.

His two male companions were Messer Corsario, his tutor, a foxy-faced man of thirty, whose rich purple gown would have been more proper to a courtier than a pedant, and the Lord Castruccio da Fenestrella, a young man of perhaps five and twenty, very gorgeous in a scarlet houppelande, and not unhandsome, despite his pallid cheeks, thin lank hair, and rather shifty eyes. It was upon him that Giacomo now turned in peevishness.

"Do not laugh, Castruccio."

Meanwhile the captain was flinging out an arm in command to his followers. "Two of you to search the enclosure yonder about the gate. Beat up the hedges. Two of you with me." He swung to the lady before she could answer her brother. "You have seen no one, highness?"

Her highness was guilty of an evasion. "Should I not tell you if I had?"

"Yet a man certainly entered here not many minutes since by the gardendoor."

"You saw him enter?"

"I saw clear signs that he had entered."

"Signs? What signs?"

He told her. Her mobile lips expressed a doubt before she uttered it.

"A poor warrant that for this intrusion, Ser Bernabó."

The captain grew uncomfortable. "Highness, you mistake my motives."

"I hope I do," she answered lightly, and turned her shoulder to him.

He commanded his two waiting followers. The others were already in the enclosed garden. "To the temple!"

At that she turned again, her eyes indignant. "Without my leave? The temple, sir, is my own private bower."

The captain hesitated, ill-at-ease. "Hardly at present, highness. It is in the hands of the workmen; and this fellow may be hiding there."

"He is not. He could not be in the temple without my knowledge. I am but come from there."

"Your memory, highness, is at fault. As I approached, you were coming along the terrace from the enclosed garden."

She flushed under the correction. And there was a pause before she slowly answered him: "Your eyes are too good, Bernabó." In a tone that made him change countenance she added: "I shall remember it, together with your reluctance to accept my word." Contemptuously she dismissed him. "Pray, make your search without regard for me."

The captain stood a moment hesitating. Then he bowed stiffly from the hips, tossed his head in silent command to his men, and so led them off, over the marble bridge.

After he had drawn blank, like the soldiers he had sent to search the enclosure, he returned, baffled, with his four fellows at his heels. The Princess Valeria wandered now in company with those other gay ones along the terrace by the balustrade.

"You come empty-handed, then," she rallied him.

"I'll stake my life he entered the garden," said the captain sullenly.

"You are wise in staking something of no value."

He disregarded alike the taunt and the titter it drew from her companions. "I must report to his highness. Do you say positively, madonna, that you did not see this fellow?"

"Lord, man! Do you still presume to question me? Besides, if you're so confident, why waste time in questions? Continue your search."

The captain addressed himself to her companions. "You, sirs and ladies, did you have no glimpse of this knave—a tall youngster, dressed in green?"

"In green!" cried the Lady Valeria. "Now that is interesting. In green? A dryad, perhaps; or, perhaps my brother here."

The captain shook his head. "That is not possible."

"Nor am I in green," added the young marquis. "Nor have I been outside the garden. She mocks you, Messer Bernabó. It is her cursed humour. We have seen no one."

"Nor you, Messer Corsario?" Pointedly now the captain addressed the pedant, as by his years and office the likeliest to return him a serious answer.

"Indeed, no," the gentleman replied. "But then," he added, "we were some way off, as you observed. Madonna, however, who was up here, asserts that she saw no one."

"Ah! But does she so assert it?" the captain insisted.

The Lady Valeria looked him over in chill disdain. "You all heard what I said. Repetition is a weariness."

"You see," the captain appealed to them.

Her brother came to his assistance. "Why can't you answer plainly, and have done, Valeria? Why must you forever remember to be witty? Why can't you just say 'no'?"

"Because I've answered plainly enough already, and my answer has been disregarded. Ser Bernabó shall have no opportu-

nity to repeat an offence I am not likely to forget." She turned away. "Come, Dionara, and you, Isotta. It is growing chill."

With her ladies obediently following her she descended towards the lower gardens and the palace.

Messer Bernabó stroked his chin, a man nonplussed. The Lord Castruccio chided him.

"You're a fool, Bernabó, to anger her highness. Besides, man, what mare's nest are you hunting?"

The soldier was pale with vexation. "You saw as I did that, as we crossed the gardens, her highness was coming from that enclosure."

"Yes, booby," said Corsario, "and we saw as you did that she came alone. If a man entered by that gate as you say, he got no farther than the enclosed garden, and this your men have searched already. You gain nothing by betraying suspicions. Who and what do you suppose this man?"

"Suppose! I know."

"What do you know?"

"That he is a rogue, a brigand scoundrel, associate of Lorenzaccio da Trino who slipped through our fingers an hour ago."

"By the Host!" cried Corsario, in genuine surprise. "I thought . . ." He checked abruptly, and dissembled the break by a laugh. "And can you dream that the Lady Valeria would harbour a robber?"

"Can I dream, can any man dream, what the Lady Valeria will do?"

"I could dream that she'll put your eyes out if ever the power is hers," lisped the Lord of Fenestrella with the malice that was of his nature. "You heard her say they are too good, and that she'll remember it. You should be less ready to tell her all you see. He is a fool who helps to make a woman wise."

The Marquis laughed to applaud his friend's philosophy, and his glance approved him fawningly.

The young soldier considered them.

"Sirs, I will resume my search."

When they had searched until night closed in upon the world, investigating every hedge and bush that might afford conceal-ment, the captain came to think that either he had been at fault in concluding that the fugitive had sought shelter in the garden, or else the rogue had found some way out and was now beyond their reach.

He retired crestfallen, and the three gentlemen who had ac-companied his search and who did not conceal their amusement at its failure went in to supper.

Chapter V

The Princess

At about the time that the young Lord of Montferrat was sitting down belatedly to table with his tutor and his gentleman-in-waiting, a very bedraggled and chilled Bellarion, who for two hours had been standing immersed to the chin in water, his head amid the branches of the alder-bush, came cautiously forth at last. He ventured no farther, however, than the shallow tongue of land behind the marble pavilion, ready at the first alarm to plunge back into his watery concealment.

There he lay, shivering in the warm night, and taking stock of his plight, an exercise which considerably diminished him in his self-confidence and self-esteem.

"Experience," he had been wont to say—being rather addicted, I gather, to the making of epigrammatic formulæ—"is the hornbook of fools, unnecessary for the practical purposes of life to the man of wit."

It is possible that he was tempted to revise this dictum in the light of the events of that disastrous day, recognising that a little of the worldly experience he despised might have saved him most if not all of its disasters. If he admitted this without yet admitting the fallacy of his aphorism, it was only to reach a conclusion even more humiliating. He had strayed from lack of experience, therefore it followed, he told himself, that he was a fool. That is one of the dangers of reasoning by syllogism.

He had accepted the companionship of a man whose face pronounced him a scoundrel, and whose various actions in the course of the day confirmed the message of his face, and this for no better reason than that the man wore a Franciscan's frock. If his sense did not apprise him that a Franciscan's habit does not necessarily cover a Saint Francis, there was a well-known proverb—*cucullus non facit monachum*—which he might have remembered. Because sense and memory had alike failed him, he had lost his purse, he had lost the letter which was his passport for the long and arduous journey before him, he had narrowly escaped losing his liberty, and he would be lucky if he were quit of all this mischief without losing his life. The lesser evils of the ruin of a serviceable suit of clothes and the probability of taking a rheum as the result of his immersion went for the moment disregarded.

Next he considered the rashness, the senselessness, of his seeking sanctuary in this garden. Was worldly experience really necessary, he wondered, to teach a man that the refuge of which he does not know the exit may easily become a trap? Had he not excelled at the Grazie as a chessplayer from his care and ability in

pondering the moves that must follow the immediate one? Had he read—amongst other works on the art of war which had ever held his mind in fascination—the *De Re Militari* of Silvius Faustus to so little purpose that he could not remember one of its first axioms, to the effect that he is an imprudent leader who goes into action without making sure that his line of retreat is open?

By such questions as these did Bellarion chastise himself as he crouched shivering in the dark. Still lower did he crouch, making himself one with the earth itself, when presently a moon, like a golden slice of melon, emerged from behind the black bulk of the palace, and shed a ghostly radiance upon those gardens. He set himself then at last to seek a course by which he might extricate himself from this trap and from this city of Casale.

He was still far from any solution of that problem when a sound of voices recalled him to more immediate things. Two figures mounting the steps of the terrace had to him the appearance of two black human silhouettes that were being slowly pushed up out of the ground. Their outline defined them for women, even before he made out their voices to be feminine. He wondered would one of them be the gracious and beautiful lady who had given him sanctuary, a lady whose like hitherto he had seen only painted on canvas above altars and in mural frescoes, the existence of whose living earthly counterparts had been to him a matter of some subconscious doubt.

At the height of the bridge, so tremulously reflected in silver on the black water below, the ladies paused, speaking the while in subdued voices. Then they came down the nearer steps and vanished into the temple, whence presently one of them emerged upon that narrow, shallow promontory, calling softly, and very vaguely:

"Olà! Olà! Messer! Messer!"

He recognised the voice, and recognising it realised that its quality was individual and unforgettable.

To the Lady Valeria as she stood there, it seemed that a part of the promontory's clay at her feet heaved itself up amorphously, writhed into human shape, and so resolved itself into the man she sought. She checked a startled outcry, as she understood the nature of this materialisation.

"You will be very wet, sir, and cold." Her voice was gentle and solicitous, very different from that in which she had addressed her brother's companions and the captain.

Bellarion was quite frank. "As wet as a drowned man, and very nearly as cold." And he added: "I would I could be sure I shall not yet be hung up to dry."

The lady laughed softly at his rueful humour. "Nay, now, we have brought the means to make you dry more comfortably. But it was very rash of you to have entered here without first making sure that you were not observed."

"I was not observed, madonna. Else be sure I should not have entered."

He caught in the gloom the sound of her breath indrawn with the hiss of sudden apprehension. "You were not observed? And yet . . . Oh, it is just as I was fearing." And then, more briskly, and before he could reply, "But come," she urged him. "We have brought fresh clothes for you. When you are dry you shall tell me all."

Readily enough he allowed himself to be conducted within the single circular chamber of the marble pavilion, where Madonna Dionara, her lady, awaited. The place was faintly lighted

by a lantern placed on a marble table. It contained besides this some chairs that were swathed in coarse sheets, and a long wooden coffer, carved and painted, in shape and size like a sarcophagus, from which another such sheet had just been swept. The three open spaces, between twin pillars facing towards the palace, were now closed by leather curtains. The circular marble floor was laid out as a dial, with the hours in Roman figures of carved brass sunk into the polished surface, a matter which puzzled him. He was not to guess that this marble pavilion was a copy in minia-ture of a Roman temple of Apollo, and that in the centre of the domed roof there was a circular opening for the sun, through which its rays so entered that as the day progressed a time-telling shadow moved across the hours figured in their circle on the floor.

Overhead there was a confusion of poles and scaffolding and trailing dust-sheets, and in a corner an array of pails and buckets, and all the litter of suspended painters' work. Dimly, on one of the walls, he could make out a fresco that was half painted, the other half in charcoal outline.

On the table, which was swathed like all the other furnishings, the lantern revealed a bundle of red garments lately loosed from a confining cloak of black. Into these he was bidden to change at once. Red, he was told, had been deliberately chosen because all that the captain seemed to know of him was that he had been dressed in green. So that not merely would his protectress render him dry and warm again; she would disguise him. The ladies meanwhile would keep watch in the garden immediately below. They had brought a lute. If one of them should sing to it, this would mean that she sounded the alarm, and he must hide in the coffer, taking with him everything that might betray his presence, including the lantern which he must extinguish. Flint and steel and tinder had not been forgotten, so that light might be rekindled when the danger was overpast. Her highness raised the lid of the coffer to reveal to him the mechanism of the snap lock. This was released, of course, by the key, which should then be withdrawn. Provided he did this, once he allowed the lid to close upon him, none would be able to open it from the outside; whilst from the inside it was an easy matter, even in the dark, to release the catch. Meanwhile the keyhole would provide him with suffi-cient air and at the same time permit him to judge by sounds of what was happening. The wet garments he removed were to be made into a bundle and dropped into the coffer, whence they would afterwards be taken and destroyed. Finally he was given ten minutes in which to make the change.

Abruptly he found himself alone, and so impressed by her commands that already his fingers were swiftly untrussing his points. He went briskly to work, first to strip himself, then to rub himself dry and restore his chilled circulation, for which purpose he heedlessly employed the black cloak in which the fresh gar-ments had been bundled. Then he set about donning that scarlet raiment of fine quality and modish fashion, all the while lost in wonder of her graciousness and resource. She revealed herself, he reflected, as a woman fit to lead and to command, a woman with a methodical mind and a well-ordered intelligence which many a captain of men might envy. And she revealed herself, too, as in-tensely womanly, an angel of compassion. Although clearly a lady of great rank, she nevertheless went to so much pains and thought to save a wretched fugitive like himself, and this without pausing to ascertain if he were worthy of compassion.

As abruptly as she had left him did she now return, even as he was completing his hasty toilet. And she came alone, having left her lady with the lute on guard below.

He stood now before her a brave figure, despite his tumbled black locks and the fact that the red hose of fine cloth was a little short for his long shanks, and therefore a little cramping. But the kilted tunic became him well with its girdle of steel and leather which he was buckling even as she entered.

She swept forward to the table, and came straight to business. "And now, sir, your message?"

His fingers stood arrested on the buckle, and his solemn dark eyes opened wide as they searched her pale face.

"Message?" quoth he slowly.

"Message, yes." Her tone betrayed the least impatience. "What has happened? What has become of Ser Giuffredo? Why has he not been near me this fortnight? What did the Lord Barbaresco bid you tell me? Come, come, sir. You need not hesitate. Surely you know that I am the Princess Valeria of Montferrat?"

All that he understood of this was that he stood in a princely presence, before the august sister of the sovereign Marquis of Montferrat. Had he been reared in the world he might have been awe-stricken by the circumstances. But he knew princes and princesses only from books written by chroniclers and historians, who treat them familiarly enough. If anything about her commanded his respect, it was her slim grace and her rather elusive beauty, a beauty that is not merely of colour and of features, but of the soul and mind alive in these.

His hands fell limply away from the buckle, which he had made fast at length. His lively countenance looked almost foolish as dimly seen in the yellow light of the lantern.

"Madonna, I do not understand. I am no messenger. I . . ."

"You are no messenger?" Her tawny head was thrust forward, her dark eyes glowed. "Were you not sent to me? Answer, man! Were you not sent?"

"Not other than by an inscrutable Providence, which may desire to preserve me for better things than a rope."

The whimsical note of the answer may have checked her stirring anger. There was a long pause in which she pondered him with eyes that were become unfathomable. Mechanically she loosed the long black cloak that covered her low-cut sheathing gown of sapphire blue.

"Why, then, did you come? Was it to spy . . . No, no. You are not that. A spy would have gone differently to work. What are you, then?"

"Just a poor scholar on his travels, studying life at first hand and a trifle more rapidly than he can digest it. As for how I came into your garden, let me tell you."

And he told her with admirable succinctness the sorry tale of that day's events. It drove the last vestige of wrath from her face, and drew the ghost of a smile to the corners of a mouth that could be as tender as imperious. Observing it, he realised that whilst she had given him sanctuary under a misapprehension, yet she was not likely to visit her obvious disappointment too harshly upon him.

"And I thought . . ." She broke off and trilled a little laugh, between mirth and bitterness. "It was a lucky chance for you, master fugitive." She considered him again, and it may be that his stalwart young male beauty had a hand unconsciously in shap-

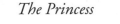

ing her resolves concerning him. "What am I to do with you?" she asked him.

He answered simply and directly, speaking not as a poor nameless scholar to a high-born princess, but as equal to equal, as a young man to a young woman.

"If you are what your face tells me, madonna, you will let me profit by an error that entails no less for yourself beyond that of these garments, which, if you wish it . . ."

She waved the proposal aside before it was uttered. "Pooh, the garments. What are they?" She frowned thoughtfully. "But I named names to you."

"Did you? I have forgotten them." And in answer to the hard incredulity of her stare, he explained himself. "A good memory, madonna, lies as much in an ability to forget as in a capacity to remember. And I have an excellent memory. By the time I shall have stepped out of this garden I shall have no recollection that I was ever in it."

Slowly she spoke after a pause. "If I were sure that I can trust you . . ." She left it there.

Bellarion smiled. "Unless you are certain that you can, you had better call the guard. But then, how could you be sure that in that case I should not recall the names you named, which are now forgotten?"

"Ah! You threaten!"

The sharp tone, the catch in her breath, the sudden movement of her hand to her breast showed him that his inference was right.

This lady was engaged in secret practices. And the inference itself displayed the swift activity of his wits; just as his answer displayed them.

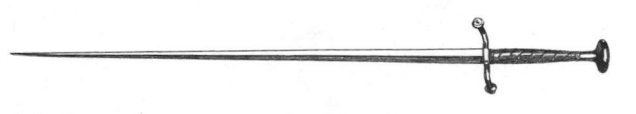

"Nay, lady. I show you only that trust me you must, since if you mistrust me you can no more order my arrest than you can set me free."

"My faith, sir, you are shrewd, for one who's convent-bred."

"There's a deal of shrewdness, lady, to be learned in convents." And then, whether the beauty and charm of her so wrought upon him as to breed in him the desire to serve her, or whether he merely offered a bargain, a return for value received and to be received, it is probable that he did not know himself. But he made his proposal. "If you would trust me, madonna, you might even use me, and so repay yourself."

"Use you?"

"As a messenger. In the place of him whom you expected. That is, if you have messages to send, as I think you should have."

"You think it?"

"From what you have said."

"I said so little." She was clearly suspicious.

"But I inferred so much. Too much, perhaps. Let me expose my reasoning." The truth is he was a little vain of it. "You expected a messenger from one Lord Barbaresco. You left the garden gate ajar to facilitate his entrance when he came, and you were on the watch for him, and alone. Your ladies, one of whom at least is in your confidence, were beguiling the gentlemen and keeping them in the lower garden, whilst you loitered watchful by the hedged enclosure. Hence I argue on your part anxiety and secrecy. You were anxious because no message had come for a fortnight, nor had Messer Giuffredo, the usual messenger, been seen. Almost you may have feared that some evil had befallen Messer Giuffredo, if not the Lord Barbaresco, himself. Which shows that the secret practices of which these messages are the subject may themselves be dangerous. Do I read the signs fluently enough?"

There was little need for his question. Her face supplied the answer.

"Too fluently, I think. Too fluently for one who is no more than you represent yourself."

"It is, madonna, that you are not accustomed to the exercise of pure reason. It is rare enough."

"Pure reason!" Her scorn where his fatuity had expected wonder was like a searing iron. "And do you know, sir, what pure reason tells me?"

"I can believe anything, madonna," he said, alluding to the tone she used with him.

"That you were sent to set a trap for me."

He perceived exactly by what steps she had come to that conclusion. He smiled reassuringly, and shook his moist head.

"The reasoning is not pure enough. If I had been so sent, should I have been pursued and hunted? And should I not have come prepared with some trivial message, to assure you that I am the messenger you were so very ready to believe me?"

She was convinced. But still she hesitated.

"But why, concluding so much and so accurately, should you offer to serve me?"

"Say from gratitude to one who has saved perhaps my life."

"But I did so under a misapprehension. That should compel no gratitude."

"I like to think, madonna, that you would have shown me the same charity even if there had been no misapprehension. I

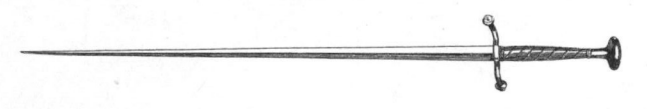

am the more grateful for what you have done because I choose to believe that in any case you would have done it. Then there is this handsome suit to be paid for, and, lastly and chiefly, the desire to serve a lady in need of service, which I believe is not an altogether strange desire in a man of sensibility. It has happened aforetime."

That was as near as he would go to the confession that she had beglamoured him. Since it was a state of mind that did not rest upon pure reason, it is one to which he would have been reluctant to confess even to himself.

She pondered him, and it seemed to him that her searching glance laid bare all that he was and all that he was likely to be.

"These are slight and unworldly reasons," she said at last.

"I am possibly an unworldly fellow."

"You must be, indeed, to propose knight-errantry."

But her need, as he had already surmised and as he was later fully to understand, was great and urgent. It may almost have seemed to her, indeed, as if Providence had brought her this young man, not only for his own salvation, but for hers.

"The service may entail risk," she warned him, "and a risk far greater than any you have run tonight."

"Risk sweetens enterprise," he answered, "and wit can conquer it."

Her smile broadened, almost she laughed. "You have a high confidence in your wit, sir."

"Whereas, you would say, the experience of the last four and twenty hours should make me humble. Its lesson, believe me, has not been lost. I am not again to be misled by appearances."

"Well, here's to test you, then." And she gave him her mes-

sage, which was after all a very cautious one, the betrayal of which could hardly harm her. He was to seek the Lord Barbaresco, of whom she told him nothing beyond the fact that the gentleman dwelt in a house behind the cathedral, which any townsman would point out to him. He was to inquire after his health, about which, he was to add, the absence of news was making her uneasy. As a credential to the Lord Barbaresco she gave him the broken half of a gold ducat.

"Tomorrow evening," she concluded, "you will find the garden gate ajar again at about the same hour, and I shall be waiting."

Chapter VI

The Winds of Fate

You behold Messer Bellarion treading the giddy slope of high and mysterious adventure, fortuitously launched upon a course whose end he was very far from discerning, but which most certainly was not the University of Pavia, the pursuit of Greek studies, and the recovery of an unblemished faith.

Lorenzaccio da Trino has more to answer for than the acts of brigandage for which the law pursued him.

In the gloom of that September night, after the moon had set, Bellarion, in raiment which already might be taken to symbolise the altered aim and purpose of his life, whereof himself, poor straw upon the winds of Fate, he was as yet unconscious, slipped from a gateway that was no longer guarded and directed his steps towards the heart of the town.

Coming in the Cathedral Square upon a company of the

watch, going the rounds with pikes and lanterns, he staggered a little in his gait and broke raucously into song to give himself the air of a belated, carefree reveller. Knowing no bawdy worldly songs proper to a man of his apparent circumstances and condition, he broke into a Gregorian chant, which he rendered in anything but the unisonous manner proper to that form of plain-song. The watch deeming him, as he computed that they would, an impudent parodist, warned him against disturbing the peace of the night, and asked who he was, whence he came, and whither he went.

Unprepared for these questions, he rose magnificently and rather incoherently to the occasion.

He knew that there was a house of Augustinian fathers in Casale. And boldly he stated that he had been supping there. Thus launched, his invention soared. The Prior's brother was married to his sister, and he had borne messages to the Prior from that same brother who dwelt in Cigliano, and was, like himself, a subject of the Duke of Savoy. He was lodged with his cousin-german, the Lord Barbaresco, whose house, having arrived but that day in Casale, he was experiencing some difficulty in finding.

"Body of Bacchus! Is that the reason?" quoth the leader of the patrol to the infinite amusement of his men.

They were as convinced as he himself was appalled by the fluency of his lying. Perhaps from that sympathy which men in his supposed state so commonly command, perhaps from the hope of reward, they volunteered to escort him to his cousin's dwelling.

To the narrow street behind the cathedral of which the Lord

Barbaresco's was the most imposing house, they now conducted him, and loudly they battered on his lordship's iron-studded door, until from a window overhead a quavering voice desired to know who knocked.

"His lordship's cousin returning home," replied the officer of the watch. "Make haste to open."

There was a mutter of voices in the dark overhead, and Bellarion awaited fearfully the repudiation that he knew must come.

"What cousin?" roared another, deeper voice. "I am expecting no cousin at this hour."

"He is angry with me," Bellarion explained. "I had promised to return to sup with him." He threw back his head, called up into the night in a voice momentarily clear. "Although the hour is late, I pray you, cousin, do not leave me standing here. Admit me and all, all, shall be explained." He stressed the verb, which for the Lord Barbaresco should have one meaning and for the too pertinacious watch another. And then he added certain mystic words to clinch the matter: "And bring a ducat to reward these good fellows. I have promised them a ducat, and have upon me only half a ducat. The half of a ducat," he repeated, as if with drunken insistence. "And what is half a ducat? No more than a broken coin."

The soldiers grinned at his drunken whimsicality. There was a long moment's pause. Then the deep voice above said, "Wait!" and a casement slammed.

Soon came a rasping of bolts, and the heavy door swung inwards, revealing a stout man in a purple bedgown, who shaded a candle-flame with his hand. The light was thrown up into a red

fleshly face that was boldly humorous, with a hooked nose and alert blue eyes under arched black brows.

Bellarion was quick to supply the cue. "Dear cousin, my excuses. I should have returned sooner. These good fellows have been most kind to me in this strange town."

Standing a little in front of the unsuspecting members of the watch, he met the Lord Barbaresco's searching glance by a grimace of warning.

"Give them the ducat for their pains, cousin, and let them go with God."

His lordship came prepared, it seemed.

"I thank you, sir," he said to the antient, "for your care of my cousin, a stranger here." And he dropped a gold coin into the readily projected palm. He stood aside, his hand upon the edge of the door. "Come you in, cousin."

But once alone with his enforced visitor in the stone passage, dimly lighted by that single candle, his lordship's manner changed.

"Who the devil are you, and what the devil do you seek?"

Bellarion showed his fine teeth in a broad smile, all sign of his intoxication vanished. "If you had not already answered those questions for yourself, you would neither have admitted me nor parted with your ducat, sir. I am what you were quick to suppose me. To the watch, I am your cousin, lodging with you on a visit to Casale. Lest you should repudiate me, I mentioned the half-ducat as a password."

"It was resourceful of you," Barbaresco grunted. "Who sent you?"

"Lord! The unnecessary questions that you ask! Why, the Lady Valeria, of course. Behold!" Under the eyes of Messer Barbaresco

he flashed the broken half of a ducat.

His lordship took the golden fragment, and holding it near the candle-flame read the half of the date inscribed upon it, then returned it to Bellarion, inviting him at last to come abovestairs.

They went up, Barbaresco leading, to a long, low-ceilinged chamber of the mezzanine, the walls of which were hung with soiled and shabby tapestries, the floor of which had been unswept for weeks. His lordship lighted a cluster of candles in a leaden candle-branch, and their golden light further revealed the bareness of the place, its sparse and hard-worn furnishings heavy with dust. He drew an armchair to the table where writing-implements and scattered papers made an untidy litter. He waved his guest to a seat, and asked his name.

"Bellarion."

"I never heard of the family."

"I never heard of it myself. But that's no matter. It's a name that serves as well as another."

"Ah!" Barbaresco accepted the name as assumed. He brushed the matter aside by a gesture. "Your message?"

"I bring no message. I come for one. Her highness is distracted by the lack of news from you, and by the fact that, although she has waited daily for a fortnight, in all that time Messer Giuffredo has not been near her."

Bellarion was still far from surmising who this Messer Giuffredo might be or what. But he knew that mention of the name must confirm him in Barbaresco's eyes, and perhaps lead to a discovery touching the identity of its owner. Because of the interest which the tawny-headed, sombre-eyed princess inspired in him, Bellarion was resolved to go beyond the precise extent of his mission as defined by her.

"Giuffredo took fright. A weak-stomached knave. He fancied himself observed when last he came from the palace garden, and nothing would induce him to go again."

So that whatever the intrigue, Bellarion now perceived, it was not amorous. Giuffredo clearly was a messenger and nothing more. Barbaresco himself, with his corpulence and his fifty years, or so, was incredible as a lover.

"Could not another have been sent in his place?"

"A messenger, my friend, is not readily found. Besides, nothing has transpired in the last two weeks of which it was urgently necessary to inform her highness."

"Surely, it was urgently necessary to inform her highness of just that, so as to allay her natural anxiety?"

Leaning back in his chair, his plump hands, which were red like all the rest of him that was visible, grasping the ends of its arms, the gentleman of Casale pondered Bellarion gravely.

"You assume a deal of authority, young sir. Who and what are you to be so deeply in the confidence of her highness?"

Bellarion was prepared for the question. "I am an amanuensis of the palace, whose duties happen to have brought me closely into touch with the Princess."

It was a bold lie, but one which he could support at least and at need by proofs of scholarliness.

Barbaresco nodded slowly.

"And your precise interest in her highness?"

Bellarion's smile was a little deprecating.

"Now, what should you suppose it?"

"I am not supposing. I am asking."

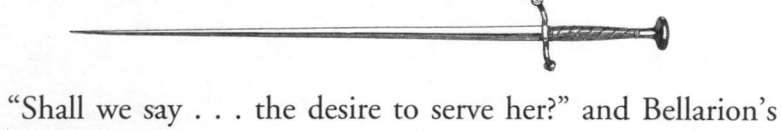

"Shall we say . . . the desire to serve her?" and Bellarion's smile became at once vague and eloquent. This, taken in conjunction with his reticence, might seem to imply a romantic attachment. Barbaresco, however, translated it otherwise.

"You have ambitions! So. That is as it should be. Interest is ever the best spur to endeavour."

And he, too, now smiled; a smile so oily and cynical that Bellarion set him down at once for a man without ideals, and mistrusted him from that moment. But he was strategist enough to conceal it, even to reflect something of that same cynicism in his own expression, so that Barbaresco, believing him a kindred spirit, should expand the more freely. And meanwhile he drew a bow at a venture.

"That which her highness looks to me to obtain is some explanation of your . . . inaction."

He chose the most noncommittal word; but it roused the Lord Barbaresco almost to anger.

"Inaction!" He choked, and his plethoric countenance deepened to purple. To prove the injustice of the charge, he urged his past activities of which he thus rendered an account. Luring him thence, by skilful question, assertion, and contradiction, along the apparent path of argument upon matters of which he must assume the young man already fully informed, gradually Bellarion drew from him a full disclosure of what was afoot. He learnt also a good deal of history of which hitherto he had been in ignorance, and he increased considerably his not very elevating acquaintance with the ways of men.

It was an evil enough thing which the Princess Valeria had set herself to combat with the assistance of some dispossessed

Guelphic gentlemen of Montferrat, the chief of whom was this Lord Barbaresco; and it magnified her in the eyes of Bellarion that she should evince the high courage necessary for the combat.

The extensive and powerful State of Montferrat was ruled at this time by the Marquis Theodore as regent during the minority of his nephew Gian Giacomo, son of that great Ottone who had been slain in the Neapolitan wars against the House of Brunswick.

These rulers of Montferrat, from Guglielmo, the great crusader, onwards, had ever been a warlike race, and Montferrat itself a school of arms. Nor had their proud belligerent nature been diluted by the blood of the Paleologi when on the death without male issue of Giovanni the Just a hundred years before, these dominions had passed to Theodore I, the younger son of Giovanni's sister Violante, who was married to the Emperor of the East, Andronicus Comnenus Paleologus.

The present Regent Theodore, however, combined with the soldierly character proper to his house certain qualities of craft and intrigue rarely found in knightly natures. The fact is, the Marquis Theodore had been ill-schooled. He had been reared at the splendid court of his cousin the Duke of Milan, that Gian Galeazzo whom Francesco da Carrara had dubbed "the Great Viper," in allusion as much to the man's nature as to the colubrine emblem of his house. Theodore had observed and no doubt admired the subtle methods by which Gian Galeazzo went to work against those whom he would destroy. If he lacked the godlike power of rendering them mad, at least he possessed the devilish craft of rendering them by their own acts detestable, so that in the end it was their own kin or their own subjects who pulled them down.

Witness the manner in which he had so poisoned the mind of Alberto of Este as to goad him into the brutal murder of almost all his relatives. It was his aim thus to render him odious to his Ferrarese subjects that by his extinction Ferrara might ultimately come under the crown of Milan. Witness how he forged love letters, which he pretended had passed between the wife and the secretary of his dear friend Francesco Gonzaga, Lord of Mantua, whereby he infuriated Gonzaga into murdering that innocent lady—who was Galeazzo's own cousin and sister-in-law—and tearing the secretary limb from limb upon the rack, so that Mantua rose against this human wolf who governed there. Witness all those other Lombard princes whom by fraud and misrepresentation, ever in the guise of a solicitous and loving friend, he lured into crimes which utterly discredited them with their subjects. This was an easier and less costly method of conquest than the equipping of great armies, and also it was more effective, because an invader who imposes himself by force can never hope to be so secure or esteemed as one whom the people have invited to become their ruler.

All this the Marquis Theodore had observed and marked, and he had seen Gian Galeazzo constantly widening his dominions by these means, ever increasing in power and consequence until in the end he certainly would have made of all Northern Italy a kingdom for his footstool had not the plague pursued him into the Castle of Melegnano, where he had shut himself up to avoid it, and there slain him in the year of grace 1402.

Trained in that school, the Marquis Theodore had observed and understood many things that would have remained hidden from an intelligence less acute.

He understood, for instance, that to rise by the pleasure of the people is the only way of reaching stable eminence, and that to accomplish this, noble qualities must be exhibited. For whilst men singly may be swayed by vicious appeals, collectively they will respond only to appeals of virtue.

Upon this elementary truth, according to Barbaresco, the Marquis Theodore was founding the dark policy which, from a merely temporary regent during the minority of his nephew, should render him the absolute sovereign of Montferrat. By the lavish display of public and private virtues, by affability towards great and humble, by endowments of beneficences, by the careful tempering of justice with mercy where this was publicly desired, he was rendering himself beloved and respected throughout the state. And step by step with this he was secretly labouring to procure contempt for his nephew, to whom in the ordinary course of events he would presently be compelled to relinquish the reins of government.

Nature, unfortunately, had rendered the boy weak. It was a weakness which training could mend as easily as increase. But to increase it were directed all the efforts which Theodore took care should be applied. Corsario the tutor, a Milanese, was a venal scoundrel, unhealthily ambitious. He kept the boy ignorant of all those arts that mature and grace the intellect, and confined instruction to matters calculated to corrupt his mind, his nature, and his morals. Castruccio, Lord of Fenestrella, the boy's first gentleman-in-waiting, was a vicious and depraved Savoyard, who had gamed away his patrimony almost before he had entered upon the enjoyment of it. It was easy to perceive the purpose for which the Regent had made him the boy's constant and intimate companion.

Here Bellarion, with that assumption of knowledge which had served to draw Barbaresco into explanations, ventured to interpose a doubt. "In that matter, I am persuaded that the Regent overreaches himself. The people know that he permits Castruccio to remain; and when they settle accounts with Castruccio they will also present a reckoning to the Regent."

Barbaresco laughed the argument to scorn.

"Either you do not realise Theodore's cunning, or you are insufficiently observant. Have not representations been made already to the Regent that Castruccio is no fit companion for the future Lord of Montferrat, or indeed for any boy? It merely enables Messer Theodore to parade his own paternal virtues, his gentleness of character, the boy's wilfulness, and the fact that he is, after all, no more than Regent of Montferrat. He would dismiss, he protests, Messer Castruccio, but the Prince is so devoted and attached to him that he would never be forgiven. And, after all, is that not true?"

"Aye, I suppose it is," Bellarion confessed.

Barbaresco was impatient of his dullness. "Of course it is. This Castruccio has known how to conquer the boy's love and wonder, by pretended qualities that fire youth's imagination. The whole world could hardly have yielded a better tool for the Regent or a worse companion for the little Prince."

Thus were the aims of the Marquis Theodore revealed to Bellarion, and the justifications for the movement that was afoot to thwart him. Of this movement for the salvation of her brother, the Princess Valeria was the heart and Barbaresco the brain. Its object was to overthrow the Marquis Theodore and place the government in the hands of a council of regency during the re-

mainder of Gian Giacomo's minority. Of this council Barbaresco assumed that he would be the president.

Sorrowfully Bellarion expressed a doubt.

"The mischief is that the Marquis Theodore is already so well established in the respect and affection of the people."

Barbaresco reared his head and threw out his chest. "Heaven will befriend a cause so righteous."

"My doubt concerns not the supernatural, but the natural means at our command."

It was a sobering reminder. Barbaresco left the transcendental and attempted to be practical. Also a subtle change was observable in his manner. He was no longer glibly frank. He became reserved and vague. They were going to work, he said, by laying bare the Regent's true policy. Already they had at least a dozen nobles on their side, and these were labouring to diffuse the truth. Once it were sufficiently diffused the rest would follow as inevitably as water runs downhill.

And this assurance was all the message that Bellarion was invited to take back to the Princess. But Bellarion was determined to probe deeper.

"That, sir, adds nothing to what the Lady Valeria already knows. It cannot allay the anxiety in which she waits. She requires something more definite."

Barbaresco was annoyed. Her highness should learn patience, and should learn to trust them. But Bellarion was so calmly insistent that at last Barbaresco angrily promised to summon his chief associates on the morrow, so that Bellarion might seek from them the further details he desired on the Lady Valeria's behalf.

Content, Bellarion begged a bed for the night, and was conducted to a mean, poverty-stricken chamber in that great empty house. On a hard and unclean couch he lay pondering the sad story of a wicked regent, a foolish boy, and a great-hearted lady, who, too finely reckless to count the cost of the ill-founded if noble enterprise to which she gave her countenance, would probably end by destroying herself together with her empty brother.

Chapter VII

Service

Stimulated by the insistence of this apparently accredited and energetic representative of the Princess, Messer Barbaresco assembled in his house in the forenoon of the following day a half-dozen gentlemen who were engaged with him upon that crack-brained conspiracy against the Regent of Montferrat. Four of these, including Count Enzo Spigno, were men who had been exiled because of Guelphic profession, and who had returned by stealth at Barbaresco's summons.

They talked a deal, as such folk will; but on the subject of real means by which they hoped to prevail they were so vague that Bellarion, boldly asserting himself, set about provoking revelation.

"Sirs, all this leads us nowhere. What, indeed, am I to convey to her highness? Just that here in Casale at my Lord Barbaresco's house some gentlemen of Montferrat hold assemblies to discuss

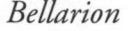

her brother's wrongs? Is that all?"

They gaped and frowned at him, and they exchanged dark glances among themselves, as if each interrogated his neighbour. It was Barbaresco at last who answered, and with some heat.

"You try my patience, sir. Did I not know you accredited by her highness I would not brook these hectoring airs . . ."

"If I were not so accredited, there would be no airs to brook." Thus he confirmed the impression of one deeper than they in the confidence of the Lady Valeria.

"But this is a sudden impatience on the Lady Valeria's part!" said one.

"It is not the impatience that is sudden. But the expression of it. I am telling you things that may not be written. Your last messenger, Giuffredo, was not sufficiently in her confidence. How should she have opened her mind to him? Whilst you, sirs, are all too cautious to approach her yourselves, lest in a subsequent miscarriage of your aims there should be evidence to make you suffer with her."

The first part of that assertion he had from themselves; the second was an inference, boldly expressed to search their intentions. And because not one of them denied it, he knew what to think—knew that their aims amounted to more, indeed, than they were pretending.

In silence they looked at him as he stood there in a shaft of morning sunlight that had struggled through the curtain of dust and grime on the blurred glass of the mullioned window. And then at last, Count Spigno, a lean, tough, swarthy gentleman, whose expressions had already revealed him the bitterest enemy there of the Marquis Theodore, loosed a short laugh.

"By the Host! He's in the right." He swung to Bellarion. "Sir, we should deserve the scorn you do not attempt to dissemble if our plans went no farther than . . ."

The voices of his fellow conspirators were raised in warning. But he brushed them contemptuously aside, a bold rash man.

"A choicely posted arbalester will . . ."

He got no further. This time his utterance was smothered by their anger and alarm. Barbaresco and another laid rough hands upon him, and through the general din rang the opprobrious epithets they bestowed upon him, of which 'fool' and 'madman' were the least. Amongst them they cowed him, and when it was done they turned again to Bellarion who had not stirred from where he stood, maintaining a frown of pretended perplexity between his level black brows.

It was Barbaresco, oily and crafty, who sought to dispel, to deviate any assumption Bellarion might have formed.

"Do not heed his words, sir. He is forever urging rash courses. He, too, is impatient. And impatience is a dangerous mood to bring to such matters as these."

Bellarion was not deceived. They would have him believe that Count Spigno had intended no more than to urge a course, whereas what he perceived was that the Count had been about to disclose the course already determined, and had disclosed enough to make a guess of the remainder easy. No less did he perceive that to betray his apprehension of this fact might be never to leave that house alive. He could read it in their glances, as they waited to learn from his answer how much he took for granted.

Therefore he used a deep dissimulation. He shrugged ill-humouredly.

"Yet patience, sirs, can be exceeded until from a virtue it becomes a vice. I have more respect for an advocate of rash courses"—and he inclined his head slightly to Count Spigno—"than for those who practise an excessive caution whilst time is slipping by."

"That, sir," Barbaresco rebuked him, "is because you are young. With age, if you are spared, you will come to know better."

"Meanwhile," said Bellarion, completely to reassure them, "I see plainly enough that your message to her highness is scarce worth carrying." And he flung himself down into his chair with simulated petulance.

The conference came to an end soon afterwards, and the conspirators went their ways again singly. Shortly after the departure of the last of them, Bellarion took his own, promising that he would return that night to Messer Barbaresco's house to inform him of anything her highness might desire him to convey. One last question he asked his host at parting.

"The pavilion in the palace gardens is being painted. Can you say by whom?"

Barbaresco's eyes showed that he found the question odd. But he answered that most probably one Gobbo, whose shop was in the Via del Cane, would be entrusted with the work.

Into that shop of Gobbo's, found by inquiry, Bellarion penetrated an hour later. Old Gobbo himself, amid the untidy litter of the place, was engaged in painting an outrageous scarlet angel against a star-flecked background of cobalt blue. Bellarion's first question ascertained that the painting of the pavilion was indeed in Gobbo's hands.

"My two lads are engaged upon it now, my lord."

Bellarion winced at the distinguished form of address, which took him by surprise until he remembered his scarlet suit with its imposing girdle and gold-hilted dagger.

"The work progresses all too slowly," said he sharply.

"My lord! My lord!" The old man was flung into agitation. "It is a beautiful fresco, and . . ."

"They require assistance, those lads of yours."

"Assistance!" The old man flung his arms to heaven. "Where shall I find assistants with the skill?"

"Here," said Bellarion, and tapped his breast with his forefinger.

Amazed, Gobbo considered his visitor more searchingly. Bellarion leaned nearer, and lowered his voice to a tone of confidence.

"I'll be frank with you, Ser Gobbo. There is a lady of the palace, a lady of her highness . . ." He completed his sentence, by roguishly closing an eye.

Gobbo's lean brown old face cracked across in a smile, as becomes an old artist who finds himself face to face with romance.

"You understand, I see," said Bellarion, smiling in his turn. "It is important that I should have a word with this lady. There are grave matters . . . I'll not weary you with these and my own sad story. Perform a charitable act to your own profit."

But Gobbo's face had grown serious. "If it were discovered . . ." he was beginning.

"It shall not be. That I promise you full confidently. And to compensate you . . . five ducats."

"Five ducats!" It was a great sum, and confirmed Master Gobbo in the impression made by Bellarion's appearance, dress, and manner, that here he dealt with a great lord. "For five ducats . . ." He broke off, and scratched his head.

85

Bellarion perceived that he must not be given time for thought.

"Come, my friend, lend me the clothes for the part and a smock such as is proper, and do you keep these garments of mine in pledge for my safe return and for the five ducats that shall then be yours."

He knew how to be irresistible, and he was fortunate in his present victim. He went off a half-hour or so later in the garb of his suddenly assumed profession and bearing a note from Gobbo to his sons.

Late in the afternoon Bellarion lounged in the pavilion in the palace garden to which his pretence had gained him easy admission. He mixed some colours for the two young artists under their direction. But beyond that he did nothing save wait for sunset when the light would fail and the two depart. Himself, though not without the exertion of considerable persuasions based upon a display of his amorous intentions, he remained behind to clear things up.

Thus it happened that, as the Lady Dionara was walking by the lake, she heard herself addressed from the bridge that led to the pavilion.

"Madonna! Gracious madonna!"

She turned to behold a tall young man with tumbled black hair and a smear of paint across his face in a smock that was daubed with every colour of the rainbow, waving a long-handled brush in a gesture towards the temple.

"Would not her highness," he was asking, "graciously condescend to view the progress of the frescoes?"

The Lady Dionara looked down her nose at this greatly presumptuous fellow until he added softly: "And receive news at the

same time of the young man she befriended yesterday?" That changed her expression, so swift and ludicrously that Bellarion was moved to silent laughter.

To view those frescoes came the Lady Valeria alone, leaving Monna Dionara to loiter on the bridge. Within the temple her highness found the bedaubed young painter dangling his legs from a scaffold and flourishing a brush in one hand, a mahlstick in the other. She looked at him in waiting silence. He did not try her patience.

"Madonna, you do not recognise me." With the sleeve of his smock he wiped the daub of paint from across his features. But already his voice had made him known.

"Messer Bellarion! Is it yourself?"

"Myself." He came to the ground. "To command."

"But . . . why this? Why thus?" Her eyes were wide; she was a little breathless.

"I have had a busy day, madonna, and a busy night, and I have more to report than may hurriedly be muttered behind a hedge."

"You bring messages?"

"The message amounts to nothing. It is only to say that Messer Giuffredo, fancying himself followed and watched on the last occasion, is not to be induced to come again. And in the meanwhile nothing has happened of which it was worthwhile to inform you. Messer Barbaresco desires me further to say that everything progresses satisfactorily, which I interpret to mean that no progress whatever is being made."

"You interpret . . ."

"And I venture to add, having been entertained at length, not only by Messer Barbaresco, but also by the other out-at-elbow nobles in this foolish venture, that it never will progress in the sense you wish, nor to any end but disaster."

He saw the scarlet flame of indignation overspread her face, he saw the anger kindle in her great dark eyes, and he waited calmly for the explosion. But the Lady Valeria was not explosive. Her rebuke was cold.

"Sir, you presume upon a messenger's office. You meddle in affairs that are not your concern."

"Do you thank God for it," said Bellarion, unabashed. "It is time someone gave these things their proper names so as to re- move all misconception. Do you know whither Barbaresco and these other fools are thrusting you, madonna? Straight into the hands of the strangler."

Having conquered her anger once, she was not easily to be betrayed into it again.

"If that is all you have to tell me, sir, I will leave you. I'll not remain to hear my friends and peers maligned by a base knave to whom I speak by merest accident."

"Not accident, madonna." His tone was impressive. "A base knave I may be. But base by birth alone. These others whom you trust and call your peers are base by nature. Ah, wait! It was no accident that brought me!" he cried, and this with a sincerity from which none could have suspected the violence he did to his beliefs. "Ask yourself why I should come again to do more than is required of me, at some risk to myself? What are your affairs, or the affairs of the State of Montferrat, to me? You know what I am and what my aims. Why, then, should I tarry here? Because I cannot help myself. Because the will of Heaven has imposed itself upon me."

His great earnestness, his very vehemence, which seemed to invest his simple utterances with a tone of inspiration, impressed her despite herself, as he intended that they should. Nor did she deceive him when she dissembled this in light derision.

"An archangel in a painter's smock!"

"By Saint Hilary, that is nearer the truth than you suppose it."

She smiled, yet not entirely without sourness. "You do not lack a good opinion of yourself."

"You may come to share it when I've said all that's in my mind. I have told you, madonna, whither these crack-brained adventurers are thrusting you, so that they may advance themselves. Do you know the true import of the conspiracy? Do you know what they plan, these fools? The murder of the Marquis Theodore."

She stared at him round-eyed, afraid. "Murder?" she said in a voice of horror.

He smiled darkly. "They had not told you, eh? I knew they dared not. Yet so indiscreet and rash are they that they betrayed it to me—to me of whom they know nothing save that I carried as an earnest of my good faith your broken half-ducat. What if I were just a scoundrel who would sell to the Marquis Theodore a piece of information for which he would no doubt pay handsomely? Do you still think that it was accident brought me to interfere in your concerns?"

"I can't believe you! I can't!" and again she breathed, aghast, that horrid word: "Murder!"

"If they succeeded," said Bellarion coldly, "all would be well. Your uncle would have no more than his deserts, and you and your brother would be rid of an evil incubus. The notion does not shock me at all. What shocks me is that I see no chance of success for a plot conducted by such men with such inadequate resources. By joining them you can but advance the Regent's aims, which you believe to be the destruction of your brother. Let the attempt be made, and fail, or even let evidence be forthcoming of the conspiracy's existence and true purpose, and your brother is at the Regent's mercy. The people themselves might demand his outlawry or even his death for an attempt upon the life of a prince who has known how to make himself beloved."

"But my brother is not in this," she protested. "He knows nothing of it."

Bellarion smiled compassionately. "*Cui bono fuerit?* That is the first question which the law will ask. Be warned, madonna! Dissociate yourself from these men while it is time or you may enable the Regent at a single stride to reach his ultimate ambition."

The pallor of her face, the heave of her breast, were witnesses to her agitation. "You would frighten me if I did not know how false is your main assumption: that they plot murder. They would never dare to do this thing without my sanction, and this they have never sought."

"Because they intend to confront you with an accomplished fact. Oh, you may believe me, madonna. In the last twenty-four hours and chiefly from these men I have learnt much of the history of Montferrat. And I have learnt a deal of their own histories too. There is not one amongst them who is not reduced in circumstances, whose state has not been diminished by lack of fortune or lack of worth."

But for this she had an answer, and she delivered it with a slow, wistful smile.

"You talk, sir, as if you contained all knowledge, and yet you have not learnt that the fortunate desire no change, but labour to uphold the state whence their prosperity is derived. Is it surprising, then, that I depend upon the unfortunate?"

"Say also the venal, those greedy of power and of possessions, whose only spur is interest; desperate gamblers who set their heads upon the board and your own and your brother's head with theirs. Almost they divided among themselves in their talk the offices of State. Barbaresco promised me that the ambition he perceived in me should be fully gratified. He assumed that I, too, had no aim but self-aggrandisement, simply because he could assume no other reason why a man should expose himself to risks. That told me all of him that I required to know."

"Barbaresco is poor," she answered. "He has suffered wrongs. Once, in my father's time he was almost the greatest man in the State. My uncle has stripped him of his honours and almost of his possessions."

"That is the best thing I have heard of the Marquis Theodore yet."

She did not heed him, but went on: "Can I desert him now? Can I . . . ?" She checked and stiffened, seeming to grow taller. "What am I saying? What am I thinking?" She laughed, and there was scorn of self in her laugh. "What arts do you employ, you, an unknown man, a self-confessed starveling student, base and nameless, that upon no better warrant than your word I should even ask such a question?"

"What arts?" said he, and smiled in his turn, though without scorn. "The art of pure reason based on truth. It is not to be resisted."

"Not if based on truth. But yours is based on prejudice."

"Is it prejudice that they are plotting murder?"

"They have been misled by their devotion . . ."

"By their cupidity, madonna."

"I will not suffer you to say that." Anger flared up again in her, loyal anger on behalf of those she deemed her only friends in her great need. She checked it instantly, "Sir, I perceive your interest, and I am grateful. If you would still do me a service, go, tell Messer Barbaresco from me that this plot of assassination must go no further. Impose it upon him as my absolute command. Tell him that I must be obeyed and that, rather than be a party to such an act, I would disclose the intention to the Marquis Theodore."

"That is something, madonna. But if when you have slept upon it . . ."

She interrupted him. "Upon whatever course I may determine I shall find means to convey the same to my Lord Barbaresco. There will not be the need to trouble you again. For what you have done, sir, I shall remain grateful. So, go with God, Messer Bellarion."

She was turning away when he arrested her.

"It is a little personal matter this. I am in need of five ducats."

He saw the momentary frown, chased away by the beginnings of a smile.

"You are consistent in that you misunderstand me, though I have once reminded you that if I needed money for myself I could

sell my information to the Regent. The five ducats are for Gobbo who lent me this smock and these tools of my pretended trade." And he told her the exact circumstances.

She considered him more gently. "You do not lack resource, sir?"

"It goes with intelligence, madonna," he reminded her as an argument in favour of what he said. But she ignored it.

"And I am sorry that I . . . You shall have ten ducats, unless your pride is above . . ."

"Do you see pride in me?"

She looked him over with a certain haughty amusement. "A monstrous pride, an overweening vanity in your acuteness."

"I'll take ten ducats to convince you of my humility. I may yet need the other five in the service of your highness."

"That service, sir, is at an end, or will be when you have conveyed my message to the Lord Barbaresco."

Bellarion accepted his dismissal in the settled conviction that her highness was mistaken and would presently be glad to admit it.

She was right, you see, touching that vanity of his.

Chapter VIII

Stalemate

Bellarion and Barbaresco sat at supper, waited upon by an untidy and unclean old man who afforded all the service of that decayed establishment. The fare was frugal, more frugal far than the Convent of Cigliano had afforded out of Lent, and the wine was thin and sharp.

When the repast was done and the old servant, having lighted candles, had retired, Bellarion startled his host by the portentous gravity of his tone.

"My lord, you and I must talk. I told you that her highness sends no answer to your message, which is the truth, and all that you could expect, since there was no message and consequently could be no answer. I did not tell you, however, that she sends you a message which is in some sense an answer to certain suspicions that I voiced to her."

Barbaresco's mouth fell open, and the stare of his blue eyes grew fixed. Clearly he was startled, and clearly paused to command himself before asking:

"Why did you not tell me this before?"

"I preferred to wait so as to make sure of not going supperless. It may, of course, offend you that I should have communicated my suspicions to her highness. But the poor lady was so downcast by your inaction, that to cheer her I ventured the opinion that you are perhaps not quite so aimless as you wish to appear."

Whatever his convent education may have done for him, it does not seem—as you will long since have gathered—that it had inculcated a strict regard for exactitude. Dissimulation, I fear, was bred in the bones of him; although he would have answered any such charge by informing you that Plato had taught him to distinguish between the lie on the lips and the lie in the heart.

"Oh, but proceed! The opinion?" Barbaresco fiercely challenged him.

"You'll remember what Count Spigno said before you others checked him. The arbalester . . . You remember." Bellarion appeared to falter a little under the glare of those blue eyes and the fierce set of that heavy jaw. "So I told her highness, to raise her drooping spirits, that one of these fine days her friends in Casale might cut the Gordian knot with a crossbow shaft."

Barbaresco suggested by his attitude a mastiff crouching for a spring.

"Ah!" he commented. "And she said?"

"The very contrary of what I expected. Where I looked for elation, I found only distress. It was in vain I pleaded with her that thus a consummation would speedily be reached; that if such

95

a course had not yet been determined, it was precisely the course that I should advocate."

"Oh! You pleaded that! And she?"

"She bade me tell you that if such a thing were indeed in your minds, you must dismiss it. That she would be no party to it. That sooner she would herself denounce the intention to the Marquis Theodore."

"Body of God!" Barbaresco came to his feet, his great face purple, the veins of his temples standing forth like cords.

Whilst appearing unmoved, Bellarion braced his muscles for action.

The attack came. But only in words. Barbaresco heaped horrible and obscene abuse upon Bellarion's head. "You infamous fool! You triple ass! You chattering ape!" With these, amongst other terms, the young man found himself bombarded. "Get you back to her, and tell her, you numskulled baboon, that there was never any such intention."

"But was there not?" Bellarion cried with almost shrill ingenuousness of tone. "Yet Count Spigno . . ."

"Devil take Count Spigno, fool. Heed me. Carry my message to her highness."

"I carry no lies," said Bellarion firmly, and rose with great dignity.

"Lies!" gurgled Barbaresco.

"Lies," Bellarion insisted. "Let us have done with them. To her highness I expressed as a suspicion what in my mind was a clear conviction. The words Count Spigno used, and your anxiety to silence him, could leave no doubt in any man of wit, and I am that, I hope, my lord. If you will have this message carried, you will first show me the ends you serve by its falsehood, and let me, who am in this thing as deep as any, be the judge of whether it is justified."

Before this firmness the wrath went out of Barbaresco. Weakly he wrung his hands a moment, then sank sagging into his chair.

"If the others, if Cavalcanti or Casella, had known how much you had understood, you would never have left this house alive, lest you should do precisely what you have done."

"But if it is on her behalf—hers and her brother's—that you plan this thing, why should you not take her feeling first? What else is right or fair?"

"Her feeling?" Barbaresco sneered, and Bellarion understood that the sneer was for himself. "God deliver me from the weariness of reasoning with a fool. Our bolt would have been shot, and none could have guessed the hands that loosed it. Now you have made it known, and you need to be told what will happen if we were mad enough to go through with it. Why, the Princess Valeria would be our instant accuser. She would come forth at once and denounce us. That is the spirit of her; wilful, headstrong, and mawkish. And I am a fool to bid you go back to her and persuade her that you were mistaken. When the blow fell, she would see that what you had first told her was the truth, and our heads would pay."

He set his elbows on the table, took his head in his hands, and fetched a groan from his great bulk. "The ruin you have wrought! God! The ruin!"

"Ruin?" quoth Bellarion.

"Of all our hopes," Barbaresco explained in petulance. "Can't you see it? Can you understand nothing for yourself, animal, save

the things you were better for not understanding? And can't you see that you have ruined yourself with us? With your face and shape and already close in the Lady Valeria's confidence as you are, there are no heights in the State to which you might not have climbed."

"I had not thought of it," said Bellarion, sighing.

"No, nor of me, nor of any of us. Of me!" The man's grief became passionate. "At last I might have sloughed this beggary in which I live. And now . . ." He banged the table in his sudden rage, and got to his feet again. "That is what you have done. That is what you have wrecked by your silly babbling."

"But surely, sir, by other means . . ."

"There are no other means. Leastways, no other means at our command. Have we the money to levy troops? Oh, why do I waste my breath upon you? You'll tell the others tomorrow what you've done, and they shall tell you what they think of it."

It was a course that had its perils. But if once in the stillness of the night Bellarion's shrewd wits counselled him to rise, dress, and begone, he stilled the coward counsel. It remained to be seen whether the other conspirators would be as easily intimidated as Barbaresco. To ascertain this, Bellarion determined to remain. The Lady Valeria's need of him was not yet done, he thought, though why the Lady Valeria's affairs should be the cause of his exposing himself to the chances of a blade between the ribs was perhaps more than he could satisfactorily have explained.

That the danger was very far from imaginary the next morning's conference showed him. Scarcely had the plotters realised the nature of Bellarion's activities than they were clamouring for his blood. Casella, the exile, breathing fire and slaughter, would have sprung upon him with dagger drawn, had not Barbaresco bodily interposed.

"Not in my house!" he roared. "Not in my house!" his only concern being the matter of his own incrimination.

"Nor anywhere, unless you are bent on suicide," Bellarion calmly warned them. He moved from behind Barbaresco, to confront them. "You are forgetting that in my murder the Lady Valeria will see your answer. She will denounce you, sirs, not only for this, but for the intended murder of the Regent. Slay me, and you just as surely slay yourselves." He permitted himself to smile as he looked upon their stricken faces. "It's an interesting situation, known in chess as a stalemate."

In their baffled fury they turned upon Count Spigno, whose indiscretion had created this situation. Enzo Spigno, sitting there with a sneer on his white face, let the storm rage. When at last it abated, he expressed himself.

"Rather should you thank me for having tested the ground before we stand on it. For the rest, it is as I expected. It is an ill thing to be associated with a woman in these matters."

"We did not bring her in," said Barbaresco. "It was she who appealed to me for assistance."

"And now that we are ready to afford it her," said Casella, "she discovers that it is not of the sort she wishes. I say it is not hers to choose. Hopes have been raised in us, and we have laboured to fulfil them."

How they all harped on that, thought Bellarion. How concerned was each with the profit that he hoped to wrest for himself, how enraged to see himself cheated of this profit. The Lady Valeria, the State, the boy who was being corrupted that he might

be destroyed, these things were nothing to these men. Not once did he hear them mentioned now in the futile disorderly debate that followed, whilst he sat a little apart and almost forgotten.

At last it was Spigno, this Spigno whom they dubbed a fool—but who, after all, had more wit than all of them together—who discovered and made the countermove.

"You there, Master Bellarion!" he called. "Here is what you are to tell your lady in answer to her threat: We who have set our hands to this task of ridding the State of the Regent's thraldom will not draw back. We go forward with this thing as seems best to us, and we are not to be daunted by threats. Make it clear to this arrogant lady that she cannot betray us without at the same time betraying herself; that whatever fate she invokes upon us will certainly overtake her as well."

"It may be that she has already perceived and weighed that danger," said Bellarion.

"Aye, as a danger; but perhaps not as a certainty. And tell her also that she as certainly dooms her brother. Make her understand that it is not so easy to play with the souls of men as she supposes, and that here she has evoked forces which it is not within her power to lay again." He turned to his associates. "Be sure that when she perceives precisely where she stands, she will cease to trouble us with her qualms either now or when the thing is done."

Bellarion had mockingly pronounced the situation interesting when by a shrewd presentment of it he had given pause to the murderous rage of the conspirators. Considering it later that day as he took the air along the river-brink, he was forced to confess it more disturbingly interesting even than he had shown it to be.

He had not been blind to that weakness in the Lady Valeria's position. But he had been foolishly complacent, like the skilful chessplayer who, perceiving a strong move possible to his opponent, takes it for granted that the opponent himself will not perceive it.

It seemed to him that nothing remained but to resume his interrupted pilgrimage to Pavia, leaving the State of Montferrat and the Lady Valeria to settle their own affairs. But in that case, her own ruin must inevitably follow, precipitated by the action of those ruffians with whom she was allied, whether that action succeeded or failed.

Then he asked himself what to him were the affairs of Montferrat and its princess, that he should risk his life upon them.

He fetched a sigh. The Abbot had been right. There is no peace in this world outside a convent wall. Certainly there was no peace in Montferrat. Let him shake the dust of that place of unrest from his feet, and push on towards Pavia and the study of Greek.

And so, by olive grove and vineyard, he wandered on, assuring himself that it was towards Pavia that he now went, and repeating to himself that he would reach the Sesia before nightfall and seek shelter in some hamlet thereabouts.

Yet dusk saw him reëntering Casale by the Lombard Gate which faces eastwards. And this because he realised that the service he had shouldered was a burden not so lightly to be cast aside: if he forsook her now, the vision of her tawny head and wistful eyes would go with him to distract him with reproach.

Chapter IX

The Marquis Theodore

The High and Mighty Marquis Theodore Paleologo, Regent of Montferrat, gave audience as was his gracious custom each Saturday to all who sought it, and received petitions from all who proffered them.

A fine man, this Marquis Theodore, standing fully six feet tall, of a good shape and soldierly carriage, despite his fifty years. His countenance was amiable and open with boldly chiselled features and healthily tanned skin. Affable of manner, accessible of person, he nowise suggested the schemer. The privilege of audience which he granted so freely was never abused, so that on the Saturday of this week with which we are dealing the attendance in the audience chamber was as usual of modest proportions. His highness came, attended by his Chancellor and his Captain of Justice, and followed by two secretaries; he made a leisurely progress through the chamber, pausing at every other step to receive this one, or to say a word to that one; and at the end of an hour departed again, one of his secretaries bearing away the single petition that had been proffered, and this by a tall, dark-haired young man who was vividly dressed in scarlet.

Within five minutes of the Regent's withdrawal, that same secretary returned in quest of the tall young man in red.

"Are you named Cane, sir?"

The tall young man bowed acknowledgment, and was ushered into a small, pleasant chamber, whose windows overlooked the gardens with which Bellarion had already made acquaintance. The secretary closed the door, and Bellarion found himself under the scrutiny of a pair of close-set pale eyes whose glance was crafty and penetrating. Cross-legged, the parti-coloured hose revealed by the fall of the rich gown of mulberry velvet, the Regent sat in a high-backed chair of leather wrought with stags' heads in red and gold, his left elbow resting upon a carved writing-pulpit.

Between hands that were long and fine, he held a parchment cylinder, in which Bellarion recognised the pretended petition he had proffered.

"Who are you, sir?" The voice was calm and level; the voice of a man who does not permit his accents to advertise his thoughts.

"My name is Bellarion Cane. I am the adoptive son of Bonifacio Cane, Count of Biandrate."

Since he had found it necessary for his present purposes to adopt a father, Bellarion had thought it best to adopt one whose name must carry weight and at need afford protection. Therefore he had conferred this honour of paternity upon that great soldier, Facino Cane, who was ducal governor of Milan.

There was a flash of surprise from the eyes that conned him. "You are Facino's son! You come from Milan, then?"

"No, my lord. From the Augustinian Convent at Cigliano, where my adoptive father left me some years ago whilst he was still in the service of Montferrat. It was hoped that I might take the habit. But a restlessness of spirit has urged me to prefer the world." Thus he married pure truth to the single falsehood he had used, the extent of which was to clothe the obscure soldier who had befriended him with the identity of the famous soldier he had named.

"But why the world of Montferrat?"

"Chance determined that. I bore letters from my abbot to help me on my way. It was thus I made the acquaintance of the Lord Barbaresco, and his lordship becoming interested in me, and no doubt requiring me for certain services, desired me to remain. He urged that here was a path already open to my ambition, which if steadily pursued might lead to eminence."

There was no falsehood in the statement. It was merely truth untruly told, truth unassailable under test, yet calculated to convey a false impression.

A thin smile parted the Prince's shaven lips. "And when you had learnt sufficient, you found that a surer path to advancement might lie in the betrayal of these poor conspirators?"

"That, highness, is to set the unworthiest interpretation upon my motives." Bellarion made a certain show in his tone and manner of offended dignity, such as might become the venal rascal he desired to be considered.

"You will not dispute that the course you have taken argues more intelligence than honesty or loyalty."

"Your highness reproaches me with lack of loyalty to traitors?"

"What was their treason to you? What loyalty do you owe to me? You have but looked to see where lies your profit. Well, well, you are worthy to be the son, adoptive or natural, of that rascal Facino. You follow closely in his footsteps, and if you survive the perils of the journey you may go as far."

"Highness! I came to serve you . . ."

"Silence!" The pleasant voice was scarcely raised. "I am speaking. I understand your service perfectly. I know something of men, and if I choose to use you, it is because your hope of profit may keep you loyal, and because I shall know how to detect disloyalty and how to punish it. You engage, sir, in a service full of perils." The Regent seemed faintly to sneer. "But you have thrust yourself willingly into it. It will test you sternly and at every step. If you survive the tests, if you conquer the natural baseness and dishonesty of your nature, you shall have no cause to complain of my generosity."

Bellarion flushed despite himself under the cold contempt of that level voice and the amused contempt of those calm, pale eyes.

"The quality of my service should lead your highness to amend your judgment."

"Is it at fault? Will you tell me, then, whence springs the regard out of which you betray to me the aims and names of these men who have befriended you?"

Bellarion threw back his head and in his bold dark eyes was kindled a flame of indignation. Inwardly he was a little uneasy to find the Regent accepting his word so readily and upon such slight examination.

"Your highness," he choked, "will give me leave to go."

But his highness smiled, savouring his power to torture souls where lesser tyrants could torture only bodies.

"When I have done with you. You came at your own pleasure. You abide at mine. Now tell me, sir: Besides the names you have here set down of these men who seek my life, do you know of any others who work in concert with them?"

"I know that there are others whom they are labouring to seduce. Who these others are I cannot say, nor, with submission, need it matter to your highness. These are the leaders. Once these are crushed, the others will be without direction."

"A seven-headed hydra, of which these are the heads. If I lop off these heads . . ." He paused. "Yes, yes. But have you heard none others named in these councils?" He leaned forward a little, his eyes intent upon Bellarion's face. "None who are nearer to me? Think well, Master Bellarion, and be not afraid to name names, however great."

Bellarion perceived here, almost by instinct, the peril of too great a reticence.

"Since they profess to labour on behalf of the Marquis Gian Giacomo, it is natural they should name him. But I have never heard it asserted that he has knowledge of their plot."

"Nor any other?" The Marquis was singularly insistent. "Nor any other?" he repeated.

Bellarion showed a blank face. "Why? What other?"

"Nay, sir. I am asking you."

"No, highness," he slowly answered. "I recall the mention of no other."

The Prince sank back into his chair, his searching eyes never quitting the young man's face. Then he committed what in a man so subtle was a monstrous indiscretion, giving Bellarion the explanation that he lacked.

"You are not deep enough in their confidence yet. Return to their councils, and keep me informed of all that transpires in them. Be diligent, and you shall find me generous."

Bellarion was genuinely aghast. "Your highness will delay to strike when by delay you may imperil . . . ?"

He was sternly silenced. "Is your counsel sought? You understand what I require of you. You have leave to go."

"But, highness! To return amongst them now, after openly coming here to you, will not be without its danger."

The Regent did not share his alarm. He smiled again.

"You have chosen a path of peril as I told you. But I will help you. I discover that I have letters from Facino humbly soliciting my protection for his adoptive son whilst in Casale. It is a petition I cannot disregard. Facino is a great lord in Milan these days. My court shall be advised of it, and it will not be considered strange that I make you free of the palace. You will persuade your confederates that you avail yourself of my hospitality so that you may abuse it in their interests. That should satisfy them, and I shall look to see you here this evening. Now go with God."

Bellarion stumbled out distracted. Nothing had gone as he intended after that too promising beginning. Perhaps had he not disclosed himself as Facino Cane's adoptive son, he would not have supplied the Regent with a pretence that should render plausible his comings and goings. But the necessity for that disclosure was undeniable. His conduct had been dictated by the conviction that he could do for the Lady Valeria what she could not without self-betrayal do for herself. Confidently he had counted

upon instant action of the Regent to crush the conspirators, and so make the Princess safe from the net in which their crazy ambitions would entangle her. Instead he had made the discovery—from the single indiscretion of the Regent—that the Marquis Theodore was already fully aware of the existence of the conspiracy and of the identity of some, if not all, of the chief conspirators. That was why he had so readily accepted Bellarion's tale. The disclosure agreed so completely with the Regent's knowledge that he had no cause to doubt Bellarion's veracity. And finding him true in these most intimate details, he readily believed true the rest of his story and the specious account of his own intervention in the affair. Possibly Bellarion's name was already known to him as that of one of the plotters who met at Barbaresco's house.

Far, then, from achieving his real purpose, all that Bellarion had accomplished was to offer himself as another and apparently singularly apt instrument for the Regent's dark purposes.

It was a perturbed Bellarion, a Bellarion who perceived in what dangerous waters he was swimming, who came back that noontide to Barbaresco's house.

Chapter X

The Warning

They were very gay that night at the hospitable court of the Marquis Theodore. A comedy was performed early in the evening, a comedy which Fra Serafino in his chronicle describes as lascivious, by which he may mean no more than playful. Thereafter there was some dancing in the long hall, of which the Regent himself set the example, leading forth the ugly but graceful young Princess of Morea.

His nephew, the Marquis Gian Giacomo, followed with the Countess of Ronsecco, who would have declined the honour if she had dared, for the boy's cheeks were flushed, his eyes glazed, his step uncertain, and his speech noisy and incoherent. And there were few who smiled as they observed the drunken antics of their future prince. Once, indeed, the Regent paused, grave and concerned of countenance, to whisper an admonition. The boy answered him with a bray of insolent laughter, and flung away, dragging the pretty countess with him. It was plain to all that the gentle, knightly Regent found it beyond his power to control his unruly, degenerate nephew.

Amongst the few who dared to smile was Messer Castruccio da Fenestrella, radiant in a suit of cloth of gold, who stood watching the mischief he had made. For it was he who had first secretly challenged Gian Giacomo to a drinking-bout during supper, and afterwards urged him to dance with the pretty wife of stiff-necked Ronsecco.

Awhile he stood looking on. Then, wearying of the entertainment, he sauntered off to join a group apart of which the Lady Valeria was the centre. Her ladies, Dionara and Isotta, were with her, the pedant Corsario, looking even less pedantic than his habit, and a half-dozen gallants who among them made all the chatter. Her highness was pale, and there was a frown between her eyes that so wistfully followed her unseemly brother, inattentive of those about her, some of whom from the kindliest motives sought to distract her attention. Her cheeks warmed a little at the approach of Castruccio, who moved into the group with easy, insolent grace.

"My lord is gay tonight," he informed them lightly. None answered him. He looked at them with his flickering, shifty eyes, a sneering smile on his lips. "So are not you," he informed them. "You need enlivening." He thrust forward to the Princess, and bowed. "Will your highness dance?"

She did not look at him. Her eyes were fixed, and their glance went beyond him and was of such intensity that Messer Castruccio turned to seek the object of that curious contemplation.

Down the hall came striding Messer Aliprandi, the Orator of Milan, and with him a tall, black-haired young man, in a suit of red that was more conspicuous than suitable of fashion to the place or the occasion. Into the group about the Princess they came, whilst the exquisite Castruccio eyed this unfashionable young man with frank contempt, bearing his pomander-ball to his nostrils, as if to protect his olfactory organs from possible offence.

Messer Aliprandi, trimly bearded, elegant in his furred gown, and suavely mannered, bowed low before the Lady Valeria.

"Permit me, highness, to present Messer Bellarion Cane, the son of my good friend Facino Cane of Biandrate."

It was the Marquis Theodore, who had requested the Orator of Milan—as was proper, seeing that by reason of his paternity Bellarion was to be regarded as Milanese—to present his assumed compatriot to her highness.

Bellarion, modelling himself upon Aliprandi, executed his bow with grace.

As Fra Serafino truthfully says of him: "He learnt manners and customs and all things so quickly that he might aptly be termed a fluid in the jug of any circumstance."

The Lady Valeria inclined her head with no more trace of recognition in her face than there was in Bellarion's own.

"You are welcome, sir," she said with formal graciousness, and then turned to Aliprandi. "I did not know that the Count of Biandrate had a son."

"Nor did I, madonna, until this moment. It was the Marquis Theodore who made him known to me." She fancied in Aliprandi's tone something that seemed to disclaim responsibility.

But she turned affably to the newcomer, and Bellarion marvelled at the ease with which she dissembled.

"I knew the Count of Biandrate well when I was a child, and I hold his memory very dear. He was in my father's service once, as you will know. I rejoice in the greatness he has since achieved. It should make a brave tale."

"*Per aspera ad astra* is ever a brave tale," Bellarion answered soberly. "Too often it is *per astra ad aspera*, if I may judge by what I have read."

"You shall tell me of your father, sir. I have often wished to hear the story of his advancement."

"To command, highness." He bowed again.

The others drew closer, expecting entertainment. But Bellarion, who had no such entertainment to bestow, nor knew of Facino's life more than a fragment of what was known to all the world, extricated himself as adroitly as he could.

"I am no practised troubadour or story-singer. And this tale of a journey to the stars should be told under the stars."

"Why, so it shall, then. They shine brightly enough. You shall show me Facino's and perhaps your own." She rose and commanded her ladies to attend her.

Castruccio fetched a sigh of relief.

"Give thanks," he said audibly to those about him, "for Heaven's mercy which has spared you this weariness."

The door at the end of the hall stood open to the terrace and the moonlight. Thither the Princess conducted Bellarion, her ladies in close attendance.

Approaching the threshold they came upon the Marquis Gian Giacomo, reeling clumsily beside the Countess of Ronsecco, who

112

was almost on the point of tears. He paused in his caperings that he might ogle his sister.

"Where do you go, Valeria? And who's this long-shanks?"

She approached him. "You are tired, Giannino, and the Countess, too, is tired. You would be better resting awhile."

"Indeed, highness!" cried the young Countess, eagerly thankful.

But the Marquis was not at all of his sister's wise opinion.

"Tired? Resting! You're childish, Valeria. Always childish. Childish and meddlesome. Poking your long nose into everything. Someday you'll poke it into something that'll sting it. And what will it look like when it's stung? Have you thought of that?" He laughed derisively, and caught the Countess by the arm. "Let's leave long-nose and long-shanks. Ha! Ha!" His idiotic laughter shrilled up. He was ravished by his own humour. He let his voice ring out that all might hear and share the enjoyment of his comical conceit. "Long-nose and long-shanks! Long-nose and long-shanks!"

> "Said she to him, your long-shanks I adore.
> Said he to her, your long-nose I deplore."

Screaming with laughter he plunged forward to resume the dance, trod upon one of his trailing, exaggerated sleeves, tripped himself, and went sprawling on the tessellated floor, his laughter louder and more idiotic than ever. A dozen ran to lift him.

The Princess tapped Bellarion sharply on the arm with her fan of ostrich-plumes. Her face was like graven stone.

"Come," she commanded, and passed out ahead of him.

On the terrace she signed to her ladies to fall behind whilst

with her companion she moved beyond earshot along the marble balustrade, whose moonlit pallor was here and there splashed by the black tide of trailing plants.

"Now, sir," she invited in a voice of ice, "will you explain this new identity and your presence here?"

He answered in calm, level tones: "My presence explains itself when I tell you that my identity is accepted by his highness the Regent. The son of Facino Cane is not to be denied the hospitality of the Court of Montferrat."

"Then why did you lie to me when . . ."

"No, no. This is the lie. This false identity was as necessary to gain admission here as was the painter's smock I wore yesterday: another lie."

"You ask me to believe that you . . ." Indignation choked her. "My senses tell me what you are; an agent sent to work my ruin."

"Your senses tell you either more or less, or else you would not now be here."

And then it was as if the bonds of her self-control were suddenly snapped by the strain they sought to bear. "Oh, God!" she cried out. "I am near distraction. My brother . . ." She broke off on something akin to a sob.

Outwardly Bellarion remained calm. "Shall we take one thing at a time? Else we shall never be done. And I should not remain here too long with you."

"Why not? You have the sanction of my dear uncle, who sends you."

"Even so." He lowered his voice to a whisper. "It is your uncle is my dupe, not you."

"That is what I expected you to say."

"You had best leave inference until you have heard me out. Inference, highness, as I have shown you once already, is not your strength."

If she resented his words and the tone he took, she gave no expression to it. Standing rigidly against the marble balustrade, she looked away from him and down that moonlit garden with its inky shadows and tall yew hedges that were sharp black silhouettes against the faintly irradiated sky.

Briefly, swiftly, lucidly, Bellarion told her how her message had been received by the conspirators.

"You thought to checkmate them. But they perceived the move you have overlooked, whereby they checkmate you. This proves what already I have told you: that they serve none but themselves. You and your brother are but the instruments with which they go to work. There was only one way to frustrate them; only one way to serve and save you. That way I sought."

She interrupted him there. "You sought? You sought?" Her voice held bewilderment, unbelief, and even some anger. "Why should you desire to save or serve me? If I could believe you, I must account you impertinent. You were a messenger, no more."

"Was I no more when I disclosed to you the true aims of these men and the perils of your association with them?"

"Aye, you were more," she said bitterly. "But what were you?"

"Your servant, madonna," he answered simply.

"Ah, yes. I had forgotten. My servant. Sent by Providence, was it not?"

"You are bitter, lady," said Bellarion.

"Am I?" She turned at last to look at him. But his face was no more than a faint white blur. "Perhaps I find you too sweet to be real."

He sighed. "The rest of my tale will hardly change that opinion. Is it worthwhile continuing?" He spoke without any heat, a little wistfully.

"It should be entertaining if not convincing."

"For your entertainment, then: what you could not do without destroying yourself was easily possible to me." And he told her of his pretended petition, giving the Regent the names of those who plotted against his life.

He saw her clutch her breast, caught the gasp of dread and dismay that broke from her lips.

"You betrayed them!"

"Was it not what you announced that you would do if they did not abandon their plan of murder? I was your deputy, no more. When I presented myself as Facino Cane's adopted son I was readily believed—because the Regent cared little whether it were true or not, since in me he perceived the very agent that he needed."

"Ah, now at last we have something that does not strain belief."

"Will it strain belief that the Regent was already fully informed of this conspiracy?"

"What!"

"Why else should he have trusted or believed me? Of his own knowledge he knew that what I told him was true."

"He knew and he held his hand?" Again the question was made scornful by unbelief.

"Because he lacked evidence that you, and, through you, your

brother, were parties to the plot. What to him are Barbaresco's shabby crew? It is the Marquis Gian Giacomo who must be removed in such a manner as not to impair the Lord Regent's credit. To gather evidence am I now sent."

She tore an ostrich-plume from her fan in her momentary passion.

"You do not hesitate to confess how you betray each in turn; Barbaresco to the Regent; the Regent to me; and now, no doubt, me to the Regent."

"As for the last, madonna, to betray you I need not now be here. I could have supplied the Regent with all the evidence he needs against you at the same time that I supplied the evidence against the others."

She was silent, turning it over in her mind. And because her mind was acute, she saw the proof his words afforded. But because afraid, she mistrusted proof.

"It may be part of the trap," she complained. "If it were not, why should you remain after denouncing my friends? The aims you pretend would have been fully served by that."

His answer was prompt and complete.

"If I had departed, you would never have known the answer of those men whom you trust, nor would you have known that there is a Judas amongst them already. It was necessary to warn you."

"Yes," she said slowly. "I see, I think." And then in sudden revolt against the conviction he was forcing upon her, and in tones which if low were vehement to the point of fierceness: "Necessary!" she cried, echoing the word he had used. "Necessary! How was it necessary? Whence this necessity of yours? A week ago you did not know me. Yet for me, who am nothing to you, whose service carries no reward, you pretend yourself prepared to labour and to take risks involving even your very life. That is what you ask me to believe. You suppose me mad, I think."

As she faced him now, she fancied that a smile broke upon that face so indistinctly seen. His voice, as he answered her, was very soft.

"It is not mad to believe in madness. Madness exists, madonna. Set me down as suffering from it. The air of the world is proving too strong and heady, perhaps, for one bred in cloisters. It has intoxicated me, I think."

She laughed chillingly. "For once you offer an explanation that goes a little lame. Your invention is failing, sir."

"Nay, lady; my understanding," he answered sadly.

She set a hand upon his arm. He felt it quivering there, which surprised him almost as much as the change in her voice, now suddenly halting and unsteady.

"Messer Bellarion, if my suspicions wound you, set them down to my distraction. It is so easy, so dangerously easy, to believe what we desire to believe."

"I know," he said gently. "Yet when you've slept on what I've said, you'll find that your safety lies in trusting me."

"Safety! Am I concerned with safety only? Tonight you saw my brother . . ."

"I saw. If that is Messer Castruccio's work . . ."

"Castruccio is but a tool. Come, sir. We talk in vain." She began to move along the terrace towards her waiting ladies. Suddenly she paused. "I must trust you, Ser Bellarion. I must or I shall go mad in this ugly tangle. I'll take the risk. If you are not

true, if you win my trust only to abuse it and work the evil will of the Regent, then God will surely punish you."

"I think so, too," he breathed.

"Tell me now," she questioned, "what shall you say to my uncle?"

"Why, that I have talked with you fruitlessly; that either you have no knowledge of Barbaresco or else you withheld it from me."

"Shall you come again?"

"If you desire it. The way is open now. But what remains to do?"

"You may discover that." Thus she conveyed that, having resolved to give him her trust, she gave it without stint.

They came back into the hall, where stiff and formally Bellarion made his valedictory bow, then went to take his leave of the Regent.

The Regent disengaged himself from the group of which he was the centre, and, taking Bellarion by the arm, drew him apart a little.

"I have made a sounding," Bellarion informed him. "Either she mistrusts me, or else she knows nothing of Barbaresco."

"Be sure of the former, sir," said the Regent softly. "Procure credentials from Barbaresco, and try again. It should be easy, so."

Chapter XI

Under Suspicion

At Barbaresco's a surprise awaited Messer Bellarion. The whole company of plotters swarmed about him as he entered the long dusty room of the mezzanine, and he found himself gripped at once between the fierce Casella and the reckless Spigno. He did not like their looks, nor those of any man present. Least of all did he like the looks of Barbaresco who confronted him, oily and falsely suave of manner.

"Where have you been, Master Bellarion?"

He realised that he had need of his wits.

He looked round with surprise and contempt in his stare.

"Oh, yes, you're conspirators to the life," he told them. "You see a spy in every neighbour, a betrayal in every act. Oh, you have eyes; but no wit to inform your vision. God help those who trust you! God help you all!" He wrenched at the arms that held him.

"Let me go, fools."

Barbaresco licked his lips. His right hand was held behind his back. Stealthily almost he came a step nearer, so that he was very close.

"Not until you tell us where you have been. Not then, unless you tell us more."

Bellarion's sneer became more marked; but no fear showed in his glance. "Where I have been, you know. Hence these tragical airs. I've been to court."

"To what end, Bellarion?" Barbaresco softly questioned. The others preserved a frozen, watchful silence.

"To betray you, of course." He was boldly ironical. "Having done so, I return so that you may slit my throat."

Spigno laughed, and released the arm he held.

"I for one am answered. I told you from the first I did not believe it."

Casella, however, hung on fiercely. "I'll need a clear answer before I . . ."

"Give me air, man," cried Bellarion impatiently, and wrenched his arm free. "No need to maul me. I'll not run. There are seven of you to prevent me, and reflection may cool your humours. Reflect, for instance, that, if I were for running, I should not have come back."

"You tell us what you would not or did not do. We ask you what you did," Barbaresco insisted.

"I'll tell you yet another thing I would not have done if my aim had been betrayal. I should not have gone openly to court so that you might hear of my presence there."

"The very argument I employed," Spigno reminded them,

with something of Bellarion's own scorn in his manner now. "Let the boy tell his tale."

They muttered among themselves. Bellarion crossed the room under their black looks, moving with the fearless air of a man strong in the sense of his own integrity. He slid into a chair.

"There is nothing to tell that is not self-evident already. I went to carry your message to the Princess Valeria; to point out to her the position of checkmate in which you hold her; to make her realize that being committed to this enterprise, she cannot now either draw back or dictate to us the means by which our aims are to be reached. All this, I rejoice to tell you, I have happily accomplished."

Again it was Barbaresco who was their spokesman. "All this we may believe when you tell us why you chose to go to court to do it, and how, being what you represent yourself to be, you succeeded in gaining admission."

"God give me patience with you, dear Saint Thomas!" said Bellarion, sighing. "I went to court because the argument I foresaw with the Princess was hardly one to be conducted furtively behind a hedge. It threatened to be protracted. Besides, for furtive dealing, sirs, bold and open approaches are best when they are possible. They were possible to me. It happens, sirs, that I am indeed the adoptive son of Facino Cane, and I perceived how I might use that identity to present myself at court and there move freely."

A dozen questions rained upon him. He answered them all in a phrase.

"The Ambassador of Milan, Messer Aliprandi, was there to sponsor me."

There was a silence, broken at last by Barbaresco. "Aliprandi may have been your sponsor there. He cannot be your sponsor here, and you know it."

"Aye," growled white-haired Lungo. "An impudent tale!"

"And a lame one," added Casella. "If you had this means of going to court, why did you wait so long to seize it?"

"Other ways were open on former occasions. You forget that Madonna Valeria was not expecting me; the garden gate would not be ajar. And I could not this time go as a painter, which was the disguise I adopted on the last occasion. Besides, it is too expensive. It cost me five ducats."

Again their questions came together, for it was the first they had heard of the disguise which he had used. He told them at last the story. And he saw that it pleased them.

"Why did you not tell us this before?" quoth one.

Bellarion shrugged. "Is it important? So that I was your Mercury, did it matter in what shape I went? Why should I trouble you with trivial things? Besides, let me remind you—since you can't perceive it for yourselves—that if I had betrayed you to the Marquis Theodore, the Captain of Justice would now be here in my place."

"That, at least, is not to be denied," said Spigno, and in his vehemence carried two or three others with him.

But the fierce Casella was not of those, nor Lungo, nor Barbaresco.

The latter least of all, for a sudden memory had stirred in him. His blue eyes narrowed until they were almost hidden in his great red cheeks.

"How does it happen that none at court recognised in you

the palace amanuensis?"

Bellarion perceived his danger, and learnt the lesson that a lie may become a clumsy obstacle to trip a man. But of the apprehension he suddenly felt, no trace revealed itself upon his countenance.

"It is possible some did. What then? Neither identity contradicts the other. And remember, pray, that Messer Aliprandi was there to avouch me."

"But he cannot avouch you here," Barbaresco said again, and sternly asked: "Who can?"

Bellarion looked at him, and from him to the others who seemed to await almost in breathlessness his answer.

"Do you demand of me proof that I am the adoptive son of Facino Cane?" he asked.

"So much do we demand it that unless you can afford it your sands are run, my cockerel," Casella answered him, his fingers on his dagger as he spoke.

It was a case for bold measures if he would gain time. Given this, he knew that all things may become possible, and there was one particular thing his shrewd calculations accounted probable here if only he could induce them to postpone until tomorrow the slitting of his throat.

"So be it. From here to Cigliano it is no more than a day's ride on a good horse. Let one of you go ask the Abbot of the Grazie the name of him Facino left in the convent's care."

"A name?" cried Casella, sneering. "Is that all the proof?"

"All if the man who goes is a fool. If not he may obtain from the Abbot a minute description of this Bellarion. If more is needed I'll give you a note of the clothes I wore and the gear and money with which I left the Grazie that you may obtain confirmation of that, too."

But Barbaresco was impatient. "Even so, what shall all this prove? It cannot prove you true. It cannot prove that you are not a spy sent hither to betray and sell us."

"No," Bellarion agreed. "But it will prove that the identity on which I won to court is what I represent it, and that will be something as a beginning. The rest—if there is more—can surely wait."

"And meanwhile . . . ?" Casella was beginning.

"Meanwhile I am in your hands. You're never so bloodthirsty that you cannot postpone murdering me until you've verified my tale?"

That was what they fell to discussing among themselves there in his very presence, affording him all the excitement of watching the ball of his fate tossed this way and that among the disputants.

In the end the game might have gone against him but for Count Spigno, who laboured Bellarion's own argument that if he had betrayed them he would never have incurred the risk of returning amongst them.

In the end they deprived Bellarion of the dagger which was his only weapon, and then Barbaresco, Casella, and Spigno jointly conducted him abovestairs to a shabby chamber under the roof. It had no windows, whence an evasion might be attempted, and was lighted by a glazed oblong some ten feet overhead at the highest part of the sharply sloping ceiling. It contained no furniture, nor indeed anything beyond some straw and sacking in a corner which he was bidden to regard as his bed for that night and probably for the next.

They pinioned his wrists behind him for greater safety, and Casella bade him be thankful that the cord was not being tightened about his neck instead. Upon that they went out, taking the light with them, locking the door, and leaving him a prisoner in the dark.

He stood listening to their footsteps receding down the stairs, then he looked up at the oblong of moonlight in his ceiling. If the glass were removed, there would be room for a man to pass through and gain the roof. But considering the slope of it, the passage might as easily lead to a broken neck as to liberty, and in any case he had neither the power nor the means to reach it.

He squatted upon the meagre bedding, with his chin almost upon his knees, in an attitude of extreme discomfort, making something in the nature of an assessment of his mental and emotional equipment. Seen now from the point of view of cold reason to which danger had sharply brought him, his career since leaving the peace of the Grazie a week ago seemed fantastic and incredible. Destiny had made sport with him. Sentimentality had led him by the nose. He had mixed himself in the affairs of a state through which he was no more than a wayfarer, because moved to interest in the fortunes of a young woman of exalted station who would probably dismiss his memory with a sigh when she came to learn how his throat had been cut by the self-seeking fools with whom so recklessly she had associated herself. It was, he supposed, a manifestation of that romantic and unreasonable phenomenon known as chivalry. If he extricated himself alive from this predicament, he would see to it that whatever follies he committed in the future, chivalry would certainly not be found amongst them. Experience had cured him of any leanings in that

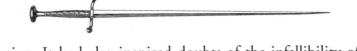

direction. It had also inspired doubts of the infallibility of his syllogism on the subject of evil. He suspected a flaw in it somewhere. For evil most certainly existed. His respect for the value of experience was rapidly increasing.

He shifted his position, stretched himself out, and lay on his side, contemplating the patch of moonlight on the floor, and speculating upon his chances of winning out of this deathtrap. Of these he took an optimistic view. The assistance upon which Bellarion chiefly counted was that of the traitor amongst the conspirators, whom he strove vainly to identify in the light of their behaviour that evening. Spigno had been the only one who by advocating Bellarion's cause had procured him this respite. Yet Spigno was one of the first to spring upon him dagger in hand, on his return from court. But the traitor, whoever he might be, would probably report the event to the Marquis Theodore, and the Marquis should take steps directly or indirectly to procure the release of one whom he must now regard as a valuable agent.

That, thought Bellarion, was the probability. Meanwhile he would remember that probabilities are by no means certainties, and he would be watchful for an opportunity to help himself.

On these reflections he must have fallen asleep, and he must have slept for some time, for, when suddenly he awakened, the patch of moonlight was gone from the floor. That was his first conscious observation; his second what that something was stirring near at hand. He raised himself on his elbow, an operation by no means easy with pinioned wrists, and turned his head in the direction of the sound, to perceive a faint but increasing rhomb of light from the direction of the doorway, and to understand with the next heartbeat that the door was being slowly and stealthily pushed open.

That was, he afterwards confessed, his first real acquaintance with the emotion of fear; fear that roughened his skin and chilled his spine; fear inspired by the instantaneous conviction that here came some one to murder him as he lay there bound and helpless.

The suspense was but of seconds, yet in those seconds Bellarion seemed to live an age as he watched that slowly widening gap and the faint light which increased in area but hardly in illumination. Then the shadowy form of a man slipped through, darkly discernible in the faint glow from the veiled light he carried.

Very softly came his voice: "Sh! Quiet! Make no sound!"

The note of warning partially calmed the tumult of Bellarion's heart, which was thudding in his throat as if to suffocate him.

As quietly as it had been opened the door was closed again, a thin and partially translucent mantle was pulled from the lantern it had been muffling, and the light beating through the horn panes was reflected from the floor and walls upon the lean, aquiline features of Count Spigno.

Bellarion uttered something that sounded like a chuckle.

"I was expecting you," said he.

Chapter XII

Count Spigno

Spigno set the lantern on the floor, and came forward. "No need to talk," he muttered. "Roll over so that I can free your hands." He drew his dagger and with it cut Bellarion's bonds.

"Take off your shoes. Make haste."

Bellarion squatted upon his bedding, and with blundering fingers, still numb from the thong, he removed his footgear. His wits worked briskly, and it was not at all upon the subject of his escape that they were busy. Despite his late resolves, and although still far from being out of peril, with the chance of salvation no more than in sight, he was already at his knight-errantry again.

He stood up at last, and Spigno was whispering urgently.

"Wait! We must not go together. Give me five minutes to win clear; then follow."

Bellarion considered him, and his eyes were very grave.

"But when my evasion is discovered . . ." he was beginning.

Spigno impatiently broke in, explaining hurriedly.

"I am the last they will suspect. The others are all here to-night. But I pleaded urgent reasons why I could not remain. I made a pretence of departing; then hid below until all were asleep. They will be at each other's throats in the morning over this." He smiled darkly in satisfaction of his cunning. "I'll take the light. You know your way about this house better than I do. Tread softly when you come."

He was turning to take up the lantern when Bellarion arrested him.

"You'll wait for me outside?"

"To what end? Nay, now. There is no purpose in that."

"Let me come with you, then. If I should stumble in the dark they'll be upon me."

"Take care that you do not."

"At least leave me your dagger since you take the light."

"Here, then." Spigno unsheathed and surrendered the weapon to him.

Bellarion gripped the hilt. With very sombre eyes he considered the Count. Then the latter turned aside again for the lantern.

"A moment," said Bellarion.

"What now?"

Impatiently Spigno faced once more the queer glance of those dark eyes, and in that moment Bellarion stabbed him.

It was a swift, hard-driven, merciful stroke that found the unfortunate man's heart and quenched his life before he had time to realise that it was threatened.

Without a sound he reeled back under the blow. Bellarion's

left arm went round his shoulders to ease him to the ground. But Spigno's limbs sagged under him. He sank through Bellarion's embrace like an empty sack, and then rolled over sideways.

The murderer choked back a sob. His legs were trembling like empty hose with which the wind makes sport. His face was leaden-hued and his sight was blurred by tears. He went down on his knees beside the dead count, turned him on his back, straightened out the twitching limbs, and folded the arms across the breast. Nor did he rise when this was done.

In slaying Count Spigno, he had performed a necessary act; necessary in the service to which he had dedicated himself. Thus at a blow he had shattered the instrument upon which the Marquis Theodore was depending to encompass his nephew's ruin; and the discovery tomorrow of Spigno's death and Bellarion's own evasion, in circumstances of unfathomable mystery, must strike such terror into the hearts of the conspirators that there would probably be an end to the plotting which served no purpose but to advance the Regent's schemes.

Yet, despite these heartening reflections, Bellarion could not shake off his horror. He had done murder, and he had done it in cold blood, deliberate and calculatingly. Worse than all—his convent rearing asserting itself here—he had sent a man unshriven to confront his Maker. He hoped that the unexpectedness with which Spigno's doom had overtaken him would be weighed in the balance against the sins which death had surprised upon him.

That is why he remained on his knees and with joined hands prayed fervently and passionately for the repose of the soul which he had despatched to judgment. So intent was he that he took no heed of the precious time that was meanwhile speeding. For per-

haps a quarter of an hour he continued there in prayer, then crossing himself he rose at last and gave thought to his own escape.

Thrusting his shoes into his belt and muffling the lantern as Spigno had muffled it, he set out, the naked dagger in his right hand.

A stair creaked under his step and then another, and each time he checked and caught his breath, listening intently. Once he fancied that he heard a movement below, and the sound so alarmed him that it was some moments before he could proceed.

He gained the floor below in safety, and rounding the balusters continued his cautious descent towards the mezzanine, where, as he knew, Barbaresco slept. Midway down he heard that sound again, this time unmistakably the sound of some one moving in the passage to the right, in the direction of Barbaresco's room. He stopped abruptly, and thrust the muffled lantern behind him, so that the faint glow of it might not beat downwards upon the gloom to betray him. He was conscious of pulses drumming in his temples, for shaken by the night's events he was now become an easy prey to fear.

Suddenly to his increasing horror, another, stronger light fell along the passage. It grew steadily as he watched it, and with it came a sound of softly shod feet, a mutter in a voice that he knew for Barbaresco's, and an answering mutter in the high-pitched voice of Barbaresco's old servant.

His first impulse was to turn and flee upwards, back the way he had come. But thus he would be rushing into a trap, which would be closed by Barbaresco's guests, who slept most probably above.

Then, bracing himself for whatever fate might send, he

bounded boldly and swiftly forward, no longer troubling to tread lightly. His aim was to round the stairs and thereafter trust to speed to complete the descent and gain the street. But the noise he made brought Barbaresco hurrying forward, and at the foot of that flight they confronted each other, Bellarion's way barred by the gentleman of Casale who loosed at sight of him a roar that roused the house.

Barbaresco was in bedgown and slippers, a candle in one hand, his servant following at his heels. He was unarmed. But not on that account could he shirk the necessity of tackling and holding this fugitive, whose flight itself was an abundant advertisement of his treachery, and whose evasion now might be attended by direst results.

He passed the candle to his servant, and flung himself bodily upon Bellarion, pinning the young man's arms to his sides, and roaring lustily the while. Bellarion struggled silently and grimly in that embrace which was like the hug of a bear, for despite his corpulence Barbaresco was as strong as he was heavy. But the grip he had taken, whilst having the advantage of pinning down the hand that held the dagger, was one that it is impossible long to maintain upon an opponent of any vigour; and before he could sufficiently bend him to receive his weight, Bellarion had broken loose. Old Andrea, the servant, having set the candle upon the floor, was running in now to seize Bellarion's legs. He knocked Andrea over, winded by a well-directed kick in the stomach, then swung aloft his dagger as Barbaresco rushed at him again. It was in his mind, as he afterwards declared, that he did not desire another murder on his soul that night. But if another murder there must be, he preferred that it should not be his own. So he

struck without pity. Barbaresco swerved, throwing up his right arm to parry the blow, and received the long blade to the hilt in his fleshy forearm.

He fell back, clapping his hand to the bubbling wound and roaring like a bull in pain, just as Casella, almost naked, but sword in hand, came bounding down the stairs with Lungo and yet another following.

For a second it seemed to Bellarion that he had struck too late. If he attempted now to regain the staircase he must inevitably be cut off, and how could he hope with a dagger to meet Casella's sword? Then, on a new thought, he darted forward, and plunged into the long room of that mezzanine. He slammed the door, and shot home the bolts, before Casella and Lungo brought up against it on the other side.

He uncovered at last his lantern and set it down. He dragged the heavy table across the door, so as to reënforce it against their straining shoulders. Then snatching up the cloak in which the lantern had been muffled he made for the window, and threw it open.

He paused to put on his shoes, what time the baffled conspirators were battering and straining at the door. Then he forced the naked dagger as far as it would go into the empty sheath that dangled from his own belt, and tied a corner of the cloak securely to one of the stone mullions so that some five or six feet of it dangled below the sill. Onto this sill he climbed, turned, knelt, and laid hold of the cloak with both hands.

He had but to let himself down hand over hand for the length of cloth, and then only an easy drop of a few feet would lie between himself and safety.

But even as he addressed himself to this, the housedoor below was opened with a clatter, and out into the street sprang two of the conspirators.

He groaned as he looked down upon them from his precarious position. Whilst they, in their shirts, capering fantastically as it seemed to him in the shaft of light that cut athwart the gloom from the open door, brandished their glittering blades and waited.

Since there could be no salvation in climbing back, he realised that he was at the end of the wild career he had run since leaving the peace of the Grazie a week ago. A week! He had lived a lifetime in that week, and he had looked more than once in the face of death. He thought of the Abbot's valedictory words: *Pax multa in cella, foris autem plurima bella.* What would he not give now to be back in the peace of that convent cell!

As he hung there, between two deaths, he sought to compose his mind to prayer, to prepare his soul for judgment, by an act of contrition for his sins. Nor could he in that supreme hour take comfort in his old heresy that sin is a human fiction.

And then, even as his despair of body and spirit touched its nadir, he caught a sound that instantly heartened him: the approach of regularly tramping feet.

Those below heard it, too. The watch was on its rounds. The murderous twain took counsel for a moment. Then, fearing to be surprised there, they darted through the doorway, and closed the door again, just as the patrol with lanterns swinging from their halberts came round the corner not a dozen yards away.

With nothing to fear from these, Bellarion now let himself swiftly down the length of the cloak and dropped lightly to the ground.

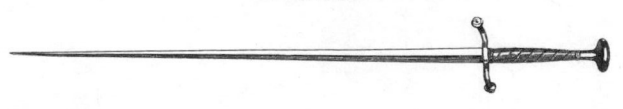

He was breathing easily and oddly disposed to laugh when the officer came up with him, and the patrol of six made a half-circle round him.

"What's this?" he was challenged. "Why do you prefer a window to a door, my friend?"

Bellarion was still seeking a plausible answer when the officer's face came nearer to his own upon which the light was beating down. Recognition was mutual. It was that same officer who had hunted him from the tavern of the Stag to the Palace gardens.

"By the Blood!" cried Messer Bernabó. "It is Lorenzaccio's fleet young friend. Well met, my cockerel! I've been seeking you this week. You shall tell me where you've been hiding."

Chapter XIII

The Trial

The court of the Podestà of Casale was commonly well attended, and often some of the attendance would be distinguished. The Princess Valeria, for instance, would sometimes sit with the ladies in the little minstrels' gallery of what had once been the banqueting-hall of the Communal Palace, and by her presence attest her interest in all that concerned the welfare of the people of Montferrat. Occasionally, too, as became a prince who desired to be regarded as a father of his people, the Marquis Theodore would come to observe for himself how justice was administered in his name, or in the name of the boy whose deputy he was.

On the morning after that affray at Messer Barbaresco's house, both the Regent and his niece were to be seen in that hall of justice, the latter aloft in the gallery, the former in a chair placed on the dais alongside of the Podestà's seat of state. The Regent's countenance was grave, his brow thoughtful. This was proper to the occasion, but hardly due to the causes supposed by the spectators. Disclosures now inevitable might win him an increase of the public sympathy he enjoyed. But because premature they temporarily wrecked his real aims, wrecked in any case by the death of his agent Spigno.

There were other notabilities present. Messer Aliprandi—who had expressly postponed his departure for Milan—was seated beside the Regent. Behind them against the grey stone wall lounged a glittering group of courtiers, in which Castruccio da Fenestrella was conspicuous.

In the body of the court seethed a crowd composed of citizens of almost every degree, rigidly kept clear of the wide space before the dais by a dozen men-at-arms forming a square with partisans held horizontally.

On the left of the Podestà, who was clothed in a scarlet robe and wore a flat round scarlet cap that was edged with miniver, sat his two assessors in black, and below these two scriveners. The Podestà himself, Angelo de' Ferraris, a handsome, bearded man of fifty, was a Genoese, to comply with the universal rule throughout Italy that the high office of justiciary should ever be held by one who was a foreigner to the State, so as to ensure the disinterestedness and purity of the justice he dispensed.

Some minor cases had briefly been heard and judged, and the court now awaited the introduction of that prisoner who was responsible for this concourse above the average in numbers and quality.

He came in at last, between guards, tall, comely, with thick

glossy black hair that fell to the nape of his neck, his brave red suit considerably disordered and the worse for wear. He was pale from lack of sleep, for he had spent what was left of the night in the town gaol among the vermin-infested scourings of Casale, where he had deemed it prudent to maintain himself awake. Perhaps because of this, too, he suffered a moment's loss of his admirable self-command when upon first entering there he found himself scanned by eyes so numerous and so varied. For an instant he paused, disconcerted, experiencing something of that shyness which is a mixture of mistrust and resentment, peculiar to wild creatures. But the emotion was transient. Before it could be remarked, he had recovered his normal poise, and advanced to the place assigned him on the broad stone flags, bowed to the Regent and the Podestà, then waited, his head high, his glance steady.

On the hush that fell came the Podestà's voice, sternly calm. "Your name?"

"Bellarion Cane." Since that was the name he had given himself when he had sought the Regent, the lie must be maintained. It was dangerous, of course. But dangers hemmed him in on every side.

"Your father's name?"

"Facino Cane is my adoptive father's name. The name of my carnal parents I do not know."

Desired to explain himself, he did so, and his explanation was a model of brevity and lucidity. It bore witness to a calm which argued to his listeners an easy conscience. But the Podestà was to deal with certain facts rather than uncertain personal impressions.

"You came hither a week ago in the company of one Lorenzaccio da Trino, a bandit with a price on his head. To this one of my officers who is present bears witness. Do you deny it?"

"I do not. It is possible for an honest man to travel in the company of a rogue."

"You were with him at a house in the district of Casale where a theft was committed and the owner of which was subsequently murdered here in the hostelry of the Stag by this same Lorenzaccio whilst in your company. The murdered man recognised you before he died. Do you confess to this?"

"Confession implies sin and the seeking of forgiveness. I admit the facts freely. They nowise contradict my previous statement. But that is not a confession."

"Yet if you were innocent of evil why did you run away from my officer? Why did you not remain, and state then what you have stated now?"

"Because the appearances were against me. I acted upon impulse, and foolishly as men act when they do not pause first to reflect."

"You found shelter in the house of the Lord Annibale Barbaresco. No doubt you told him your story, represented yourself as an innocent man betrayed by appearances, and so moved his compassion."

The Podestà paused. Bellarion did not answer. He let the statement pass. He knew the source of it. Last night when the officer had roused the house and announced to Barbaresco his prisoner's supposed association with Lorenzaccio, Barbaresco had fastened upon it to explain the events.

"Last night you attempted to rob him, and being caught in

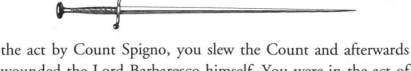

the act by Count Spigno, you slew the Count and afterwards wounded the Lord Barbaresco himself. You were in the act of escaping from the house by one of its windows when the watch supervened and caught you. Do you admit all this?"

"I do not. Nor will the circumstances. I am a robber, it is said. I spend a week in Messer Barbaresco's house. On any night of that week I was alone with him, save only for his decrepit old servant. Yet it is pretended that I chose as the occasion for robbing him a night on which seven able-bodied friends are with him. Your potency must see that the facts are mocked by likelihood."

His potency saw this, as did all present. They saw more. This young man's speech and manner were those of the scholar he proclaimed himself rather than of the robber he was represented.

The justiciary leaned forward, combing his short pointed beard.

"What, then, do you say took place? Let us hear you."

"Is it not within the forms of law that we should first hear my accuser—this Messer Barbaresco?" Bellarion's bold dark eyes raked the court, seeking the stout person of his late host.

The Podestà smiled a little, and his smile was not quite nice.

"Ah, you know the law? Trust a rogue to know the law."

"Which is to make a rogue of every lawyer in the land," said Bellarion, and was rewarded by a titter from the crowd, pleased with a sarcasm that contained more truth than he suspected. "I know the law as I know divinity and rhetoric and other things. Because I have studied it."

"Maybe," said the Podestà grimly. "But not as closely as you are to study it now." Messer de' Ferraris, too, could deal in sarcasm.

An officer with excitement spread upon his face came bustling into the court. But paused upon perceiving that the justiciary was speaking.

"Your accuser," said Messer de' Ferraris, "you have heard already, or at least his accusation, which I have pronounced to you. That accusation you are now required to answer."

"Required?" said Bellarion, and all marvelled at the calm of this man who knew no fear of persons. "By what am I so required? Not by the law, which prescribes that an accused shall hear his accuser in person and be given leave to question him upon his accusations. Your excellency should not be impatient that I stand upon the rights of an accused. Let Messer Barbaresco come forth, and out of his own mouth he shall destroy his falsehood."

His manner might impress the general, but it did not conciliate his judge.

"Why, rogue, do you command here?"

"The law does," said Bellarion, "and I voice the law."

"You voice the law!" The Podestà smiled upon him. "Well, well! I will be patient as you bid me in your impudence. Messer Barbaresco shall be heard." There was an infinite threat in his tone. He leaned back, and looked round the court. "Let Messer Barbaresco stand forth."

There was a rustle and mutter of expectation through the court, for this stiff-necked young cockerel promised to give good entertainment. Then the excited officer who had lately entered thrust forward into the open space.

"Excellency, Messer Barbaresco is gone. He left Casale at sunrise, as soon as the gates were opened, and with him went the six whose names were on Messer Bernabó's list. The captain of the

Lombard Gate is here to speak to it."

Bellarion laughed, and was sternly bidden to remember where he stood and to observe the decencies.

The captain of the Lombard Gate stood forth to confirm the other's tale. A party of eight had ridden out of the town soon after sunrise, taking the road to Lombardy. One who rode with his arm in a sling he had certainly recognised for my Lord Barbaresco, and he had recognised three others whom he named and a fourth whom he knew for Barbaresco's servant.

The Regent stroked his chin and turned to the Podestà, who was clearly taken aback.

"Why was this permitted?" he asked sternly.

The Podestà was ill-at-ease. "I had no news of this man's arrest until long after sunrise. But in any case it is not usual to detain accusers."

"To detain them, no. But to take certain precautions where the features are so peculiar."

"Their peculiarity, highness, with submission, becomes apparent only in this flight."

The Regent sank back in his chair, and his pale blue eyes were veiled behind lowered lids. "Well, well! I interrupt the course of justice. The prisoner waits."

A little bewildered, not only by the turn of events, but by the Regent's attitude, the Podestà addressed Bellarion with a little less judicial sternness.

"You have heard, sir, that your accuser is not here to speak in person."

Again Bellarion laughed. "I have heard that he has spoken. His flight is an eloquent testimony to the falsehood of his charge."

"Sir, sir," the Podestà admonished him. "You are to satisfy this court. You are to afford us your own version of what took place that the ends of justice may be served."

Now here was a change of tone, thought Bellarion, and he was no longer addressed contemptuously as 'rogue.' He took full advantage of it.

"I am to testify? Why, so I will." He looked at the Regent, and found the Regent's eyes upon him, stern and commanding in a face that was set. He read its message.

"But there is little to which I can speak, for I do not know the cause of the quarrel that broke out between Count Spigno and Messer Barbaresco. I was not present at the beginnings. I was drawn to it by the uproar, and when I arrived, Count Spigno was already dead. At sight of me, perhaps because I was a witness and might inform against them, I was set upon by Messer Barbaresco and his friends. I wounded Barbaresco, and so got away, locking myself in a room. I was escaping thence by a window when the watch came up. That is all I can say."

It was a tale, he thought, that must convey to the Regent the full explanation. But whatever it may have done in that quarter, it did not satisfy the Podestà.

"I could credit this more easily," said the latter, "but for the circumstance that Count Spigno and yourself were fully dressed, whilst Messer Barbaresco and the others were in their shirts. That in itself suggests who were the aggressors, who the attacked."

"It might but for the flight of Messer Barbaresco and the others. Innocent men do not run away."

"Out of your own mouth you have pronounced it," thundered the Podestà. "You profess innocence of association with

Lorenzaccio. Yet you ran away on that occasion."

"Oh, but the difference . . . The appearances against a single man unknown in these parts . . ."

"Can you explain how you and the dead count came to be dressed and the others not?" It was more than a question. It was a challenge.

Bellarion looked at the Regent. But the Regent made no sign. He continued to eye Bellarion coldly and sternly. Ready enough to tell the full lie he had prepared, yet he had the wit to perceive that the Regent, whilst not suspecting its untruth, might find the disclosure inconvenient, in which case he would certainly be lost. As a spy, he reasoned, he could only be of value to the Regent as long as this fact remained undisclosed. So he took his resolve.

"Why Count Spigno was dressed, I cannot say. My own condition was the result of accident. I had been to court last night. I returned late, and I was tired. I fell asleep in a chair, and slept until the uproar aroused me."

Bellarion fancied that the Regent's glance approved him. But the Podestà slowly shook his head.

"A convenient tale," he sneered, "but lame. Can you do no better?"

"Can any man do better than the truth?" demanded Bellarion firmly and in the circumstances impudently. "You ask me to explain things that are outside my knowledge."

"We shall see." The tone was a threat. "The hoist has often been known to stimulate a man's memory and to make it accurate."

"The hoist?" Bellarion's spirit trembled, for all that his mien preserved its boldness. He looked again at the Regent, this time for succour. The Regent was whispering to Messer Aliprandi, and almost at once the Orator of Milan leaned forward to address the Podestà.

"May I speak a word in your court, my lord?"

The Podestà turned to him in some surprise. It was not often that an ambassador intervened in the trial of a rogue accused of theft and murder.

"At your good pleasure, my lord."

"With submission, then, may I beg that, considering the identity claimed by this prisoner and the relationship urged with his magnificence the Count of Biandrate, the proceedings against him be suspended until this identity shall have been tested by ordinary means?"

The ambassador paused. The Podestà, supreme autocrat of justice, had thrown up his head, resentful of such very definite interference. But before he could answer, the Regent was adding the weight of his support to the Orator's request.

"However unusual this may be, Messer de' Ferraris," he said, in his quiet, cultured voice, "you will realise with me that if the prisoner's identity prove to be as he says, and if his present position should be the result of a chain of unfortunate circumstances, we should by proceeding to extremes merely provoke against Montferrat the resentment of our exalted friend the Count of Biandrate."

Thus was it demonstrated to Bellarion how much may hang upon a man's wise choice of a parent.

The Podestà bowed his head. There was a moment's silence before he spoke.

"By what means is it proposed that the accused's pretended

identity shall be tested?"

It was Bellarion who spoke. "I had a letter from the Abbot of the Grazie of Cigliano, which this Lorenzaccio stole from me, but which the officer . . ."

"We have that letter," the Podestà interrupted, his voice harsh. "It says nothing of your paternity, and for the rest it can prove nothing until you prove how it was acquired!"

"He claims," Aliprandi interposed again, "to come from the Convent of the Grazie of Cigliano, where Messer Facino Cane placed him some years ago. It should not be difficult, nor greatly delay the satisfaction of justice, to seek at the convent confirmation of his tale. If it is confirmed, let one of the fathers who knows him attend here to say whether this is the same man."

The Podestà combed his beard in silence. "And if so?" he inquired at last.

"Why, then, sir, your mind will be delivered at least of the prejudice created by this young man's association with a bandit. And you will be in better case to judge his share in last night's events."

There, to the general disappointment, ended for the moment the odd affair of Bellarion Cane, which in the disclosures it foreshadowed had promised such unusual entertainment.

The Regent remained in court after Bellarion's removal, lest it be supposed that his interest in the administration of justice had been confined to that case alone. But Messer Aliprandi withdrew, as did most of those others who came from the palace, and amongst them, pale and troubled, went the Princess Valeria. To Dionara she vented something of her dismay and anger.

"A thief, a spy, a murderer," she said. "And I trusted him that he might ruin all my hopes. I have the wages of a fool."

"But if he were what he claims to be?" Monna Dionara asked her.

"Would that make him any less what he is? He was sent to spy on me, that he might discover what was plotting. My heart told me so. Yet to the end I heeded rather his own false tongue."

"But if he were a spy, why should he have urged you to break off relations with these plotters?"

"So that he might draw from me a fuller revelation of my intentions. It was he who murdered Spigno; Spigno the shrewdest, the most loyal and trustworthy of them all. Spigno upon whom I depended to curb their recklessness and yet to give them audacity in season. And this vile creature of my uncle's has murdered him." Her eyes were heavy with unshed tears.

"But if so, why was he arrested?"

"An accident. That was not in the reckoning. I went to see how they would deal with that. And I saw."

Madonna Dionara's vision, however, was less clear, or else clearer.

"Yet I do not understand why he should murder the Count."

"Do you not?" The Princess laughed a little, quite mirthlessly. "It is not difficult to reconstruct the happening. Spigno was dressed, and so was he. Spigno suspected him, and followed him last night to watch him. The scoundrel's bold appearance at court was his one mistake, his inexplicable imprudence. Spigno taxed him with it on his return, pressed him, perhaps, with questions that unmasked him, and so to save his own skin this Bellarion slew the Count. Why else are the others all fled? Because they know themselves detected. Is it not all crystal clear?"

The Lady Dionara shook her head. "If it was your brother's ruin the Marquis Theodore plotted, this surely frustrates his own ends. If it were as you say, Messer Bellarion would have spoken out boldly in court, and told his tale. Why, being what you suppose him, should he keep silent, when by speaking he could best serve the Regent's purposes?"

"I do not know," the Princess confessed, "nor does any ever know the Regent's purposes. He works quietly, craftily, slowly, and he will never strike until he is sure that the blow must be final. This rogue's conduct was an obedience to the Regent's commands. Did you not see the looks that passed between them? Did you not see that when Messer Aliprandi intervened it was after a whisper from my uncle?"

"But if this man were not what he says he is, what can the intervention avail in the end?"

Madonna Valeria was wholly scornful now. "He may be what he claims and yet at the same time what I know him to be. Why not? Where is the contradiction? Yet I dare to prophesy. This Messer Bellarion will not again be brought to trial. The means will be afforded him of breaking prison."

Chapter XIV

Evasion

Bellarion was returned to the common gaol, which was perched high upon the city's red wall, to herd once more with the vile pariahs there incarcerated. But not for long. Within an hour came an order for his removal to a diminutive stone chamber whose barred, unglazed window looked out upon a fertile green plain through which the broad, silvery ribbon of the river Po coiled its way towards Lombardy.

Thither a little later in the afternoon came the Marquis Theodore to visit him, in quest of the true facts. Bellarion lied to him as fluently as he had lied earlier to the Podestà. But no longer with the same falsehoods.

His tale now went very near the truth. He had come under the suspicion of the conspirators last night as a result of his visit to court. Explanations had been demanded, and he had afforded them, as he exactly stated. But conscience making cowards of the conspirators, they bound him and locked him in a room until from Cigliano they should have confirmation of his tale. Count Spigno, fearing that his life might be in danger, came in the night to set him free.

"Which leads me to suspect," said Bellarion, "that Count Spigno, too, was an agent of your potency's. No matter. I keep to the events."

The conspirators, he continued, were more watchful than Spigno suspected. They came upon the twain just as Bellarion's bonds had been cut, and Spigno had, fortunately, thrust a dagger into his hand. They fell upon Spigno, and one of them—the confusion at the moment did not permit him to say which—stabbed the unfortunate count. Bellarion would have shared his fate but that he hacked right and left with fist and dagger, wounding Barbaresco and certainly one other, possibly two others. Thus he broke through them, flung down the stairs, locked himself in the room on the mezzanine, and climbed out of the window into the arms of the watch.

"If your highness had not desired me to go to court, this would not have happened. But at least the conspirators are fled and the conspiracy is stifled in panic. Your highness is now safe."

"Safe!" His highness laughed hard and cruelly. There was now in his mien none of that benignity which Montferrat was wont to admire in it. The pale blue eyes were hard as steel, a furrow at the base of his aquiline nose rendered sinister and predatory the whole expression of his countenance.

"Your blundering has destroyed the evidence by which I might have made myself safe."

"My blundering! Here's justice! Besides, if I were to give the evidence I withheld from the Podestà, if I were to give a true account of what happened at Barbaresco's . . ."

"If you did that!" The Regent interrupted angrily. "How would it look, do you suppose? A vagrant rogue, the associate of a bandit was closeted yesterday with me, and so far received my countenance that he was bidden to court. It would disclose a plot, indeed. It would be said that I plotted to fashion evidence against my nephew. Do you think that I have no enemies here in Casale and elsewhere in Montferrat besides Barbaresco and his plotters? If Spigno had lived, it would have been different, or even if we had Barbaresco and the others and could now wring the truth from them under torment. But Spigno is dead and the others gone."

Bellarion deemed him bewildered by his own excessive subtleties.

"Does Barbaresco's flight give no colour to my tale?" he asked quietly.

"Only until some other tale is told, as told it would be. Then what of the word of a rascal like yourself? And what of me who depend upon the word of so pitiful a knave?"

"Your highness starts at shadows." Bellarion was almost contemptuous. "In the end it may be necessary to tell my tale if I am to save my neck."

The Regent's look and tone made Bellarion feel cold.

"Your neck? Why, what does your neck matter?"

"Something to me, however little to your highness."

The Regent sneered, and the hard eyes grew harder still. "You become inconvenient, my friend."

Bellarion perceived it. The Regent feared lest investigation should reveal that he had actually fostered the conspiracy for purposes of his own, using first Count Spigno and then Bellarion as his agents.

"Aye, you become inconvenient," he repeated. "Duke Gian Galeazzo would never have boggled over dealing with you. He would have wrung this precious neck by which you lay such store. Do you thank God that I am not Gian Galeazzo."

He took the cloak from his left arm. From within its folds he let fall at Bellarion's feet a coil of rope; from his breast he drew two stout files which he placed upon Bellarion's stool.

"If you remove one of those bars, that should give you passage. Attach the rope to another, and descend by it at dusk. When you touch ground, you will be outside the walls. Go your ways and never cross the frontiers of Montferrat again. If you do, my friend, I promise you that you shall be hanged out of hand for having broken prison."

"I should deserve it," said Bellarion. "Your highness need have no anxiety."

"Anxiety, you dog!" The Regent measured him with that cold glance a moment, then swung on his heel and left him.

Next morning, when it was learnt that the prisoner had escaped, wild and varied were the speculations in Casale to explain it, and stern, searching, and fruitless the inquiry conducted by the governor of the prison. None was known to have visited Bellarion save only the Marquis Theodore, and only one person was so mad as to suppose that the Regent had made possible the evasion.

"You see," said the Princess Valeria to her faithful Dionara.

"Has my prophecy been fulfilled? Was I not right in my reading of this sordid page?" But in her dark eyes there was none of the exultation that verified conjecture so often brings.

And at about the same time, Bellarion, having found a fisherman to put him across the Po beyond Frassinetto, was trudging mechanically along, safe now in the territory of Milan. But his thoughts went back to Montferrat and the Princess Valeria.

"In her eyes I am a rogue, a spy, a trickster, and perhaps worse, which matters nothing, for in her eyes I never could have been anything that signifies. Nor does it really matter that she should know why Spigno died. Let her think what she will. I have made her and her brother safe for the present."

That night he lay at an inn at Candia, and reflected that he lay there at the Princess Valeria's charges, for he still possessed three of the five ducats she had given him for his needs.

"Someday," he said, "I shall repay that loan."

Next morning he was up betimes to resume at last in earnest his sorely interrupted journey to Pavia. But he found that the Muses no longer beckoned him as alluringly as hitherto. He had in the last few days tasted stronger waters than those of Castalia's limpid spring. He had also made the discovery that in fundamental matters all his past learning had but served to lead him astray. He questioned now his heresy on the score of sin. It was possible that, after all, the theologians might be right. Whether sin and evil were convertible terms he could not be sure. But not only was he quite sure that there was no lack of evil in the world; he actually began to wonder if evil were not the positive force that fashions the destinies of men, whilst good is but a form of resistance which, however strong, remains passive, or else, when active, commonly operates through evil that it may ultimately prevail.

So much for his syllogism which had seemed irrefragable. It had fallen to dust at the first touch of worldly experience. Yet, for all his apprehension of the world's wickedness it was with a sigh of regret that he turned his back upon it. The school of living, striving men called him now with a voice far stronger than that of Pavia and the learned Chrysolaras, and reminded him that he was pledged to a service which he could not yet consider fully rendered.

Book II

BOOK II

Chapter I

The Miracle of the Dogs

Bellarion took his way through the low-lying and insalubrious marshlands about Mortara where the rice-fields flourished as they had flourished almost ever since the grain was first
introduced from China some three hundred years before. It
touched his imagination to know himself treading the soil of the
great State of Milan, a state which Gian Galeazzo Visconti had
raised to such heights of fame and power.

From the peace which Gian Galeazzo had enforced at home,
as much as from his conquests abroad, there had ensued a prosperity such as Milan had never known before. Her industries
throve apace. Her weavers of silk and wool sent their products to
Venice, to France, to Flanders, and to England; the work of her
armourers was sought by all Europe; great was the trade driven
with France in horses and fat Lombardy cattle. Thus the wealth

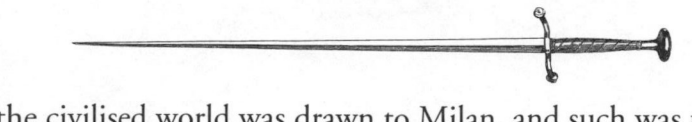

of the civilised world was drawn to Milan, and such was the development there of banking that soon there was scarcely an important city in Europe that had not its Lombard Street, just as in every city of Europe the gold coins of Gian Galeazzo, bearing his snake device, circulated freely, coming to be known as ducats in honour of this first Duke of Milan.

His laws, if tinctured by the cruelty of an age which held human lives cheap, were nevertheless wise and justly administered; and he knew how to levy taxes that should enrich himself without impoverishing his subjects, perceiving with an intuition altogether beyond his age that excessive taxation serves but to dry up the sources of a prince's treasury. His wealth he spent with a staggering profusion, creating about himself an environment of beauty, of art, and of culture which overwhelmed the rude French and ruder English of his day with the sense of their own comparative barbarism. He spent it also in enlisting into his service the first soldiers of his time; and by reducing a score of petty tyrannies and some that were of consequence, the coils of the viper came to extend from the Alps to the Abruzzi. So wide, indeed, were his dominions become that they embraced the greater part of Northern Italy, and justified their elevation to the status of a kingdom and himself to the assumption of the royal crown.

In the Castle of Melegnano, where he had shut himself up to avoid the plague that was crawling over the face of Italy, the regalia was already prepared when this great prince, whom no human enemy had yet been able to approach, was laid low by the invincible onslaught of that foul disease.

Because at the time of their great father's death Gian Maria was thirteen and Filippo Maria twelve years of age, they remained, as Gian Galeazzo's will provided against such a contingency, under the tutelage of a council of regency composed of the condottieri and the Duchess Catherine.

Dissensions marked the beginnings of that council's rule, and dissensions at a time when closest union was demanded. For in the death of the redoubtable Gian Galeazzo the many enemies he had made for Milan perceived their opportunity, whilst Gian Galeazzo's great captains, disgusted with the vacillations of the degenerate Gian Maria, who was the creature now of this party, now of that, furthered the disintegration of his inheritance by wrenching away portions of it to make independent states for themselves. Five years of misrule had dissipated all that Gian Galeazzo had so laboriously built, and of all the great soldiers who had helped him to build, the only one who remained loyal—sharing with the bastard Gabriello the governorship of the duchy—was that Facino Cane, Count of Biandrate, whom Bellarion had in his need adopted for his father.

Bellarion lay at Vigevano on the second night from Casale, and on the morrow found a boatman to put him across the broad waters of the Ticino, then took the road to Abbiategrasso, where the Lords of Milan possessed a hunting seat.

He sang as he tramped; not from any joyousness of heart, but to dispel the loneliness that increased upon him with every step that took him from Casale towards this great city of Milan, this Rome of the North, which it was his intention to view on his way to Pavia.

Beyond Abbiategrasso, finding that he was growing footsore on the hard and dusty road, he forsook it for the meadows, where fat cattle, the like of which for bulk he had never seen, were con-

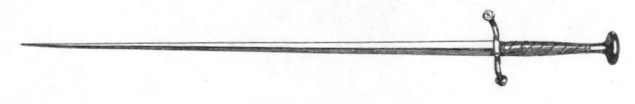

tentedly grazing. Early in the afternoon by one of the many watercourses that here intersected the ground, he sat munching the bread and cheese which he had stuffed into his scrip before leaving Abbiategrasso.

From the wood crowning the slight eminence beyond the stream came presently a confused sound of voices human and canine, a cracking of whips and other vaguer noises. Suddenly the figure of a man all in brown broke from the little belt of oaks and came racing down the green slope towards the water. He was bareheaded, and a mane of black hair streamed behind him as he ran.

He was more than midway across that open space between wood and water when his pursuers came in sight; not human pursuers, but three great dogs, three bloodhounds, bounding silently after him.

And then from the wood emerged at last a numerous mounted company led by one who seemed little more than a boy, very richly dressed in scarlet-and-silver, whose harsh and strident voice urged on the dogs. Of those who followed, and half perhaps were gay and richly clad like himself, the rest were grooms in leather, and two of them as they rode held each in leash six straining, yelping hounds. Immediately behind the youth who led rode a powerfully built fellow, black-bearded and black-browed, on a big horse, wielding a whip with a long lash, who seemed neither groom nor courtier and yet something of both. He, too, was shouting, and cracking that long whip of his to urge the dogs to bring down the human quarry before it could reach the water.

But terror lent wings to the heels of the hunted man. He gained the edge of the deep, sluggish stream a dozen yards ahead

of the hounds, and without pause or backward glance leapt wide, and struck the water cleanly, head foremost. Through it he clove, swimming desperately and strongly, using in the effort the last remnants of his strength. After him came the dogs, taking the water almost together.

Bellarion, in horror and pity, ran to the spot where the swimmer must land, and proffered a hand to him as he reached the bank. The fugitive clutched it and was drawn vigorously upwards.

"May God reward you, sir!" he gasped, and again, in a voice of extraordinary fervour, considering how little really had been accomplished: "May God reward you!" Then he dropped on hands and knees, panting, exhausted, just as the foremost of the dogs came clambering up the slippery clay of the bank to receive in its throat the dagger with which Bellarion awaited it.

A shout of rage from across the water did not deter him from slitting the throat of the second dog that landed, and he had hurled the body of it after the first before that cavalcade brought up on the far side, vociferous and angry.

The third dog, however, a great black-and-yellow hound, had climbed the bank whilst Bellarion was engaged with the second. With a deep-throated growl it was upon him, in a leap which bore him backwards and stretched him supine under the brute's weight. Instinctively Bellarion flung his left arm across his throat to shield it from those terrible fangs, whilst with his right he stabbed upwards into the beast's vitals. There was a howl of pain, and the dog shrank together a little, suspending its attack. Bellarion stabbed again, and this time his dagger found the beast's heart. It sank down upon him limp and quivering, and the warm, gushing blood soaked him almost from head to foot. He heaved aside

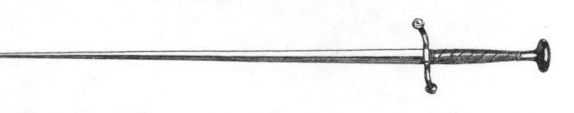

the carcass, which was almost as heavy as a man's, and got slowly to his feet, wondering uneasily what might be the sequel.

The young man in red-and-silver was blaspheming horribly. He paused to scream an order.

"Loose the pack on them! Loose the pack, Squarcia!"

But the big man addressed, on his own responsibility, had already decided on action of another sort. From his saddlebow he unslung an arbalest, which was ready at the stretch, fitted a bolt, and levelled it at Bellarion. And never was Bellarion nearer death. It was the youth he had compassionated who now saved him, and this without intending it.

Having recovered something of his breath, and urged on by the terror of those dread pursuers, he staggered to his feet, and without so much as a backward glance was moving off to resume his flight. The movement caught the eye of the black-browed giant Squarcia, just as he was about to loose his shaft. He swung his arbalest to the fugitive, and, as the cord hummed, the young man span round and dropped with the bolt in his brain.

Before Squarcia had removed the stock from his shoulder, to wind the weapon for the second shot he intended, he was slashed across the face by the whip of young red-and-silver.

"By the Bones of God! Who bade you shoot, brute beast? My order was to loose the pack. Will you baulk me of sport, you son of a dog? Did I track him so far to have him end like that?" He broke into obscenest blasphemy, from which might be extracted an order to the grooms to unleash the beasts they held.

But Squarcia, undaunted either by blasphemy or whiplash, interposed.

"Will your highness have that knave kill some more of your

dogs before they pull him down? He's armed, and the dogs are at his mercy as they climb the bank."

"He killed my dogs, and dog shall avenge dog upon him, the beast!"

From that pathetic heap at his feet Bellarion realised the fate that must overtake him if he attempted flight. Fear in him was blent with loathing and horror of these monsters who hunted men like stags. Whatever the crime of the poor wretch so ruthlessly slain under his eyes, it could not justify the infamy of making him the object of such a chase.

One of the grooms spoke to Squarcia, and Squarcia turned to his young master.

"Checco says there is a ford at the turn yonder, Lord Duke."

The form of address penetrated the absorption of Bellarion's feelings. A duke, this raging, blaspheming boy, whose language was the language of stables and brothels! What duke, then, but Duke of Milan? And Bellarion remembered tales he had lately heard of the revolting cruelty of this twenty-year-old son of the great Gian Galeazzo.

Four grooms were spurring away towards the ford, and across the stream came the thunder of Squarcia's voice, as the great ruffian again levelled his arbalest.

"Move a step from there, my cockerel, and you'll stand before your Maker."

Through the ford the horses splashed, the waters, shrunken by a protracted drought, scarce coming above their fetlocks. And Bellarion, waiting, bethought him that, after all, the real ruler of Milan was Facino Cane, and took the daring resolve once more to use that name as a scapulary.

When the grooms reached him, they found themselves intrepidly confronted by one who proclaimed himself Facino's son, and bade them sternly have a care how they dealt with him. But if he had proclaimed himself son of the Pope of Rome it would not have moved these brutish oafs, who knew no orders but Squarcia's and whose intelligence was no higher than that of the dogs they tended. With a thong of leather they attached his right wrist to a stirrup, and compelled him, raging inwardly, to trot with them. He neither struggled nor protested, realising the futility of both at present. At one part of the ford the water rose to his thighs, whilst the splashing of the horses about him added to his discomfort. But though soaked in blood and water, he still carried himself proudly when he came to stand before the young Duke.

Bellarion beheld a man of revolting aspect. His face was almost embryonic, the face of a man prematurely born whose features in growing had preserved their half-modelled shape. A bridgeless nose broad as a negro's splayed across his fresh-complexioned face, immediately above the enormous purple lips of his shapeless mouth. Round, pale-coloured eyes bulged on the very surface of his face; his brow was sloping and shallow and his chin receded. From his handsome father he inherited only the red-gold hair that had distinguished Gian Galeazzo.

Bellarion stared at him, fascinated by that unsurpassable ugliness, and, meeting the stare, a frown descended between the thick sandy eyebrows.

"Here's an insolent rogue! Do you know who I am?"

"I am supposing you to be the Duke of Milan," said Bellarion, in a tone that was dangerously near contempt.

"Ah! You are supposing it? You shall have assurance of it before we are done with each other. Did you know it when you slew my dogs?"

"Less than ever when I perceived that you hunted with them deliberately."

"Why so?"

"Could I suspect that a prince should so hunt a human quarry?"

"Why, you bold dog . . ."

"Your highness knows my name!"

"Your name, oaf? What name?"

"What your highness called me. Cane." Thus again, with more effectiveness than truth, did he introduce the identity that had served so well before. "I am Bellarion Cane, Facino Cane's son."

It was an announcement that produced a stir in that odd company.

A handsome, vigorous young man in mulberry velvet, who carried a hooded falcon perched on his left wrist, pushed forward on his tall black horse to survey this blood-smeared ragamuffin with fresh interest.

The Duke turned to him.

"You hear what he says, Francesco?"

"Aye, but I never heard that Facino had a son."

"Oh, some by-blow, maybe. No matter." A deepening malice entered his evil countenance, the mere fact of Bellarion's parentage would give an added zest to his maltreatment. For deep down in his dark soul Gian Maria Visconti bore no love to the great soldier who dominated him. "We'll rid Facino of the inconvenient incubus. Fall back there, you others. Line the bank."

167

The company spread itself in a long file along the water's edge, like beaters, to hinder the quarry's escape in that direction.

Grim fear took hold of Bellarion. He had shot his bolt, and it had missed its mark. He was defenceless and helpless in the hands of this monster and his bestial crew. At a command from the Duke they loosed the thong that bound him to the stirrup, and he found himself suddenly alone and free, with more than a glimmering in his mind of the ghastly fate intended for him.

"Now, rogue," the Duke shrilled at him, "let us see you run." He swung to Squarcia. "Two dogs," he commanded.

Squarcia detached two hounds from a pack of six which a groom held in leash. Holding each by its collar, he went down on one knee between them, awaiting the Duke's command for their release.

Bellarion meanwhile had not moved. In fascinated horror he watched these preparations, almost incredulous of their obvious purport. He was not to know that the love of the chase which had led Bernabó Visconti to frame game laws of incredible barbarity had been transmitted to his grandson in a form that was loathsomely depraved. The deer and the wild boar which had satisfied the hunting instincts of the terrible Bernabó were inadequate for the horrible lusts of Gian Maria; the sport their agonies yielded could not compare in his eyes with the sport to be drawn from the chase of human quarries, to which his bloodhounds were trained by being fed on human flesh.

"You are wasting time," the Duke admonished him. "In a moment I shall loose the dogs. Be off while you may, and if you are fleet enough, your heels may save your throat." But he laughed slobberingly over the words, which were merely intended to befool

the wretched victim with a false hope that should stimulate him to afford amusement.

Bellarion, white-faced, with such a terror in his soul as he had never known and should never know again in whatever guise he should find death confronting him, turned at last, and broke wildly, instinctively, into a run towards the wood. The Duke's bestial laughter went after him, before he had covered twenty yards and before the dogs had been loosed. His manhood, his human dignity, rose in revolt, conquering momentarily even his blind terror. He checked and swung round. Not another yard would he run to give sport to that pink-and-silver monster.

The Duke, seeing himself thus in danger of being cheated, swore at him foully.

"He'll run fast enough, highness, when I loose the dogs," growled Squarcia.

"Let go, then."

As Bellarion stood there, the breeze ruffling the hair about his neck, the hounds bounded forward. His senses swam, a physical nausea possessed him. Yet, through swooning reason, he resolved to offer no resistance so that this horror might be the sooner ended. They would leap for his throat, he knew, and so that he let them have their way, it would speedily be done.

He closed his eyes. He groaned. "Jesus!" And then his lips began to shape a prayer, the first that occurred to him, mechanically almost: *"In manus tuas, Domine . . ."*

The dogs had reached him. But there was no impact. The eager, furious leaps with which they started had fallen to a sedate and hesitating approach. They sniffed the air, and, at close quarters now, they crouched down, nosing him, their bellies trailing in the grass, their heavy tails thumping the ground, in an attitude of fawning submission.

There were cries of amazement from the ducal party. Amazement filled the soul of Bellarion as he looked down upon those submissive dogs, and he sought to read the riddle of their behaviour, thought, indeed, of divine intervention, such as that by which the saints of God had at times been spared from the inhumanities of men.

And this, too, was the thought of more than one of the spectators. It was the thought of the brutal Squarcia, who, rising from the half-kneeling attitude in which he had remained, now crossed himself mechanically.

"Miracle!" he cried in a voice that was shaken by supernatural fears.

But the Duke, looking on with a scowl on his shallow brow, raged forth at that. The Visconti may never have feared man; but most of them had feared God. Gian Maria was not even of these.

"We'll test this miracle, by God!" he cried. "Loose me two more dogs, you fool."

"Highness . . ." Squarcia was beginning a protest.

"Loose two more dogs, or I'll perform a miracle on you."

Squarcia's fear of the Duke was even greater than his fear of the supernatural. With fumbling, trembling fingers he did as he was bidden. Two more dogs were launched against Bellarion, incited by the Duke himself with his strident voice and a cut of his whip across their haunches.

But they behaved even as the first had behaved, to the increasing awe of the beholders, but no longer to Bellarion's awe or mystification. His wits recovered from their palsy, and found a

physical explanation for the sudden docility of those ferocious beasts. Right or wrong, his conclusions satisfied him, and it was without dread that he heard the Duke raging anew. So long as they sent only dogs against him, he had no cause for fear.

"Loose Messalina," the Duke was screaming in a frenzy now that thickened his articulation and brought froth and bubbles to his purple lips.

Squarcia was protesting, as were, more moderately, some of the members of his retinue. The handsome young man with the falcon opined that here might be witchcraft, and admonished his highness to use caution.

"Loose Messalina!" his highness repeated, more furiously insistent.

"On your highness's head the consequences!" cried Squarcia, as he released that ferocious bitch, the fiercest of all the pack.

But whilst she came loping towards him, Bellarion, grown audacious in his continued immunity, was patting the heads and flanks of the dogs already about him and speaking to them coaxingly, in response to which the Duke beheld them leaping and barking in friendliness about him. When presently the terrible Messalina was seen to behave in the same fashion, the excitement in the Duke's following shed its last vestige of restraint. Opinions were divided between those who cried "Miracle!" with the impious yet credulous Squarcia, and those who cried "Witchcraft!" with Messer Francesco Lonate, the gentleman of the falcon.

In the Duke's own mind some fear began to stir. Whether of God or devil, only supernatural intervention could explain this portent.

He spurred forward, his followers moving with him, and

Bellarion, as he looked upon the awe-stricken countenances of that ducal company, was moved to laughter. Reaction from his palsy of terror had come in a mental exaltation, like the glow that follows upon immersion in cold water. He was contemptuous of these fellows, and particularly of Squarcia and his grooms who, whilst presumably learned in the ways of dogs, were yet incapable of any surmise by which this miracle might be naturally explained. Mockery crept into that laugh of his, a laugh that brought the scowl still lower upon the countenance of the Duke.

"What spells do you weave, rascal? By what artifice do you do this?"

"Spells?" Bellarion stood boldly before him. He chose to be mysterious, to feed their superstition. He answered with a proverb that made play upon the name he had assumed. "Did I not tell you that I am Cane? Dog will not eat dog. That is all the magic you have here."

"An evasion," said Lonate, like one who thinks aloud.

The Duke flashed him a sidelong glance of irritation. "Do I need to be told?" Then to Bellarion: "This is a trick, rogue. God's Blood! I am not to be fooled. What have you done to my dogs?"

"Deserved their love," said Bellarion, waving a hand to the great beasts that still gambolled about him.

"Aye, aye, but how?"

"How? Does anyone know how love is deserved of man or beast? Loose the rest of your pack. There's not a dog in it will do more than lick my hands. Dogs," he added, again with a hint of mysteries, "have perceptions oft denied to men."

"Perceptions, eh? But what do they perceive?"

172

And Bellarion yielding to his singular exaltation laughed again as he answered: "Ah! Who shall say?"

The Duke empurpled. "Do you mock me, filth?"

Lonate, who was afraid of wizardry, laid a hand upon his arm. But the Duke shook off that admonitory grasp. "You shall yield me your secret. You shall so, by the Host!" He turned to the gaping Squarcia. "Call off the dogs, and make the knave fast. Fetch him along."

On that the Duke rode off with his gentlemen, leaving the grooms to carry out his orders. They stood off reluctantly, despite Squarcia's commands, so that in the end for all his repugnance the kennel-master was constrained, himself, to take the task in hand. He whistled the dogs to heel, and left one of his knaves to leash them again. Then he approached Bellarion almost timidly.

"You heard the orders of his highness," he said in the resigned voice of one who does a thing because he must.

Bellarion proffered his wrists in silence. The Duke and his following had almost reached the wood, and were out of earshot.

"It is the Duke who does this," that black-browed scoundrel excused himself. "I am but the instrument of the Duke." And cringing a little he proceeded to do the pinioning, but lightly so that the thong should not hurt the prisoner, a tenderness exercised probably for the first time in his career as the villainous servant of a villainous master. His hands trembled at the task, which again was a thing that had never happened yet. The truth is that Squarcia was inspired by another fear as great as his dread of the supernatural. On both counts he desired to stand well with this young man.

He cast a glance over his shoulder to satisfy himself that the grooms were out of earshot.

"Be sure," he muttered in his dense black beard, "that his excellency the Count of Biandrate shall know of your presence within an hour of our arrival in Milan."

Chapter II

Facino Cane

On the ground that they had far to travel, but in reality to
spare this unwelcome prisoner, Bellarion was mounted on
the crupper of Squarcia's great horse, his lightly pinioned wrists
permitting him to hang on by the kennel-master's belt.

Thus he made his first entrance into the fair city of Milan as
dusk was descending. Some impression of the size and strength
of it Bellarion gathered when, a couple of miles away, they made
a momentary halt on a slight eminence in the plain. And though
instruction had prepared him for an imposing spectacle, it had
not prepared for what he actually beheld. He gazed in wonder on
the great spread of those massive red walls reflected in a broad
navigable moat, which was a continuation of the Ticinello, and,
soaring above these, the spires of a half-dozen churches, among
which he was able from what he had read to identify the slender

belfry of Sant' Eustorgio and the octagonal brick and marble tower, surmounted by its headless gilded angel, belonging to the church of Saint Gothard, built in honour of the sainted protector of the gouty by the gout-ridden Azzo Visconti a hundred years ago.

They entered the city by the Porta Nuova, a vast gateway, some of whose stonework went back to Roman times, having survived Barbarossa's vindictive demolition nearly three centuries ago. Over the drawbridge and through the great archway they came upon a guard-house that was in itself a fortress, before whose portals lounged a group of brawny-bearded mercenaries, who talked loudly amongst themselves in the guttural German of the Cantons. Then along Borgo Nuovo, a long street in which palace stood shoulder to shoulder with hovel, and which, though really narrow by comparison with other streets of Milan, appeared generously broad to Bellarion. The people moving in this thoroughfare were as oddly assorted as the dwellings that flanked it. Sedately well-nourished, opulent men of the merchant class, glittering nobles attended by armed lackeys with blazons on their breasts, some mounted, but more on foot, were mingled here with aproned artisans and with gaunt, ragged wretches of both sexes whose aspect bespoke want and hunger. For there was little of the old prosperity left in Milan under the rule of Gian Maria.

Noble and simple alike stood still to bare and incline their heads as the Duke rode past. But Bellarion, who was sharply using his eyes, perceived few faces upon which he did not catch a reflection, however fleeting, of hatred or of dread.

From this long street they emerged at length upon a great open space that was fringed with elms, on the northern side of

which Bellarion beheld, amid a titanic entanglement of poles and scaffolding, a white architectural mass that was vast as a city in itself. He knew it at a glance for the great cathedral that was to be the wonder of the world. It was built on the site of the old basilica of Saint Ambrose, dedicated to Mariæ Nascenti: a votive offering to the Virgin Mother for the removal of that curse upon the motherhood of Milan, as a result of which the women bore no male children, or, if they bore them, could not bring them forth alive. Gian Galeazzo had imagined his first wife, the sterile Isabella of Valois, to lie under the curse. Bellarion wondered what Gian Galeazzo thought of the answer to that vast prayer in marble when his second wife Caterina brought forth Gian Maria. There are, Bellarion reflected, worse afflictions than sterility.

Gian Galeazzo had perished before his stupendous conception could be brought to full fruition, and under his degenerate son the work was languishing, and stood almost suspended, a monument as much to the latter's misrule as to his father's colossal ambition and indomitable will.

They crossed the great square, which to Bellarion, learned in the history of the place, was holy ground. Here in the now vanished basilica the great Saint Augustine had been baptised. Here Saint Ambrose, that Roman prefect upon whom the episcopate had been almost forced, had entrenched himself in his great struggle with the Empress Justina, which marked the beginnings of that strife between Church and Empire, still kept alive by Guelph and Ghibelline after the lapse of a thousand years.

Flanking the rising cathedral stood the Old Broletto, half palace, half stronghold, which from the days of Matteo Visconti had been the residence of the Lords of Milan.

They rode under the portcullis into the great courtyard of the Arrengo, which derived a claustral aspect from its surrounding porticoes, and passed into the inner quadrangle known as the Court of Saint Gotthard. Here the company dismounted, and to Lonate, who held his stirrup for him, Gian Maria issued his orders concerning the prisoner before entering the palace.

This bewitcher of dogs, he announced, should make entertainment for him after supper.

Bellarion was conducted to a stone cell underground, which was supplied with air and as much light as would make a twilight of high noon by a grating set high in the massive door. It was very cold and pervaded by a moist, unpleasant, fungoid odour. The darkness and chill of the place struck through him gradually to his soul. He was very hungry, too, which did not help his courage, for he had eaten nothing since midday, and not so much as a crust of bread did his gaolers have the charity to offer him.

At long length—at the end of two hours or more—the Duke's magnificence came to visit him in person. He was attended by Messer Lonate and four men in leather jerkins, one of whom was Squarcia. His highness sought to make up in gaudiness of raiment for what he lacked of natural endowments. He wore a trailing, high-necked velvet houppelande, one half of which was white, the other red, caught about his waist by a long-tongued belt of fine gold mail that was studded with great rubies. From waist to ground the long gown fell open as he moved showing his legs which were cased, the one in white, the other in scarlet. They were the colours of his house, colours from which he rarely departed in his wear, following in this the example set him by his illustrious sire. On his head he wore a bulging scarlet cap tufted

at the side into a jagged, upright mass like a cock's comb.

His goggling eyes measured the prisoner with a glance which almost sent a shudder through Bellarion.

"Well, rogue? Will you talk now? Will you confess what was the magic that you used?"

"Lord Duke, I used no magic."

The Duke smiled. "You need a lenten penance to bring you to a proper frame of mind. Have you never heard of the Lent of my invention? It lasts for forty days, and is a little more severe than mere fasting. But very salutary with obstinate or offending rogues, and it teaches them such a contempt of life that in the end they are usually glad to die. We'll make a beginning with you now. I dare make oath you'll be as sorry that you killed my dogs as that my dogs did not kill you." He turned to Squarcia. "Bring him along," he commanded, and stalked stiffly out.

They dragged Bellarion into a larger stone chamber that was as anteroom to the cell. Here he now beheld a long wooden engine, standing high as a table, and composed of two oblong wooden frames, one enclosed within the other and connected by colossal wooden screws. Cords trailed from the inner frame.

The Duke growled an order.

"Lay the rogue stark."

Without waiting to untruss his points, two of the grooms ripped away his tunic, so that in a moment he was naked to the waist. Squarcia stood aloof, seeking to dissemble his superstitious awe, and expecting calamity or intervention at any moment.

The intervention came. Not only was it of a natural order, but it was precisely the intervention Squarcia should have been expecting, since it resulted from the message he had secretly carried.

The heavy studded door at the top of a flight of three stone steps swung slowly open behind the Duke, and a man of commanding aspect paused on the threshold. Although close upon fifty years of age, his moderately tall and vigorous, shapely frame, his tanned, shaven face, squarely cut with prominent bone structures, his lively, dark eyes, and his thick, fulvid hair, gave him the appearance of no more than forty. A gown of mulberry velvet edged with brown fur was loosely worn over a dress of great richness, a figured tunic of deep purple and gold with hose of the colour of wine.

A moment he stood at gaze, then spoke, in a pleasant, resonant voice, its tone faintly sardonic.

"Upon what beastliness is your highness now engaged?"

The Duke span round; the grooms stood arrested in their labours. The gentleman came sedately down the steps.

"Who bade you hither?" the Duke raged at him.

"The voice of duty. First there is my duty as your governor, to see that . . ."

"My governor!" Sheer fury rang in the echoing words. "My governor! You do not govern me, my lord, though you may govern Milan. And you govern that at my pleasure, you'll remember. I am the master here. It is I who am Duke. You'll be wise not to forget it."

"Perhaps I am not wise. Who shall say what is wisdom?" The tone continued level, easy, faintly mocking. Here was a man very sure of himself. Too sure of himself to trouble to engage in argument. "But there is another duty whose voice I have obeyed. Parental duty. For they tell me that this prisoner with whom you are proposing to be merry after your fashion claims to be my son."

"They tell you? Who told you?" There was a threat to that unknown person in the inquiry.

"Can I remember? A court is a place of gossip. When men and women discover a piece of unusual knowledge they must be airing it. It doesn't matter. What matters to me is whether you, too, had heard of this. Had you?" The pleasant voice was suddenly hard; it was the voice of the master, of the man who holds the whip. And it intimidated, for whilst the young Duke stormed and blustered and swore, yet he did so in a measure of defence.

"By the bones of Saint Ambrose! Did you not hear that he slew my dogs? Slew three of them, and bewitched the others."

"He must have bewitched you, Lord Duke, at the same time, since, although you heard him claim to be my son, yet you venture to practise upon him without so much as sending me word."

"Is it not my right? Am I not lord of life and death in my dominions?"

The dark eyes flashed in that square, shaven face. "You are . . ." He checked. He waved an imperious hand towards Squarcia Giramo. "Go, you, and your curs with you."

"They are here in attendance upon me," the Duke reminded him.

"But they are required no longer."

"God's Light! You grow daily more presumptuous, Facino."

"If you will dismiss them, you may think differently."

The Duke's prominent eyes engaged the other's stern glance, until, beaten by it, he swung sullenly to his knaves: "Away with you! Leave us!" Thus he owned defeat.

Facino waited until the men had gone, then quietly admonished the Duke.

"You set too much store by your dogs. And the sport you make with them is as dangerous as it is bestial. I have warned your highness before. One of these fine days the dogs of Milan will turn upon you and tear out your throat."

"The dogs of Milan? On me?" His highness almost choked.

"On you, who account yourself lord of life and death. To be Duke of Milan is not quite the same thing as to be God. You should remember it." Then he changed his tone. "That man you were hunting today beyond Abbiate was Francesco da Pusterla, I am told."

"And this rogue who calls himself your son attempted to rescue him, and slew three of my best dogs. . . ."

"He was doing you good service, Lord Duke. It would have been better if Pusterla had escaped. As long as you hunt poor miscreants, guilty of theft or violence or of no worse crime than being needy and hungry, retribution may move slowly against you. But when you set your dogs upon the sons of a great house, you walk the edge of an abyss."

"Do I so? Do I so? Well, well, my good Facino, as long as a Pusterla remains aboveground, so long shall my hounds be active. I don't forget that a Pusterla was castellan of Monza when my mother died there. And you, that hear so much gossip about the town and court, must have heard what is openly said: that the scoundrel poisoned her."

Facino looked at him with such grim significance that the Duke's high colour faded under the glance. His face grew ashen. "By the Bones of God!" he was beginning, when Facino interrupted.

"This young man here was not to know your motives. In-

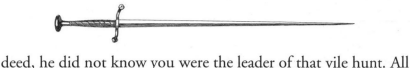

deed, he did not know you were the leader of that vile hunt. All that he saw was a fellow-creature inhumanly pursued by dogs. None would call me a gentle, humane man. But I give you my word, Lord Duke, that he did what in his place I hope I should have had the courage to do, myself. I honour him for it. Apart from that, he told you that his name was Cane. It is a name that deserves some respect in Milan, even from the Duke." His voice grew cold and hard as steel. "Hunt the Pusterla all you please, magnificent, and at your own peril. But do not hunt the Cane without first giving me warning of the intention."

He paused. The Duke, slow-witted ever, stood between shame and rage before him, silent. Facino turned to Bellarion, his tone and manner expressing contempt of his ducal master. "Come, boy. His highness gives you leave. Put on your tunic and come with me."

Bellarion had waited in a fascinated amazement that held a deal of fear, based on the conviction that he escaped Scylla to be wrecked upon Charybdis. For a long moment he gazed now into that indolently good-humoured, faintly mocking countenance. Then, with mechanical obedience, he took up the garment, which had been reduced almost to rags, and followed the Count of Biandrate from that stone chamber.

Sedately Facino went up the narrow staircase with no word for the young man who followed in uneasy wonder and dread speculation of what was now to follow.

In a fine room that was hung with Flemish tapestries, and otherwise furnished with a richness such as Bellarion had never yet beheld, lighted by great candles in massive gilt candlesticks that stood upon the ground, the masterful Facino dismissed a couple of waiting lackeys, and turned at last to bestow a leisurely scrutiny upon his companion.

"So you have the impudence to call yourself my son," he said, between question and assertion. "It seems I have more family than I suspected. But I felicitate you on your choice of a father. It remains for you to tell me upon whom I conferred the honour of being your mother."

He threw himself into a chair, leaving Bellarion standing before him, a sorry figure in his tattered red tunic pulled loosely about him, his flesh showing in the gaps.

"To be frank, my lord, in my anxiety to avoid a violent death I overstated our relationship."

"You overstated it?" The heavy eyebrows were raised. The humour of the countenance became more pronouncedly sardonic. "Let me judge the extent of this overstatement."

"I am your son by adoption only."

Down came the eyebrows in a frown, and all humour passed from the face.

"Nay, now! That I know for a lie. I might have got me a son without knowing it. That is always possible. I was young once, faith, and a little careless of my kisses. But I could scarcely have adopted another man's child without being aware of it."

And now Bellarion, judging his man, staked all upon the indolent good-nature, the humorous outlook upon life which he thought to perceive in Facino's face and voice. He answered him with a studied excess of frankness.

"The adoption, my lord, was mine; not yours." And then, to temper the impudence of that, he added: "I adopted you, my lord, in my hour of peril and of need, as we adopt a patron saint.

My wits were at the end of their resources. I knew not how else to avert the torture and death to which wanton brutality exposed me, save by invoking a name in itself sufficiently powerful to protect me."

There was a pause in which Facino considered him, half angrily, so that Bellarion's heart sank and he came to fear that in his bold throw with Fortune he had been defeated. Then Facino laughed outright, yet there was an edge to his laugh that was not quite friendly. "And so you adopted me for your father. Why, sir, if every man could choose his parents . . ." He broke off. "Who are you, rogue? What is your name?"

"I am called Bellarion, my lord."

"Bellarion? A queer name that. And what's your story? Continue to be frank with me, unless you would have me toss you back to the Duke for an impostor."

At that Bellarion took heart, for the phrase implied that if he were frank this great soldier would befriend him at least to the extent of furthering his escape. And so Bellarion used an utter frankness. He told his tale, which was in all respects the true tale which he had told Lorenzaccio da Trino.

It was, when all is said, an engaging story, and it caught the fancy of the Lord Facino Cane, as Bellarion, closely watching him, perceived.

"And in your need you chose to think that this rider who befriended you was called Facino!" The condottiero smiled now, a little sardonically. "It was certainly resourceful. But this business of the Duke's dogs? Tell me what happened there."

Bellarion's tale had gone no farther than the point at which he had set out from Cigliano on his journey to Pavia. Nor now, in answer to this question, did he mention his adventure in Montferrat and the use he had made there already of Facino's name, but came straight to the events of that day in the meadows by Abbiategrasso. To this part of his narrative, and particularly to that of Bellarion's immunity from the fierce dogs, Facino listened in incredulity, although it agreed with the tale he had already heard.

"What patron did you adopt to protect you there?" he asked, between seriousness and derision. "Or did you use magic, as they say?"

"I answered the Duke on that score with more literal truth than he suspected when I told him that dog does not eat dog."

"How? You pretend that the mere name of Cane. . . ?"

"Oh, no. I reeked, I stank of dog. The great hound I had ripped up when it was upon me had left me in that condition, and the other hounds scented nothing but dog in me. The explanation, my lord, lies between that and miracle."

Facino slowly nodded. "And you do not believe in miracles?" he asked.

"Your lordship's patience with me is the first miracle I have witnessed."

"It is the miracle you hoped for when you adopted me for your father?"

"Nay, my lord. My hope was that you would never hear of the adoption."

Facino laughed outright. "You're a frank rogue," said he, and heaved himself up. "Yet it would have gone ill with you if I had not heard that a son had suddenly been given to me." To Bellarion's amazement the great soldier came to set a hand upon his

shoulder, the dark eyes, whose expression could change so swiftly from humour to melancholy, looked deeply into his own. "Your attempt to save Pusterla's life without counting the risk to yourself was a gallant thing, for which I honour you, and for which you deserve well of me. And they are to make a monk of you, you say?"

"That is the Abbot's hope." Bellarion had flushed a little under the sudden, unexpected praise and the softening of the voice that bestowed it. "And it may follow," he added, "when I return from Pavia."

"The Abbot's hope? But is it your own?"

"I begin to fear that it is not."

"By Saint Gotthard, you do not look a likely priest. But that is your own affair." The hand fell from his shoulder, Facino turned, and sauntered away in the direction of the loggia, beyond which the night glowed luminously blue as a sapphire. "From me you shall have the protection you invoked when you adopted me, and tomorrow, well-accredited and equipped, you shall resume the road to Pavia and your studies."

"You establish, my lord, my faith in miracles," said Bellarion.

Facino smiled as he beat his hands together. Lackeys in his blue-and-white liveries appeared at once in answer to that summons. His orders were that Bellarion should be washed and fed, whereafter they would talk again.

Chapter III

The Countess of Biandrate

Facino Cane and Bellarion talked long together on the night of their first meeting, and as a result the road to Pavia was not resumed upon the morrow, nor yet upon the morrow's morrow. It was written that some years were yet to pass before Bellarion should see Pavia, and then not at all with the eyes of the student seeking a seat of learning.

Facino believed that he discovered in the lad certain likenesses to himself: a rather whimsical, philosophical outlook, a readiness of wit, and an admirable command of his person such as was unusual amongst even the most cultured quattrocentists. He discovered in him, too, a depth and diversity of learning, which inspired respect in one whose own education went little beyond the arts of reading and writing, but who was of an intelligence to perceive the great realms that lie open to conquest by the mind.

He admired also the lad's long, clean-limbed grace and his boldly handsome, vivid countenance. Had God given him a son, he could not have desired him other than he found Bellarion. From such a thought in this childless man—thrust upon him, perhaps, by the very manner of Bellarion's advent—it was but a step to the desire to bind the boy to himself by those ties of adoption which Bellarion had so impudently claimed. That step Facino took with the impulsiveness and assurance that were his chief characteristics. He took it on the third day of Bellarion's coming, at the end of a frank and detailed narrative by Bellarion of the events in Montferrat. He had for audience on that occasion not only Facino, but Facino's young and languidly beautiful countess. His tale moved them sometimes to laughter, sometimes to awe, but always to admiration of Bellarion's shrewdness, resource, and address.

"A sly fox the Marquis Theodore," Facino had commented. "Subtlety curbs ambition in him. Yet his ambition is such that one of these days it will curb his subtlety, and then Messer Theodore may reap his deserts. I know him well. Indeed, it was in his father's service that I learnt the trade of arms. And that's a better trade for a man than priesthood."

Thus from the subject of Theodore he leapt abruptly to the subject of Bellarion, and became direct at once. "With those limbs and those wits of yours, you should agree with that. Will you let them run to waste in cloisters?"

Bellarion sighed thoughtfully. He scented the inspiration of that question, which fell so naturally into place in this dream in which for three days he had been living. It was all so different, so contrary to anything that he could have imagined at the

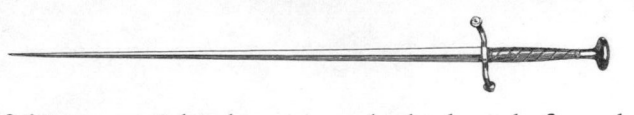

hands of this man with whose name he had made free, this man who daily bade him postpone the resumption of his journey until the morrow.

Softly now, in answer to that question, be quoted the Abbot: "*Pax multa in cella, foris autem plurima bella.* And yet . . . And yet is the peace of the cloisters really better than the strife of the world? Is there not as much service to be done in righting wrongs? Is not peace stagnation? Are not activity and strife the means by which a man may make his soul?" He sighed again. His mention of righting wrongs was no vague expression, as it seemed, of an ideal. He had a particular wrong very vividly in mind.

Facino, watching him almost hungrily, was swift to argue.

"Is not he who immures himself to save his soul akin to the steward who buried his talents?"

He developed the argument, and passed from it to talk of feats of arms, of great causes rescued, of nations liberated, of fainting right upheld and made triumphant.

From broad principles his talk turned, as talk will, to details. He described encounters and actions, broad tactical movements and shrewd stratagems. And then to his amazement the subject was caught up, like a ball that is tossed, by Bellarion; and Bellarion the student was discoursing to him, the veteran of a score of campaigns and a hundred battles, upon the great art of war. He was detailing, from Thucydides, the action of the Thebans against Platæa, and condemning the foolish risk taken by Eurymachus, showing how the disastrous result of that operation should have been foreseen by a commander of any real military sense. Next he was pointing the moral to be drawn from the Spartan invasion of Attica which left the Peloponnesus uncovered to the at-

tack of the Athenians. From that instance of disastrous impetuosity he passed to another of a different kind and of recent date in the battle of Tagliacozzo, and, revealing a close acquaintance with Primatus and Bouquet, he showed how a great army when it thrust too deeply into hostile territory must do so always at the risk of being unable to extricate itself in safety. Then from the broad field of strategy, he ran on, aglow now with a subject of his predilection, to discourse upon tactics, and chiefly to advocate and defend the more general use of infantry, to enlarge upon the value of the hedgehog for defensive purposes against cavalry, supporting his assertions by instancing the battle of Sempach and other recent actions of the Swiss.

It could not be expected that a great leader like Facino, who had depended all his life upon the use of cavalry, should agree with such views as these. But the knowledge displayed by this convent-reared youngster, and the shrewd force and lucidity with which Bellarion, who had never seen a pitched battle, argued upon matters that were regarded as mysteries hidden from all but the initiates in the difficult science of arms, amazed him so profoundly that he forgot to argue at all.

Facino had learnt the trade of war by actual practice in a long and hard apprenticeship. It had never even occurred to him that there was a theory to be learnt in the quiet of the study, to be culled from the records of past failure and achievement in the field. Nor now that this was revealed to him was he disposed to attach to it any considerable importance. He regarded the young man's disquisitions merely in the light of interesting mental exercises. But at the same time he concluded that one who showed such understanding and critical appreciation of strategy and tac-

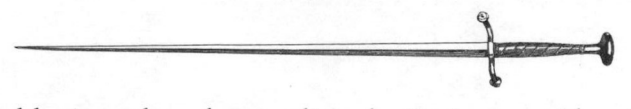

tics should, given the other qualities by Facino considered necessary, be quick to gather experience and learn the complex military art. Now every man who truly loves the trade by which he lives is eager to welcome a neophyte of real aptitude. And thus between Facino and Bellarion another link was forged.

Deep down in Bellarion's soul there was that vague desire, amounting as yet to little more than a fantastic hope, to consummate his service to that brave Princess of Montferrat. It was a dream, shadowy, indefinite, almost elusive to his own consciousness. But the door Facino now held so invitingly open might certainly lead to its ultimately becoming a reality.

They were occupying at the time the loggia of Facino's apartments above the court of Saint Gotthard. Facino and his lady were seated, one at each end of that open space. Bellarion stood equidistant from either, leaning against one of the loggia's slender pillars that were painted red and white, his back to the courtyard, which lay peaceful now in the bright sunlight and almost forsaken, for it was the rest hour of early afternoon. He was dressed in very courtly fashion in a suit of purple which Facino's wardrobe had supplied. The kilted tunic was caught about his waist by a belt of violet leather with gold trimmings, and his long black hair had been carefully combed and perfumed by one of Facino's servants. He made a brave figure, and the languid sapphire eyes of the Countess as they surveyed him confirmed for her the conviction already gathered from his frank and smoothly told tale that between himself and her husband there existed no relationship such as she had at first suspected, and such as the world in general would presently presume.

"My Lord Count advises you shrewdly, Ser Bellarion," she

ventured, seeing him thoughtful and wavering. "You make it very plain that you are not meant for cloisters."

She was a handsome woman of not more than thirty, of middle height with something feline in her beautifully proportioned litheness, and something feline too in the blue-green eyes that looked with sleepy arrogance from out of her smoothly pallid face set within a straight frame of ebony black hair.

Bellarion considered her, and the bold, direct, appraising glance of his hazel eyes, which seemed oddly golden in that light, stirred an unaccountable uneasiness in this proud daughter of the Count of Tenda who had married out of ambition a man so much older than herself. Languidly she moved her fan of peacock feathers, languidly surveyed herself in the mirror set in the heart of it.

"If I were to await further persuasions I must become ridiculous," said Bellarion.

"A courtly speech, sir," she replied with her slow smile. Slowly she rose. "You should make something of him, Facino."

Facino set about it without delay. He was never dilatory when once he had taken a resolve. They removed themselves next day— Facino, his lady, his household, and Bellarion—to the ducal hunting-palace at Abbiategrasso, and there the secular education of Bellarion was at once begun, and continued until close upon Christmastide, by when some of the sense of unreality, of dream experiences, began at last to fade from Bellarion's mind.

He was taught horsemanship, and all that concerns the management of horses. Followed a training in the use of arms, arduous daily exercises in the tiltyard supervised by Facino himself, superficially boisterous, impatient, at times even irascible in his zeal, but fundamentally of an infinite patience. He was taught such crude swordsmanship as then obtained, an art which was three parts brute force and one part trickery; he was instructed in ballistics, trained in marksmanship with the crossbow, informed in the technicalities of the mangonel, and even initiated into the mysteries of that still novel weapon the cannon, an instrument whose effects were moral rather than physical, serving to terrify by its noise and stench rather than actually to maim. A Swiss captain in Facino's service named Stoffel taught him the uses of the short but formidable Swiss halbert, and from a Spaniard named de Soto he learnt some tricks with a dagger.

At the same time he was taken in hand by the Countess for instruction in more peaceful arts. An hour each evening was devoted to the dance, and there were days when she would ride forth with him in the open meadows about the Ticino to give him lessons in falconry, a pursuit in which she was greatly skilled; too skilled and too cruelly eager, he thought, for womanhood, which should be compassionate.

One autumn day when a northerly wind from the distant snows brought a sting which the bright sunshine scarcely sufficed to temper, Bellarion and the Countess Beatrice, following the flight of a falcon that had been sent soaring to bring down a strong-winged heron, came to the edge of an affluent of the Ticino, now brown and swollen from recent rains, on the very spot where Duke Gian Maria had loosed his hounds upon Bellarion.

They brought up there perforce just as overhead the hawk stooped for the third time. Twice before it had raked wide, but now a hoarse cry from the heron announced the strike almost before it could be seen, then both birds plumbed down to earth, the spread of the falcon's great wings steadying the fall.

One of the four grooms that followed sprang down, lure in hand, to recapture the hawk and retrieve the game.

Bellarion looked on in silence with brooding eyes, heedless of the satisfaction the Countess was expressing with almost childish delight.

"A brave kill! A brave kill!" she reiterated, and looked to him in vain for agreement. A frown descended upon the white brow of that petulant beauty, rendered by vanity too easily sensitive to disapproval and too readily resentful. Directly she challenged him. "Was it not a brave kill, Bellarion?"

He roused himself from his abstraction, and smiled a little. He found her petulance amusing ever, and commonly provoked her by the display of that amusement.

"I was thinking of another heron that almost fell a victim here." And he told her that this was the spot on which he had met the dogs.

"So that we're on holy ground," said she, enough resentment abiding to provoke the sneer.

But it went unheeded. "And from that my thoughts ran on to other things." He pointed across the river. "That way I came from Montferrat."

"And why so gloomy about that? You've surely no cause to regret your coming?"

"All cause, indeed, for thankfulness. But one day I shall hope to return, and in strength enough to hood a hawk that's stooping there."

"That day is not yet. Besides, the sun is sinking, and we're far from home. So if you're at the end of your dreams we had best be moving."

There was a tartness in her tone that did not escape him. It had been present lately whenever Montferrat was mentioned. It arose, he conceived, from some misunderstanding which he could not fathom. Either to fathom or to dispel it, he talked now as they rode, unfolding all that was in his mind, more than he knew was in his mind, until actual utterance discovered it for him.

"Are you telling me that you have left your heart in Montferrat?" she asked him.

"My heart?" He looked at her and laughed. "In a sense you may say that. I have left a tangle which I desire one day to unravel. If that is to have left my heart there . . ." He paused.

"A Perseus to deliver Andromeda from the dragon! A complete knight-errant aflame to ride in the service of beauty in duress! Oh, you shall yet live in an epic."

"But why so bitter, lady?" wondered Bellarion.

"Bitter? I? I laugh, sir, that is all."

"You laugh. And the matter is one for tears, I think."

"The matter of your lovesickness for Valeria of Montferrat?"

"My . . ." He gasped and checked, and then he, who a moment ago had gently chided her for laughing, himself laughed freely.

"You are merry on a sudden, sir!"

"You paint a comic picture, dear madonna, and I must laugh. Bellarion the nameless in love with a princess! Have you discovered any other signs of madness in me?"

He was too genuinely merry for deceit, she thought, and looked at him sideways under her long lashes.

"If it is not love that moves you to these dreams, what then?"

His answer came very soberly, austerely, "Whatever it may be, love it certainly is not, unless it be love of my own self. What should I know of love? What have I to do with love?"

"There speaks the monk they almost made of you. I vow you shuddered as you spoke the word. Did the fathers teach you the monkish lie that love is to be feared?"

"Of love, madonna, they taught me nothing. But instinct teaches me to endeavour not to be grotesque. I am Bellarion the nameless, born in squalor, cradled in a kennel, reared by charity . . ."

"Beatific modesty! Saintly humility! Even as the dust am I, you cry, in false self-abasement that rests on pride of what you are become, of what you may yet become, pride of the fine tree grown from such mean soil. Survey yourself, Bellarion."

"That, lady, is my constant endeavour."

"But you bring no honesty to the task, and so your vision's warped."

"Should I be honest if I magnified myself in my own eyes?"

"Magnified? Why, where's the need? Was Facino more than you are when he was your age? His birth could not have been less lowly, and he had not the half of your endowments, not your beauty, nor your learning, nor your address."

"Lady, you will make me vain."

"Then I shall advance your education. There is Ottone Buonterzo, who was Facino's brother in arms. Like you he, too, was born in the mud. But he kept his gaze on the stars. Men go whither they look, Bellarion. Raise your eyes, boy."

"And break my nose in falling over the first obstacle in my path."

"Did they do this? Ottone is Tyrant of Parma, a sovereign prince. Facino could be the same if his heart were big enough.

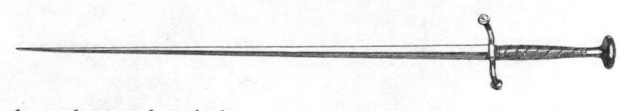

Yet in other things he did not want for boldness. He married me, for instance, the only daughter of the Count of Tenda, whose rank is hardly less than that of your lady of Montferrat. But perhaps she is better endowed. Perhaps she is more beautiful than I am. Is she?"

"Lady," said Bellarion, "I have never seen any one more beautiful than you." The slow solemnity of his delivery magnified and transformed the meaning of his words.

A scarlet flush swept across the ivory pallor of the Countess. She veiled her eyes behind lids which were lowered until the long lashes swept her cheek; a little smile crept into the corners of her full and perfect lips. She reached out a hand, and momentarily let it rest upon his own as he rode beside her.

"That is the truth, Bellarion?"

He was a little bewildered to see so much emotion evoked so lightly. It testified, he thought, to a consuming vanity.

"The truth," he said shortly and simply.

She sighed and smiled again. "I am glad, so glad to have you think well of me. It is what I have desired of you, Bellarion. But I have been afraid. Afraid that your Princess of Montferrat might . . . supply an obstacle."

"Could any supply an obstacle? I scarcely understand. All that I have and am I owe to my Lord Count. Am I an ingrate that I could be less than your slave, yours and my Lord Count's?"

She looked at him again, and now she was oddly white, and there was a hard brightness in her eyes which a moment ago had been so soft and melting.

"Oh! You talk of gratitude!" she said.

"Of what else?"

"Of what else, indeed? It is a great virtue, gratitude; and a rare one. But you have all the virtues. Have you not, Bellarion?"

He fancied that she sneered.

They passed from the failing sunlight into the shadows of the wood. But the chill that fell between them was due to deeper causes.

Chapter IV

The Champion

Facino Cane took his ease at Abbiategrasso in those declining days of 1407 and zestfully devoted himself to the training and education of Bellarion. It was the first rest the great soldier had known in ten years, a rest he would never have taken but for the novel occupation which Bellarion provided him. For Facino was of those who find no peace in utter idleness. He was of a restless, active mind, and being no scholar found no outlet for his energy save in physical directions. Here at Abbiategrasso, away from turbulence, and able for the first time since Gian Galeazzo's death to live without being perpetually on guard, he confessed himself happier than he could remember to have been.

"If this were life," he said to Bellarion one evening as they sauntered through the parklands where the red deer grazed, "a man might be content."

"Content," said Bellarion, "is stagnation. And man was not made for that. I am coming to perceive it. The peace of the convent is as the peace of the pasture to the ox."

Facino smiled. "Your education progresses."

"I have left school," said Bellarion. "You relish this lull in your activities, as a tired man relishes sleep. But no man would he glad to sleep his life away."

"Dear philosopher, you should write a book of such sayings for man's entertainment and information."

"I think I'll wait until I am a little older. I may change my mind again."

It was not destined that the rest by which Facino was setting such store should endure much longer. Rumours of trouble in Milan began to reach them daily, and in the week before Christmas, on a morning when a snowstorm kept them within doors about a great hissing fire in the main hall, Facino wondered whether he should not be returning. The bare suggestion seemed to anger his countess, who sat brooding in a chair of brown walnut set at one of the corners of the hearth.

"I thought you said we should remain here until spring." Her tone revealed the petulance that was ever just under the surface of her nature.

"I was not to know," he answered her, "that in the meantime the duchy would go to pieces."

"Why should you care? It is not your duchy. Though a man might have made it so by this."

"To make you a duchess, eh?" Facino smiled. His tone was quiet, but it bore the least strain of bitterness. This was an old argument between them, though Bellarion heard it now for the

first time. 'There are obstacles supplied by honour. Shall I enu-
merate them?"

"I know them by heart, your obstacles of honour." She thrust
out a lip that was very full and red, suggesting the strong life
within her. "They did not suffice to curb Pandolfo or Buonterzo,
and they are at least as well-born as you."

"We will leave my birth out of the discussion, madonna."

"Your reluctance to be reminded of it is natural enough," she
insisted with malice.

He turned away, and moved across to one of the tall mullioned windows, trailing his feet through the pine-needles and
slim boughs of evergreens with which the floor was strewn in
place of rushes, unprocurable at this season of the year. His thumbs
were thrust into the golden girdle that cinctured his trailing
houppelande of crimson velvet edged with lynx fur.

He stood a moment in silence, his broad square shoulders to
the room, looking out upon the wintry landscape.

"The snow is falling more heavily," he said at last.

But even upon that her malice fastened. "It will be falling still
more heavily in the hills about Bergamo where Pandolfo rules . . ."

He span round to interrupt her, and his voice rasped with
sarcasm.

"And not quite so heavily in the plain about Piacenza, where
Ottone Buonterzo is tyrant. If you please, madonna, we will
change the subject."

"I do not please"

"But I do." His voice beat upwards to the tones that had
reduced whole squadrons to instant obedience.

The lady laughed, and none too tunefully. She drew her rich

cloak of ermine more closely about her shapely figure.

"And of course what you please is ever to be the law. We come when you please, and we depart again as soon as you are tired of country solitude."

He stared at her frowning, a little puzzled. "Why, Bice," he said slowly, "I never before knew you attached to Abbiategrasso. You have ever made a lament of being brought hither, and you deafened me with your complaints three months ago when we left Milan."

"Which, nevertheless, did not restrain you from forcing me to come."

"That does not answer me." He advanced towards her. "What is this sudden attachment to the place? Why this sudden reluctance to return to the Milan you profess to love, the gaieties of the court in which you strain to shine?"

"I have come to prefer peace, if you must know, if you must have reason for all things. Besides, the court is not gay these days. And I am reminded there of what it might be; of what you might make it if you had a spark of real spirit. There's not one of them, not Buonterzo, nor Pandolfo, nor dal Verme, nor Appiano, who would not be Duke by now if he had the chance accorded to you by the people's love."

Bellarion marvelled to see him still curb himself before this display of shameless cupidity.

"The people's love is mine, Bice, because the people believe me to be honest and loyal. That faith would leave them the moment I became a usurper, and I should have to rule by terror, with an iron hand, as—"

"So that you ruled . . ." she was interrupting him, when he

swept on:

"I should be as detested as is Gian Maria today. I should have wars on my hands on every side, and the duchy would become a parade ground."

"It was so in Gian Galeazzo's early days. Yet upon that he built the greatness of Milan and his own. A nation prospers by victorious war."

"Today Milan is impoverished. Gian Maria's misrule has brought her down. However you squeeze her citizens, you cannot make them yield what they lack, the gold that will hire and furnish troops to defend her from a general attack. But for that, would Pandolfo and Buonterzo and the others have dared what they have dared? I have made you Countess of Biandrate, my lady, and you'll rest content with that. My duty is to the son of the man to whom I owe all that I have."

"Until that same son hires someone to murder you. What loyalty does he give you in return? How often has he not tried to shake you from the saddle?"

"I am not concerned so much with what he is as with what I am."

"Shall I tell you what you are?" She leaned towards him, contempt and anger bringing aging lines into her lovely white face.

"If it will ease you, lady, you may tell me what you think I am. A woman's breath will neither make nor unmake me."

"A fool, Facino!"

"My patience gives proof of that, I think. Do you thank God for it."

And on that he wheeled and sauntered out of the long grey room.

She sat huddled in the chair, her elbows on her knees, her dark blue eyes on the flames that leapt about the great sizzling logs. After a while she spoke.

"Bellarion!"

There was no answer. She turned. The long, high-backed form on which he had sat over against the wall was vacant. The room was empty. She shrugged impatiently, and swung again to the fire.

"And he's a fool, too. A blind fool," she informed the flames.

It was dinnertime when they returned together. The table was spread, and the lackeys waited.

"When you have dined, madonna," Facino quietly informed her, "you will prepare to leave. We return to Milan today."

"Today!" There was dismay in her voice. "Oh! You do this to vex me, to assert your mastership. You . . ."

His raised hand interrupted her. It held a letter—a long parchment document. He dismissed the servants, then briefly told her his news.

There was trouble in Milan, dire trouble. Estorre Visconti, Bernabò's bastard, together with young Giovanni Carlo, Bernabò's grandson, were harassing the city in the Ghibelline interest. In a recent raid Estorre had fired the quarter about the Ticinese Gate. There was want in the city, and this added to insecurity was rendering the citizens mutinous. And now, to crown all, was news that, taking advantage of the distress and unrest, Ottone Buonterzo was raising an army to invade the duchy.

"It is Gabriello who writes, and in the Duke's interest begs me to return immediately and take command."

"Command!" She laughed. "And the faithful lackey runs to

serve his master. You deserve that Buonterzo should whip you again as he whipped you a year ago. If he does, I have a notion who will be Duke of Milan. He's a man, this Buonterzo."

"When he's Duke of Milan, Bice, I shall be dead," said Facino, smiling. "So you may marry him then, become his duchess, and be taught how to behave to a husband. Call the servants, Bellarion."

They dined in haste, a brooding silence presiding over the meal, and within an hour of dining they were ready to set out.

There was a mule litter for the Countess, horses for Facino and Bellarion, a half-dozen mounted grooms, and a score of lances to serve as escort. The company of a hundred Swiss, which Facino had taken with him to Abbiategrasso, were to follow on the morrow under their own captain, Werner von Stoffel, to guard the baggage which would be brought in bullock-carts.

But at the last moment Facino, who, since rising from table had worn a thoughtful, undecided air, drew Bellarion aside.

"Here's a commission for you, boy," he said, and drew a letter from his breast. "Take ten lances for escort, and ride hard for Genoa with this letter for Boucicault, who is Vicar there for the King of France. Deliver it in person, and at need supplement it. Listen: It is to request from him the hire of a thousand French lances. I have offered him a fair price in this letter. But he's a greedy fellow, and may require more. You have authority, at need, to pledge my word for twice the sum stated. I am taking no risks this time with Buonterzo. But do not let Boucicault suspect that we are menaced, or he will adapt the price to our need. Let him suppose that I require the men for a punitive expedition against some of the rebellious Milanese fiefs."

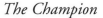

Bellarion asked a question or two, and then professed himself not only ready, but honoured by the trust reposed in him.

They embraced, and parted, Facino to mount and ride away, Bellarion to await the groom who was to fetch his horse and Werner von Stoffel who was to detail the men for his special escort.

As Facino gave the word to ride, the Countess thrust her head between the leather curtains of her litter.

"Where is Bellarion?"

"He does not ride with us."

"He doesn't. . . ? You are leaving him at Abbiate?"

"No. But I have other work for him. I am sending him on a mission."

"Other work?" Her usually sleepy eyes grew wide awake and round. "What work?"

"Nothing that will imperil him." He spurred his horse forward to avoid further questions. "Push on there!"

They reached Milan as dusk was falling, and the snow had ceased. They entered by Porta Nuova, and went at a trot through the slush and filth of the borgo. But miraculously the word of Facino's coming ran ahead. They found the great square thronged with people who had turned out to acclaim him.

Never yet since Gian Galeazzo's death had it happened to Facino to enter Milan unacclaimed. But never yet had he received so terrific a manifestation of affection and good will as this. It expressed reaction from the terror sown by a rumour lately current that even Facino had at last forsaken Gian Maria's service, leaving the people at the mercy of their maniacal Duke and of such men as della Torre and Lonate as well as of the enemies now known to be rising against them. Facino was the people's only hope. In war he had proved himself a bulwark. In peace he had been no less their champion, for he had known how to curb the savagery of his master, and how to bring some order out of the chaos into which Gian Maria's misrule was plunging the duchy.

His presence now in the very hour of crisis, in one of the darkest hours which Gian Maria's dark reign had provided for them, uplifted them on wings of confidence to exaggerated heights of hope.

As the thunders of the acclamations rolled across the great square to the Old Broletto, from one of whose windows the Duke looked down upon his people, Facino, bareheaded, his fulvid hair tossed by the breeze, his square-cut, shaven face looking oddly youthful for his fifty years, smiled and nodded, whilst his Countess, drawing back the curtains of her litter, showed herself too, and for Facino's sake was acclaimed with him.

As the little troop reached the gateway, Facino raised his eyes and met the glance of the Duke at the window above. Its malevolence dashed the glow from his spirit. And he had a glimpse of the swarthy, saturnine countenance of della Torre, who was looking over Gian Maria's shoulder.

They rode under the gloomy archway and the jagged teeth of the portcullis, across the Court of the Arrengo and into the Court of Saint Gotthard. Here they drew up, and it was a gentleman of Milan and a Guelph, one of the Aliprandi, who ran forward to hold the stirrup of Facino the Ghibelline champion.

Facino went in his turn to assist his Countess to alight. She leaned on his arm more heavily than was necessary. She raised

her eyes to his, and he saw that they were aswim in tears. In a subdued but nonetheless vehement voice she spoke to him.

"You saw! You heard! And yet you doubt. You hesitate."

"I neither doubt nor hesitate," he quietly answered. "I know where my path lies, and I follow it."

She made a noise in her throat. "And at the window? Gian Maria and that other. Did you see them?"

"I saw. I am not afraid. It would need more courage than theirs to express in deed their hatred. Besides, their need of me is too urgent."

"One day it may not be so."

"Let us leave that day until it dawn."

"Then it will be too late. This is your hour. Have they not told you so?"

"They have told me nothing that I did not know already— those in the streets and those at the window. Come, madonna."

And the Countess, raging as she stepped beside him, from between her teeth cursed the day when she had mated with a man old enough to be her father who at the same time was a fool.

Chapter V

The Commune of Milan

They deafen us with their acclamations of you, those sons of dogs!"

Thus the Duke, in angry greeting of the great condottiero, who was not only the last of his father's captains to stand beside him in his hour of need, but the only one who had refrained from taking arms against him. Nor did he leave it there. "Me they distracted with their howling lamentations when I rode abroad this morning. They need a lesson in loyalty, I think. I'll afford it them one of these fine days. I will so, by the bones of Saint Ambrose! I'll show them who is Duke of Milan."

There was a considerable concourse in the spacious chamber known as the Hall of Galeazzo, in which the Duke received the condottiero, and, as Facino's wide-set, dark eyes raked their ranks, he perceived at once the influence that had been at work during his few months of absence. Here at the Duke's elbow was the sinister della Torre, the leader of the Guelphic party, the head of the great House of the Torriani, who had striven once with the Visconti for supremacy in Milan, and in the background wherever he might look Facino saw only Guelphs: Casati, Bigli, Aliprandi, Biagi, Porri, and others. They were at their ease, and accompanied by wives and daughters, these men who two years ago would not have dared come within a mile of the Visconti Palace. Indeed, the only noteworthy Ghibelline present, and he was a man so amiably weak as to count for little in any party, was the Duke's natural brother, Gabriello Maria, the son who had inherited the fine slender height, good looks, and red-gold hair of Gian Galeazzo.

Facino was moved to anger. But he dissembled it.

"The people perceive in me the possible saviour of your duchy." He was smiling, but his eyes were hard. "It is well to propitiate those who have the power to serve us."

"Do you reprove his highness?" wondered della Torre, scowling.

"Do you boast your power?" growled the Duke.

"I rejoice in it since it is to be used in your potency's service, unlike Buonterzo's which is being used against you."

Behind Facino his Countess watched, and inwardly smiled. These fools were stirring her lord, it seemed, where she could not stir him.

Gabriello, however, interposed to clear the air. "And you are very welcome, Lord Count; your coming is most timely."

The Duke flashed him a sidelong glance, and grunted: "Huh!"

But Gabriello went on, his manner affable and courtly. "And his highness is grateful to you for the despatch you have used in

responding to his call."

After all, as titular governor, Gabriello spoke with the voice of authority, in matters of administration being even superior to the Duke. And Facino, whose aim was far from provocative, was glad enough to pass through the door Gabriello held for him.

"My despatch is natural enough since I have no object but the service of his highness and the duchy."

Later, however, when Facino attended a council that evening to determine measures a certain asperity was again in his tone.

He came to the business exacerbated by another scene with his Countess, in which again she had upbraided him for not dealing with these men as their ill will deserved by seizing upon the duchy for himself.

Della Torre's undisguised malice, the Duke's mean, vindictive, unreasoning jealousy, scarcely held in curb even by his needs, and Gabriello's hopeless incompetence, almost drove Facino to conclude that Beatrice was in the right and that he was a fool to continue to serve where he might command.

Trouble came when the question arose of the means at their command to resist Buonterzo, and Gabriello announced that the whole force under their hands amounted to the thousand mercenaries of Facino's own condotta, commanded by his lieutenant, Francesco Busone of Carmagnola, and some five hundred foot made up of Milanese levies.

Facino denounced this force as utterly inadequate, and informed the Council that to supplement it he had sent to Boucicault for a thousand men.

"A thousand men!" Gabriello was aghast, and so were the others. "But a thousand men will cost the treasury . . ."

Facino interrupted him. "I have offered fifteen gold florins a month for each man and fifty for the officer commanding them. But my messenger is authorised to pay twice that sum if necessary."

"Fifteen thousand florins, and perhaps thirty thousand! Why, you're surely mad! That is twice the sum contributed by the Commune. Whence is the remainder to come? His highness's allowance is but two thousand five hundred florins a month."

"The Commune must be made to realise that the duchy is in danger of utter shipwreck. If Buonterzo sacks Milan, it will cost them fifty times the hire of these troops. So they must provide the means to defend it. It is your business, my lord, as one of the ducal governors, to make that clear to them."

"They will take the view that this levy is far beyond the needs of the case."

"You must persuade them of their error."

Gabriello became impatient in his turn. "How can I persuade them of what I do not, myself, believe? After all, Buonterzo cannot be in great strength. I doubt if his whole force amounts to more than a thousand men."

"You doubt!" Facino stormed now, and banged the table in his wrath. "Am I to get myself and my condotta cut to pieces because you allow conjecture to fill the place of knowledge? You set my reputation on the board in your reckless gambling."

"Your reputation stands high, Lord Count," Gabriello sought to mollify him.

"But how long will you let it stand so? I shall presently be known for improvidence and carelessness in estimating the enemy forces and in opposing my troops to impossible odds. Once

I am given that character, where do you think I shall be able to hire men to follow me? Mercenaries who make a trade of war do not go into battle to get themselves slaughtered, and they do not follow leaders under whom this happens. That, my lord, you should know. I suffered enough last year against this same Buonterzo, when your reckless lack of information sent me with six hundred men to meet his four thousand. Then, as now, you argued that he was in small strength. That is not an error into which a condottiero is suffered to fall twice. Let it happen again, and I shall never be able to raise another condotta."

Gian Maria laughed softly, secretly nudged by della Torre. Facino span round on his stool to face the Duke, and his face was white with anger, for he read the meaning of that laugh. In his stupid jealousy the loutish prince would actually welcome such a consummation, unable to perceive its inevitable consequence to himself.

"Your highness laughs! You will not laugh when it is accomplished. You will discover that when there is an end to me as a condottiero, there will be an end to your highness as Duke of Milan. Do you think these will save you?" And rising in his passion he swept a hand to indicate Gabriello, della Torre, and Lonate. "Who will follow Gabriello when he takes the field? All the world knows that his mother was a better soldier than he, and that when she died he could not hold Pisa. And how will these two poor pimps who fawn upon you serve you in your need?"

Gian Maria, livid with anger was on his feet, too, by now. "By God! Facino, if you had dared say the half of this before my father's face, your head would have been on the Broletto Tower."

"If I had said it before him, I should have deserved no less. I should deserve no less if I did not say it now. We need plain speaking here to clear away these vapours of suspicion and ill will."

Gian Maria's wits, which ever worked sluggishly and crookedly, were almost paralysed now under the eyes of this stern soldier. Facino had ever been able to whistle him to heel, which was the thing he most detested in Facino. It was an influence which lately, during Facino's absence, he had been able to shake off. But he found himself cowed now, despite the support he received from the presence of Facino's enemies.

It was della Torre who answered for him.

"Is that a threat, Lord Count? Dare you suggest to his highness that you might follow the example of Buonterzo and the others? You plead for plain speaking. Be plain, then, so that his highness may know precisely what is in your mind."

"Aye!" cried his highness, glad enough to be supplied with this command. "Be plain."

Facino controlled his wrath until he found it transmuted into contempt.

"Does your highness heed this witling? Did it require the welcome given me today to prove my loyalty?"

"To prove it? How does it prove it?"

"How?" Facino looked at the others, taking his time to answer. "If I had a disloyal thought, all I need is to go down into the streets and unfurl my banner. The banner of the dog. How long do you think would the banner of the snake be seen in Milan after that?"

Gian Maria sat down abruptly, making incoherent noises

in his throat, like a hound snarling over a bone. The other three, however, came to their feet, and della Torre spoke the thought of all.

"A subject who proclaims himself a danger to his prince has forfeited the right to live."

But Facino laughed at them. "To it, then, sirs," he invited. "Out with your daggers! There are three of you, and I am almost unarmed." He paused and smiled into their sullen eyes. "You hesitate. You realise, I see, that having done it, you would need to make your souls and prepare yourselves to be torn in pieces by the mob." He turned again to the Duke, who sat glowering. "If I boast the power which comes to me from the people's love, it is that your highness may fully appreciate a loyalty which has no thought of using that power but to uphold your rights. These councillors of yours, who have profited by my absence to inspire in you black thoughts against me, take a different view. I will leave your highness to deliberate with them."

He stalked out with a dignity which left them in confusion.

At last it was della Torre who spoke. "A hectoring bully, swollen with pride! He forces his measures down our throats, commits us to extravagance whose only purpose is to bolster his reputation as a condottiero, and proposes to save the duchy from ruin in one way by ruining it as effectively in another."

But Gabriello, weak and incompetent though he might be, and although sore from Facino's affronts, yet realised the condottiero's indubitable worth and recognised the cardinal fact that a quarrel with him now would mean the end of all of them. He said so, thereby plunging his half-brother into deeper mortification and stirring his two fellow-councillors into resentful opposition.

"What he is doing we could do without him," said Lonate. "Your highness could have hired these men from Boucicault, and used them to put down Facino's insolence at the same time as Buonterzo's."

But Gabriello showed him the weakness of his argument. "Who would have led them? Do you dream that Boucicault would hire out the troops of the King of France without full confidence in their leader? As Facino himself says, mercenaries do not hire themselves out to be slaughtered."

"Boucicault himself might have been hired," suggested the fop.

"At the price of setting the heel of the King of France upon our necks. No, no," Gabriello was emphatic, which did not, however, restrain della Torre from debating the point with him.

In the midst of the argument Gian Maria, who had sat gnawing his nails in silence, abruptly heaved himself up.

"A foul plague on you and your wrangles! I am sick of both. Settle it as you like. I've something better to do than sit here listening to your vapourings." And he flung out of the room, in quest of the distractions which his vapid spirit was ever craving.

In his absence those three, the weakling, the fop, and the schemer, settled the fortunes of his throne. Della Torre, realising that the moment was not propitious for intrigue against Facino, yielded to Gabriello. It was decided that the Commune's confirmation should be sought for Facino's action in increasing his condotta.

So Gabriello summoned the Communal Council, and because he feared the worst, demanded the maximum sum of thirty thousand florin monthly for Facino's troops.

The Commune of Milan, so impoverished by the continuous rebellious depredations of the last five years, was still wrangling over the matter, its members were still raising their hands and wagging their heads, when three days later Bellarion rode into Milan with a thousand horse, made up chiefly of Gascons and Burgundians, and captained by one of Boucicault's lieutenants, an amiable gentleman named Monsieur de la Tour de Cadillac.

The people's fear of storm and pillage, whilst diminished by Facino's presence, was not yet entirely subdued. Hence there was a glad welcome for the considerable accretion to the defensive strength represented by this French legion.

That gave the Commune courage, and presently it was also to be afforded relief upon hearing that not thirty thousand florins monthly as Gabriello Maria Visconti had stated, but fifteen thousand was to be the stipend of the French lances.

Facino was delightedly surprised when he learnt this from Bellarion.

"You must have found that French pedlar in a singularly easy humour that he should have let you have the men on my own terms: and low terms they are."

Bellarion rendered his accounts.

"I found him anything but easy, and we spent the best part of two days haggling. He began by laughing at your offer; described it as impudent; wondered if you took him for a fool. Thereupon I made shift to take my leave of him. That sobered him. He begged me not to be hasty; confessed that he could well spare the men; but that I must know the price was not more than half the worth of his soldiers. At thirty florins a month for each man he would appoint a leader for them at his own charges. I said little beyond

asserting that no such price was possible; that it was beyond the means of the Commune of Milan. He then proposed twenty-five florins, and finally twenty, below which he swore by all the saints of France that he would not go. I begged him to take time for thought, and as the hour was late to let me know his decision in the morning. But in the morning I sent him a note of leave-taking, informing him that, as his terms were beyond our means and as our need was none so pressing, I was setting out for the Cantons to raise the men there."

Facino's mouth fell open. "Body of God! That was a risk!"

"No risk at all. I had the measure of the man. He was so covetous, so eager to drive the bargain, that I almost believe I could have got the men for less than your price if you had not stated it in writing. I was not suffered to depart. He sent a messenger to beg me wait upon him before leaving Genoa, and the matter was concluded on your terms. I signed the articles in your name, and parted such good friends with the French Vicar that he presented me with a magnificent suit of armour, as an earnest of his esteem of Facino Cane and Facino Cane's son."

Facino loosed his great full-throated laugh over the discomfiture of the crafty Boucicault, slapped Bellarion's shoulder, commended his guile, and carried him off at once to the Palace of the Ragione in the New Broletto where the Council awaited him.

By one of six gates that pierced this vast walled enclosure, which was the seat of Milan's civic authority, they came upon the multitude assembled there and to the Palace of the Ragione in its middle. This was little more than a great hall carried upon an open portico, to which access was gained by an exterior stone staircase. As they went up, Bellarion, to whom the place was new, looked over the heads of the clamorous multitude in admiring wonder at the beautiful loggia of the Osii with its delicately pointed arcade in black and white marble and its parapet hung with the shields of the several quarters of the city.

Before the assembled Council, with the handsome Gabriello Maria richly robed beside the President, Facino came straight to the matter nearest his heart at the moment.

"Sirs," he said, "you will rejoice to see in the increase of our strength by a thousand lances hired from the King of France an assurance of Milan's safety. For with a force now of some three thousand men with which to take the field against Buonterzo, you may tell the people from me that they may sleep tranquil o' nights. But that is not the end of my good tidings." He took Bellarion by the shoulder, and thrust him forward upon the notice of those gentlemen. "In the terms made with Monsieur Boucicault, my adoptive son here has saved the Commune of Milan the sum of fifteen thousand florins a month, which is to say a sum of between thirty and fifty thousand florins, according to the length of this campaign." And he placed the signed and sealed parchment which bore the articles on the council table for their inspection.

This was good news, indeed; almost as good, considering their depleted treasury, as would have been the news of a victory. They did not dissemble their satisfaction. It grew as they considered it. Facino dilated upon Messer Bellarion's intelligent care of their interests. Such foresight and solicitude were unusual in a soldier, and were usually left by soldiers contemptuously to statesmen. This the President of the Council frankly confessed in the little

speech in which he voiced the Commune's thanks to Messer Bellarion, showing that he took it for granted that a son of Facino's, by adoption or nature, must of necessity be a soldier.

Nor was the expression of that gratitude confined to words. In the glow of their enthusiasm, the Communal Council ended by voting Messer Bellarion a sum of five thousand florins as an earnest of appreciation of his care of their interests.

Thus, suddenly and without warning Bellarion found not merely fame but—as it seemed to his modest notions—riches thrust upon him. The President came to shake him by the hand, and after the President there was the Ducal Governor, the Lord Gabriello Maria Visconti, sometime Prince of Pisa.

For once he was almost disconcerted.

Chapter VI

The Fruitless Wooing

To have done what Bellarion had done was after all no great matter to the world of the court and would have attracted no attention there. But to have received the public thanks of Milan's civic head and a gift of five thousand florins in recognition of his services was instantly to become noteworthy. Then there was the circumstance that he was the son of the famous Facino—for "adoptive" was universally accepted as the euphemism for "natural," and this despite the Countess Beatrice's vehement assertions of the contrary; and lastly, there was the fact that he was so endowed by nature as to commend himself to his fellow-men and no less to his fellow-women. He moved about the court of Milan during those three or four weeks of preparation for the campaign against Buonterzo with the ease of one who had been bred in courts. With something of the artist's love

of beauty, he was guilty almost of extravagance in his raiment, so that in no single detail now did he suggest his lowly origin and convent rearing. Rendered conspicuous at the outset by events and circumstances, he became during those few weeks almost famous by his own natural gifts and attractions. Gabriello Maria conceived an attachment for him; the Duke himself chose to be pleasant and completely to forget the incident of the dogs. Even della Torre, Facino's mortal but secret enemy, sought to conciliate him.

Bellarion, whose bold, penetrating glance saw everything, whose rigid features betrayed nothing, steered a careful course by the aid of philosophy and a sense of humour which grew steadily and concurrently with the growth of his knowledge of men and women.

If he had a trouble in those days when he was lodged in Facino's apartments in the ducal palace, it lay in the too assiduous attentions of the Countess Beatrice. She was embittered with grievances against Facino, old natural grievances immeasurably increased by a more recent one; and to his discomfort it was to Bellarion that she went with her plaints.

"I am twenty years younger than is he," she said, which was an exaggeration, the truth being that she was exactly fifteen years her husband's junior. "I am as much of an age to be his daughter as are you, Bellarion, to be his son."

Bellarion refused to perceive in this the assertion that she and Bellarion were well matched in years.

"Yet, madonna," said he gently, "you have been wed these ten years. It is a little late to repine. Why did you marry him?"

"Ten years ago he seemed none so old as now."

"He wasn't. He was ten years younger. So were you."

"But the difference seemed less. We appeared to be more of an age until the gout began to trouble him. Ours was a marriage of ambition. My father compelled me to it. Facino would go far, he said. And so he would, so he could, if he were not set on cheating me."

"On cheating you, madonna?"

"He could be Duke of Milan if he would. Not to take what is offered him is to cheat me, considering why I married him."

"If this were so, it is the price you pay for having cheated him by taking him to husband. Did you tell him this before you were wed?"

"As if such things are ever said! You are dull sometimes, Bellarion."

"Perhaps. But if they are not said, how are they to be known?"

"Why else should I have married a man old enough to be my father? It was no natural union. Could a maid bring love to such a marriage?"

"Ask someone else, madonna." His manner became frosty. "I know nothing of maids and less of love. These sciences were not included in my studies."

And then, finding that hints were wasted against Bellarion's armour of simplicity—an armour assumed like any other panoply—she grew outrageously direct.

"I could repair the omission for you, Bellarion," she said, her voice little more than a tremulous whisper, her eyes upon the ground.

Bellarion started as if he had been stung. But he made a good recovery.

"You might; if there were no Facino."

She flashed him an upward glance of anger, and the colour flooded her face. Bellarion, however, went calmly on.

"I owe him a debt of loyalty, I think; and so do you, madonna. I may know little of men, but from what I have seen I cannot think that there are many like Facino. It is his loyalty and honesty prevents him from gratifying your ambition."

It is surprising that she should still have wished to argue with him. But so she did.

"His loyalty to whom?"

"To the Duke his master."

"That animal! Does he inspire loyalty, Bellarion?"

"To his own ideals, then."

"To anything in fact but me," she complained. "It is natural enough, perhaps. Just as he is too old for me, so am I too young for him. You should judge me mercifully when you remember that, Bellarion."

"It is not mine to judge you at all, madonna, and Heaven preserve me from such presumption. It is only mine to remember that all I have and all I am, I owe to my Lord Count, and that he is my adoptive father."

"You'll not, I hope, on that account desire me to be a mother to you," she sneered.

"Why not? It is an amiable relationship."

She flung away in anger at that. But only to return again on the morrow to invite his sympathy and his consolation, neither of which he was prepared to afford her. Her wooing of him grew so flagrant, so reckless in its assaults upon the defences behind which he entrenched himself, that one day be boldly sallied forth

to rout her in open conflict.

"What do you seek of me that my Lord Count cannot give you?" he demanded. "Your grievance against him is that he will not make you a duchess. Your desire in life is to become a duchess. Can I make you that if he cannot?"

But it was he, himself, who was routed by the counterattack.

"How you persist in misunderstanding me! If I desire of him that he make me a duchess, it is because it is the only thing that he can make me. Cheated of love, must I be cheated also of ambition?"

"Which do you rate more highly?"

She raised that perfect ivory-coloured face, from which the habitual insolent languor had now all been swept; her deep blue eyes held nothing but entreaty and submission.

"That must depend upon the man who brings it."

"To the best of his ability my Lord Facino has brought you both."

"Facino! Facino!" she cried out in sudden petulance. "Must you always be thinking of Facino?"

He bowed a little. "I hope so, madonna," he answered with a grave finality.

And meanwhile the profligate court of Gian Maria observed this assiduity of Facino's lady, and the Duke himself set the fashion of making it a subject for jests. It is not recorded of him that he made many jests in his brief day and certainly none that were not lewd.

"Facino's adoptive son should soon be standing in nearer relationship to him," he said. "He will be discovering presently

that his wife has become by Messer Bellarion's wizardry his adoptive daughter."

So pleased was his highness with that poor conceit that he repeated it upon several occasions. It became a theme upon which his courtiers played innumerable variations. Yet, as commonly happens, none of these reached the ears of Facino. If any had reached them, it would have been bad only for him who uttered it. For Facino's attachment to his quite unworthy lady amounted to worship. His trust in her was unassailable. Judging the honesty of others after his own, he took it for granted that Beatrice's attitude towards his adoptive son was as motherly as became the wife of an adoptive father.

This, indeed, was his assumption even when the Countess supplied what any other man must have accounted grounds for suspicion.

The occasion came on an evening of early April. Bellarion had received a message by a groom to wait upon Facino. He repaired to the Count's apartments, to find him not yet returned, whereupon with a manuscript of Alighieri's *Comedy* to keep him company he went to wait in the loggia, overlooking the inner quadrangle of the Broletto, which was laid out as a garden, very green in those first days of April.

Thither, a little to his chagrin, for the austere music of Dante's Tuscan lines was engrossing him, came the Countess, sheathed in a gown of white samite, with great sapphires glowing against the glossy black of her hair to match the dark mysterious blue of her languid eyes.

She came alone, and brought with her a little lute, an instrument which she played with some expertness. And she was gifted, too, in the making of little songs, which of late had been excessively concerned with unrequited love, despair, and death.

The Count, she informed Bellarion, had gone to the Castle, by which she meant, of course, the great fortress of Porta Giovia built and commonly inhabited by the late Duke. But he would be returning soon. And meanwhile, to beguile the tedium of his waiting, she would sing to him.

Singing to him Facino found her, and he was not to guess with what reluctance Bellarion had suffered her voice to substitute the voice of Dante Alighieri. Nor, in any case, was he at all concerned with that.

He came abruptly into the room from which the loggia opened, his manner a little pressed and feverish. And the suddenness of his entrance, acting upon a conscience not altogether at rest, cropped her song in mid-flight. The eyes she raised to his flushed and frowning face were startled and uneasy. Bellarion, who sat dreaming, holding the vellum-bound manuscript which was closed upon his forefinger, sprang up, with something in his manner of that confusion usually discernible in one suddenly recalled from dreams to his surroundings.

Facino strode out to the loggia, and there loosed his news at once.

"Buonterzo is moving. He left Parma at dawn yesterday, and is advancing towards Piacenza with an army fully four thousand strong."

"Four thousand!" cried Bellarion. "Then he is in greater strength than you even now."

"Thanks to the French contingent and the communal militia, the odds do not perturb me. Buonterzo is welcome to the advantage. He'll need a greater when we meet. That will be in two days' time, in three at latest. For we march at midnight. All is in readiness. The men are resting between this and then. You had best do the same, Bellarion."

Thus, with a complete change from his usual good-tempered, easygoing manner, already the commander rapping out his orders without waste of words, Facino delivered himself.

But now his Countess, who had risen when he announced the imminence of action, expressed her concern.

"Bellarion?" she cried. Her face was white to the lips, her rounded bosom heaving under its close-fitting sheath; there was dread in her eyes. "Bellarion goes with you?"

Facino looked at her, and the lines between his brows grew deeper. It wounded him sharply that in this hour concern for another should so completely override concern for himself. Beyond that, however, his resentment did not go. He could think no evil where his Bice was concerned, and, indeed, Bellarion's eager interposition would have supplied the antidote had it been necessary.

"Why, madonna, you would not have me left behind! You would not have me miss such an occasion!" His cheeks were aglow; his eyes sparkled.

Facino laughed. "You hear the lad? Would you be so cruel as to deny him?"

She recaptured betimes the wits which surprise had scattered, and prudently dissembled her dismay. On a more temperate note, from which all passion was excluded, she replied:

"He's such a child to be going to the wars!"

"A child! Pooh! Who would become master should begin early. At his age I was leader of a troop."

He laughed again. But he was not to laugh later, when he recalled this trivial incident.

Chapter VII

Manœuvres

Shortly before midnight they rode out from the Palace of the old Broletto: Facino, attended by Bellarion for his esquire, a page bestriding a mule that was laden with his armour, and a half-dozen men-at-arms.

Facino was silent and pensive. His lady's farewell had lacked the tenderness he craved, and the Duke whose battles he went to fight had not even been present to speed him. He had left the palace to go forth upon this campaign, slinking away like a discharged lackey. The Duke, he had been told, was absent, and for all that he was well aware of the Duke's detestable pernoctations, he preferred to believe that this was merely another expression of that ill will which, despite all that he had done and all that it lay in his power to do, the Duke never failed to display towards him.

But as the little company rode in the bright moonlight down

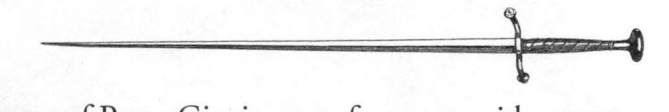

the borgo of Porta Giovia, out of a narrow side street emerged a bulky man, almost dragged along by three great hounds straining at the leash and yelping eagerly, their noses to the ground. A slender figure in a cloak followed after him, calling petulantly as he came:

"Not so fast, Squarcia! Body of God! Not so fast, I say. I am out of breath!"

There was no mistaking that strident voice. It was the Duke, himself, and close upon his heels came six armed lackeys to make a bodyguard.

Squarcia and his powerful hounds crossed the main street of the borgo, almost under the head of Facino's horse, the brawny huntsman panting and swearing as he went.

"I cannot hold them back, Lord Duke," he answered. "They're hot upon the scent, and strong as mules, devil take them!"

He vanished down the dark gulf of an alley. From the leader of the Duke's bodyguard came a challenge:

"Who goes there at this hour?"

Facino loosed a laugh that was full of bitterness.

"Facino Cane, Lord Duke, going to the wars."

"It makes you laugh, eh?" The Duke approached him. He had missed the bitterness of the laughter, or else the meaning of that bitterness.

"Oh yes, it makes me laugh. I go to fight the battles of the Duke of Milan. It is my business and my pleasure. I leave you, Lord Duke, to yours."

"Aye, aye! Bring me back the head of that rogue Buonterzo. Good fortune to you!"

"Your highness is gracious."

"God be with you!" He moved on. "That rogue Squarcia is getting too far ahead. Ho, there! Squarcia! Damn your vile soul! Not so fast!" The gloom of the alley absorbed him. His body-guard followed.

Again Facino laughed. "'God be with me,' says the Duke's magnificence. May the devil be with him. I wonder upon what foulness he is bent tonight, Bellarion." He touched his horse with the spur. "Forward!"

They came to the Castle of Porta Giovia, the vast fortress of Gian Galeazzo, built as much for the city's protection from with-out as for his own from the city. The drawbridge was lowered to receive them, and they rode into the great courtyard of San Donato, which was thronged with men-at-arms and bullock-carts laden with the necessaries of the campaign. Here, in the inner courtyard and in the great plain beyond the walls of both castle and city, the army of Facino was drawn up, marshalled by Carmagnola.

Facino rode through the castle, issuing brief orders here and there as he went, then, at the far end of the plain beyond, at the very head of the assembled forces, he took up his station attended by Bellarion, Beppo the page, and his little personal bodyguard. There he remained for close upon an hour, and in the moon-light, supplemented by a dozen flaring barrels of tar, he reviewed the army as it filed past and took the road south towards Melegnano.

The order of the going had been preconcerted between Facino and his lieutenant Carmagnola, and it was Carmagnola who led the vanguard, made up of five hundred mounted men of the civic militia of Milan and three hundred German infantry, a mixed force composed of Bavarians, Swabians, and Saxons, trailing the ponderous German pike which was fifteen feet in length. They were uniform at least in that all were stalwart, bearded men, and they sang as they marched, swinging vigorously to the rhythm of their outlandish song. They were commanded by a Swabian named Koenigshofen.

Next came de Cadillac with the French horse, of whom eight hundred rode in armour with lances erect, an imposing array of mounted steel which flashed ruddily in the flare from the tar barrels; the remaining two hundred made up a company of mounted arbalesters.

After the French came an incredibly long train of lumbering wagons drawn by oxen, and laden, some with the ordinary baggage of the army—tents, utensils, arms, munitions, and the like—and the others with mangonels and siege implements including a dozen cannon.

Finally came the rear guard composed of Facino's own condotta, increased by recent recruitings to twelve hundred men-at-arms and supplemented by three hundred Switzers under Werner von Stoffel, of whom a hundred were arbalesters and the remainder infantry armed with the short but terribly effective Swiss halbert.

When the last had marched away to be absorbed into the darkness, and the song of the Germans at the head of the column had faded out of earshot, muffled by the tramp of the rearguard, Facino with his little knot of personal attendants set out to follow.

Towards noon of the following day, with Melegnano well behind them, they came to a halt in the hamlet of Ospedaletto, having covered twenty-five miles in that first almost unbroken

march. The pace was not one that could be maintained, nor would it have been maintained so long but that Facino was in haste to reach the south bank of the Po before Buonterzo could cross. Therefore, leaving the main army to rest at Ospedaletto, he pushed on with five hundred lances as far as Piacenza. With these at need he could hold the bridgehead, whilst waiting for the main army to join him on the morrow.

At Piacenza, however, there was still no sign of the enemy, and in the Scotti who held the city—one of the possessions wrested from the Duchy of Milan—Facino found an unexpected ally. Buonterzo had sent to demand passage of the Scotti. And the Scotti, with the true brigand instinct of their kind, had replied by offering him passage on terms. But Buonterzo, the greater brigand, had mocked the proposal, sending word back that, unless he were made free of the bridge, he would cross by force and clean up the town in passing. As a consequence, whilst Buonterzo's advance was retarded by the necessity of reaching Piacenza in full force, Facino was given free and unhindered passage by the Scotti, so that he might act as a buckler for them.

Having brought his army on the morrow safely across the Po, Facino assembled it on the left bank of the little river Nure. He destroyed the bridge by which the Æmilian Way crosses the stream at Pontenure, and sat down to await Buonterzo, who was now reported to be at Firenzuola, ten miles away.

Buonterzo, however, did not come directly on, but, quitting the Æmilian Way, struck south, and, crossing the shallow hills into the valley of the Nure, threatened thence to descend upon Facino's flank.

That was the beginning of a series of movements, of marchings

and countermarchings, which endured for a full week without ever bringing the armies in sight of each other. These manœuvres carried them gradually south, and their operations became a game of hide-and-seek among the hills.

At first it bewildered Bellarion that two commanders, each of whom had for aim the destruction of the other, should appear so sedulously to avoid an engagement. But in the end, he came to understand the spirit actuating them. Each fought with mercenary troops, and just as it is not the business of mercenaries to get themselves killed, neither is it their business to slay if slaughter can be avoided. They fought for profit, and whilst prisoners were profitable, since they yielded not only arms and horses, but also ransoms, dead men yielded nothing beyond their harness. Therefore they demanded that their commanders should lead them as nearly as possible into a position of such strategical advantage that the enemy, perceiving himself at their mercy, should have no choice but to surrender. To this general rule the only exception was afforded by the Swiss, who were indifferent to bloodshed. But of Swiss there were only a few on Facino's side, and none at all on Buonterzo's.

At the end of a week, after endless manœuvres, matters were very much as they had been at the beginning. Buonterzo had fallen back again on Firenzuola, hoping to draw Facino into open country, whilst Facino, refusing to be drawn, lay patiently at San Nicoló.

Three days Facino waited there, to be suddenly startled by the news that Buonterzo was at Aggazano, eight miles away. Suspecting here an attempt to slip past him and, by crossing perhaps at Stradella, to invade the territory of Milan, and also because he conceived that Buonterzo had placed himself in a disadvanta-geous position, leaving an opening for attack, Facino decided upon instant action.

In the best house of San Nicoló, which he had temporarily adopted for his quarters, Facino assembled on the morning of the 10th of May his chief officers, Francesco Busone of Car-magnola, Koenigshofen, the Swiss Werner von Stoffel, and the French commander de Cadillac.

In a small plain room on the ground floor, darkened by semi-closed shutters to exclude the too ardent sun, they were gathered, Bellarion with them, about the plain deal table at which Facino sat. On the table's white surface the condottiero with a stick of charcoal had drawn a map which if rough was fairly accurate of scale. In the past week Bellarion had seen and studied a half-dozen such charts and had come to read them readily.

Charcoal stick in hand, Facino expounded.

"Buonterzo lies here, and the speed at which he has moved from Firenzuola will constrain him to rest there, whatever his ultimate intention."

Carmagnola interposed. He was a large young man, hand-some, florid, and self-assured.

"He is too favourably placed for an attack from the plain. At Aggazano he holds the slopes, whence he can roll down like an avalanche."

"You are interrupting me, Francesco." Facino's voice was dry and cold. "And you point out the obvious. It is not my intention to make a frontal attack; but merely to simulate one. Here is my plan: I divide the army into two battles. One of these, composed of the French horse, the civic militia, and Koenigshofen's pikes, you shall lead, Francesco, marching directly upon Aggazano, as if intending to attack. Thus you engage Buonterzo's attention, and pin him there. Meanwhile with the remainder of the forces I, myself, march up the valley of the Trebbia as far as Travo, and then, striking over the hills, descend thence upon Buonterzo's camp. That will be the moment of your simulated attack from the plain below to become real, so that whichever way Buonterzo turns, we are upon his rear."

There was a murmur of approval from the four officers.

Facino looked from one to another, smiling a little. "No situation could be better suited for such a manœuvre."

And now Bellarion, the chessplayer and student of the art of war, greatly daring, yet entirely unconscious of it, presumed to advance a criticism.

"The weakness lies in the assumption that this situation will be maintained until action is joined."

Carmagnola gasped, and with Koenigshofen and de Cadillac gave the young man a stare of haughty, angry amazement. Facino laughed outright, at so much impudence.

Werner von Stoffel, between whom and Bellarion a certain friendship had sprung up during the months they had spent together at Abbiategrasso, was the only one who spared his feelings, whilst Facino, having vented his scorn in laughter, condescended to explain.

"We ensure that by the speed of our onset, which will leave him no time to move. It is the need for rest that has made him take up this strong position. Its very strength is the trap in which we'll take him." He rose, brushing the matter aside. "Come! The details each of you can work out for himself. What imports is that we should move at once, leave camp and baggage so that we may march unhampered. Here speed is all."

But Bellarion was so little abashed by their contempt that he actually returned to the attack.

"If I were in Buonterzo's place," he said, "I should have scouts along the heights from Rivergaro to Travo. Upon discovering your intentions from your movements, I should first descend upon Carmagnola's force, and, having routed it, I should come round and on, to engage your own. Thus the division of forces upon which you count for success might easily be made the cause of your ruin."

Again there was a silence of amazement at this babe in war-like matters who thrust his opinions upon the notice of tried soldiers.

"Let us thank God," said Carmagnola with stinging sarcasm, "that you do not command Buonterzo's troops, or our overthrow would be assured." And he led the rather cruel laughter, which at last silenced Bellarion.

The two battles into which the army was divided moved at dusk, leaving all baggage and even the cannon, of which Facino judged that he would have no need in operations of the character intended. Before midnight Carmagnola had reached his station within a mile of Aggazano, and Facino was at Travo, ready to breast the slopes at dawn, and from their summit descend upon Buonterzo's camp.

Meanwhile the forces rested, and Facino himself snatched a few hours' sleep in a green tent which had hurriedly been pitched for him.

Bellarion, however, too excited by the prospect of action to think of sleeping, and rendered uneasy by his apprehensions, paced by the river which murmured at that point over a broad shallow, its waters sadly shrunken by the recent drought. Here in his pacings he was joined by Stoffel.

"I did not laugh at you today," the Swiss reminded him.

"I have to thank you for that courtesy," said Bellarion gravely.

"Courtesy wasn't in my mind."

A patriotic Swiss and an able soldier, Stoffel had the appearance of neither. He was of middle height and a gracefully slim figure which he dressed with elegance and care. His face was shaven, long and olive-skinned with a well-bridged nose and dark pensive eyes under straight black eyebrows. There was about him something mincing and delicate, but entirely pleasant, for with it all he was virile and intrepid.

"You voiced," he said now, "a possibility which should not have been left outside their calculations."

"I have never seen a battle," said Bellarion. "But I do not need to see one to know that all strategy is bad which does not consider and provide for every likely countermove that is discernible."

"And the counter-move you suggested was discernible enough—at least, when you suggested it."

Bellarion looked at the Swiss so far as the Swiss was visible in the faint radiance of that warm summer night.

"Thinking as you do, why did you not support me, Stoffel?"

"Carmagnola and de Cadillac are soldiers of repute, and so is even Koenigshofen, whilst I am but the captain of a small body of Swiss infantry whose office it is to carry out the duties imposed upon him. I do not give advice unasked, which is why

even now I dare not suggest to Facino that he repair his omission to place scouts on the heights. He takes Buonterzo's vulnerability too much for granted."

Bellarion smiled. "Which is why you seek me; hoping that I will suggest it to him."

"I think it would be well."

Bellarion considered. "We could do better, Stoffel. We could go up ourselves, and make observations."

They came an hour or so later to the crest of the hill, and there remained on watch for some two hours until the light of dawn was strong enough to disclose to them in detail the slopes towards Aggazano. And what they saw in that cold grey light was the realisation, if not of the exact possibility Bellarion had voiced, at least of something very near akin. The difference lay in that, instead of moving first against Carmagnola and later against Facino, Buonterzo was beginning with the latter course. And Bellarion instantly perceived the advantages of this. Buonterzo could descend upon Facino from above in a position of enormous tactical advantage, and, having destroyed him, go round to meet Carmagnola on level terms of ground.

The order of the movements, however, was a detail of comparative unimportance. What mattered was that Buonterzo was actually moving to destroy severally the two battles into which Facino had divided his army. In the upland valley to the north, a couple of miles away, already breasting the gentle slopes towards the summit from which Bellarion and Stoffel observed them, swarmed the whole army of Ottone Buonterzo.

The watchers waited for no more. Down the hill again to Travo they raced and came breathless into the tent where Facino

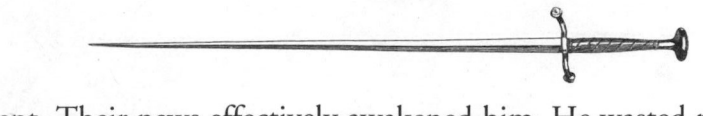

slept. Their news effectively awakened him. He wasted no time in futile raging, but, summoning his officers, issued orders instantly to marshal the men and march down the valley so as to go round to effect a reunion with Carmagnola's battle.

"It will never be effected that way," said Bellarion quietly.

Facino scowled at him, dismissed the officers to their tasks, and, when only Stoffel remained, angrily demanded of Bellarion what the devil he meant by constantly intruding opinions that were not sought.

"If the last opinion I intruded had been weighed," said Bellarion, "you would not now be in this desperate case."

"Desperate!" Facino almost exploded on the word. "How is it desperate?"

"Come outside, my lord."

To humour his self-sufficiency, to allow it to swell into a monstrous bubble which when fully swollen he would reduce to nothing by a single prick, Facino went with him from the tent, Stoffel gravely following. And in the open, by the river under that long line of shallow hills, Bellarion expounded the situation in the manner of a pedant lecturing a scholar.

"Already, by his present position, Buonterzo has driven the wedge too deeply between yourself and Carmagnola. A reunion of forces is no longer possible by marching down the valley. In less than an hour Buonterzo will command the heights, and observe your every movement. He will be at a centre, whence he can hurl his force along a radius to strike you at whatever point of the periphery you chance to occupy. And he will strike you with more than twice your numbers, falling upon your flank from a position of vantage which would still render him irresistible if he had half your strength. Your position, my lord, with the river on your other flank, is much as was the position of the Austrians at Morgarten when they were utterly broken by the Swiss."

Facino's impatience and anger had gradually undergone a transmutation into wonder and dismay, and he knew not whether to be more dismayed because he had failed to perceive the situation for himself, or because it was pointed out to him by one whose knowledge of the art of war was all derived from books.

Without answering, he stood there brooding, chin in hand, striving to master his bitter vexation.

"If you had heeded me yesterday—" Bellarion was beginning, which was very human, but hardly generous, when Facino roughly cut him short.

"Peace!" he growled. "What is done is done. We have to deal with what we find." He turned to Stoffel. "We must retreat across the river before Buonterzo thrusts us into it. There is a ford here above Travo at this height of water."

"That," ventured Stoffel, "is but to increase our separation from Carmagnola."

"Don't I know it?" roared Facino, now thoroughly in a rage with himself and all the world. "Do you suppose I can perceive nothing? Let a messenger ride at once to Carmagnola, ordering him to fall back, and cross below Rivergaro. The river should be fordable just below the islands. Thus it is possible he might be able to rejoin me."

"It should certainly be possible," the Swiss agreed, "if Buonterzo pursues us across the ford, intent upon delivering battle whilst the odds are so heavily in his favour."

"I am counting upon that. We draw him on, refusing battle

until Carmagnola is also across and in his rear. Thus we'll snatch victory from defeat."

"But if he doesn't follow?" quoth Bellarion. And again, in spite of what had happened, Facino frowned his haughty impatience of this fledgling's presumption. Unintimidated, Bellarion went on: "If you were in Buonterzo's place, would you follow, when, by remaining on this bank and marching down the valley, you might keep the two enemy battles apart so as to engage each at your convenience?"

"If Buonterzo were to do that, I should recross, and he would then have me upon his rear. After all, if his position has advantages, it has also disadvantages. However he turns he will be between two forces."

"Which is no disadvantage to him unless the two can operate simultaneously, and this he can prevent once you have crossed the river by leaving a force to watch you and dispute your passage should you attempt to return. And for that a small force will suffice. With a hundred well-posted arbalesters I could hold that ford for a day against an enemy."

"You could?" Facino almost laughed.

"I could, and I will if the plan commends itself to you."

"What plan?"

It was a plan that had occurred to Bellarion even as they argued, inspired by the very arguments they had used. He had been conning the ground beyond the water, a line of shallow hills, with a grey limestone bluff crowned by a dense wood of lofty elms commanding the ford itself.

"Buonterzo should be drawn to pursue you across the river, which might easily happen if you cross in full sight of his forces and with all the appearance of disorder. An army in flight is an almost irresistible lure to an overwhelming force. It was thus that Duke William of Normandy ensured his own ultimate victory at Senlac. The slopes across the water offer no difficulty to a pursuer, and the prospect of bringing you to an engagement before Carmagnola can rejoin you should prove too seductive. It should even render Buonterzo obstinate when he finds his passage disputed. And for this, as I have said, a hundred arbalesters will suffice. In the end he must either force a passage, or decide to abandon the attempt and go instead against Carmagnola first. But before either happens, if you act promptly, you may have rejoined Carmagnola by crossing to him at Rivergaro, and then come round the hills upon Buonterzo's rear, thus turning the tables upon him. Whether he is still here, attempting to cross, or whether he is marching off down the valley, he will be equally at your mercy if you are swift. And I will undertake to hold him until sunset with a hundred crossbowmen."

Overwhelmed with amazement by that lucid exposition of a masterly plan, Facino stood and stared at him in silence. Gravely, at last, he asked him: "And if you fail?"

"I shall still have held him long enough to enable you to extricate yourself from the trap in which you are now caught."

Facino's bewildered glance sought the dark, comely face of Stoffel. He smiled grimly. "Am I a fool, Stoffel, that a boy should instruct me in the art by which I have lived? And would you trust a hundred of your Swiss to this same boy?"

"With confidence."

But still Facino hesitated. "You realise, Bellarion, that if the passage is forced before I arrive, it will go very hard with you?"

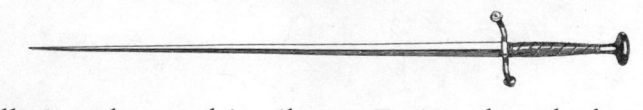

Bellarion shrugged in silence. Facino thought he was not understood.

"Such an action as you propose will entail great slaughter, perhaps. Buonterzo will be impatient of that, and he may terribly avenge it."

Bellarion smiled. "He will have to cross first, and meanwhile I shall count upon his impatience and vindictiveness to hold him here when he should be elsewhere."

Chapter VIII

The Battle of Travo

The morning sunlight falling across the valley flashed on the arms of Buonterzo's vanguard, on the heights, even as Facino's rear guard went splashing through the ford, which at its deepest did not come above the bellies of the horses or the breasts of Bellarion's hundred Swiss, who, with arbalests above their heads, to keep the cords dry, were the last to cross.

From his eyrie Buonterzo saw the main body of Facino's army straggling in disorder over the shallow hill beyond the water, and, persuaded that he had to deal with a rabble disorganised by fear, he gave the order to pursue.

A squadron of horse came zigzagging down the hillside at speed, whilst a considerable body of infantry dropped more directly.

The last stragglers of the fugitive army had vanished from view when that cavalry gained the ford and entered the water.

But before the head of the column had reached midstream there was a loud hum of arbalest cords, and fifty bolts came to empty nearly as many saddles. The column checked, and, whilst it hesitated, another fifty bolts from the enemy invisible in the woods that crowned the bluff dealt fresh destruction.

There was a deal of confusion after that, a deal of raging and splashing, some seeking to turn and retreat, others, behind, who had not been exposed to that murderous hail, clamouring to go on. So that by the time Bellarion's men had drawn their cords anew and set fresh bolts, the horsemen in the water had gone neither forward nor back. And now Bellarion let them have a full hundred in a single volley, and thereby threw them into such panic that there was an end to all hesitation. They turned about, those that were still able to do so, and, driving riderless horses before them and assisting wounded comrades to regain the shore, they floundered their way back.

The effect of this upon Buonterzo was precisely that upon which Bellarion in his almost uncanny knowledge of men had counted. He was filled with fury, which he expressed to those about him denouncing the action as insensate.

From the eminence on which he sat his horse he could see that over the shallow hills across the river the disorderly flight of Facino's troops continued, and, raging at the delay in the pursuit, Buonterzo rode down the hill with the remainder of his forces.

Excited officers met him below to deafen him with facts which he had already perceived. The ford was held against them by a party of crossbowmen, rendering impossible the pursuit his potency had commanded.

"I'll show you," Buonterzo savagely promised them, and he ordered a hundred men into the village of Travo to bring thence every door and shutter the place contained.

Close upon three hours were spent in that measure of preparation. But Buonterzo counted upon speedily making up for that lost time once the bluff were cleared of those pestilential crossbowmen.

His preparations completed, Buonterzo launched the attack, sending a body of three hundred foot to lead it, each man bearing above his head one of the cumbrous improvised shields, and trailing after him his pike, attached now to his belt.

From the summit of the bluff Bellarion looked down upon what appeared to be a solid roof of timber thrusting forward across the stream. A troop of horse was preparing to follow as soon as the pikemen should have cleared the way. Bellarion drew two thirds of his men farther off along the river. Thus, whilst lengthening the range, rendering aim less certain and less effective, at least it enabled the arbalesters to shoot at the vulnerable flank of the advancing host.

The attack was fully two thirds of the way across the ford, which may have been some two hundred yards in width, before Bellarion's men were in their new positions. He ordered a volley of twenty bolts, so as to judge the range; and although only half of these took effect, yet the demoralisation created, in men who had been conceiving themselves invulnerably sheltered, was enough to arrest them. A second volley followed along the low line of exposed flank, and, being more effective than the first, flung the column into complete disorder.

Dead men lay awash where they had fallen; wounded men

were plunging in the water, shouting to their comrades for help, what time their comrades cursed and raved, rousing the echoes of that normally peaceful valley, as they had been roused before when the horsemen found themselves in similar plight. Odd shutters and doors went floating down the stream, and the continuity of the improvised roof having been broken, those immediately behind the fallen found themselves exposed now in front as well as on the flank.

A mounted officer spurred through the water, shouting a command repeatedly as he came, and menacing the disordered ranks with his sword. At last his order was understood, and the timber shields were swung from overhead to cover the flank that was being assailed. That, thought Buonterzo, should checkmate the defenders of the ford, who with such foresight had shifted their position. But scarcely was the manoeuvre executed when into them came a volley from the thirty men Bellarion had left at the head of the bluff in anticipation of just such a countermovement. Because the range here was short, not a bolt of that volley failed to take effect, and by the impression it created of the ubiquity of this invisible opponent it completed the discomfiture of the assailants. They turned, flung away their shields, and went scrambling back out of range as fast as they could breast the water. To speed them came another volley at their flanks, which claimed some victims, whilst several men in their panic got into deep water and two or three were drowned.

Livid with rage and chagrin, Buonterzo watched this second repulse. He knew from his earlier observations and from the extent of the volleys that it was the work of a negligible contingent posted to cover Facino's retreat, and his wrath was deepened by

the reflection that, as a result of this delay, Facino might, if not actually escape, at least compel him now to an arduous pursuit. No farther than that could Buonterzo see, in the blindness of his rage, precisely as Bellarion had calculated. And because he could see no farther, he stood obstinately firm in his resolve to put a strong force across the river.

The sun was mounting now towards noon, and already over four hours had been spent at that infernal ford. Yet realising, despite his impatience, that speed is seldom gained by hastiness, Buonterzo now deliberately considered the measures to be taken, and he sent men for a mile or more up and down streams to seek another passage. Another hour was lost in this exploration, which proved fruitless in the end. But meanwhile Buonterzo held in readiness a force of five hundred men-at-arms in full armour, commanded by an intrepid young knight named Varallo.

"You will cross in spite of any losses," Buonterzo instructed him. "I compute them to number less than two hundred men, and if you are resolute you will win over without difficulty. Their bolts will not take effect save at short range, and by then you will be upon them. You are to give no quarter and make no prisoners. Put every man in that wood to the sword."

An ineffective volley rained on breastplate and helmet at the outset, and, encouraged by this ineffectiveness, Varallo urged forward his men-at-arms. Thus he brought them steadily within a range whereat arbalest bolt could pierce their protecting steel plates. But Bellarion, whose error in prematurely loosing the first volley was the fruit of inexperience, took no chances thereafter. He ordered his men to aim at the horses.

The result was a momentary check when a half-score of

stricken chargers reared and plunged and screamed in pain and terror, and flung off as many riders to drown helplessly in their armour, weighed down by it and unable to regain their feet.

But Varallo, himself scatheless, urged them on with a voice of brass, and brought them after that momentary pause of confusion to the far bank. Here another dozen horses were brought down, and two or three men directly slain by bolts before Varallo had marshalled them and led them charging up and round the shallow hill, where the ascent was easy to the wood that crowned the bluff.

The whole of Buonterzo's army straggling along the left bank of the river cheered them lustily on, and the dominant cry that rang out clearly and boldly was "No quarter!"

That cry rang in the ears of Facino Cane, as he mounted the hilltop above and behind Buonterzo's force. He had made such good speed, acting upon Bellarion's plan, that crossing at Rivergaro he had joined Carmagnola, whom he met between there and Agazzano, and sweeping on, round, and up he had completed a circuit of some twelve miles in a bare five hours.

And here below him, at his mercy now, the strategic position of that day's dawn completely reversed, lay Buonterzo's army, held in check there by the skill and gallantry of Bellarion and his hundred Swiss. But it was clear that he had arrived barely in time to command victory, and possible that he had arrived too late to save Bellarion.

Instantly he ordered de Cadillac to cleave through, and cross in a forlorn attempt to rescue the party in the wood from the slaughter obviously intended. And down the hill like an avalanche went the French horse upon an enemy too stricken by surprise to

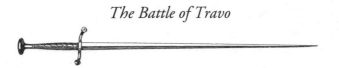

take even such scant measures of defence as the ground afforded.

Over and through them went de Cadillac, riding down scores, and hurling hundreds into the river. Through the ford his horses plunged and staggered at almost reckless speed, to turn Varallo's five hundred, who, emerging from the wood, found themselves cut off by a force of twice their strength. Back into the wood they plunged and through it, with de Cadillac following. Out again beyond they rode, and down the slope to the plain at breakneck speed. For a mile and more de Cadillac pursued them. Then, bethinking him that after all his force amounted to one third of Facino's entire army, and that his presence might be required on the main scene of action, he turned his men and rode back.

They came again by way of the wood, and along the main path running through it they found nigh upon a score of Swiss dead, all deliberately butchered, and one who still lived despite his appalling wounds, whom they brought back with them.

By the time they regained the ford, the famous Battle of Travo—as it is known to history—was all but over.

The wide breach made in Buonterzo's ranks by de Cadillac's charge was never healed. Perceiving the danger that was upon them from Facino's main army, the two broken ends of that long line went off in opposite directions, one up the valley and the other down, and it must be confessed that Buonterzo, realising the hopelessness of the position in which he had been surprised, himself led the flight of the latter and more numerous part of his army. It may have been his hope to reach the open plains beyond Rivergaro and there reform his men and make a stand that should yet retrieve the fortunes of the day. But Facino himself with his own condotta of twelve hundred men took a converging line along

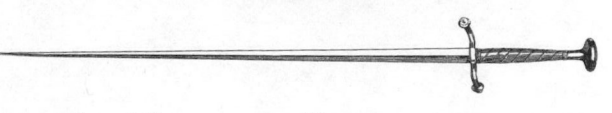

the heights, to head Buonterzo off at the proper moment. When he judged the moment to have arrived, Facino wheeled his long line and charged downhill upon men who were afforded in that narrow place no opportunity of assuming a proper formation.

Buonterzo and some two hundred horse, by desperate spurring, eluded the charge. The remainder amounting to upwards of a thousand men were rolled over, broken, and hemmed about, so that finally they threw down their arms and surrendered before they were even summoned to do so.

Meanwhile Koenigshofen, with the third battle into which the army had been so swiftly divided, dealt similarly with the fugitives who had attempted to ascend the valley.

Two thousand prisoners, fifteen hundred horses, a hundred baggage-carts well laden, a score of cannon besides some tons of armour and arms, was the booty that fell to Facino Cane at Travo. Of the prisoners five hundred Burgundian men-at-arms were taken into his own service. A thousand others were stripped of arms, armour, and horses, whilst the remainder, among whom were many officers and knights of condition, were held for ransom.

The battle was over, but Facino had gone off in pursuit of Buonterzo; and Carmagnola, assuming command, ordered the army to follow. They came upon their leader towards evening between Rivergaro and Piacenza, where he had abandoned the pursuit, Buonterzo having crossed the river below the islands.

Carmagnola, flushed and exultant, gave him news of the completeness of the victory and the richness of the booty.

"And Bellarion?" quoth Facino, his dark eyes grave.

De Cadillac told of the bodies in the wood; Stoffel with sorrow on his long swarthy face repeated the tale of the wounded

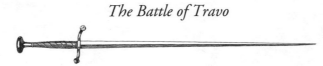

Swiss who had since died. The fellow had reported that the men-at-arms who rode in amongst them shouting "No quarter!" had spared no single life. There could be no doubt that Bellarion had perished with the rest.

Facino's chin sank to his breast, and the lines deepened in his face.

"It was his victory," he said, slowly, sorrowfully. "His was the mind that conceived the plan which turned disaster into success. His the gallantry and self-sacrifice that made the plan possible." He turned to Stoffel who more than any other there had been Bellarion's friend. "Take what men you need for the task, and go back to recover me his body. Bring it to Milan. The whole nation shall do honour to his ashes and his memory."

Chapter IX

De Mortuis

There are men to whom death has brought a glory that would never have been theirs in life. An instance of that is afforded by the history of Bellarion at this stage.

Honest, loyal, and incapable of jealousy or other kindred meanness, Facino must have given Bellarion a due measure of credit for the victory over Buonterzo if Bellarion had ridden back to Milan beside him. But that he would have given him, as he did, a credit so full as to make the achievement entirely Bellarion's, could hardly be expected of human nature or of Facino's. A living man so extolled would completely have eclipsed the worth of Facino himself; besides which to the man who in achieving lays down his life, we can afford to be more generous—because it is less costly—than to the man who survives his achievement.

Never, perhaps, in its entire history had the Ambrosian city been moved to such a delirium of joy as that in which it now hailed the return of the victorious condottiero who had put an end to the grim menace overhanging a people already distracted by internal feuds.

News of the victory had preceded Facino, who reached Milan ahead of his army two days after Buonterzo's rout.

It had uplifted the hearts of all, from the meanest scavenger to the Duke, himself. And yet the first words Gian Maria addressed to Facino in the audience chamber of the Broletto, before the assembled court, were words of censure.

"You return with the work half done. You should have pursued Buonterzo to Parma and invested the city. This was your chance to restore it to the crown of Milan. My father would have demanded a stern account of you for this failure to garner the fruits of victory."

Facino flushed to the temples. His jaw was thrust forward as he looked the Duke boldly and scathingly between the eyes.

"Your father, Lord Prince, would have been beside me on the battlefield to direct the operations that were to preserve his crown. Had your highness followed his illustrious example there would be no occasion now for a reproach that must recoil upon yourself. It would better become your highness to return thanks for a victory purchased at great sacrifice."

The goggle eyes looked at him balefully until their glance faltered as usual under the dominance of the condottiero's will, the dominance which Gian Maria so bitterly resented. Ungracefully the slender yet awkward body sprawled in the great gilded chair, red leg thrown over white one.

It was della Torre, tall and dark at his master's side, who came

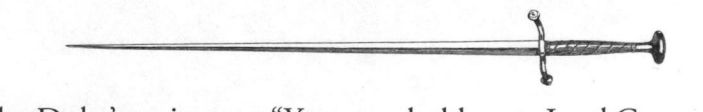

to the Duke's assistance. "You are a bold man, Lord Count, so to address your prince."

"Bold, aye!" growled the Duke, encouraged by that support. "Body of God! Bold to recklessness. One of these days . . ." He broke off, the coarse lips curling in a sneer. "But you spoke of sacrifices?" The cunning that lighted his brutishness fastened upon that. It boded, he hoped, a tale of losses that should dim the lustre of this popular idol's achievement.

Facino rendered his accounts, and it was then that he proclaimed Bellarion's part; he related how Bellarion's wit had devised the whole plan which had reversed the positions on the Trebbia, and he spoke sorrowfully of how Bellarion and his hundred Swiss had laid down their lives to make Facino's victory certain.

"I commend his memory to your highness and to the people of Milan."

If the narrative did not deeply move Gian Maria, at least it moved the courtiers present, and more deeply still the people of Milan when it reached them later.

The outcome was that after a *Te Deum* for the victory, the city put on mourning for the martyred hero to whom the victory was due; and Facino commanded a Requiem to be sung in Saint Ambrose for this Salvator Patriæ, whose name, unknown yesterday, was by now on every man's lips. His origin, rearing, and personal endowments were the sole subjects of discussion. The tale of the dogs was recalled by the few who had ever heard of it and now widely diffused as an instance of miraculous powers which disposed men almost to canonise Bellarion.

Meanwhile, however, Facino returning exacerbated from that

audience was confronted by his lady, white-faced and distraught.

"You sent him to his death!" was the furious accusation with which she greeted him.

He checked aghast both at the words and the tone. "I sent him to his death!"

"You knew to what you exposed him when you sent him to hold that ford."

"I did not send him. Himself he desired to go; himself proposed it."

"A boy who did not know the risk he ran!"

The memory of the protest she had made against Bellarion's going rose suddenly invested with new meaning. Roughly, violently, he caught her by the wrist. His face suddenly inflamed was close to her own, the veins of his brow standing out like cords.

"A boy, you say. Was that what you found him, lady?"

Scared, but defiant, she asked him: "What else?"

"What else? Your concern suggests that you discovered he's a man. What was Bellarion to you?"

For once he so terrified her that every sense but that of self-preservation abandoned her on the instant.

"To me?" she faltered. "To me?"

"Aye, to you. Answer me." There was death in his voice, and in the brutal crushing grip upon her wrist.

"What should he have been, Facino?" She was almost whimpering. "What lewdness are you dreaming?"

"I am dreaming nothing, madam. I am asking."

White-lipped she answered him. "He was as a son to me." In her affright she fell to weeping, yet could be glad of the ready

tears that helped her to play the part so suddenly assumed. "I have no child of my own. And so I took him to my empty mother's breast."

The plaint, the veiled reproach, overlaid the preposterous falsehood. After all, if she was not old enough to be Bellarion's mother, at least she was his senior by ten years.

Facino loosed his grip, and fell back, a little abashed and ashamed.

"What else could you have supposed him to me?" she was complaining. "Not . . . not, surely, that I had taken him for my lover?"

"No," he lied lamely. "I was not suspecting that."

"What then?" she insisted, playing out her part.

He stood looking at her with feverish eyes. "I don't know," he cried out at last. "You distract me, Bice!" and he stamped out.

But the suspicion was as a poison that had entered his veins, and it was a moody, silent Facino who sat beside his lady at the State supper given on the following night in the old Broletto Palace. It was a banquet of welcome to the Regent of Montferrat, his nephew the Marquis Gian Giacomo, and his niece the Princess Valeria, whose visit was the result of certain recent machinations on the part of Gabriello Maria.

Gabriello Maria had lately been exercised by the fundamental weakness of Gian Maria's position, and he feared lest the victor in the conflict between Facino and Buonterzo might, in either case, become a menace to the Duchy. No less was he exercised by the ascendancy which was being obtained in Milan by the Guelphs under della Torre, an ascendancy so great that already there were rumours of a possible marriage between the Duke and the daughter of Malatesta of Rimini, who was regarded as the leader of the Guelphic party in Italy. Now Gabriello, if weak and amiable, was at least sincere in his desire to serve his brother as in his desire to make secure his own position as ducal governor. For himself and his brother he could see nothing but ultimate disaster from too great a Guelphic ascendancy.

Therefore, had he proposed an alliance between Gian Maria and his father's old ally and friend, the Ghibelline Prince of Montferrat. Gian Maria's jealous fear of Facino's popularity had favourably disposed him, and letters had been sent to Aliprandi, the Orator of Milan at Casale.

Theodore, on his side, anxious to restore to Montferrat the cities of Vercelli and Alessandria which had been wrested from it by the all-conquering Gian Galeazzo, and having also an eye upon the lordship of Genoa, once an appanage of the crown of Montferrat, had conceived that the restoration of the former should be a condition of the treaty of alliance which might ultimately lead to the reconquest of the latter.

Accordingly he had made haste, in response, to come in person to Milan that he might settle the terms of the treaty with the Duke. With him he had brought his niece and the nephew on whose behalf he ruled, who were included in Gabriello's invitation. Gabriello's aim in this last detail was to avert the threatened Malatesta marriage. A marriage between the Duke and the Princess of Montferrat might be made by Theodore an absolute condition of that same treaty, if his ambition for his niece were properly fired.

At the banquet that night, Gabriello watched his brother, who sat with Theodore on his right and the Princess Valeria on his left, for signs from which he might calculate the chances of bringing the secret part of his scheme to a successful issue. And signs were not wanting to encourage him. It was mainly to the Princess that Gian Maria addressed himself. His glance devoured the white beauty of her face with its crown of red-gold hair; his pale goggle eyes leered into the depths of her own which were so dark and inscrutable, and he discoursed the while, loud and almost incessantly, in an obvious desire to dazzle and to please.

And perhaps because the lady remained unmoved, serenely calm, a little absent almost, and seldom condescending even to smile at his gross sallies, he was piqued into greater efforts for her entertainment, until at last he blundered upon a topic which obviously commanded her attention. It was the topic of the hour.

"There sits Facino Cane, Count of Biandrate," he informed her. "That square-faced fellow yonder, beside the dark lady who is his countess. An overrated upstart, all puffed up with pride in an achievement not his own."

The phrase drew the attention of the Marquis Theodore.

"But if not his own, whose, then, the achievement, highness?"

"Why a fledgling's, one whom he claims for his adoptive son." The adjective was stressed with sarcasm. "A fellow named Bellarion."

"Bellarion, eh?" The Regent betrayed interest. So, too, did the Princess. For the first time she faced her odious host. Meanwhile Gian Maria ran on, his loud voice audible even to Facino, as he no doubt intended.

"The truth is that by his rashness Facino was all but out fought, when this Bellarion showed him a trick by which he might turn the tables on Buonterzo."

"A trick?" said she, in an odd voice, and Gian Maria, over-joyed to have won at last her attention, related in detail the strat-egy by which Facino's victory had been snatched.

"A trick, as your highness said," was her comment. "Not a deed of arms in which there was a cause for pride."

Gian Maria stared at her in surprise, whilst Theodore laughed aloud.

"My niece is romantic. She reads the poets, and from them conceives of war as a joyous joust, or a game of chivalry, with equal chances and a straightforward encounter."

"Why, then," laughed the Duke, "the tale should please you, madonna, of how with a hundred men this rascal held the ford against Buonterzo's army for as long as the trick's suc-cess demanded."

"He did that?" she asked, incredulous.

"He did more. He laid down his life in doing it. He and his hundred were massacred in cold blood. That is why on Wednes-day, at Saint Ambrose, a Requiem Mass is to be sung for him who in the eyes of my people deserves a place in the Calendar beside Saint George."

His aim in this high praise was less to bestow laurels upon Bellarion than to strip them from Facino. "And I am not sure that the people are wrong. *Vox populi, vox Dei.* This Bellarion was oddly gifted, oddly guarded." In illustration of this he passed on to relate that incident which had come to be known by then in Milan as "The Miracle of the Dogs." He told the tale without any shame at the part he had played, without any apparent sense that to hunt human beings with hounds was other than a proper sport for a prince.

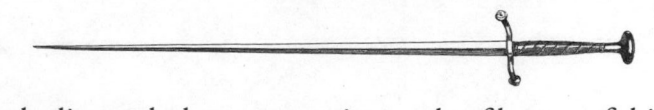

As she listened, she was conscious only of horror of this monstrous boy, so that the flesh of her arm shrank under the touch of his short, broad-jewelled paw, from which the fingernails had been all but entirely gnawed. Anon, however, in the solitude of the handsome chamber assigned to her, she came to recall and weigh the things the Duke had said.

This Bellarion had laid down his life in the selfless service of adoptive father and country, like a hero and a martyr. She could understand that in one of whom her knowledge was what it was of Bellarion as little as she could understand the miracle of the dogs.

Chapter X

The Knight Bellarion

That Requiem Mass at Saint Ambrose's for the repose of the soul of Bellarion was never sung. And this because, whilst the bells were solemnly tolling in summons to the faithful, Messer Bellarion, himself, very much in the flesh, and accompanied by Werner von Stoffel, who had been sent to recover his body, marched into the city of Milan by the Ticinese Gate at the head of some seventy Swiss arbalesters, the survivors of his hundred.

There was some delay in admitting them. When that dusty company came in sight, swinging rhythmically along, in steel caps and metal-studded leather tunics, crossbows shouldered, the officer of the gate assumed them to be one of the marauding bands which were continually harassing the city by their incursions.

By the time that Bellarion had succeeded in persuading him of his identity, rumour had already sped before him with the

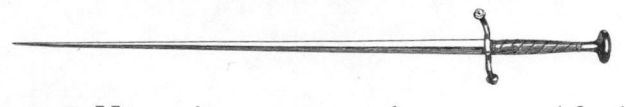

amazing news. Hence, in a measure as he penetrated further into the city, the greater was his difficulty in advancing through the crowd which turned out to meet him and to make him acquainted with the fame to which his supposed death had hoisted him.

In the square before the cathedral, the crowd was so dense that he could hardly proceed at all. The bells had ceased. For news of his coming had reached Saint Ambrose, and the intended service was naturally abandoned. This Bellarion deplored, for a sermon on his virtues would have afforded him an entertainment vouchsafed to few men.

At last he gained the Broletto and the courtyard of the Arrengo, which was thronged almost as densely as the square outside. Thronged, too, were the windows overlooking it, and in the loggia on the right Bellarion perceived the Duke himself, standing between the tall, black, saturnine della Torre and the scarlet Archbishop of Milan, and, beside the Archbishop, the Countess Beatrice, a noble lady sheathed in white samite with black hair fitting as close and regularly to her pale face as a cap of ebony. She was leaning forward, one hand upon the parapet, the other waving a scarf in greeting.

Bellarion savoured the moment critically, like an epicure in life's phenomena. Fra Serafino rightly described the event as one of those many friendly contrivings of Fortune, as a result of which be came ultimately to be known as Bellarion the Fortunate.

Similarly he savoured the moment when he stood before the Duke and his assembled court in the great frescoed chamber known as the Hall of Galeazzo, named after that son of Matteo Visconti who was born *ad cantu galli*.

Facino, himself, had fetched him thither from the court of

the Arrengo, and he stood now dusty and travel-stained, in steel cap and leather tunic, still leaning upon the eight-foot halbert which had served him as a staff. Calm and unabashed under the eyes of that glittering throng, he rendered his account of this fresh miracle—as it was deemed—to which he owed his preservation. And the account was as simple as that which had explained to Facino the miracle of the dogs.

When Buonterzo's men-at-arms had forced the passage of the ford, Bellarion had been on the lower part of the bluff with some two thirds of his band. He had climbed at once to the summit, so as to conduct the thirty men he had left there to the shelter on the southern slope. But he came too late. The vindictive soldiers of Buonterzo were already pursuing odd survivors through the trees to the cry of "No quarter!" To succour them being impossible, Bellarion conceived it his duty to save the men who were still with him. Midway down the wooded farther slope he had discovered, at a spot where the descent fell abruptly to a ledge, a cave whose entrance was overgrown and dissembled by a tangle of wild vine and jessamine. Thither he now led them at the double. The cave burrowed deeply into the limestone rock.

"We replaced," he related, "the trailing plants which our entrance had disturbed, and retired into the depths of the cave to await events, just as the first of the horsemen topped the summit. From the edge of the wood they surveyed the plain below. Seeing it empty, they must have supposed that those they had caught and slain composed the entire company which had harassed them. They turned, and rode back, only to return again almost at once, their force enormously increased as it seemed to us who could judge only by sounds.

"I realise now that in reality they were in flight before the French cavalry which had been sent across to rescue us.

"For an hour or more after their passage we remained in our concealment. At last I sent forth a scout, who reported a great body of cavalry advancing from the Nure. This we still assumed to be Buonterzo's horse brought back by news of Facino's real movements. For another two hours we remained in our cave, and then at last I climbed to the summit of the bluff, whence I could survey the farther bank of the Trebbia. To my amazement I found it empty, and then I became aware of men moving among the trees near at hand, and presently found myself face to face with Werner von Stoffel, who told me of the battle fought and won whilst we had lain in hiding."

He went on to tell them how they had crossed the river and pushed on to Travo in a famished state. They found the village half wrecked by the furious tide of war that had swept over it. Yet some food they obtained, and towards evening they set out again so as to overtake Facino's army. But at San Giorgio, which they reached late at night, and where they were constrained to lie, they found that Facino had not gone that way, and that, therefore, they were upon the wrong road. Next morning, consequently, they decided to make their own way back to Milan.

They crossed the Po at Piacenza, only to find themselves detained by the Scotti for having marched into the town without permission. The Scotti knew of the battle fought, but not of its ultimate issue. Buonterzo was in flight; but he might rally. And so, for two days Bellarion and his little band were kept in Piacenza until it was definitely known there that Buonterzo's rout was complete. Then, at last, his departure was permitted, since to have detained him longer must provoke the resentment of the victorious Facino.

"We have made haste on the march since," he concluded, "and I rejoice to have arrived at least in time to prevent a Requiem, which would have been rendered a mockery by my obstinate tenacity to life."

Thus, on a note of laughter, he closed a narrative that was a model of lucid brevity and elegant, Tuscan delivery.

But there were two among the courtly crowd who did not laugh. One was Francesco Busone of Carmagnola, Facino's handsome, swaggering lieutenant, who looked sourly upon this triumph of an upstart in whom he had already feared a rival. The other was the Princess Valeria, who, herself unseen in that concourse, discovered in this narrative only an impudent confession of trickery from one whom she had known as a base trickster. Almost she suspected him of having deliberately contrived that men should believe him dead to the end that by this sensational resurrection he should establish himself as the hero of the hour.

Gabriello Maria, elegant and debonair, came to shake him by the hand, and after Gabriello came the Duke with della Torre, to praise him almost fawningly as the Victor of Travo.

"That title, Lord Duke, belongs to none but my Lord Facino."

"Modesty, sir," said della Torre, "is a garment that becomes a hero."

"If my Lord Facino did not wear it, sir, you could not lie under your present error. He must have magnified to his own cost my little achievement."

But they would not have him elude their flattery, and when at last they had done with him he was constrained to run the gauntlet of the sycophantic court, which must fawn upon a man whom the Duke approved. And here to his surprise he found the Marquis Theodore, who used him very civilly and with no least allusion to their past association.

At last Bellarion escaped, and sought the apartments of Facino. There he found the Countess alone. She rose from her seat in the loggia when he entered, and came towards him so light and eagerly that she seemed almost to drift across the floor.

"Bellarion!"

There was a flush on her usually pale cheeks, a glitter in her bright slanting eyes, and she came holding out both hands in welcome.

"Bellarion!" she cried again, and her voice throbbed like the plucked chords of a lute.

Instantly he grew uneasy. "Madonna!" He bowed stiffly, took one of her proffered hands, and bore it formally to his lips. "To command!"

"Bellarion!" This time that melodious voice was pitched reproachfully. She seized him by his leather-clad arms, and held him so, confronting him.

"Do you know that I have mourned you dead? That I thought my heart would break? That my own life seemed to have gone out with yours? Yet all that you can say to me now—in such an hour as this—so cold and formally is 'to command'! Of what are you made, Bellarion?"

"And of what are you made, madonna?" Roughly almost, he disengaged himself from her grip. He was very angry, and anger was a rare emotion in his cold, calculating nature. "O God! Is there no loyalty in all this world? Below, there was the Duke to

nauseate me with flattery which was no more than base disloyalty to my lord. I escape from it to meet here a disloyalty which wounds me infinitely more."

She had fallen back a little, and momentarily turned aside. Suddenly she faced him again, breathless and very white. Her long narrow eyes seemed to grow longer and narrower. Her expression was not nice.

"Why, what are you assuming?" There was now no music in her voice. It was harshly metallic. "Has soldiering made you fatuous by chance?" She laughed unpleasantly, as upon a sudden scorn-provoking revelation. "I see! I see! You thought that I. . .! You thought. . . ! Why, you fool! You poor, vain fool! Shall I tell Facino what you thought, and how you have dared to insult me with it?"

He stood bewildered, aghast, and indignant. He sought to recall her exact expressions. "You used words, madonna . . ." he was beginning hotly when suddenly he checked, and when he resumed the indignation had all gone out of him. "What you have said is very just. I am a fool, of course. You will give me leave?"

He made to go, but she had not yet done with him.

"I used words, you say. What words? What words that could warrant your assumptions? I said that I had mourned you. It is true. As a mother might have mourned you. But you . . . You could think . . ." She swung past him, towards the open loggia. "Go, sir. Go wait elsewhere for my lord."

He departed without another word, not indeed to await Facino, whom he did not see again until the morrow, a day which for him was very full.

Betimes he was sought by the Lord Gabriello Maria, who came at the request of the Commune of Milan to conduct him to the Ragione Palace, there to receive the thanks of the representatives of the people.

"I desire no thanks, and I deserve none." His manner was almost sullen.

"You'll receive them nonetheless. To disregard the invitation were ungracious."

And so the Lord Gabriello carried off Bellarion, the son of nobody, to the homage of the city. In the Communal Palace he listened to a recital by the President of his shining virtues and still more shining services, in token of their appreciation of which the fathers of the Ambrosian city announced that they had voted him the handsome sum of ten thousand gold florins. In other words, they had divided between himself and Facino the sum they had been intending to award the latter for delivering the city from the menace of Buonterzo.

After that, and in compliance with the request of the Council, the rather bewildered Bellarion was conducted by his noble escort to receive the accolade of knighthood. Empanoplied for the ceremony in the suit of black armour which had been Boucicault's gift to him, he was conducted into the court of the Arrengo, where Gian Maria in red and white attended by the nobility of Milan awaited him. But it was Facino, very grave and solemn, who claimed the right to bestow the accolade upon one who had so signally and loyally served him as an esquire. And when Bellarion rose from his knees, it was the Countess of Biandrate, at her husband's bidding, who came to buckle the gold spurs to the heels of the new knight.

For arms, when invited to choose a device, he announced that he would adopt a variant of Facino's own: a dog's head argent on a field azure.

At the conclusion a herald proclaimed a joust to be held in the Castle of Porta Giovia on the morrow when the knight Bellarion would be given opportunity of proving publicly how well he deserved the honour to which he had acceded.

It was a prospect which he did not relish. He knew himself without skill at arms, in which he had served only an elementary apprenticeship during those days at Abbiategrasso.

Nor did it increase his courage that Carmagnola should come swaggering towards him, his florid countenance wreathed in smiles of simulated friendliness, to claim for the morrow the honour of running a course and breaking a lance with his new brother-knight.

He smiled, nevertheless, as falsely as Carmagnola himself.

"You honour me, Ser Francesco. I will do my endeavour."

He noted the gleam in Carmagnola's eyes, and went, so soon as he was free, in quest of Stoffel, with whom his friendship had ripened during their journey from Travo.

"Tell me, Werner, have you ever seen Carmagnola in the tilt-yard?"

"Once, a year ago, in the Castle of Porta Giovia."

"Ha! A great hulking bull of a man."

"You describe him. He charges like a bull. He bore off the prize that day against all comers. The Lord of Genestra had his thigh broken by him."

"So, so!" said Bellarion, very thoughtful. "It's my neck he means to break tomorrow. I read it in his smile."

"A swaggerer," said Stoffel. "He'll take a heavy fall one day."

"Unfortunately that day is not tomorrow."

"Are you to ride against him, then?" There was concern in Stoffel's voice.

"So he believes. But I don't. I have a feeling that tomorrow I shall not be in case to ride against anyone. I have a fever coming on: the result of hardships suffered on the way from Travo. Nature will compel me, I suspect, to keep my bed tomorrow."

Stoffel considered him with grave eyes. "Are you afraid?"

"What else?"

"And you confess it?"

"It asks courage. Which shows that whilst afraid I am not a coward. Life is full of paradox, I find."

Stoffel laughed. "No need to protest your courage to me. I remember Travo."

"There I had a chance to succeed. Here I have none. And who accepts such odds is not a brave man, but a fool. I don't like broken bones; and still less a broken reputation. I mean to keep what I've won against the day when I may need it. Reputation, Stoffel, is a delicate bubble, easily pricked. To be unhorsed in the lists is no proper fate for a hero."

"You're a calculating rogue!"

"That is the difference between me and Carmagnola, who is just a superior man-at-arms. Each to his trade, Werner, and mine isn't of the tiltyard, however many knighthoods they bestow on me. Which is why tomorrow I shall have the fever."

This resolve, however, went near to shipwreck that same evening.

In the Hall of Galeazzo the Duke gave audience, which was

to be followed by a banquet. Bidden to this came the new knight Bellarion, trailing a splendid houppelande of sapphire velvet edged with miniver that was caught about his waist by a girdle of hammered silver. He had dressed himself with studied care in the azure and argent of his new blazon. His tunic, displayed at the breast, where the houppelande fell carelessly open, and at the arms which protruded to the elbow from the wide short sleeves of his upper garment, was of cloth of silver, whilst his hose was in broad vertical stripes of alternating blue and white. Even his thick black hair was held in a caul of fine silver thread that was studded with sapphires.

Imposingly tall, his youthful lankness dissembled by his dress, he drew the eyes of the court as he advanced to pay homage to the Duke.

Thereafter he was held awhile in friendly talk by della Torre and the Archbishop. It was in escaping at last from these that he found himself suddenly looking into the solemn eyes of the Princess Valeria, of whose presence in Milan this was his first intimation.

She stood a little apart from the main throng under the fretted minstrel's gallery, at the end of the long hall, with the handsome Monna Dionara for her only companion.

Startled, he turned first red, then white, under the shock of that unexpected encounter. He had a feeling, under those inscrutable eyes, of being detected, stripped of his fine trappings and audacious carriage, and discovered for an upstart impostor, the son of nobody, impudently ruffling it among the great.

Thus an instant. Then, recovering his poise, he went forward with leisurely dignity to make his bow, in which there was nothing rustic.

She coloured slightly. Her eyes kindled, and she drew back as if to depart. A single interjectory word escaped her: "Audacious!"

"Lady, I thank you for the word. It shall supply the motto I still lack: *Audax*, remembering that *Audaces fortuna juvat*."

She had not been a woman had she not answered him.

"Fortune has favoured you already. You prosper, sir."

"By God's grace, madonna."

"God has less to do with it, I think, than your own arts."

"My arts?" He questioned not the word, but the meaning she applied to it.

"Such arts as Judas used. You should study the end he made."

On that she would have gone, but the sharpness of his tone arrested her.

"Madonna, if ever I practised those arts, it was in your service, and a reproach is a poor requital."

"In my service!" Her eyes momentarily blazed. "Was it in my service that you came to spy upon me and betray me? Was it in my service that you murdered Enzo Spigno?" She smiled with terrible bitterness. "I have, you see, no illusions left of the service that you did me."

"No illusions!" His voice was wistful. She reasoned much as he had feared that she would reason. "Lord God! You are filled with illusions; the result of inference; and I warned you, madonna, that inference is not your strength."

"You poor buffoon! Will you pretend that you did not murder Spigno?"

"Of course I did."

The admission amazed her where she had expected denial.

"You confess it? You dare to confess it?"

"So that in future you may assert with knowledge what you have not hesitated to assert upon mere suspicion. Shall I inform you of the reason at the same time? I killed Count Spigno because he was the spy sent by your uncle to betray you, so that your brother's ruin might be accomplished."

"Spigno!" she cried in so loud a voice of indignation that her lady clutched her arm to impose caution. "You say that of Spigno? He was the truest, bravest friend I ever knew, and his murder shall be atoned if there is a justice in Heaven. It is enough."

"Not yet, madonna. Consider only that one circumstance which intrigued the Podestà of Casale: that at dead of night, when all Barbaresco's household was asleep, only Count Spigno and I were afoot and fully dressed. Into what tale does that fit besides the lie I told the Podestà? Shall I tell you?"

"Shall I listen to one who confesses himself a liar and murderer?"

"Alas! Both: in the service of an ungracious lady. But hear now the truth."

Briefly and swiftly he told it.

"I am to believe that?" she asked him in sheer scorn. "I am to be so false to the memory of one who served me well and faithfully as to credit this tale of his baseness upon no better word than yours? Why, it is a tale which even if true must brand you for a beast. This man, whatever he may have been, was moved to rescue you, you say, from certain doom; and all the return you made him for that act of charity was to stab him!"

He wrung his hands in despair. "Oh, the perversity of your reasoning! But account me a beast if you will for the deed. Yet admit that the intention was selfless. Judge the result. I killed Count Spigno to make you safe, and safe it has made you. If I

had other aims, if I were an agent to destroy you, why did I not speak out in the Podestà's court?"

"Because your unsupported word would hardly have sufficed to doom persons of our condition."

"Which again is precisely why I killed Count Spigno: because if he had lived, he would have supported it. Is it becoming clear?"

"Clear? Shall I tell you what is clear? That you killed Spigno in self-defence when he discovered you for the Judas that you were. Oh, believe me, it is very clear. To make it so there are your lies to me, your assertion that you were a poor nameless scholar who had imposed himself upon the Marquis Theodore by the pretence of being Facino Cane's son. A pretence you said it was. You'll deny that now."

Some of his assurance left him. "No. I don't deny it."

"You'll tell me, perhaps, that you deceived the Lord Facino himself with that pretence?" And now without waiting for an answer, she demolished him with the batteries of her contempt. "In so great a pretender even that were possible. You pretended to lay down your life at Travo, yet behold you resurrected to garner the harvest which that trick has earned you."

"Oh, shameful!" he cried out, stirred to anger by a suspicion so ignoble.

"Are you not rewarded and knighted for the stir that was made by the rumour of your death? You are to give proof of your knightly worth in the lists tomorrow. It will be interesting."

On that she left him standing there with wounds in his soul that would take long to heal. When at last he swung away, a keen eye observed the pallor of his face and the loss of assurance from his carriage; the eye of Facino's lady who approached him on her lord's arm.

"You are pale, Bellarion," she commented in pure malice, having watched his long entertainment with the Princess of Montferrat.

"Indeed, madonna, I am none so well."

"Not ailing, Bellarion?" There was some concern in Facino's tone and glance.

And there and then the rogue saw his opportunity and took it.

"It will be nothing." He passed a hand across his brow. "The excitement following upon the strain of these last days."

"You should be abed, boy."

"It is what I tell myself."

He allowed Facino to persuade him, and quietly departed. His sudden illness was rumoured later at the banquet when his place remained vacant, and consequently there was little surprise when it was known on the morrow that a fever prevented him from bearing his part in the jousts at Porta Giovia.

By the doctor who ministered to him, he sent a message to Carmagnola of deepest and courtliest regret that he was not permitted to rise and break a lance with him.

Chapter XI

The Siege of Alessandria

G abriello Maria Visconti's plans for the restoration of
Ghibelline authority suffered shipwreck, as was to be expected in a council mainly composed of Guelphs.

The weapon placed in their hands by Gabriello Maria for his
own defeat was the Marquis Theodore's demand, as the price of
his alliance, that he should be supported in the attempt to recover Genoa to Montferrat.

Della Torre laughed the proposal to scorn. "And thereby in-
cur the resentment of the King of France!" He developed that
argument so speciously that not even Facino, who was present,
suspected that it did not contain the true reason of della Torre's
opposition.

In hiring a French contingent to strengthen the army which
he had led against Buonterzo, Facino had shown the uses that

could be made of Boucicault. What Facino had done della Torre could do, nominally on the Duke's behalf. He could hire lances from Boucicault to set against Facino himself when the need for this arose.

"Possibly," ventured Gabriello, the surrender of Vercelli and certain other guarantees would suffice to bring Montferrat into alliance."

But dellaTorre desired no such alliance. "Surrender Vercelli! We have surrendered too much already. It is time we sought alliances that will restore to Milan some of the fiefs of which she has been robbed."

"And where," Facino quietly asked him, "will you find such allies?"

Della Torre hesitated. He knew as well as any man that policies may be wrecked by premature disclosure. If his cherished scheme of alliance with Malatesta of Rimini were suspected, Facino, forewarned, would arm himself to frustrate it. He lowered his glance.

"I am not prepared to say where they may be found. But I am prepared to say that they are not to be found in Theodore of Montferrat at the price demanded by that Prince."

Gabriello Maria was left to make what excuses he could to the Marquis Theodore; and the Marquis Theodore received them in no pleasant manner. He deemed himself slighted, and said so, hinting darkly that Milan counted enemies enough already without wantonly seeking to add to them. Thus in dudgeon he returned to Montferrat.

Della Torre's patient reticence was very shortly justified.

In the early days of June came an urgent and pitiful appeal

from the Duke's brother, Filippo Maria, Count of Pavia, for assistance against the Vignati of Lodi, who were ravaging his territories and had seized the city of Alessandria.

The Duke was in his closet with della Torre and Lonate when that letter reached him. He scowled and frowned and grunted over the parchment awhile, then tossed it to della Torre.

"A plague on him that wrote it! Can you read the scrawl, Antonio?"

Della Torre took it up. "It is from your brother, highness; the Lord Filippo Maria."

"That skin of lard!" Gian Maria was contemptuous. "If he remembers my existence, he must be in need of something."

Della Torre gravely read the letter aloud. The Prince guffawed once or twice over a piteous phrase, meanwhile toying with the head of a great mastiff that lay stretched at his feet.

He guffawed more heartily than ever at the end, the malice of his nature finding amusement in the calamities of his brother. "His Obesity of Pavia is disturbed at last! Let the slothful hog exert himself, and sweat away some of his monstrous bulk."

"Do not laugh yet, my lord." Della Torre's lean, crafty, swarthy face was grave. "I have ever warned you against the ambition of Vignate, and that it would not be satisfied with the reconquest of Lodi. He is in arms, not so much against your brother as against the house of Visconti."

"God's bones!" Goggle-eyed, the Duke stared at his adviser. Then to vent unreasoning fury he rose and caught the dog a vicious kick which drove it yelping from him. "By Hell, am I to go in arms against Vignate? Is that your counsel?"

"No less."

"And this campaign against Buonterzo scarcely ended! Am I to have nothing but wars and feuds and strife to distract my days? Am I to spend all in quelling brigandage? By the Passion! I'd as soon be Duke of Hell as reign in Milan."

"In that case," said della Torre, "do nothing, and the rest may follow."

"Devil take you, Antonio!" He caught up a hawk-lure from the table, and set himself to strip it as he talked, scattering the feathers about the room. "Curb him, you say? Curb this damned thief of Lodi? How am I to curb him? The French lances are gone back to Boucicault. The parsimonious fathers of this miserly city were in haste to dismiss them. They think of nothing but ducats, may their souls perish! They think more of ducats than of their duke." Inconsequently, peevishly, he ranted on, reducing the hawk-lure to rags the while, and showing the crafty della Torre his opportunity.

"Vignate," he said at last, when the Duke ceased, "can be in no great strength when all is reckoned. Facino's own condotta should fully suffice to whip him out of Alessandria and back to Lodi."

Gian Maria moved restlessly about the room.

"What if it should not? What if Facino should be broken by Vignate? What then? Vignate will be at the gates of Milan."

"He might be if we could not prepare for the eventuality."

With a sudden curious eagerness Gian Maria glared at his mentor. "Can we? In God's name, can we? If we could . . ." He checked. But the sudden glow of hate and evil hope in his prominent pale eyes showed how he was rising to the bait.

Della Torre judged the moment opportune. "We can," he answered firmly.

"How, man? How?"

"In alliance with Malatesta your highness would be strong enough to defy all comers."

"Malatesta!" The Duke leapt as if stung. But instantly he curbed himself. The loose embryonic features tightened, reflecting the concentration of the embryonic wicked mind within. "Malatesta, eh?" His tone was musing. He let himself drop once more into his broad armchair, and sat there, cross-legged, pondering.

Della Torre moved softly to his side, and lowered his voice to an impressive note.

"Indeed, your highness should consider whether you will not in any event bring in Malatesta so soon as Facino has departed on this errand."

The handsome, profligate Lonate, lounging, a listener by the window, cleared up all ambiguity: "And so make sure that this upstart does not return to trouble you again."

Gian Maria's head sank a little between his shoulders. Here was his chance to rid himself for all time of the tyrannical tutelage of that condottiero, made strong by popular support.

"You speak as if sure that Malatesta will come."

Della Torre put his cards on the table at last. "I am. I have his word that he will accept a proposal of alliance from your highness."

"You have his word!" The ever-ready suspicions of a weak mind were stirring.

"I took his feeling against the hour when your potency might need a friend."

"And the price?"

Della Torre spread his hands. "Malatesta has ambitions for his daughter. If she were Duchess of Milan . . ."

"Is that a condition?" The Duke's voice was sharp.

"A contingency only," della Torre untruthfully assured him. "Yet if realised the alliance would be consolidated. It would become a family affair."

"Give me air! Let me think." He rose, thrusting della Torre away by a sweep of his thin arm.

Ungainly in his gaudy red and white, shuffling his feet as he went, he crossed to the window where Lonate made way for him. There he stood a moment looking out, whilst between Lonate and della Torre a look of intelligence was flashed.

Suddenly the boy swung round again, and his grotesque countenance was flushed. "By God and His Saints! What thought does it ask?" He laughed, slobberingly, at the picture in his mind of a Facino Cane ruined beyond redemption. Nor could he perceive, poor fool, that he would be but exchanging one yoke for another, probably heavier.

Still laughing, he dismissed della Torre and Lonate, and sent for Facino. When the condottiero came, he was given Filippo Maria's letter, which he spelled out with difficulty, being little more of a scholar than the Duke.

"It is grave," he said when he had reached the end.

"You mean that Vignate is to be feared?"

"Not so long as he is alone. But how long will he so continue? What if he should be joined by Estorre Visconti and the other malcontents? Singly they matter nothing. United they become formidable. And this bold hostility of Vignate's may be the signal for a league."

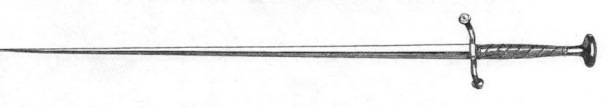

"What then?"

"Smash Vignate and drive him out of Alessandria before it becomes a rallying-ground for your enemies."

"About it, then," rasped the Duke. "You have the means."

"With the Burgundians enlisted after Travo, my condotta stands at two thousand three hundred men. If the civic militia is added . . ."

"It is required for the city's defence against Estorre and the other roving insurgents."

Facino did not argue the matter.

"I'll do without it, then."

He set out next day at early morning, and by nightfall, the half of that march to Alessandria accomplished, he brought his army, wearied and exhausted by the June heat, to rest under the red walls of Pavia.

To proceed straight against the very place which Vignate had seized and held was a direct course of action in conflict with ideas which Bellarion did not hesitate to lay before the war-experienced officers composing Facino's council. He prefaced their exposition by laying down the principle, a little didactically, that the surest way to defeat an opponent is to assault him at the weakest point. So much Facino and his officers would have conceded on the battleground itself. But Bellarion's principle involved a wider range, including the enemy's position before ever battle was joined so as to ensure that the battleground itself should be the enemy's weakest point. The course he now urged entailed an adoption of the strategy employed by the Athenians against the Thebans in the Peloponnesian war, a strategy which Bellarion so much admired and was so often to apply.

In its application now, instead of attacking Alessandria behind whose walls the enemy lay in strength, he would have invaded Vignate's own temporarily unguarded Tyranny of Lodi.

Facino laughed a little at his self-sufficiency, and, emboldened by that, Carmagnola took it upon himself to put the fledgling down.

"It is in your nature, I think, to avoid the direct attack." He sneered as he spoke, having in mind the jousts at Milan and the manner in which Bellarion had cheated him of the satisfaction upon which he counted. "You forget, sir, that your knighthood places you under certain obligations."

"But not, I hope," said Bellarion innocently, "under the obligation of being a fool."

"Do you call me that?" Carmagnola's sudden suavity was in itself a provocation.

"You boast yourself the champion of the direct attack. It is the method of the bull. But I have never heard it argued from this that the bull is intelligent even among animals."

"So that now you compare me with a bull?" Carmagnola flushed a little, conscious that Koenigshofen and Stoffel were smiling.

"Quiet!" growled Facino. "We are not here to squabble among ourselves. Your assumptions, Bellarion, sometimes become presumptions."

"So you thought on the Trebbia."

Facino brought his great fist down upon the table. "In God's name! Will you be pert? You interrupt me. Battering-ram tactics are not in my mind. I choose a different method. But I attack Alessandria nonetheless, because Vignate and his men are there."

Discreetly Bellarion said no more, suppressing the argument that by reducing unguarded Lodi and restoring it to the crown of Milan from which it had been ravished, a moral effect might be produced of far-reaching effect upon the fortunes of the duchy.

After a conference with Filippo Maria in his great castle of Pavia, Facino resumed his march, his army now increased by six hundred Italian mercenaries under a soldier of fortune named Giasone Trotta, whom Filippo Maria had hired. He took with him a considerable train of siege artillery, of mangonels, rimbaults, and cannon, to which the Count of Pavia had materially added.

Nevertheless, he did not approach Alessandria within striking distance of such weapons. He knew the strength to withstand assault of that fortress-city, built some three hundred years before on the confines of the Pavese and Montferrat to be a Guelphic stronghold in the struggle between Church and Empire. Derisively then the Ghibellines had dubbed it a fortress of straw. But astride of the river Tanaro, above its junction with the Bormida, this Alessandria of Straw had successfully defied them.

Facino proposed to employ the very strength of her strategic position for the undoing of her present garrison if it showed fight. And meanwhile he would hem the place about, so as to reduce it by starvation.

Crossing the Po somewhere in the neighbourhood of Bassignara, he marched up the left bank of the Tanaro to Pavone, a village in the plain by the river just within three miles of Alessandria. There he took up his quarters, and thence on a radius of some three miles he drew a cordon throughout that low-lying, insalubrious land, intersected with watercourses, where only rice-fields flourished. This cordon crossed the two rivers just above

their junction, swept thence to Marengo, recrossing the Bormida, ran to Aulara in the south and on to Casalbagliano in the west, just beyond which it crossed the Tanaro again, and, by way of San Michele in the north, went on to complete the circle at Pavone.

So swift had been the movement that the first intimation to the Alessandrians that they were besieged was from those who, issuing from the city on the morrow, were stopped at the lines and ordered to return.

From information obtained from these, in many cases under threat of torture, it became clear that the populous city was indifferently victualled, and unequal, therefore, to a protracted resistance. And this was confirmed during the first week by the desperate efforts made by Vignate, who was raging like a trapped wolf in Alessandria. Four times he attempted to break out in force. But within the outer circle, and close to the city so as to keep it under observation, Facino had drawn a ring of scouts, whose warning in each case enabled him to concentrate promptly at the point assailed. The advantage lay with Facino in these engagements, since the cavalry upon which Vignate chiefly depended found it impossible to operate successfully in those swampy plains. Over ground into which the horses sank to their fetlocks at every stride, a cavalry charge was a *brutum fulmen*. Horses were piked by Koenigshofen's foot, and formations smashed and hurled back by an enemy upon whom their impact was no more than a spent blow.

If they escaped it was because Facino would make no prisoners. He would not willingly relieve Alessandria of a single mouth that would help to eat up its power of endurance. For the same

reason he enjoined it upon his officers that they should be as sparing as possible of life.

"That is to say, of human life," said Bellarion, raising his voice in council for the first time since last rebuked.

They looked at him, not understanding.

"What other life is in question?" asked Carmagnola.

"There are the horses. If allowed to survive, they may be eaten in the last extremity."

They acted upon that reminder when Vignate made his next sally. Facino did not wait as hitherto to receive the charge upon his pikes, but raked the enemy ranks, during their leisurely advance and again during their subsequent retreat with low-aimed arbalest bolts which slew only horses.

Whether Vignate perceived the reason, or whether he came to realise that the ground was not suitable for cavalry, his fourth sally, to the north in the direction of San Michele, was made on foot. He had some two thousand men in his following, and had they been lightly armed and properly led it is probable that they would have broken through, for the opposing force was materially less. But Vignate, unaccustomed to handling infantry, committed the error of the French at Agincourt. He employed dismounted men-at-arms in all the panoply in which normally they rode to battle. Their fate was similar to that of the French on that earlier occasion. Toiling over the clammy ground in their heavy armour, their advance became leaden-footed, and by the time they reached Facino's lines they were exhausted men easily repulsed, and as glad as they were surprised to escape death or capture.

After that failure, three representatives of the Commune of Alessandria, accompanied by one of Vignate's captains, presented themselves at Facino's quarters in the house of the Curate of Pavone, temporarily appropriated by the condottiero.

They were ushered into a plain yellow-washed room, bare of all decoration save that of a crudely painted wooden crucifix which hung upon the wall above a straight-backed wooden settle. An oblong table of common pine stood before this settle; a writing-pulpit, also of pine, placed under one of the two windows by which the place was lighted, and four rough stools and a shallow armchair completed the furniture.

The only gentle touch about that harsh interior was supplied by the sweet-smelling lemon verbena and rosemary mingled in the fresh rushes with which the floor was copiously strewn to dissemble its earthen nudity.

Carmagnola, showily dressed as usual in blue and crimson, with marvellously variegated hose and a jewelled caul confining his flaxen hair, had appropriated the armchair, and his gorgeous presence seemed to fill the place. Stoffel, Koenigshofen, Giasone Trotta, and Vougeois, who commanded the Burgundians, occupied the stools and afforded him a sober background. Bellarion leaned upon the edge of the settle, where Facino sat alone, square-faced and stern, whilst the envoys invited him to offer terms for the surrender of the city.

"The Lord Count of Pavia," he told them, "does not desire to mulct too heavily those of his Alessandrian subjects who have remained loyal. He realises the constraint of which they may have been the victims, and he will rest content with a payment of fifty thousand florins to indemnify him for the expenses of this expedition." The envoys breathed more freely. But Facino had not yet done. "For myself I shall require another fifty thousand florins for distribution among my followers, to ransom the city from pillage."

The envoys were aghast. "One hundred thousand gold florins!" cried one. "My lord, it will . . ."

He raised his hand for silence. "That as regards the Commune of Alessandria. Now, as concerns the Lord Vignate, who has so rashly ventured upon this aggression. He is allowed until noon tomorrow to march out of Alessandria with his entire following, but leaving behind all arms, armour, horses, bullocks, and war material of whatsoever kind. Further, he will enter into a bond for one hundred thousand florins, to be paid either by himself personally or by the Commune of Lodi to the Lord Count of Pavia's city of Alessandria, to indemnify the latter for the damages sustained by this occupation. And my Lord Vignate will further submit to the occupation of the city of Lodi by an army of not more than two thousand men, who will be housed and fed and salaried at the city of Lodi's charges until the indemnity is paid. With the further condition that if payment is not made within one month, the occupying army shall take it by putting the city to sack."

The officer sent by Vignate, a stiff, black-bearded fellow named Corsano, flushed indignantly. "These terms are very harsh," he complained.

"Salutary, my friend," Facino corrected him. "They are intended to show the Lord Vignate that brigandage is not always ultimately profitable."

"You think he will agree?" The man's air was truculent. The three councillors looked scared.

Facino smiled grimly. "If he has an alternative, let him take advantage of it. But let him understand that the offer of these terms is for twenty-four hours only. After that I shall not let him off so lightly."

"Lightly!" cried Corsano in anger, and would have added more but that Facino cropped the intention.

"You have leave to go." Thus, royally, Facino dismissed them.

They did not return within the twenty-four hours, nor as day followed day did Vignate make any further sign. Time began to hang heavily on the hands of the besiegers, and Facino's irritation grew daily, particularly when an attack of the gout came to imprison him in the cheerless house of the Curate of Pavone.

One evening a fortnight after the parley and nearly a month after the commencement of the siege, as Facino sat at supper with his officers, all save Stoffel, who was posted at Casalbagliano, the condottiero, who was growing impatient of small things, inveighed against the quality of the food.

It was Giasone Trotta, to whose riders fell the task of provisioning the army, who answered him. "Faith! If the siege endures much longer, it is we who will be starved by it. My men have almost cleaned up the countryside for a good ten miles in every direction."

It was a jocular exaggeration, but it provoked an explosion from Facino.

"God confound me if I understand how they hold out. With two thousand ravenous soldiers in the place, a week should have brought them to starvation."

Koenigshofen thoughtfully stroked his square red beard. "It's colossally mysterious," said he.

"Mysterious, aye! That's what plagues me. They must be fed from outside."

"That is quite impossible!" Carmagnola was emphatic. As Facino's lieutenant, it fell to his duty to see that the cordon was properly maintained.

"Yet what is the alternative," wondered Bellarion, "unless they are eating one another?"

Carmagnola's blue eyes flashed upon him almost malevolently for this further reflection upon his vigilance.

"You set me riddles," he said disdainfully.

"And you're not good at riddles, Francesco," drawled Bellarion, meeting malice with malice. "I should have remembered it."

Carmagnola heaved himself up. "Now, by the Bones of God, what do you mean?"

The ears of the ill-humoured Facino had caught a distant sound. "Quiet, you bellowing calf!" he snapped. "Listen! Listen! Who comes at that breakneck speed?"

It was a hot, breathless night of July, and the windows stood wide to invite a cooling draught. As the four men, so bidden, grew attentive, they caught from the distance the beat of galloping hooves.

"It's not from Alessandria," said Koenigshofen.

"No, no," grunted Facino, and thereafter they listened in silence.

There was no reason for it save such colour as men's imaginings will give a sound breaking the deathly stillness of a hot dark night, yet each conceived and perhaps intercommunicated a feeling that these hooves approaching so rapidly were harbingers of portents.

Carmagnola went to the door as two riders clattered down the village street, and, seeing the tall figure silhouetted against the light from within, they slackened pace.

"The Lord Facino Cane of Biandrate? Where is he quartered?"

"Here!" roared Carmagnola, and at the single word the horses were pulled up with a rasping of hooves that struck fire from the ground.

Chapter XII

Visconti Faith

If Facino Cane's eyes grew wide in astonishment to see his countess ushered into that mean chamber by Carmagnola, wider
still did they grow to behold the man who accompanied her and
to consider their inexplicable conjunction. For this man was
Giovanni Pusterla of Venegono, cousin to that Pusterla who had
been castellan of Monza, and who by Gian Maria's orders had
procured the assassination of Gian Maria's mother.

The rest is a matter of history upon which I have already
touched.

In a vain attempt to mask his own matricide, to make the
crime appear as the work of another, Gian Maria had seized the
unfortunate castellan who had served his evil will too faithfully
and charging him with the crime caused him barbarously and without trial to be done to death. Thereafter, because he perceived that

296

this did not suffice to turn the public mind from the conviction of his own horrible guilt, Gian Maria had vowed the extermination of the Pusterla family, as a blood-offering to the manes of his murdered mother. It was a Pusterla whom he had hunted with his dogs into the arms of Bellarion in the meadows of Abbiategrasso, and that was the fifth innocent member of the family whom he had done to death in satisfaction of his abominable vow.

This Pusterla of Venegono, who now led the Countess Beatrice into her husband's presence, was a slight but vigorous and moderately tall man of not more than thirty, despite the grey that so abundantly mingled with his thick black hair. His shaven countenance was proud and resolute, with a high-bridged nose flanked perhaps too closely by dark eyes that glowed and flashed as in reflection of his super-abundant energy of body and of spirit.

Between himself and Facino there was esteem; but no other link to account for his sudden appearance as an escort to the Lady Beatrice.

From the settle which he occupied, his ailing leg stretched upon it, the amazed Facino greeted them by a rough soldier's oath on a note of interrogation.

The Countess, white and lovely, swept towards him.

"You are ailing, Facino!" Concern charged her murmuring voice as she stooped to receive his kiss.

His countenace brightened, but his tone was almost testy. To discuss his ailments now was but to delay the explanation that he craved. "That I ail is no matter. That you should be here . . . What brings you, Bice, and with Venegono there?"

"Aye, we take you by surprise," she answered him. "Yet

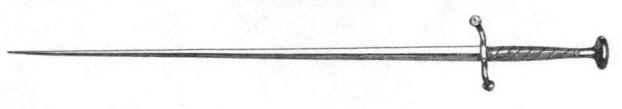

Heaven knows there would be no need for that if ever you had heeded me, if ever you had used your eyes and your wits as I bade you."

"Will you tell me what brings you, and leave the rest?"

She hesitated a moment, then swung imperially to her travelling companion.

"Tell him, Messer da Venegono."

Venegono responded instantly. He spoke rapidly, using gestures freely, his face an ever-shifting mirror of his feelings, so that at once you knew him for a brisk-minded, impulsive man. "We are here to speak of what is happening in Milan. Do you know nothing of it, my lord?"

"In Milan? Despatches reach me weekly from his highness. They report nothing that is not reassuring."

The Countess laughed softly, bitterly. Venegono plunged on.

"Is it reassuring to you that the Malatesta of Rimini, Pandolfo, and his brother Carlo are there with an army five thousand strong?"

Facino was genuinely startled. "They are moving against Milan?"

Again the Countess laughed, and this time Venegono laughed with her.

"Against it?" And he launched his thunderbolt. "They are there at the express invitation of the Duke." Without pausing for breath he completed the tale. "On the second of the month the Lady Antonia Malatesta was married to Duke Gian Maria, and her father has been created Governor of Milan."

A dead silence followed, broken at last by Facino. The thing was utterly incredible. He refused to believe it, and said so with an oath.

"My lord, I tell you of things that I have witnessed," Venegono insisted.

"Witnessed? Have you been in Milan? You?"

Venegono's features twisted into a crooked smile. "After all there are still enough staunch Ghibellines in Milan to afford me shelter. I take my precautions, Lord Count. But I do not run from danger. No Pusterla ever did, which is why this hell-hound Duke has made so many victims."

Appalled, Facino looked at him from under heavy brows. Then his lady spoke, a faint smile of bitter derision on her pale face.

"You'll understand now why I am here, Facino. You'll see that it was no longer safe in Milan for Facino's wife: the wife of the man whose ruin is determined and to be purchased by the Duke at all costs: even at the cost of putting his neck under Malatesta's heel."

Facino's mind, however, was still entirely absorbed by the main issue.

"But Gabriello?" he cried.

"Gabriello, my lord," said Venegono promptly, "is as much a victim, and has been taken as fully by surprise, as you and every Ghibelline in Milan. It is all the work of della Torre. To what end he strives only himself and Satan know. Perhaps he will lead Gian Maria to destruction in the end. It may be his way of resuming the old struggle for supremacy between Visconti and Torriani. Anyhow, his is the guiding brain."

"But did that weak bastard Gabriello never raise a hand . . ."

"Gabriello, my lord, has gone to earth for his own safety's sake in the Castle of Porta Giovia. There Malatesta is besieging him, and the city has been converted into an armed camp labouring to reduce its own citadel. That monster Gian Maria has set a price upon the head of the brother who has so often shielded him from the just wrath of the Commune and the people. There is a price, too, upon the heads of his cousins Antonio and Francesco Visconti, who are with Gabriello in the fortress, together with many other Ghibellines among whom my own cousin Giovanni Pusterla. Lord!" he ended passionately, "if the great Galeazzo could but come to life again, to see the filthy shambles his horrible son has made of the great realm he built!"

Silence followed. Facino, his head lowered, his brows knitted, was drawing a geometrical figure on the table with the point of a knife. Presently whilst so engaged he spoke, slowly, sorrowfully.

"I am the last of all those condottieri who were Gian Galeazzo's brothers-in-arms; the last of those who helped him build up the great state which his degenerate son daily dishonours. His faithless, treacherous nature drove the others away from him one by one, each taking some part of his dominions to make an independent state for himself! I alone have remained, loyally to serve and support his tottering throne, making war upon my brother condottieri in his defence, suffering for him and from him, for the sake of his great father who was my friend, for the sake of the trust which his father left me when he died. And now I have my wages. I am sent to restore Alessandria to the pestilential hands of these false Visconti from which it has been wrested, and whilst I am about this errand, my place is usurped by the greatest Guelph in Italy, and measures are taken to prevent my ever returning." His voice almost broke.

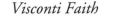

There was a long-drawn sigh from the Countess. "There is no need to tell you more," she murmured. "You begin to open your eyes, and to see for yourself at last."

And then Venegono was speaking.

"I come to you, Facino, in the name of all the Ghibellines of Milan, who look to you as to their natural leader, who trust you and have no hope save in you. Before this Guelphic outrage they cringe in terror of the doom that creeps upon them. Already Milan is a city of blood and horror. You are our party's only hope, Milan's only hope in this dreadful hour."

Facino buried the knife-blade deep in the table with sudden violence, and left it quivering there. He raised at last his eyes. They were blood-injected, and the whole expression of his face had changed. The good-nature of which it habitually wore the stamp had been entirely effaced.

"Let God but heal this leg of mine," he said, "and from my hands the Visconti shall eat the fruits of treachery until they choke them."

He stretched out his hand as he spoke towards the crucifix that hung upon the wall, making of his threat a solemn vow.

Bellarion, looking beyond him, at the Countess, read in the covert exultation of her face her assumption that her greed for empire was at last promised gratification and her insensibility that it should be purchased on terms that broke her husband's heart.

Chapter XIII

The Victuallers

In the torrid heat of the following noontide, Bellarion rode alone to visit Stoffel at Casalbagliano. He did not go round by the lines, but straight across country, which brought him past the inner posts of surveillance and as close under the red walls of Alessandria as it was safe to go.

The besieged city seemed to sleep in the breathless heat of the low-lying lands upon which it had been reared. Saving an occasional flash of steel from the weapon or breastplate of some sentinel on the battlements, there was no sign of a life which starvation must by now have reduced to the lowest ebb.

As Bellarion rode he meditated upon the odd course of unpremeditated turbulence which he had run since leaving the seclusion of Cigliano a year ago. He had travelled far indeed from his original intention, and he marvelled now at the ease with

which he had adapted himself to each new set of circumstances he met, applying in worldly practise all that he had learnt in theory by his omnivorous studies. From a mental vigour developed by those studies he drew an increasing consciousness of superiority over those with whom fate associated him, a state of mind which did not bring him to respect his fellow-man.

Greed seemed to Bellarion, that morning, the dominant impulse of worldly life. He saw it and all the stark, selfish evil of it wherever he turned his retrospective glance. Most cruelly, perhaps, had he seen it last night in the Countess Beatrice, who dignified it—as was common—by the name of ambition. She would be well served, he thought, if that ambition were gratified in such a way that she should curse its fruit with every hour of life that might be hers thereafter. Thus might she yet save her silly, empty soul.

He was drawn abruptly from the metaphysical to the physical by two intrusions upon his consciousness. The first was a spent arbalest bolt, which struck the crupper of his horse and made it bound forward, a reminder to Bellarion that he had all but got within range of those red walls. The second was a bright object gleaming a yard or two ahead of him along the track he followed.

The whole of Facino's army might have passed that way, seeing in that bright object a horseshoe and nothing more. But Bellarion's mind was of a different order. He read quite fluently in that iron shoe that it was cast from the hind hoof of a mule within the last twenty-four hours.

Two nights ago a thunderstorm had rolled down from the Montferrine hills, which were now hazily visible in the distance on his right. Had the shoe been cast before that, rust must have dimmed its polished brightness; yet, as closer examination confirmed, no single particle of rust had formed upon it. Bellarion asked himself a question: Since no strangers were allowed to come or go within the lines, what man of Facino's had during the last two days ridden to a point so barely out of range of an arbalest bolt from the city? And why had he ridden a mule?

He had dismounted, and he now picked up the shoe to make a further discovery. A thick leather-cased pad attached to the underside of it.

He did not mount again, but leading his horse he proceeded slowly on foot along the track that led to Casalbagliano.

It was an hour later when the outposts challenged him on the edge of the village. He found Stoffel sitting down to dinner when he reached the house where the Swiss was quartered.

"You keep an indifferent watch somewhere between here and Aulara," was Bellarion's greeting.

"You often bewilder me," Stoffel complained.

"Here's to enlighten you, then."

Bellarion slapped down the shoe on the table, adding precise information as to where he had found it and his reasons for supposing it so recently cast.

"And that's not all. For half a mile along that track there was a white trail in the grass, which investigation proved to be wheaten flour, dribbled from some sack that went that way perhaps last night."

Stoffel was aghast. He had not sufficient men, he confessed, to guard every yard of the line, and, after all, the nights could be very dark when there was no moon.

"I'll answer for it that you shall have more men tonight," Bellarion promised him, and, without waiting to dine, rode back in haste to Pavone.

He came there upon a council of war debating an assault upon Alessandria now that starvation must have enfeebled the besieged.

In his present impatience, Facino could not even wait until his leg, which was beginning to mend, should be well again. Therefore he was delegating the command to Carmagnola, and considering with him, as well as with Koenigshofen and Giasone Trotta, the measures to be taken. Monna Beatrice was at her siesta abovestairs in the house's best room.

Bellarion's news brought them vexation and dismay.

Soon, however, Carmagnola was grandiosely waving these aside.

"It matters little now that we have decided upon assault."

"It matters everything, I think," said Bellarion, and so drew upon himself the haughty glare of Facino's magnificent lieutenant. Always, it seemed, must those two be at odds. "Your decision rests upon the assumption that the garrison is weakened by starvation. My discovery alters that."

Facino was nodding slowly, gloomily, when Carmagnola, a reckless gambler in military matters, ready now to stake all upon the chance of distinction which his leader's illness afforded him, broke in assertively.

"We'll take the risk of that. You are now in haste, my lord, to finish here, and there is danger for you in delay."

"More danger surely in precipitancy," said Bellarion, and so put Carmagnola in a rage.

"God rid me of your presumption!" he cried. "At every turn you intrude your green opinions upon seasoned men of war."

"He was right at Travo," came the guttural tones of Koenigshofen, "and he may be right again."

"And in any case," added Trotta, who knew the fortifications of Alessandria better than any of them, "if there is any doubt about the state of the garrison, it would be madness to attack the place. We might pay a heavy price to resolve that doubt."

"Yet how else are we to resolve it?" Carmagnola demanded, seeing in delays the loss of his own opportunity.

"That," said Bellarion quietly, "is what you should be considering."

"Considering?" Carmagnola would have added more, but Facino's suddenly raised hand arrested him.

"Considering, yes," said the condottiero. "The situation is changed by what Bellarion tells us, and it is for us to study it anew."

Reluctant though he might be to put this further curb upon his impatience, yet he recognised the necessity.

Not so, however, his lieutenant. "But Bellarion may be mistaken. This evidence, after all . . ."

"Was hardly necessary," Bellarion interrupted. "If Vignate had really been in the straits we have supposed, he must have continued, and ever more desperately, his attempts to fight his way out. Having found means to obtain supplies from without, he has remained inactive because he wishes you to believe him starving so that you may attack him. When he has damaged and weakened you by hurling back your assault, then he will come out in force to complete your discomfiture."

"You have it all clear!" sneered Carmagnola. "And you see it all in the cast shoe of a mule and a few grains of wheat." He swung about to the others, flinging wide his arms. "Listen to him! Learn our trade, sirs! Go to school to Master Bellarion."

"Indeed, you might do worse," cut in Facino, and so struck him into gaping, angry amazement. "Bellarion reasons soundly enough to put your wits to shame. When I listen to him—God help me!—I begin to ask myself if the gout is in my leg or my brains. Continue, boy. What else have you to say?"

"Nothing more until we capture one of these victualling parties. That may be possible tonight, if you double or even treble Stoffel's force."

"Possible it may be," said Facino. "But how exactly do you propose that it be done?"

Bellarion took a stick of charcoal and on the pine board drew lines to elucidate his plan. "Here the track runs. From this the party cannot stray by more than a quarter-mile on either side; for here the river, and there another watercourse, thickly fringed with young poplars, will prevent it. I would post the men in an unbroken double line, along an arc drawn across this quarter-mile from watercourse to watercourse. At some point of that arc the party must strike it, as fish strike a net. When that happens, the two ends of the arc will swing inwards until they meet, thus completely enclosing their prey against the chance of any single man escaping to give the alarm."

Facino nodded, smiling through his gloom. "Does anyone suggest a better way?"

After a pause it was Carmagnola who spoke. "That plan should answer as well as any other." Though he yielded, vanity would not permit him to do so graciously. "If you approve it, my lord, I will see the necessary measures taken."

But Facino pursed his lips in doubt. "I think," he said after a moment's pause, "that Bellarion might be given charge of the affair. He has it all so clear."

Thus it fell out that before evening Bellarion was back again in Stoffel's quarters. To Casalbagliano also were moved after night had fallen two hundred Germans from Koenigshofen's command at Aulara. Not until then did Bellarion cast that wide human arc of his athwart the track exactly midway between Casalbagliano and Alessandria, from the Tanaro on the one side to the lesser watercourse on the other. Himself he took up his station in the arc's middle, on the track itself. Stoffel was given charge of the right wing, and another Swiss named Wenzel placed in command of the left.

The darkness deepened as the night advanced. Again a thunderstorm was descending from the hills of Montferrat, and the clouds blotted out the stars until the hot gloom wrapped them about like black velvet. Even so, however, Bellarion's order was that the men should lie prone, lest their silhouettes should be seen against the sky.

Thus in utter silence they waited through the breathless hours that were laden by a storm which would not break. Midnight came and went and Bellarion's hopes were beginning to sink, when at last a rhythmical sound grew faintly audible; the soft beat of padded hooves upon the yielding turf. Scarcely had they made out the sound than the mule train, advancing in almost ghostly fashion, was upon them.

The leader of the victualling party, who knowing himself well

within the ordinary lines had for some time now been account-
ing himself secure, was startled to find his way suddenly barred
by a human wall which appeared to rise out of the ground. He
seized the bridle of his mule in a firmer grip and swung the beast
about even as he yelled an order. There was a sudden stampede,
cries and imprecations in the dark, and the train was racing back
through the night, presently to find its progress barred by a line
of pikes. This way and that the victuallers flung in their desperate
endeavours to escape. But relentlessly and in utter silence the net
closed about them. Narrower and narrower and ever denser grew
the circle that enclosed them, until they were hemmed about in
no more space than would comfortably contain them.

Then at last lights gleamed. A dozen lanterns were uncovered
that Bellarion might take stock of his capture. The train con-
sisted of a score of mules with bulging panniers, and half a dozen
men captained by a tall, loose-limbed fellow with a bearded, pock-
marked face. Sullenly they stood in the lantern light, realising
the futility of struggling and already in fancy feeling the rope
about their gullets.

Bellarion asked no questions. To Stoffel, who had approached
him as the ring closed, he issued his orders briefly. They were
surprising, but Stoffel never placed obedience in doubt. A hundred men under Wenzel to remain in charge of the mules at the
spot where they had been captured until Bellarion should make
known his further wishes; twenty men to escort the muleteers,
disarmed and pinioned, back to Casalbagliano; the others to be
dismissed to their usual quarters.

A half-hour later in the kitchen of the peasant's house on the
outskirts of Casalbagliano, where Stoffel had taken up his tem-

porary residence, Bellarion and the captured leader faced each other.

The prisoner, his wrists pinioned behind him, stood between two Swiss pikemen, whilst Bellarion holding a candle level with his face scanned those pallid, pock-marked features which seemed vaguely familiar.

"We've met before, I think . . ." Bellarion broke off. It was the beard that had made an obstacle for his memory. "You are that false friar who journeyed with me to Casale, that brigand named . . . Lorenzaccio. Lorenzaccio da Trino."

The beady eyes blinked in terror. "I don't deny it. But I was your friend then, and but for that blundering peasant . . ."

"Quiet!" he was curtly bidden. Bellarion set down the candle on the table, which was of oak, rough-hewn and ponderous as a refectory board, and himself sat down in the armchair that stood by its head. Fearfully Lorenzaccio considered him, taking stock of the richness of his apparel and the air of authority by which the timid convent nursling of a year ago was now invested. His fears withheld him from any philosophical reflections upon the mutability of human life.

Suddenly Bellarion's bold dark eyes were upon him, and the brigand shuddered despite the stifling heat of the night.

"You know what awaits you?"

"I know the risks I ran. But . . ."

"A rope, my friend. I tell you so as to dispel any fond doubt."

The man reeled a little, his knees sagging under him. The guards steadied him. Watching him, Bellarion seemed almost to smile. Then he took his chin in his hand, and for a long moment there was silence save for the prisoner's raucous, agitated breath-

ing. At last Bellarion spoke again, very slowly, painfully slowly to the listening man, since he discerned his fate to be wrapped up in Bellarion's words.

"You claim that once you stood my friend. Whether you would, indeed, have stood my friend to the end I do not know. Circumstances parted us prematurely. But before that happened you had stolen all that I had. Still, it is possible you would have repaid me had the chance been yours."

"I would! I would!" the wretched man protested. "By the Mother of God, I would!"

"I am so foolish as to permit myself to believe you. And you'll remember that your life hangs upon my belief. You were the instrument chosen by Fate to shape my course for me, and there is on my part a desire to stand your friend . . ."

"God reward you for that! God . . ."

"Quiet! You interrupt me. First I shall require proof of your good will."

"Proof!" Lorenzaccio was confused. "What proof can I give?"

"You can answer my questions, clearly and truthfully. That will be proof enough. But at the first sign of prevarication, there will be worse than death for you, as certainly as there will be death at the end. Be open with me now, and you shall have your life and presently your freedom."

The questions followed, and the answers came too promptly to leave Bellarion any suspicion of invention. He tested them by cross-questions, and was left satisfied that from fear of death and hope of life Lorenzaccio answered truthfully throughout. For a half-hour, perhaps, the examination continued, and left Bellarion in possession of all the information that he needed. Lorenzaccio was in the pay of Girolamo Vignate, Cardinal of Desana, a brother of the besieged tyrant, who operating from Cantalupo was sending these mule-trains of victuals into Alessandria on every night when the absence of moonlight made it possible; the mules were left in the city to be eaten together with their loads, and the men made their way back on foot from the city gates; the only one ever permitted to enter was Lorenzaccio himself, who invariably returned upon the morrow in possession of the password to gain him admission on the next occasion. He had crossed the lines, he confessed, more than a dozen times in the last three weeks. Further, Bellarion elicited from him a minute description of the Cardinal of Desana, of Giovanni Vignate of Lodi, and of the principal persons usually found in attendance upon him, of the topography of Alessandria, and of much else besides. Many of his answers Bellarion took down in writing.

Chapter XIV

The Muleteer

It wanted less than an hour to dawn when the mule-train came up to the southern gate of Alessandria, and its single leader disturbed the silence of the night by a shrill whistle thrice repeated.

A moment later a light showed behind the grating by the narrow postern gate, built into the wall beside the portcullis. A voice bawled a challenge across the gulf.

"Who comes?"

"Messenger from Messer Girolamo," answered the muleteer.

"Give the word of the night."

"Lodi triumphant."

The light was moved, and presently followed a creaking of winches and a rattle of heavy chains. A great black mass, faintly discernible against the all-encompassing darkness, slowly descended outwards and came to rest with a thud almost at the very feet of the muleteer. Across that lowered drawbridge the archway of the guard-house glowed in light, and revealed itself aswarm with men-at-arms under the jagged teeth of the raised portcullis.

The muleteer spoke to the night. He took farewell of men who were not with him, and called instructions after someone of whom there was no sign, then drove his laden mules across the bridge, and himself came last into the light amid the men-at-arms drawn up there to ensure against treachery, ready to warn those who manned the winches above in the event of an attempt to rush the bridge.

The muleteer, a tall fellow, as tall as Lorenzaccio, but much younger, dressed in a loose tunic of rough brown cloth with leg-clothing of the same material cross-gartered to the knees, found himself confronted by an officer who thrust a lantern into his face.

"You are not Lorenzaccio!"

"Devil take you," answered the muleteer, "you needn't burn my nose to find that out."

His easy impudence allayed suspicion. Besides, how was a besieged garrison to suspect a man who brought in a train of mules all laden with provisions?

"Who are you? What is your name?"

"I am called Beppo, which is short for Giuseppe. And to-night I am the deputy of Lorenzaccio who has had an accident and narrowly escaped a broken neck. No need to ask your name, my captain. Lorenzaccio warned me I should meet here a fierce watchdog named Cristoforo, who would want to eat me alive when he saw me. But now that I have seen you I don't believe

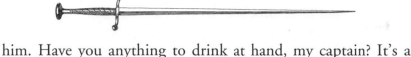

him. Have you anything to drink at hand, my captain? It's a plaguily thirsty night." And with the back of his hand the muleteer swept the beads of sweat from his broad, comely forehead, leaving it clean of much of the grime that elsewhere disfigured his countenance.

"You'll take your mules to the Communal," the captain answered him shortly, resenting his familiarity.

Day was breaking when Messer Beppo came to the Communal Palace and drove his mules into the courtyard, there to surrender them to those whom he found waiting. It was a mixed group made up of Vignate's officers and representatives of the civic government. The officers were well-nourished and vigorous, the citizens looked feeble and emaciated, from which the muleteer inferred that in the matter of rationing the citizens of Alessandria were being sacrificed to the soldiery.

Messer Beppo, who for a muleteer was a singularly self-assertive fellow, demanded to be taken at once to the Lord Giovanni Vignate. They were short with him at first for his impudence until he brought a note almost of menace into his demand, whereupon an officer undertook to conduct him to the citadel.

Over a narrow drawbridge they entered the rocca, which was the heart of that great Guelphic fortress, and from a small courtyard they ascended by a winding staircase of stone to a stone chamber whose grey walls were bare of arras, whose Gothic windows were unglazed, and whose vaulted ceiling hung so low that the tall muleteer could have touched it with his raised hand. A monkish table of solid oak, an oaken bench, and a high-backed chair were all its furniture, and a cushion of crimson velvet the only sybaritic touch in that chill austerity.

Leaving him there, the young officer passed through a narrow door to a farther room. Thence came presently a swarthy man who was squat and bowlegged with thick, pouting lips and an air of great consequence. He was wrapped in a crimson gown that trailed along the stone floor and attended by a black-robed monk and a tall lean man in a soldier's leathern tunic with sword and dagger hanging from a rich belt.

The squat man's keen, haughty eyes played searchingly over the muleteer.

"I am to suppose you have a message for me," he said, and sat down in the only chair. The monk, who was stout and elderly, found a place on the bench, leaning his elbows on the table. The captain stationed himself behind Vignate, whilst the officer who had brought Messer Beppo lingered in the background by the wall.

The tall young muleteer lounged forward, no whit abashed in the presence of the dread Lord of Lodi.

"His excellency the Cardinal of Desana desires you to understand, my lord, that this mule-train of victuals is the last one he will send."

"What?" Vignate clutched the arms of his chair and half raised himself from his seat. His countenance lost much of its chill dignity.

"It isn't that it's no longer safe; but it's no longer possible. Lorenzaccio, who has had charge of these expeditions, is a prisoner in the hands of Facino. He was caught yesterday morning on his way back from Alessandria. As likely as not he'll have been hanged by now. But that's no matter. What is important is that they've found us out, and the cordon is now so tightly drawn

316

that it's madness to try to get through."

"Yet you," said the tall captain, "have got through."

"By a stratagem that's not to be repeated. I took a chance. I stampeded a dozen mules into Facino's lines near Aulara. At the alarm there was a rush for the spot. It drew, as I had reckoned, the men on guard between Aulara and Casalbagliano, leaving a gap. In the dark I drove through that gap before it was repaired."

"That was shrewd," said the captain.

"It was necessary," said Beppo shortly. "Necessary not only to bring in these provisions, but to warn you that there are no more to follow."

Vignate's eyes looked out of a face that had turned grey. The man's bold manner and crisp speech intrigued him.

"Who are you?" he asked. "You are no muleteer."

"Your lordship is perspicacious. After Lorenzaccio was taken, no muleteer could have been found to run the gauntlet. I am a captain of fortune. Beppo Farfalla, to serve your lordship. I lead a company of three hundred lances, now at my Lord Cardinal's orders at Cantalupo. At my Lord Cardinal's invitation I undertook this adventure, in the hope that it may lead to employment."

"By God, if I am to be starved I am likely to offer you employment."

"If your lordship waits to be starved. That was not my Lord Cardinal's view of what should happen."

"He'll teach me my trade, will he, my priestly brother?"

Messer Beppo shrugged. "As to that, he has some shrewd notions."

"Notions! My Lord Cardinal?" Vignate was very savage in his chagrin. "What are these notions?"

"One of them is that this pouring of provisions into Alessandria was as futile as the torment of the Danaides."

"Danaides? Who are they?"

"I hoped your lordship would know. I don't. I quote my Lord Cardinal's words; no more."

"It's a pagan allusion out of Appollodorus," the monk explained.

"What my Lord Cardinal means," said Beppo, "is that to feed you was a sheer waste, since as long as it continued, you sat here doing nothing."

"Doing nothing!" Vignate was indignant. "Let him keep to his Mass and his breviary and what else he understands."

"He understands more than your lordship supposes."

"More of what?"

"Of the art of war, my lord."

And my lord laughed unpleasantly, being joined by his captain, but not by the monk whom it offended to see a cardinal derided.

And now Beppo went on: "He assumes that this news will be a spur you need."

"Why damn his impudence and yours! I need no spur. You'll tell him from me that I make war by my own judgment. If I have sat here inactive, it is that I have sat here awaiting my chance."

"And now that the threat of starvation will permit you to sit here no longer, you will be constrained to go out and seek that chance."

"Seek it?" Vignate was frowning darkly, his eyes aflame. He disliked this cockerel's easy, impudent tone. Captains of fortune did not usually permit themselves such liberties with him. "Where

shall I seek it? Tell me that and I'll condone your insolence."

"My Lord Cardinal thinks it might be sought in Facino's quarters at Pavone."

"Oh, yes; or in the Indies, or in Hell. They're as accessible. I have made sorties from here—four of them, and all disastrous. Yet the disasters were due to no fault of mine."

"Is your lordship quite sure of that?" quoth Messer Beppo softly, smiling a little.

The Lord of Lodi exploded. "Am I sure?" he cried, his grey face turning purple and inflating. "Dare any man suggest that I am to blame?"

"My Lord Cardinal dares. He more than suggests it. He says so bluntly."

"And your impudence no doubt agrees with him?"

"Upon the facts could my impudence do less?" His tone was mocking. The three stared at him in sheer unbelief. "Consider now, my lord: You made your sallies by day, in full view of an enemy who could concentrate at whatever point you attacked, over ground upon which it was almost impossible for your horse to charge effectively. My Lord Cardinal thinks that if you had earlier done what the threat of starvation must now compel you to do, and made a sally under cover of night, you might have been upon the enemy lines before ever your movement could be detected and a concentration made to hold you."

Vignate looked at him with heavy contempt, then shrugged: "A priest's notion of war!" he sneered.

The tall captain took it up with Messer Beppo. Less disdainful in tone, he no less conveyed his scorn of the Cardinal Girolamo's ideas.

"Such an action would have been well if our only aim had been to break through and escape leaving Alessandria in Facino's hands. But so ignoble an aim was never in my Lord Vignate's thoughts." He leaned on the tall back of his master's chair, and thrust out a deprecatory lip. "Necessity may unfortunately bring him to consider it now that . . ."

Messer Beppo interrupted him with a laugh.

"The necessity is no more present now than it has ever been. Facino Cane will lie as much at your mercy tomorrow night as he has lain on any night in all these weeks of your inaction."

"What do you say?" breathed Vignate. "At our mercy?" The three of them stared at him.

"At your mercy. A bold stroke and it is done. The line drawn out on a periphery some eighteen miles in length is very tenuous. There are strong posts at Marengo, Aulara, Casalbagliano, and San Michele."

"Yes, yes. This we know."

"Marengo and San Michele have been weakened since yesterday, to strengthen the line from Aulara to Casalbagliano in view of the discovery that Alessandria has been fed from there. Aulara and Casalbagliano are the posts farthest from Pavone, which is the strongest post of all and Facino's quarters."

Vignate's eyes began to kindle. He was sufficiently a soldier, after all, to perceive whither Messer Beppo was going. "Yes, yes," he muttered.

"Under cover of night a strong force could creep out by the northern gate, so as to be across the Tanaro at the outset, and going round by the river fall upon Pavone almost before an alarm could be raised. Before supports could be brought up you would have broken the force that is stationed there. The capture of Facino and his chief captains, who are with him, would be as certain as that the sun is rising now. After that, your besiegers would be a body without a head."

Followed a silence. Vignate licked his thick lips as he sat huddled there considering.

"By God!" he said, and again, after further thought, "By God!" He looked at his tall captain. The captain tightened his lips and nodded.

"It is well conceived," he said.

"Well conceived!" cried Beppo on that note of ready laughter. "No better conception is possible in your present pass. You snatch victory from defeat."

His confidence inspired them visibly. Then Vignate asked a question:

"What is Facino's force at Pavone? Is it known?"

"Some four or five hundred men. No more. With half that number you could overpower them if you took them by surprise."

"I do not run unnecessary risks. I'll take six hundred."

"Your lordship has decided, then?" said the tall captain.

"What else, Rocco?"

Rocco fingered his bearded chin. "It should succeed. I'd be easier if I were sure the enveloping movement could be made without giving the alarm."

Unbidden the audacious Messer Beppo broke into their counsel.

"Aye, that's the difficulty. But it can be overcome. That is where I can serve you; I and my three hundred lances. I move them round during the day wide of the lines and bring up behind Pavone, at Pietramarazzi. At the concerted hour I push them forward, right up against Facino's rear, and at the moment that you attack in front I charge from behind, and the envelopment is made."

"But how to know each other in the dark?" said Rocco. "Your force and ours might come to grips, each supposing the other to be Facino's."

"My men shall wear their shirts over their armour if yours will do the same."

"Lord of Heaven!" said Vignate. "You have it all thought out."

"That is my way. That is how I succeed."

Vignate heaved himself up. On his broad face it was to be read that he had made up his mind.

"Let it be tonight, then. There is no gain in delay, nor can our stomachs brook it. You are to be depended upon, Captain Farfalla?"

"If we come to terms," said Beppo easily. "I'm not in the business for the love of adventure."

Vignate's countenance sobered from its elation. His eyes narrowed. He became the man of affairs. "And your terms?" quoth he.

"A year's employment for myself and my condotta at a monthly stipend of fifteen thousand gold florins."

"God of Heaven!" Vignate ejaculated. "Is that all?" And he laughed scornfully.

"It is for your lordship to refuse."

"It is for you to be reasonable. Fifteen thou . . . Besides, I don't want your condotta for a year."

"But I prefer the security of a year's employment. It is secu-

rity for you, too, of a sort. You'll be well served."

"Ten thousand florins for your assistance in this job," said Vignate firmly.

"I'll be wishing you good morning," said Messer Beppo as firmly. "I know my value."

"You take advantage of my urgent needs," Vignate complained.

"And you forget what you already owe me for having risked my neck in coming here."

After that they haggled for a full half-hour, and if guarantees of Messer Beppo's good faith had been lacking, they had it in the tenacity with which he clung to his demands.

At long length the Lord of Lodi yielded, but with an ill grace and with certain mental reservations notwithstanding the bond drawn up by his monkish secretary. With that parchment in his pocket, Messer Beppo went gaily to breakfast with the Lord Vignate, and thereafter took his leave, and slipped out of the city to carry to the Cardinal at Desana the news of the decision and to prepare for his own part in it.

It was a dazzling morning, all sign of the storm having been swept from the sky, and the air being left the cleaner for its passage.

Messer Beppo smiled as he walked, presumably because on such a morning it was good to live. He was still smiling when towards noon of that same day he strode unannounced into Facino's quarters at Pavone.

Facino was at dinner with his three captains, and the Countess faced her lord at the foot of the board. He looked up as the newcomer strode to the empty place at the table.

"You're late, Bellarion. We have been awaiting you and your

report. Was there any attempt last night to put a victualling party across the lines?"

"There was," said Bellarion.

"And you caught them?"

"We caught them. Yes. Nevertheless, the mule-train and the victuals won into Alessandria."

They looked at him in wonder. Carmagnola scowled upon him. "How, sir? And this in spite of your boast that you caught them?"

Bellarion fixed him with eyes that were red and rather bleary from lack of sleep.

"In spite of it," he agreed. "The fact is, that mule-train was conducted into Alessandria by myself." And he sat down in the silence that followed.

"Do you say that you've been into Alessandria?"

"Into the very citadel. I had breakfast with the squat Lord of Lodi."

"Will you explain yourself?" cried Facino.

Bellarion did so.

Chapter XV

The Camisade

The sequel you already guess, and its telling need not keep us long.

That night Vignate and six hundred men, wearing their shirts over their armour, rode into as pretty an ambush about the village of Pavone as is to be found in the history of such operations. It was a clear night, and, although there was no moon, there was just light enough from the star-flecked sky to make it ideal, from the point of view of either party, for the business in hand.

There was some rough fighting for perhaps a half-hour, and a good deal of blood was shed, for Vignate's men, infuriated at finding themselves trapped, fought viciously and invited hard knocks in return.

Bellarion in the handsome armour of Boucicault's gift, but without a headpiece, to which as yet he had been unable to ac-

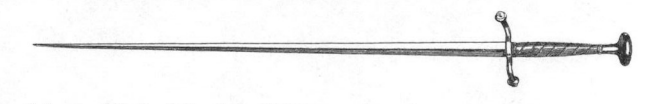

custom himself, held aloof from the furious scrimmage, just as he had held aloof from the jousts in Milan. He had a horror of personal violence and manhandling, which some contemporaries who detected it have accounted a grave flaw in his nature. Nevertheless, one blow at least for his side was forced upon him, and all things considered it was a singularly appropriate blow. It was towards the end of the fight, just as the followers of Vignate began to own defeat and throw down their weapons, that one man, all cased in armour and with a headpiece whose peaked vizor gave him the appearance of some monstrous bird, came charging furiously at the ring of enemies that confined him. He was through and over them in that terrific charge, and the way of escape was clear before him save for the aloof Bellarion, who of his own volition would have made no move to check that impetuous career. But the fool must needs drive straight at Bellarion through the gloom. Bellarion pulled his horse aside, and by that swerve avoided the couched lance which he suspected rather than saw. Then, rising in his stirrups as that impetuous knight rushed by, he crashed the mace with which he had armed himself upon the peaked vizor, and rolled his assailant from the saddle.

Thereafter he behaved with knightly consideration. He got down from his horse, and relieved the fallen warrior of his helmet, so as to give him air, which presently revived him. By the usages of chivalry the man was Bellarion's prisoner.

The fight was over. Already men with lanterns were going over the meadow which had served for battleground; and into the village of Pavone, to the great alarm of its rustic inhabitants, the disarmed survivors of Vignate's force, amounting still to close upon five hundred, were being closely herded by Facino's men.

Through this dense press Bellarion conducted his prisoner, in the charge of two Burgundians.

In the main room of Facino's quarters the two first confronted each other in the light. Bellarion laughed as he looked into that flat, swarthy countenance with the pouting lips that were frothing now with rage.

"You filthy, venal hound! You've sold yourself to the highest bidder! Had I known it was you, you might have slit my throat or ever I would have surrendered."

Facino, in the chair to which his swathed leg confined him, and Carmagnola, who had come but a moment ago to report the engagement at an end, stared now at Bellarion's raging prisoner, in whom they recognised Vignate. And meanwhile Bellarion was answering him.

"I was never for sale, my lord. You are not discerning. I was my Lord Facino's man when I sought you this morning in Alessandria."

Vignate looked at him, and incredulity was tempering the hate of his glance.

"It was a trick!" He could hardly believe that a man should have dared so much. "You are not Farfalla, captain of fortune?"

"My name is Bellarion."

"It's the name of a trickster, then, a cheat, a foul, treacherous hind, who imposed upon me with lies." He looked past his captor at Facino, who was smiling. "Is this how you fight, Facino?"

"Merciful God!" Facino laughed. "Are you to prate of chivalry and knight-errantry, you faithless brigand! Count it against him, Bellarion, when you fix his ransom. He is your prisoner. If he were mine I'd not enlarge him under fifty thousand ducats.

His people of Lodi should find the money, and so learn what it means to harbour such a tyrant."

Savage eyes glowered at Facino. Pouting lips were twisted in vicious hate. "Pray God, Facino, that you never fall prisoner of mine."

Bellarion tapped his shoulder, and he tapped hard. "I do not like you, Messer Vignate. You're a fool, and the world is troubled already by too many of your kind. So little am I venal that from a sense of duty to mankind I might send your head to the Duke of Milan you betrayed, and so forgo the hundred thousand ducats ransom you're to pay to me."

Vignate's mouth fell open.

"Say nothing more," Bellarion admonished him. "What you've said so far has already cost you fifty thousand ducats. Insolence is a costly luxury in a prisoner." He turned to the attendant Burgundians. "Take him abovestairs, strip off his armour, and bind him securely."

"Why, you inhuman barbarian! I've surrendered to you. You have my word."

"Your word!" Bellarion loosed a laugh that was like a blow in the face. Gian Galeazzo Visconti had your word, yet before he was cold you were in arms against his son. I'll trust my bonds rather than your word, my lord." He waved them out, and as he turned, Facino and Carmagnola saw that he was quivering.

"Trickster and betrayer, eh! And to be called so by such a Judas!"

Thus he showed what had stirred him. Yet not quite all. They were not to guess that he could have borne the epithets with equanimity if they had not reminded him of other lips that had uttered them.

"Solace yourself with the ransom, boy. And you're not modest, faith! A hundred thousand! Well, well!" Facino laughed. "You were in luck to take Vignate prisoner."

"In luck, indeed," Carmagnola curtly agreed, then turned to face Facino. "And so, my lord, the affair is happily concluded."

"Concluded?" There was derision in Bellarion's interjection. "Why, sir, the affair has not yet begun. This was no more than the prelude."

"Prelude to what?"

"To the capture of Alessandria. It's to be taken before daylight."

They stared at him, and Facino was frowning almost in displeasure.

"You said nothing of this."

"I thought it would be clear. Why do I lure Vignate to make a *camisade* from Alessandria with six hundred men wearing their shirts over their arms, to be met here by another three hundred under Captain Farfalla similarly bedecked? Nine hundred horsemen, or thereabouts, with their shirts over their arms will ride back in triumph to Alessandria in the dim light of dawn. And the jubilant garrison will lift up its gates to receive them."

"You intended that?" said Facino, when at last he found his voice.

"What else? Is it not a logical consummation? You should break your morning fast in Alessandria, my lord."

Facino, the great captain, looked almost with reverence at this fledgling in the art of war.

"By God, boy! You should go far. At Travo you showed your natural talent for this game of arms. But this . . ."

"Shall we come to details?" said Bellarion to remind them

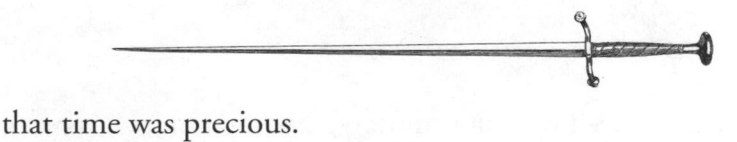

that time was precious.

Little, however, remained to be concerted. By Bellarion's contriving the entire condotta was waiting under arms. Facino offered Bellarion command of what he called the white-shirts, to be supported by Carmagnola with the main battle. Bellarion, however, thought that Carmagnola should lead the white-shirts.

"Theirs will be the honour of the affair," Facino reminded him. "I offer it to you as your due."

"Let Messer Carmagnola have it. What fighting there may be will fall to the lot of the pretended returning camisaders when the garrison discovers the imposture. That is a business which Messer Carmagnola understands better than I do."

"You are generous, sir," said Carmagnola.

Bellarion looked sharply to see if he were sneering. But for once Carmagnola was obviously sincere.

As Bellarion had planned, so the thing fell out.

In the grey light of breaking day, creeping pallid and colourless as the moonstone over the meadows about Alessandria, the anxious watchers from the walls beheld a host approaching, whose white shirts announced them for Vignate and his raiders. Down went drawbridge, up portcullis, to admit them over the timbers of the bridge they thundered, under the deep archway of the gatehouse they streamed, and the waiting soldiery of Vignate deafened the ears of the townsfolk with their cheers, which abruptly turned to cries of rage and fear. For the camisaders were amongst them, beating them down and back, breaking a way into the gatehouse, assuming possession of the machinery that controlled drawbridge and portcullis, and spreading themselves out into the square within to hold the approaches of the gate.

Their true quality was at last revealed, and in the tall armoured man on the tall horse who led and directed them Francesco Busone of Carmagnola was recognised by many.

And now as the daylight grew, another host advanced upon the city, the main battle of Facino's army. This was followed by yet a third, a force detailed to escort the disarmed camisaders of Vignate who were being brought back prisoners.

When two hours later Facino broke his fast in the citadel, as Bellarion had promised him that he should, with his officers about him, and his Countess, her beauty all aglow, at the table's foot, there was already peace and order in the captured city.

Chapter XVI

Severance

The Knight Bellarion rode alone in the hot glow of an August afternoon through the moist and fertile meadowland between Alessandria and San Michele. He was dejected by the sterility of worldly achievement and mourned the futility of all worldly endeavour. In endeavour, itself, as he had to admit from his own experience, there was a certain dynamic entertainment, affording an illusion of useful purpose. With achievement the illusion was dispelled. The purpose grasped was so much water in the hands. Man's greatest accomplishment was to produce change. Restlessness abode in him nonetheless because no one state could be shown to be better than another. The only good in life was study, because study was an endeavour that never reached fulfilment. It busied a man to the end of his days, and it aimed at the only true reality in all this world of shams and deceits.

Messer Bellarion conceived that in abandoning the road to Pavia and Master Chrysolaras he had missed his way in life. Nay, further, his first false step had been taken when driven by that heresy of his, rooted in ignorance and ridiculous, he had quitted the monastery at Cigliano. In conventual endeavour, after all, there was a definite purpose. There, mortal existence was regarded as no more than the antechamber to real life which lay in the hereafter; a brief novitiate wherein man might prepare his spirit for Eternity. By contrast with that definite, peaceful purpose, this world of blindly striving, struggling, ever-restless men, who addressed themselves to their span of mortal existence as if it were to endure forever, was no better, no more purposeful, and of no more merit in its ultimate achievement, than a clot of writhing earthworms.

Thus Messer Bellarion, riding by sparkling waters in the dappled shade of poplars standing stark against the polished azure of the summer sky, and the very beauty with which God had dressed the world made man's defilement of it the more execrable in his eyes.

Emerging from the screen of poplars, he emerged also from his gloomy reflections, dragged thence by the sight of a lady on a white horse that was gaily caparisoned in blue and silver. She was accompanied by a falconer and attended by two grooms whose liveries in the same colours announced them of the household of Messer Facino Cane, Count of Biandrate, and now by right of conquest and self-election Tyrant of Alessandria. For in accepting his tacit dismissal from the Duke of Milan, Facino had thrown off his allegiance to all Visconti and played now, at last, for his own strong hand.

Bellarion would have turned another way. It had become a habit with him whenever he espied the Countess. But the lady hailed him, consigning the hooded falcon on her wrist into the keeping of her falconer, who with the grooms fell back to a respectful distance as Bellarion, reluctantly obedient, approached.

"If you're for home, Bellarion, we'll ride together."

Uncomfortable, he murmured a gratified assent that sounded as false as he intended that it should.

She looked at him sideways as they moved on together. She spoke of hawking. Here was fine open country for the sport. A flight could be followed for miles in any direction, moving almost as directly along the ground as the birds moved in the air above. Yet sport that day had been provokingly sluggish, and quarries had been sought in vain. It would be the heat, she opined, which kept the birds under cover.

In silence he jogged beside her, letting her prate, until at last she too fell silent. Then, after a spell, with a furtive sidelong glance from under her long lashes, she asked him a question in a small voice.

"You are angry with me, Bellarion?"

He was startled, but recovered instantly. "That were a presumption, madonna."

"In you it might be a condescension. You are so aloof these days. You have avoided me as persistently as I have sought you."

"Could I suppose you sought me?"

"You might have seen."

"If I had not deemed it wiser not to look."

She sighed a little. "You make it plain that it is not in you to forgive."

"That does not describe me. I bear no malice to any living man or woman."

"But what perfection! I wonder you could bear to stray from Heaven!" It was no more than an impulsive display of her claws. Instantly she withdrew them. "No, no. Dear God, I do not mean to mock at you. But you're so cold, so placid! That is how you come to be the great soldier men are calling you. But it will not make men love you, Bellarion."

Bellarion smiled. "I don't remember to have sought men's love."

"Nor women's, eh?"

"The fathers taught me to avoid it."

"The fathers! The fathers!" Her mockery was afoot again."In God's name, why ever did you leave the fathers?"

"It was what I was asking myself when I came upon you."

"And you found no answer when you saw me?"

"None, madonna."

Her face whitened a little, and her breath came shorter.

"You're blunt!" she said, and uttered a little laugh that was hard and unpleasant.

He explained himself. "You are my Lord Facino's wife."

"Ah!" Her expression changed again. "I knew we should have that. But if I were not? If I were not?" She faced him boldly, in a sudden eagerness that he deemed piteous.

The solemnity of his countenance increased. He looked straight before him. "In all this idle world there is naught so idle as to consider what we might be if it were different."

She had no answer for a while, and they rode a little way side by side in silence, her attendants following out of earshot.

"You'll forgive, I think, when I explain," said she at last.

"Explain?" he asked her, mystified.

"That night in Milan . . . the last time we spoke together. You thought I used you cruelly."

"No more cruelly than I deserve to be used in a world where it is expected of a man that he shall be more sensible to beauty than to honour."

"I knew it was honour made you harsh," she said, and reached forth a hand to touch his own where it lay upon the pommel. "I understood. I understand you better than you think, Bellarion. Could I have been angry with you then?"

"You seemed angry."

"Seemed. That is the word. It was necessary to seem. You did not know that Facino was behind the arras that masked the little door."

"I hoped that you did not."

It was like a blow between the eyes. She snatched away her hand. Brows met over staring, glaring eyes and her nether lip was caught in sharp white teeth.

"You knew!" she gasped at last, and her voice held all the emotions.

"The arras quivered, and there was no air. That drew my eyes, and I saw the point of my lord's shoe protruding from the curtain's hem."

Her face held more wickedness in that moment than he would have thought possible to find wed with so much perfection.

"When . . . When did you see? Was it before you spoke to me as you did?"

"Your thoughts do me poor credit. If I had seen in time should I have been quite so plain and uncompromising in my words? I

did not see until after I had spoken."

The explanation nothing mollified her. "Almost I hoped you'd say that the words you used, you used because you knew of Facino's presence."

After that, he thought, no tortuous vagaries of the human mind should ever again astonish him.

"You hoped I would confess myself a bloodless coward who uses a woman as a buckler against a husband's righteous wrath!"

As she made no answer, he continued: "Each of us has been defrauded in his hopes. Mine were that you did not suspect Facino's presence, and that you spoke from a heart at last aroused to loyalty."

It took her a moment fully to understand him. Then her face flamed scarlet, and unshed tears of humiliation and anger blurred her vision. But her voice, though it quivered a little, was derisive.

"You spare me nothing," she said. "You strip me naked in your brutal scorn, and then fling mud upon me. I have been your friend, Bellarion—aye, and more. But that is over now."

"Madonna, if I have offended . . ."

"Let be." She became imperious. "Listen now. You must not continue with my Lord Facino because where he goes thither must I go, too."

"You ask me to take my dismissal from his service?" He was incredulous.

"I beg it . . . a favour, Bellarion. It is yourself have brought things to the pass where I may not meet you without humiliation. And continue daily to meet you I will not." Her ready wicked temper flared up. "You'll go, or else I swear . . ."

"Swear nothing," he thundered, very suddenly aroused.

"Threaten, and you bind me to Facino hand and foot."

Instantly she was all soft and pleading. A fool she was. Nevertheless—indeed, perhaps because of it—she had a ready grasp of the weapons of her sex.

"Oh, Bellarion, I do not threaten. I implore . . . I . . ."

"Silence were your best agent now." He was curt. "I know your wishes, and . . ." He broke off with a rough wave of his hand. "Where should I go?" he asked, but the question was addressed to Fate and not to her. She answered it, however.

"Do you ask that, Bellarion? Why, in this past month since Alessandria fell your fame has gone out over the face of Italy. The credit for two such great victories as those of Travo and Alessandria is all your own, and the means by which you won them are on every man's tongue."

"Aye! Facino is generous!" he said, and his tone was bitter.

"There's not a prince in Italy would not be glad to employ you."

"In fact the world is full of places for those we would dismiss."

After that they rode in silence until they were under the walls of the city.

"You'll go, Bellarion?"

"I am considering." He was very grave, swayed between anger and a curious pity, and weighing other things besides.

In the courtyard of the citadel he held her stirrup for her. As she came to earth, and turned, standing very close to him, she put her little hand on his.

"You'll go, Bellarion, I know. For you are generous. This, then, is farewell. Be you fortunate!"

He bowed until his lips touched her hand in formal homage.

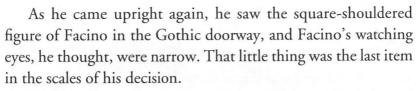

As he came upright again, he saw the square-shouldered figure of Facino in the Gothic doorway, and Facino's watching eyes, he thought, were narrow. That little thing was the last item in the scales of his decision.

Facino came to greet them. His manner was pleasant and hearty. He desired to know how the hawking had gone, how many pheasants his lady had brought back for supper, how far afield she had ridden, where Bellarion had joined her, and other similar facts of amiable commonplace inquiry. But Bellarion watching him perceived that his excessively ready smile never reached his eyes.

Throughout supper, which he took as usual in the company of his captains and his lady, Facino was silent and brooding, nor even showed great interest when Carmagnola told of the arrival of a large body of Ghibelline refugees from Milan to swell the forces which Facino was assembling against the coming struggle, whether defensive or offensive, with Malatesta and Duke Gian Maria.

Soon after the Countess had withdrawn, Facino gave his captains leave. Bellarion, however, still kept his place. His resolve was taken. That which the Countess claimed of him as a sacrifice to her lacerated vanity, he found his sense of duty to Facino claiming also, and his prudent, calculating wits confirming.

Facino raised heavy eyes from the contemplation of the board and leaned back in his chair. He looked old that night in the flickering candlelight. His first words betrayed the subject upon which his thoughts had been lingering.

"Ha, boy! I am glad to see the good relations between Bice and yourself. I had fancied a coolness between you lately."

"I am the Countess's servant, as I am yours, my lord."

"Aye, aye," Facino grunted, and poured himself wine from a jug of beaten gold. "She likes your company. She grudged you once, when I sent you on a mission to Genoa. I'm brought to think of it because I am about to repeat the offence."

"You wish me to go to Boucicault for men?" Bellarion showed his surprise.

Facino looked at him quizzically. "Why not? Do you think he will not come?"

"Oh, he'll come. He'll march on Milan with you to smash Malatesta, and afterwards he'll try to smash you in your turn, that he may remain sole master in the name of the King of France."

"You include politics in your studies?"

"I use my wits."

"To some purpose, boy. To some purpose. But I never mentioned Boucicault, nor thought of him. The men I need must be procured elsewhere. Where would you think of seeking them?"

And then Bellarion understood. Facino wanted him away, and desired him to understand it, which was why he had dragged in that allusion to the Countess. Facino was made reticent by his deep love for his unworthy lady; his need for her remained fiercely strong, however she might be disposed to stray.

Bellarion used his wits, you see, as he had lately boasted.

Why had Facino spied that night in Milan? Surely because in the relations between Bellarion and the Countess he had already perceived reason for uneasiness. That uneasiness his spying had temporarily allayed. Yet not so completely but that he continued watchful, and now, at the first sign of a renewal of that association, it took alarm. Though Facino might still be sure that he had nothing to avenge, he could be far from sure that he had nothing to avert.

A great sorrow welled up from Bellarion's heart. All that he now was, all that he possessed, his very life itself, he owed to Facino's boundless generosity. And in return he was become a thorn in Facino's flesh.

"Why, sir," he said slowly, smiling a little as if in deprecation, "this matter of levies has been lately in my thoughts. To be frank, I have been thinking of raising a condotta of my own."

Facino sat bolt upright in his surprise. Clearly his first emotion was of displeasure.

"Oho! You grow proud?"

"I have my ambitions."

"How long have you nursed this one? It's the first I hear of it."

Blandly Bellarion looked across at him, and bland was his tone.

"I matured the conceit as I rode abroad today."

"As you rode abroad?"

Facino's eyes were intently upon his face. It conserved its blandness. The condottiero's glance flickered and fell away. They understood each other.

"I wish you the luck that you deserve, Bellarion. You've done well by me. You've done very well. None knows it better than I. And it's right you should go, since you've the sense to see that it's best for . . . you."

The colour had faded from Bellarion's face, his eyes were very bright. He swallowed before he could trust himself to speak, to play the comedy out.

"You take it very well, sir—this desertion of you. But I'm your man for all my ambition."

Thereafter they discussed his future. He was for the Cantons, he announced, to raise a body of Swiss, the finest infantry in the world, and Bellarion meant to depend on infantry. As a parting favour he begged for the loan of Stoffel, who would be useful to him as a sponsor to his compatriots of Uri and the Vierwald-staetter. Facino promised him not only Stoffel himself, but fifty men of the Swiss cavalry Stoffel had latterly recruited, to be a nucleus of the condotta Bellarion went to raise.

They pledged each other in a final cup, and parted, Facino to seek his bed, Bellarion in quest of Stoffel.

Stoffel, having heard the proposal, at once engaged himself, protesting that the higher pay Bellarion offered him had no part in the decision.

"And as for men, there's not one of those who fought with you on the bluff above the Trebbia but will want to come."

They numbered sixty when they were called up, and with Facino's consent they all went with Bellarion on the morrow. For, having decided upon departure, there was no reason to delay it.

Betimes in the morning Bellarion had business with a banker of Alessandria named Torella with whom Vignate's ransom was deposited in return for certain bills of exchange negotiable in Berne. Thereafter he went to take his leave of Facino, and to lay before him a suggestion, which was the fruit of long thinking in the stillness of a wakeful night. He was guilty, he knew, of a duplicity, of serving ends very different, indeed, from those that he pretended. But his conscience was at ease, because, although he might be using Facino as a tool for the performance of his ultimate secret aims, yet the immediate aims of Facino himself would certainly be advanced.

"There is a service I can perhaps do you as I go," said Bellarion at parting. "You are levying men, my lord, which is a heavy drain upon your own resources."

"Prisoners like Vignate don't fall into the hands of each of us."

"Have you thought, instead, of seeking alliances?"

Facino was disposed to be hilarious. "With whom? With the dogs that are baying and snarling round Milan? With Estorre and Gian Carlo and the like?"

"There's Theodore of Montferrat," said Bellarion quietly.

"So there is, the crafty fox, and the price he'll want for his alliance."

"You might find it convenient to pay it. Like myself, the Marquis Theodore has ambitions. He covets Vercelli and the lordship of Genoa. Vercelli would be in the day's work in a war on Milan."

"So it would. We might begin hostilities by occupying it. But Genoa, now . . ."

"Genoa can wait until your own work is done. On those terms Montferrat comes in with you."

"Ha! God's life! You're omniscient."

"Not quite. But I know a great deal. I know, for instance, that Theodore went to Milan at Gabriello's invitation to offer alliance to Gian Maria on those terms. He left in dudgeon, affronted by Gian Maria's refusal. He's as vindictive as he's ambitious. Your proposal now might tickle both emotions."

This was sound sense, and Facino admitted it emphatically.

"Shall I go by way of Montferrat and negotiate the alliance for you with Messer Theodore?"

"You'll leave me in your debt if you succeed."

"That is what Theodore will say when I propose it to him."

"You're sanguine."

"I'm certain. So certain that I'll impose a condition. Messer Theodore shall send the Marquis Gian Giacomo to you to be your esquire. You'll need an esquire in my place."

"And what the devil am I to do with Gian Giacomo?"

"Make a man of him, and hold him as a guarantee. Theodore grows old and accidents often happen on a campaign. If he should die before it's convenient, you'll have the sovereign of Montferrat beside you to continue the alliance."

"By God! You look ahead!"

"In the hope of seeing something someday. I've said that the Regent Theodore has his ambitions. Ambitious men are reluctant to relinquish power, and in a year's time the Marquis Gian Giacomo will be of age to succeed. Have a care of him when he's with you."

Facino looked at him and blew out his cheeks. "You're bewildering sometimes. You seem to say a hundred things at once. And your thoughts aren't always nice."

Bellarion sighed. "My thoughts are coloured by the things they dwell on."

Chapter XVII

The Return

The Knight Bellarion contrasted the manner of his departure from Casale a year ago with the manner of his return, and took satisfaction in it. There was more worldliness in his heart than he suspected.

He rode, superbly mounted on a tall grey horse, with Stoffel at his side a little way ahead of the troop of sixty mounted arbalesters, all well equipped and trim in vizorless steel caps and metal-studded leather hacketons, their leader rearing a lance from which fluttered a bannerol bearing Bellarion's device, on a field azure the dog's head argent. The rear was brought up by a string of packmules, laden with tents and equipment of the company.

Clearly this tall young knight was a person of consequence, and as a person of consequence he found himself entreated in Casale.

The Regent's reception of him admirably blended the condescension proper to his own rank with the deference due to
Bellarion's. The Regent, you'll remember, had been in Milan at
the time of Bellarion's leap to fame and honour, and that was all
that he chose now to remember of Facino Cane's adoptive son.
He had heard also—as all Italy had heard by now—of how
Alessandria had been taken and his present deference was a reflection of true respect for one who displayed such shining abili-
ties of military leadership. By no word or sign did he betray
recollection of the young man's activities in Casale a year ago. A
tactful gentleman this Regent of Montferrat. His court, he professed, was honoured by this visit of the illustrious son of an illustrious sire, and he hoped that in the peace of Montferrat, Messer
Bellarion would rest him awhile from his late glorious labours.

"You may yet count me a disturber of that peace, Lord Marquis. I come on an embassy from my Lord of Biandrate."

"Its purport?"

"The aims wherein your highness failed in Milan might find
support in Alessandria."

Theodore took a deep breath.

"Well, well," said he. "We will talk of it when you have dined.
Our first anxiety is for your comfort."

Bellarion understood that he had said enough. What
Theodore really needed was time in which to weigh the proposal
he perceived before they came to a discussion of it.

They dined below in a small room contiguous to the great
hall, a cool, pleasant room whose doors stood wide to those spacious sunlit gardens into which Bellarion had fled when the
Podestà's men pursued him. They were an intimate family party:

the Princess Valeria, the Marquis Gian Giacomo, his tutor Corsario, and his gentleman, the shifty-eyed young Lord of Fenestrella. The year that was sped had brought little change to the court of Casale; yet some little change a shrewd eye might observe. The Marquis, now in his seventeenth year, had aged materially. He stood some inches taller, he was thinner and of a leaden pallor. His manner was restless, his eyes dull, his mouth sullen. The Regent might be proceeding slowly, but he proceeded surely. No need for the risk of violent measures against one who was obligingly killing himself by the profligacy so liberally supplied him.

The Princess, too, was slighter and paler than when last Bellarion had seen her. A greater wistfulness haunted her dark eyes; a listlessness born of dejection hung about her.

But when Bellarion, conducted by her uncle, had stood unexpectedly before her, straight as a lance, tall and assured, the pallor had been swept from her face, the languor from her expression. Her lips had tightened and her eyes had blazed upon this liar and murderer to whose treachery she assigned the ruin of her hopes.

The Regent, observing these signs, made haste to present the visitor to the young Marquis in terms that should ensure a preservation of the peace.

"Giacomo, this is the Knight Bellarion Cane. He comes to us as the envoy of his illustrious father, the Count of Biandrate, for whose sake as for his own you will do him honour."

The youth looked at him languidly. "Give you welcome, sir," he said without enthusiasm, and wearily proffered his princely hand, which Bellarion dutifully kissed.

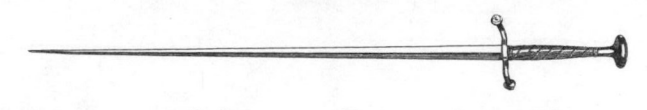

The Princess made him a stiff, unsmiling inclination of her head in acknowledgment of his low bow. Fenestrella was jocosely familiar, Corsario absurdly dignified.

It was an uncomfortable meal. Fenestrella, having recognized Bellarion for the prisoner in the Podestà's court a year ago, was beginning to recall the incident when the Regent headed him off, and swung the talk to the famous seizure of Alessandria, rehearsing the details of the affair: how Bellarion disguised as a muleteer had entered the besieged city, and how pretending himself next a captain of fortune he had proposed the *camisade* in which subsequently he had trapped Vignate; and how thereafter with his own men in the shirts of the *camisaders* he had surprised the city.

"Trick upon trick," said the Princess in a colourless voice, speaking now for the first time.

"Just that," Bellarion agreed shamelessly.

"Surely something more," Theodore protested. "Never was stratagem more boldly conceived or more neatly executed. A great feat of leadership, Ser Bellarion, deserving the renown it has procured you."

"And a hundred thousand florins," said Valeria.

So, they knew that, too, reflected Bellarion.

Fenestrella laughed. "You set a monstrous value on the Lord Vignate."

"I hoped his people of Lodi, who had to find the gold, would afterwards ask themselves if it was worthwhile to retain a tyrant quite so costly."

"Sir, I have done you wrong," the Princess confessed. "I judged you swayed by the thought of enriching yourself."

He affected to miss the sarcasm. "Your highness would have done me wrong if you had left that out."

Valeria alone did not smile at that. Her brown eyes were hard as they held his gaze.

"It was Messer Carmagnola, they tell me, who led the charge into the city. That is a gallant knight, ever to be found where knocks are to be taken."

"True," said Bellarion. "It's all he's fit for. An ox of a man."

"That is your view of a straightforward, honest fighter?"

"Perhaps I am prejudiced in favour of the weapon of intelligence."

She leaned forward a little to dispute with him. All were interested and only Theodore uneasy.

"It is surely necessary even in the lists. I remember at a tournament in Milan the valour and address of this knight Carmagnola. He bore off the palm that day. But, then, you were not present. You had a fever, or was it an ague?"

"Most likely an ague; I always shiver at the thought of a personal encounter."

The Regent led the laugh, and now even Valeria smiled, but it was a smile of purest scorn.

Bellarion remained solemn. "Why do you laugh, sirs? It is no more than true."

"True!" cried Fenestrella. "And it was you unhorsed Vignate!"

"That was an accident. I slid aside when he rode at me. He overshot his aim and I took advantage of the moment."

Valeria's eyes were still upon him, almost incredulous in their glance. Oh, he was utterly without shame. He retorted upon her with the truth; but it was by making the truth sound like a mock-

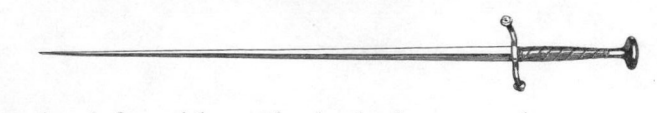

ery that he defeated her. She looked away at last, nor spoke to him again.

Delivered from her attacks, Bellarion addressed himself to the young Marquis, and by way of polite inquiry into his studies asked him how he liked Virgil.

"Virgilio?" quoth the boy, mildly surprised. "You know Virgilio, do you? Bah, he's a thieving rogue, but very good with dogs."

"I mean the poet, my lord."

"Poet? What poet? Poets are a weariness. Valeria reads me their writings sometimes. God knows why, for there's no sense in them."

"If you read them to yourself, you might . . ."

"Read them to myself? Read? God's bones, sir! You take me for a clerk! Read!" He laughed the notion contemptuously away, and buried his face in his cup.

"His highness is a backward scholar," Corsario deprecated.

"We do not thrust learning upon him," Theodore explained. "He is not very strong."

Valeria's lip quivered. Bellarion perceived that it was with difficulty she kept silent.

"Why, you know best, sir," he lightly said, and changed his subject.

Thereafter the talk was all of trivial things until the meal was done. After the Princess had withdrawn and the young Marquis and Fenestrella had begged leave to go, the Regent dismissed Messer Corsario and the servants, but retained his guest to the last.

"I will not keep you now, sir. You'll need to rest. But before

we separate you may think it well to tell me briefly what my Lord Facino proposes. Thus I may consider it until we come to talk of it more fully this evening."

Bellarion, who knew, perhaps as few men knew, the depth of Theodore's craft, foresaw a very pretty duel in which he would have need of all his wits.

"Briefly, then," said he, "your highness desires the recovery of Vercelli and similarly the restoration of the lordship of Genoa. Alone you are not in strength to gratify your aims. My Lord Facino, on the other hand, is avowedly in arms against the Duke of Milan. He is in sufficient strength to stand successfully on the defensive. But his desire is to take the offensive, drive out Malatesta, and bring the Duke to terms. An alliance with your highness would enable each of you to achieve his ends."

The Regent took a turn in the room before he spoke.

He came at last, to stand before Bellarion, his back to the Gothic doorway and the sunlight beyond, graceful and tall and so athletically spare that a boy of twenty might have envied him his figure. He looked at Bellarion with those pale, close-set eyes which to the discerning belied the studiedly benign expression of his handsome, shaven face.

"What guarantees does the Lord of Biandrate offer?" he asked quietly.

"Guarantees?" echoed Bellarion, and nothing in his blank face betrayed how his heart had leapt at the Regent's utterance of that word.

"Guarantees that when I shall have done my part, he will do his."

Calm, passionless, and indifferent he might show himself.

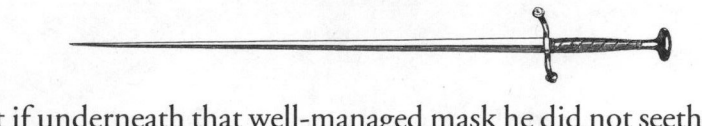

But if underneath that well-managed mask he did not seethe with eagerness, spurred on by ambition and vindictiveness, then Bellarion knew nothing. If he paused to ask for guarantees, it was because he so ardently desired the thing Facino offered that he would take no risk of being cheated.

Bellarion smiled ingenuously. "My Lord Facino proposes to open the campaign by placing you in possession of Vercelli. That is better than a guarantee. It is payment in advance."

A momentary gleam in the pale eyes was instantly suppressed.

"Part payment," said the Regent's emotionless voice. "And then?"

"Of necessity, to consolidate your possession, the next movement must be against Milan itself."

Slowly the Regent inclined his head.

"I will consider," he said gravely. "I will summon the Council to deliberate with me and we will weigh the means at our command. Meanwhile, whatever my ultimate decision, I am honoured by the proposal."

Thus calm, correct, displaying no eagerness, leaving it almost in doubt whether the consideration was due to inclination or merely to deference for Facino, the Regent quitted the matter. "You will need rest, sir." He summoned his chamberlain to whom he entrusted his guest, assured the latter that all within the Palace and City of Casale were at his orders, and ceremoniously took his leave.

Chapter XVIII

The Hostage

The golden light of eventide lay on the terraced palace gardens, on the white temple mirrored in the placid lake, on granite balustrades where roses trailed, on tall, trim boxwood hedges that were centuries old, and on smooth emerald lawns where peacocks sauntered.

Thither the Princess Valeria, trimly sheathed in russet, and her ladies Isotta and Dionara, in formally stiff brocades, had come to take the air, and thither came sauntering also the Knight Bellarion and the pedant Corsario.

The knight was discoursing Lucretius to the pedant, and the pedant did not trouble to conceal his boredom. He had no great love of letters, but displayed a considerable knowledge of Apuleius and Petronius, and smirkingly quoted lewdnesses now from the *Golden Ass*, now from *Trimalchio's Supper*.

Bellarion forsook Lucretius and became a sympathetic listener, displaying a flattering wonder at Messer Corsario's learning. Out of the corner of his eye he watched the upper terrace where the Princess lingered.

Presently he ventured a contradiction. Messer Corsario was at fault, he swore. The line he quoted was not from Petronius, but from Horace. Corsario insisted; the dispute grew heated.

"But the lines are verses," said Bellarion, "and *Trimalchio's Supper* is in prose."

"True. But verses occur in it." Corsario kept his patience with difficulty in the face of such irritating mistaken assurance.

When Bellarion laughed his assertion to scorn, he went off in a pet to fetch the book, so that he might finally silence and shame this ignorant disputant. Bellarion took his way to the terrace above, where the Princess Valeria sauntered.

She observed his approach with stern eyes; and when he bowed before her she addressed him in terms that made of the difference in their ranks a gulf between them.

"I do not think, sir, that I sent for you."

He preserved an unruffled calm, but his answering assertion sounded foolish in his own ears.

"Madonna, I would give much to persuade you that I am your servant."

"Your methods do not change, sir. But why should they? Are they not the methods that have brought you fame?"

"Will you give your ladies leave a moment, while I speak two words with you? Messer Corsario will not be absent long. I have sent him off on a fool's errand, and it may be difficult to make another opportunity."

For a long moment she hesitated. Then, swayed, perhaps, by her very mistrust of him, she waved her ladies back with her fan.

"Not in that direction, highness," he said quickly, "but in that. So they will be in line with us, and anyone looking from the Palace will not perceive the distance separating us, but imagine us together."

She smiled a little in disdainful amusement. But she gave the order.

"How well equipped you are!" she said.

"I came into the world, madonna, with nothing but my wits. I must do what I can with them." Abruptly, for there was no time to lose, he plunged into the business. "I desire to give you a word of warning in season, lest, with your great talent for misunderstanding, you should be made uneasy by what I hope to do. If I succeed in that which brings me, your brother will be sent hence tomorrow, or the next day, to my Lord Facino's care at Alessandria."

That turned her white. "O God! What now? What villainy is meant?"

"To remove him from the Regent's reach, to place him somewhere where he will be safe until the time comes for his own succession. To this end am I labouring."

"You are labouring? You! It is a trap! A trap to . . . to . . ." She was starkly terrified.

"If it were that, why should I tell you? Your foreknowledge will no more assist than it can hinder. I do this in your service. I am here to propose an alliance between my Lord Facino and Montferrat. This alliance was suggested by me for two purposes: to serve Facino's immediate needs, and to ensure the Regent's

ultimate ruin. It may be delayed; but it will come, just as surely as death comes to each of us. To make your brother safe while we wait, I shall impose it as a condition of the alliance that the Marquis Gian Giacomo goes to Facino as a hostage."

"Ah! Now I begin to understand."

"By which you mean that you begin to misunderstand. I have persuaded Facino that the Marquis will serve as a hostage for the Regent's good behaviour, and the Regent shall be made to believe that this is our sole purpose. But the real aim is as I have told you: to make your brother safe. By Facino he will be trained in all those things which it imports that a prince should learn; he will be made to forsake the habits and pursuits by which he is now being disgraced and ruined. Lady, for your peace of mind believe me!" He was emphatic, earnest, solemn.

"Believe you?" she cried out in mental torture. "I have cause to do that, have I not? My past dealings with you—indeed, all that is known of you, bear witness to your truth and candour. By falsehood, trickery, and treachery you have raised yourself to where you stand today. And you ask me to believe you . . . Why . . . why should you do this? Why? That is the only test. What profit do you look to make?"

He looked at her with pain and misery in his dark eyes.

"If in this thing there were any design to hurt your brother, I ask you again, madonna, why should I stand here to tell you what I am about to attempt?"

"Why do you tell me at all?"

"To relieve you from anxiety if I succeed in removing him. To let you know if I should fail of the attempt, of the earnest desire, to serve you, although you make it very hard."

Messer Corsario was hurrying towards them, a volume in his hands.

She stood there, silent, stricken, not knowing what to believe, desiring hungrily to trust Bellarion, yet restrained by every known action in his past.

"If I live, madonna," he said quietly, lowering his voice to a murmur, "you shall yet ask me to forgive your cruel unbelief."

Then he turned to meet Corsario's chuckling triumph, and to submit that the pedant should convict him of error.

"Not so great a scholar as he believes himself, this Messer Bellarion," Corsario noisily informed the Princess. And then to Bellarion, himself: "You'll dispute with soldiers, sir, in future, who lack the learning and the means to put you right. Here are the lines; here in *Trimalchio's Supper*, as I said. See for yourself."

Bellarion saw. He simulated confusion. "My apologies, Messer Corsario, for having given you the trouble to fetch the book. You win the trick."

It was an inauspicious word. To Valeria it was clear that the trick had lain in temporarily removing Messer Corsario's inconvenient presence, and that trick Bellarion had won.

She moved away now with her ladies who had drawn close upon Corsario's approach, and Bellarion was left to endure the pedant's ineffable company until suppertime.

Later that night Theodore carried him off to his own closet to discuss in private and in greater detail the terms of the proposed alliance.

His highness had considered and had taken his resolve now that he was prepared to enter into a treaty. He looked for a clear expression of satisfaction. But Bellarion disappointed him.

"Your highness speaks, of course, with the full concurrence of your Council?'

"My Council?" The Regent frowned over the question.

"Where the issues are so grave, my Lord Facino will require to be sure that all the terms of the treaty are approved by your Council, so that there may be no going back."

"In that case, sir," he was answered a little frostily, "you had better attend in person before the Council tomorrow, and satisfy yourself."

That was precisely what Bellarion desired, and having won the point, whose importance the shrewd Theodore was far from suspecting, Bellarion had no more to say on the subject that evening.

In the morning he attended before the Council of Five, the Reggimento, as it was called, of Montferrat. At the head of the council-table the Marquis Theodore was enthroned in a chair of State flanked by a secretary on either hand. Below these sat the councillors, three on one side and two on the other, all of them important nobles of Montferrat, and one of them, a white-bearded man of venerable aspect, the head of that great house of Carreto, which once had disputed with the Paleologi the sovereignty of the State.

When the purpose for which Bellarion came had been formally restated, there was a brief announcement of the resources at Montferrat's disposal and a demand that the occupation of Vercelli should be the first step of the alliance.

When at last Bellarion was categorically informed that Montferrat was prepared to throw her resources into an alliance which they thanked the Count of Biandrate for proposing,

Bellarion rose to felicitate the members of the Council upon their decision in terms calculated to fan their smouldering ardour into a roaring blaze. The restoration to Montferrat of Vercelli, the subsequent conquest of Genoa were not, indeed, to be the end in view, but merely a beginning. The two provinces of High and Low Montferrat into which the State at present was divided should be united by the conquest of the territory now lying between. Thus fortified, there would be nothing to prevent Montferrat from pushing her frontiers northward to the Alps and southward to the sea. Then, indeed, might she at last resuscitate and realise her old ambitions. Established not merely as the equal but as the superior of neighbouring Savoy, with Milan crumbling into ruins on her eastward frontiers, it was for Montferrat to assume the lordship of Northern Italy.

It went to their heads, and when Bellarion resumed his seat it was they who now pressed the alliance. No longer asking him what means Facino brought to it, they boasted and exaggerated the importance of those which they could offer.

Thus the treaty came there and then to be drawn up, article by article. The secretaries' pens spluttered and scratched over their parchments, and throughout it seemed to the Regent and his gleeful councillors that they were getting the better of the bargain.

But at the end, when all was done, and the documents complete, Messer Bellarion had a word to say which was as cold water on the white heat to which he had wrought their enthusiasm.

"There remains only the question of a guarantee from you to my Lord Facino."

"Guarantee!" They echoed the word in a tone which clearly

said they did not relish it. The Regent went further.

"Guarantee of what, sir?"

"That Montferrat will fulfil her part of the undertaking."

"My God, sir! Do you imply a doubt of our honour?"

"It is no question of honour, highness; but of a bargain whose terms are clearly to be set forth to avoid subsequent disputes on either side. Does the word 'guarantee' offend your highness? Surely not. For it was your highness who first used that word between us."

The councillors looked at the Regent. The Regent remembered, and was uncomfortable.

"Yesterday your highness asked me what guarantees my Lord Facino would give that he would fulfil his part. I did not cry out in wounded honour, but at once conceded that the immediate occupation of Vercelli should be your guarantee. Why, then, sirs, should it give rise to heat in you if on my lord's behalf I ask a return in kind, something tangible to back the assurance that when Vercelli is occupied you will march with my Lord Facino against Milan as he may deem best?"

"But unless we do that," said the Regent impatiently, "there can follow no conquest of Genoa for us."

"If there did not, you would still be in possession of Vercelli and that is a great deal. Counsels of supineness might desire you to rest content with that."

"Should we heed them, do you suppose?" said the Marquis of Carreto.

"I do not. Nor will my lord. But suppositions cannot be enough for him."

This interruption where all had flowed so smoothly was clearly fretting them. Another interposed: "Would it not be well, high-ness, to hear what guarantees my Lord of Biandrate will require?"

And Theodore assenting, Bellarion spoke to anxious ears.

"It is in the nature of a hostage, and one that will cover vari-ous eventualities. If, for instance, the Marquis Gian Giacomo should come to the throne before these enterprises are concluded, it is conceivable that he might decline to be bound by your un-dertakings. If there were no other reasons—and they will be plain enough to your excellencies—that one alone would justify my lord in asking, as he does, that the person of the Marquis of Montferrat be delivered into his care as a hostage for the fulfilment of this treaty."

Theodore, betrayed into a violent start, sat now pale and thoughtful, commanding his countenance by an effort. Another in his place would have raged and stormed and said upon im-pulse things from which he might not afterwards retreat. But Theodore Paleologo was no creature of impulse. He weighed and weighed again this thing, and allowed his councillors to babble, listening the while.

They were hostile, of course, to the proposal. It had no pre-cedent, they said. Whereupon Bellarion smothered them in precedents culled from the history of the last thousand years. Retreating from that assertion, then, they became defiant, and assured him that precedent or no precedent they would never lend themselves to any such course.

The Regent still said nothing, and whilst vaguely suspicious he wondered whether the emphatic refusal of the councillors was based upon some suspicion of himself. Had they, by any chance, despite his caution, been harbouring mistrust of his relations with

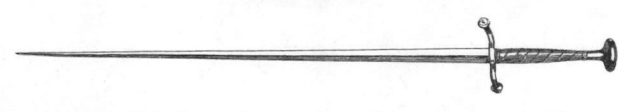

his nephew, and did they think that this proposal of Facino's was some part of his own scheming, covering some design nefarious to the boy?

One of them turned to him now: "Your highness says no word to this." And the others with one voice demanded his own pronouncement. He stirred. His face was grave.

"I am as stricken as are you. My opinion, sirs, you have already expressed for me."

Bellarion, smiling a little, as one who is entirely mystified, now answered them.

"Sirs, suffer me to say that your heat fills me with wonder. My Lord Facino had expected of you that the proposal would be welcome."

"Welcome?" cried Carreto.

"To view life in a foreign court and camp is acknowledged to be of all steps the most important in the education of a future prince. This is now offered to the Lord Gian Giacomo in such a way that two objects would simultaneously be served."

The simple statement, so simply uttered, gave pause to their opposition.

"But if harm should befall him while in Facino's hands?" cried one.

"Can you suppose, sirs, that my Lord Facino, himself, would dread the consequences of such a disaster less than you? Can you suppose that any measure would be neglected that could make for the safety and well-being of the Marquis?"

He thought they wavered a little, reassured by his words.

"However, sirs, since you feel so strongly," he continued, "my Lord Facino would be very far from wishing me to insist." One of them drew a breath of relief. The others, if he could judge their countenances, moved in apprehension. The Regent remained inscrutable. "It remains, sirs," Bellarion ended, "for you to propose an alternative guarantee."

"Time will be lost in submitting it to my Lord Facino," Carreto deplored, and the others by their nods, and one or two by words, showed the returning eagerness to seal this treaty which meant so much to Montferrat.

"Oh, no," Bellarion reassured them. "I am empowered to determine. We have no time to lose. If this treaty is not concluded by tomorrow, my orders are to assume that no alliance is possible and continue my journey to the Cantons to levy there the troops we need."

They looked at one another blankly, and at last the Regent asked a question.

"Did the Count of Biandrate, himself, suggest no alternative against our refusing him this particular guarantee?"

"It did not occur to him that you would refuse. And, frankly, sirs, in refusing that which himself he has suggested, it would be courteous to supply your reasons, lest he regard it as a reflection upon himself."

"The reason, sir, you have already been afforded," Theodore answered. "We are reluctant to expose our future sovereign to the perils of a campaign."

"That assumes perils which could not exist for him. But I am perhaps presuming. I accept your reason, highness. It is idle to debate further upon a matter which is decided."

"Quite idle," Theodore agreed with him. "That guarantee we cannot give."

"And yet . . ." began the Marquis of Carreto.

The Regent interrupted him; for once he was without suavity.

"There is no 'and yet' to that," he snapped.

Again the councillors looked at one another. They were growing uneasy. The immediate benefits, and the future glory of Montferrat which had been painted for them, were beginning to dissolve under their eyes like a mirage.

In the awkward pause that followed, Bellarion guessed their minds. He rose.

"In this matter of determining the guarantee, you will prefer, no doubt, to deliberate without me." He bowed in leave-taking. Then paused.

"It would be a sad thing, indeed, if a treaty so mutually desirable and so rich in promise to Montferrat should fail for no good reason." He bowed again. "To command, sirs."

One of the secretaries came to hold the door for him, and he passed out. An echo of the Babel that was loosed in that room on his departure reached him before he had gone a dozen paces. He smiled quietly as he sought his own apartments. He warmly approved himself. It had been shrewd of him to keep back all hint of the hostage until he stood before the Council. If he had breathed a suggestion of it in his preliminary talks with the Regent, he would have been dismissed at once. Now, however, Messer Theodore was committed to a battle in which his own conscience would fight against him, weakening him by fear of discovery of his true aims.

"The wicked flee when no man pursueth," said Bellarion to himself. "And you'll never stand to fight this out, my wicked one."

An hour and more went by before he was summoned again, to hear the decision of the Council. That decision is best given in Bellarion's own words as contained in the letter preserved for us in the Vatican Library which he wrote that same night to Facino Cane, one of the very few writings of his which are known to survive. It is couched in the pure and austere Lingua Tosca which Dante sanctioned, and it may be Englished as follows:

MY DEAR LORD: These will reach you by the hand of Wenzel who goes hence to Alessandria tomorrow together with ten of my Swiss to serve as escort for the young Prince of Montferrat. To render this escort worthy of his rank, it is supplemented by ten Montferrine lances sent by his highness the Marquis Theodore. Wenzel also bears the treaty with Montferrat, into which I have entered in your name. Its terms are as we concerted. It was not without a deal of cajolery and strategy and only by setting the Regent at odds with his Council that I was able to obtain as a hostage the person of the Marquis Gian Giacomo. The Regent, had the choice been given him, would rather, I think, have sent you his right hand. But he was constrained by the Council who see and rightly only good to the State in this alliance with your excellent lordship.

He has insisted, however, that the boy be accompanied by his tutor Corsario, a scoundrel who has schooled him in naught but lewdness, and his gentleman Fenestrella, who, though young, is an even greater preceptor in those same Stygian arts. Since it is proper that a prince on his travels should be attended by tutor and companion, there was no good objection that I could make to this. But I beg you, my dear lord, to regard these two as the agents of the Marquis Theodore, to watch them closely, and to deal with them drastically should you discover or suspect even that they practise anything against the young Marquis. It would be a good service to the boy, and acceptable, no doubt, in the sight of God, if you were to wring the necks of these two scoundrels out of hand. But difficulties with the Regent of Montferrat would follow.

As for the Prince himself, your lordship will find him soft in body, and empty in mind, or at least empty of all but viciousness. If despite your many occupations and preoccupations your lordship could trouble yourself to mend the lad's ways, or to entrust him to those who will undertake the mending of them and at the same time watch over him vigilantly, you would perform a deed for which God could not fail to reward your lordship.

I need not remind you, my dear lord, that the safety of a hostage is a very sacred matter, nor should I presume so to remind you but for my reasons for believing, as your lordship already knows, that this young Prince may be beset by perils from the very quarters which ordinarily should be farthest from suspicion. In addition to these twain, the Marquis is attended by a physician and two body servants. Of these I know nothing, wherefore they should be observed as closely as the others.

The responsibility under which you lie towards the State of Montferrat will be your justification for placing attendants of your own choosing to act jointly with these. The physician should be permitted to give the boy no physic of which he does not previously partake. In this way, and if you do not warn him of it beforehand, you may speedily and effectively be rid of him.

I am grieved that you should be plagued with this matter at

such a season. But I hope that you will not count the price too dear for the alliance of Montferrat, which puts into the field at once close upon six thousand well-equipped men, between horse and foot. You will now be in sufficient strength to deal at your pleasure with that base Duke and his Guelphic Riminese brigands.

Send me your commands by Wenzel, who is to rejoin me at Lucerne. I shall set out in the morning as soon as the Marquis Gian Giacomo has left Casale for Alessandria. Your lordship shall have news of me soon again.

Humbly I kiss the hands of my lady your Countess, and for you, my dear lord, that God may bless and prosper you is the fervent prayer of this your son and servant.

BELLARION

BOOK III

Chapter I

The Lord Bellarion

On a day of September of the year of Our Lord 1409, a
dust-laden horseman clattered into the courtyard of a palace near the Bridge of the Trinity in Florence, and announced
himself a courier with letters for the noble Lord Bellarion.

He was consigned by a man-at-arms to an usher, by the usher
to a chamberlain, and by the chamberlain to a slim young secretary. From this you will gather that access to the Lord Bellarion
was no longer a rough-and-ready business; and, from this again,
that he had travelled far since detaching himself from the Lord
Facino Cane a year ago.

At the head of the condotta which he had raised, he had fought
in the course of that year a half-score of engagements, now in this
service, now in that, and in all but one he had won easy triumphs.
Even his single failure—which was at Verruno in the pay of the

Estes of Ferrara—was such as to enhance his reputation. Forced by overwhelming numbers to admit defeat, yet by sheer skill he had baffled the great Pandolfo's attempt to surround him, and had brought off his condotta with such little loss that Pandolfo's victory was a barren one.

His condotta, now known as the "Company of the White Dog," from the device he had adopted, had grown to the number of twelve hundred men, with a heavy preponderance of infantry, his handling of which was giving the other great captains of Italy food for thought. In fame he was the rival of Piccinino, almost the rival of Sforza himself, under whose banner he had served in the war against his old opponent Buonterzo. And Fra Serafino da Imola tells us unequivocally in his chronicle that the ambush in which Buonterzo ended his turbulent life in March of that year was of Bellarion's planning. Since then he had continued in the service of the Florentine Republic at a monthly stipend which had gradually been raised with the growth of his condotta to twenty thousand gold florins.

Like all famous men, he was not without detractors. He was charged with a cold ruthlessness, which brought, it was claimed, an added horror into warfare, shocking adversaries, as it had shocked Buonterzo on the Trebbia, into ordering that no quarter should be given. So opposed, indeed, was this ruthlessness to the accepted canons of Italian warfare, that it was said Bellarion could enlist only Swiss mercenaries who notoriously were not queasy in these matters. The probable truth, however, is that he employed only Swiss because they were the best infantry in the world, and further so as to achieve in his following a solidarity and cohesion not to be found in other companies, made up of a medley of nationalities.

Lastly he was found lacking in those spectacular qualities of leadership, in that personal knightly prowess by which such men as Carmagnola took the eye. Never once had he led a charge, stimulating his followers by his own heroical example; never had he taken part in an escalade, or even been seen at work in a mêlée. At Subriso, where he had routed the revolted Pisans, it was said that he had never left the neighbourhood of his tent and never mounted his horse until the engagement was all but over.

Hence, whilst his extraordinary strategic talents were duly respected, it began to be put about that he was lacking in personal courage.

Careless of criticism, he had pursued the course he prescribed himself, gathering laurels as he went. On those laurels he was momentarily resting in the City of the Lilies when that courier rode into the courtyard of his palace with letters from the Count of Biandrate.

The Lord Bellarion, as men now called this leader grown out of the erstwhile nameless waif, in a pleated full-sleeved tunic of purple satin gripped about his loins by a golden girdle and with a massive chain of gold about his neck, stood in a window embrasure to decipher the crabbed untidy characters, indited from Alessandria on the feast of Saint Anthony.

"My dear son," Facino wrote, "I need you. So come to me at once with every man that you can bring. The Duke has called in the French. Boucicault is in Milan with six thousand men, and has been appointed ducal governor. Unless I strike quickly before I am myself stricken, Milan will be made a fief of France and the purblind Duke a vassal of the French king. It is the Duke's subjects themselves who summon me. The gout, from which I have been free for months, is troubling me again infernally. It always seizes me just when I most need my strength. Send me word by the bearer of these that you follow at speed."

Bellarion lowered the letter and gazed out across the spacious sunlit courtyard. There was a ghost of a smile on his bronzed face, which had gained in strength and virility during the year that was sped. He was faintly, disdainfully amused at the plight into which Gian Maria's evil blundering must have placed him before he could take the desperate step of calling in the French.

The Malatesta domination had not been long-lived. Their Guelphic grip had been ruthlessly crushing the city, where every office, even that of Podestà, was given into the hands of Guelphs. And that same grip had been crushing the Duke himself, who discovered belatedly that, in throwing off the yoke of Facino for that of the Malatesta, he had exchanged King Log for King Stork. Then, in his shifty, vacillating way, he sent ambassadors to beg Facino to return. But the ambassadors fell into the hands of the Malatesta spies, and the Duke was constrained to shut himself up in the fortress of Porta Giovia to evade their fury. Whereupon the Malatesta had drawn off to Brescia, which they seized, Pandolfo loudly boasting that he would not rest until he was Duke of Milan, so that Gian Maria Visconti should pay the price of breaking faith with him.

Terror now drove the Duke to lengths of viciousness and inhumanity unprecedented even in his own vile career.

Issuing from the Castle of Porta Giovia to return to his palace so soon as the immediate menace was removed, he found himself beset by crowds of his unfortunate people, distracted by

the general paralysis of industry and menaced by famine. Piteously they clamoured about him.

"Peace, Lord Duke! Peace! Give us Facino for our governor, and give us peace! Peace, Lord Duke! Peace!"

His fair face grimly set, his bulging eyes glaring venomously, he had ridden ahead with his escort, closing his ears to their cries, and more than one unfortunate was trampled under the horses' hooves as they passed on. But the cries continuing, that evil boy suddenly reined in his bravely caparisoned charger.

"You want peace, you dogs? You'll deafen me with hellcat cries of peace! What peace do you give me, you filthy rabble? But you shall have peace! Oho! You shall have it." He stood in his stirrups, and swung round to his captain. "Ho, there, you!" His face was inflamed with fury, a wicked mockery, and evil mirth hung about his swollen purple lips. So terrible, indeed, was his aspect that della Torre, who rode beside him, ventured to set upon his arm a restraining hand. But the Duke flung the hand off, snarling like a dog at his elderly mentor. He backed his horse until he was thigh to thigh with his captain.

"Give them what they ask for," he commanded. "Clear me a way through this dungheap! Use your lances. Give them the peace they want."

A great cry arose from those who stood nearest, held there by the press behind.

"Lord Duke! Lord Duke!" they wailed.

And he laughed at them, laughed aloud in maniacal mockery, in maniacal anticipation of the gratification of his unutterable bloodlust.

"On! On!" he commanded. "They are impatient for peace!"

But the captain of his guard, a gentleman of family, Bertino Mantegazza, sat his horse appalled, and issued no such order as he was bidden.

"Lord Duke . . ." he began, but got no further, for the Duke, catching the appealing note in his voice, seeing the horror in his eyes, suddenly crashed his iron glove into the young man's face. "God's blood! Will you stay to argue when I command?"

Mantegazza reeled under that cruel blow, and with blood suffusing his broken face would have fallen but that one of his men caught and supported him in the saddle.

The Duke laughed to see what he had done, and took command himself. "Into them! Charge!" he commanded in a shout on which his voice shrilled up and cracked. And the Bavarian mercenaries who composed the guard, to whom the Milanese were of no account and all civilians contemptible, lowered their lances and charged as they were bidden.

Two hundred of those poor wretches found in death the peace for which they clamoured. The others fled in panic, and the Duke rode on to the Broletto through streets which terror had emptied.

That night he issued an edict forbidding under pain of death the utterance of the word "Peace" in his City of Milan. Even from the Mass must that accursed word be expunged.

If they had not also clamoured for Facino, it is probable that to Facino fresh ambassadors would have been sent to invite him to return. But the Duke would have men know that he was Duke, that he was not to be coerced by the wishes of his subjects, and so, out of perversity so blind that it took no ac-

count of the pit he might be digging for himself, the Duke invited Boucicault to Milan.

When Boucicault made haste to answer, then the appeal to Facino which should have gone from the Duke went, instead, from the Duke's despairing subjects. Hence Facino's present summons to Bellarion.

There was no hesitation in Bellarion's mind and fortunately no obstacle in his present employment. His agreement with the Florentine Republic had been determined in the last few days. Its renewal was at present under consideration.

He went at once to take his leave of the Signory, and, four days ahead of his army, he was in Alessandria being affectionately embraced by Facino.

He arrived at the very moment at which, in council with his captains and his ally the Marquis Theodore, who had come over from Vercelli, Facino was finally determining the course of action.

"I planned in the sure belief that you would come, bringing at least a thousand men."

"I bring twelve hundred, all of them well seasoned."

"Good lad, good lad!" Facino patted his shoulder. "Come you in and let them hear it from you."

Leaning heavily upon Bellarion's arm, for the gout was troubling him, he led his adoptive son up that winding stone staircase which Bellarion so well remembered ascending on that morning when, as a muleteer, he went to fool Vignate.

"So Master Theodore is here?" said Bellarion.

"And glad to come. He's been restive in Vercelli, constantly plaguing me to place him in possession of Genoa. But I've held him off. I do not trust Master Theodore sufficiently to do all my part before he has done any of his. A sly fox that and an unscrupulous."

"And the young Marquis?" Bellarion enquired.

Facino laughed. "You will not recognise him, he has grown so demure and staid. He thinks of entering holy orders. He'll yet come to be a man."

Bellarion stared. "That he was well your letters told me. But this . . . How did you accomplish it?"

"By driving out his tutor and the others who came with him. A foul crew!" He paused on the stairs. "I took their measure at a glance, and I had your hint. When one night Fenestrella and the tutor made the boy drunk and themselves drunk with him, I sent them back to Theodore with a letter in which I invited him to deal with them as their abuse of trust deserved. I dismissed at the same time the physician and the body servants, and I informed Theodore that I would place about the Marquis in future none but persons whom I could trust. Perforce he must write to thank me. What else could he do? You laugh! Faith, it's laughable enough! I laughed, too, which didn't prevent me from being watchful."

They resumed the ascent, and Bellarion expressed the hope that the Lady Beatrice was well. Common courtesy demanded that he should conquer his reluctance to name her to Facino. He was answered that she was at Casale, Facino having removed her thither lest Alessandria should come to be besieged.

Thus they came to the chamber where the council sat.

It was the same stone chamber with its vaulted ceiling and Gothic windows open to the sky in which Vignate had given

audience to Bellarion. But it was no longer as bare as when the austere Tyrant of Lodi had inhabited it. The walls were hung with arras, and rich furnishings had been introduced by the more sybaritic Facino.

About the long oaken table sat five men, four of whom now rose. The one who remained seated, as if in assertion of his rank, was the Regent of Montferrat. To the newcomer's bow he returned a short nod.

"Ah! The Lord Bellarion!" His tone was languid, and Facino fancied that he sneered. Wherefore he made haste to snap: "And he brings twelve hundred men to the enterprise, my lord."

"That should ensure him a welcome," the Regent admitted, but without cordiality. He seemed, Bellarion observed, out of humour and disgruntled, shorn of his habitual suavity.

The others came forward to greet Bellarion. First the magnificent Carmagnola, taking the eye as ever by the splendour of his raiment, the dignity of his carriage, and the poise of his handsome fair head. He was more cordial than Bellarion had yet known him. But there was something of patronage, of tutorial commendation in his congratulatory allusions to Bellarion's achievements in the field.

"He may yet be as great a soldier as yourself, Francesco," Facino growled, as he sagged into the chair at the table's head to ease his leg.

Missing the irony, Carmagnola bowed. "You'll make me vain, my lord."

"My God!" said Facino.

Came the brawny, bearded, red-faced Koenigshofen, grinning honest welcome and taking Bellarion's hand in a grip that almost hurt. Then followed the swarthy, mercurial little Piedmontese captain, Giasone Trotta, and lastly there was a slight, graceful, sober, self-contained boy in whom Bellarion might have failed to recognise the Gian Giacomo Paleologo of a year ago but for the increased likeness he bore to the Princess Valeria. So strong was that likeness grown that Bellarion was conscious of a thrill as he met the solemn, searching gaze of those dark and rather wistful eyes.

Place at the table was found for Bellarion, and he was informed of the situation and of the resolve which had been all but reached. With his own twelve hundred, and with three thousand men that Montferrat would send after leaving a sufficient force to garrison Vercelli, Facino could put eight thousand men into the field, which should be ample for the undertaking. They were well mounted and well equipped, the equipment including a dozen cannon of three hundred pounds apiece and ten bombards throwing balls of two hundred pounds.

"And the plan of campaign?" Bellarion asked.

It was expounded to him. It was extremely simple. They were to march on Milan and reduce it. All was in readiness as he would have seen for himself; for as he rode into Alessandria he had come through the great encampment under the walls, where the army awaited the order to march.

When Facino had done, Bellarion considered a moment before speaking.

"There is an alternative," he said, at last, "which you may not have considered. Boucicault is grasping more than he can hold. To occupy Milan, whose people are hostile to a French domination, he has drawn all his troops from Genoa, where he has made

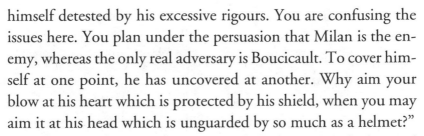

himself detested by his excessive rigours. You are confusing the issues here. You plan under the persuasion that Milan is the enemy, whereas the only real adversary is Boucicault. To cover himself at one point, he has uncovered at another. Why aim your blow at his heart which is protected by his shield, when you may aim it at his head which is unguarded by so much as a helmet?"

They made him no answer save with their eyes which urged that he, himself, should answer the question he propounded.

"March, then, not on Milan, but on Genoa, which he has so foolishly left open to attack—a folly for which he may have to answer to his master, the King of France. The Genoese themselves will offer no resistance, and you may take possession of the city almost without a blow."

Approval came warm and eagerly from the Marquis Theodore, to be cut short by Facino.

"Wait! Wait!" he rasped. The notion of Theodore's ambitions being entirely gratified before Theodore should have carried out any of his own part of the bargain was not at all in accordance with Facino's views. "How shall the possession of Genoa bring us to Milan?"

"It will bring Boucicault to Genoa," Bellarion answered. "It will draw him from his stronghold into the open, and his strength will be reduced by the fact that he must leave some force behind to keep the Milanese in subjection during his absence."

So strategically sound did the plan appear to Facino upon consideration that it overcame his reluctance to place the Regent of Montferrat at this stage in possession of Genoa.

That reluctance he afterwards expressed to Bellarion, when they were alone.

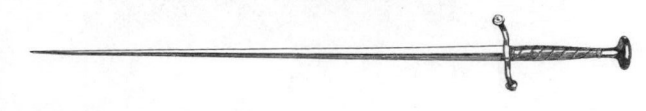

"You do it, not for Theodore, but for yourself," he was answered. "As for Theodore . . ." Bellarion smiled quietly. "You need not grudge him any advantages. They will prove very transient. Payday will come for him."

Facino looked sharply at his adoptive son. "Why, boy," said he, at last, in a voice of wonder. "What is there between you and Theodore of Montferrat?"

"Only my knowledge that he's a scoundrel."

"If you mean to make yourself the scourge of scoundrels you'll be busy in Italy. Why, it's sheer knight-errantry!"

"You may call it that," said Bellarion, and became thoughtful.

Chapter II

The Battle of Novi

The rest of this affair—this campaign against the too-ambitious vicar of the King of France—is a matter of history, which you may read in the chronicles of Messer Corio and elsewhere.

With a powerful army numbering close upon nine thousand men, Facino descended upon Genoa, which surrendered without a blow. At first there was alarm at the advance of so large an army. The fear of pillage with its attendant violence ran though the Genoese, who took the precaution of sending their women and their valuables to the ships in the harbour. Then the representatives of the people went out to meet Facino, and to assure him that they would welcome him and the deliverance from the French yoke provided that he would not bring his troops into the city.

"The only purpose for which I could wish to do so," Facino answered from the litter to which he was confined by the gout, grown worse since he had left Alessandria, "would be to enforce the rightful claims of the Marquis of Montferrat. But if you will take him for your prince, my army need advance no nearer. On the contrary, I will withdraw it towards Novi to make of it a shield against the wrath of the Marshal Boucicault when he returns!"

And so it befell that, attended only by five hundred of his own men, Theodore of Montferrat made his state entry into Genoa on the morrow, hailed as a deliverer by the multitude, whilst Facino fell back on Novi, there to lie in wait for Boucicault. Nor was his patience tried. Upon Boucicault confidently preparing for Facino's attack, the news of the happenings in Genoa fell like a thunderbolt from a clear sky.

Between fury and panic he quitted Milan, and by his very haste destroyed what little chance he may ever have had of mending the situation. By forced marches he reached the plains about Novi to find the road held against his jaded men. And here he piled error upon error. Being informed that Facino himself, incapacitated by the gout, had been carried that morning into Genoa, and that his army was commanded in his absence by his adoptive son Bellarion, the French commander decided to strike at once before Facino should recover and return to direct the operations in person.

The ground was excellent for cavalry, and entirely of cavalry some four thousand strong was Boucicault's main battle composed. Leading it in person, he hurled it upon the enemy centre in a charge which he thought must irresistibly cleave through.

Nor did the mass of infantry of which Bellarion's centre was composed resist. It yielded ground before the furious onslaught of the French lances. Indeed, as if swayed by panic, it began to yield long before any contact was established, and the French in their rash exultation never noticed the orderliness of that swift retreat, never suspected the trap, until they were fast caught in it. For whilst the centre yielded, the wings stood firm, and the wings were entirely composed of horse, the right commanded by the Piedmontese Trotta, the left by Carmagnola, who, sulky and disgruntled at his supersession in a supreme command which he deemed his right, had never wearied of denouncing this disposition of forces as an insensate reversal of all the known rules.

Back and back, ever more swiftly fell the foot. On and on pressed the French, their lances couched, their voices already clamantly mocking these opponents, who were being swept away like leaves by the mere gust of the charge.

Bellarion, riding in the rear of his retreating infantry with a mounted trumpeter beside him, uttered a single word. A trumpet blast rang out, and before its note had died the retreat was abruptly checked. Koenigshofen's men, who formed the van of that centre, suddenly drove the butts of their fifteen-foot German pikes into the ground. Each man of the two front ranks went down on one knee. A terrible hedge of spears suddenly confronted the men-at-arms of France, riding too impetuously in their confidence. Half a hundred horses were piked in the first impact. Then the impetus of those behind, striking the leading ranks which sought desperately to check, drove them forward onto those formidable German points. The entire charging mass was instantly thrown into confusion.

"That," said Bellarion grimly, "will teach Boucicault to re-spect infantry in future. Sound the charge!"

The trumpeter wound another blast, thrice repeated, and in answer, as Bellarion had preconcerted, the right and left wings, which had gradually been extending, wheeled about and charged the French on both flanks simultaneously. Only then did Boucicault perceive whither his overconfident charge had carried him. Vainly did he seek to rally and steady his staggering follow-ers. They were enveloped, smashed, ridden down before they could recover. Boucicault, himself, fighting like a man possessed, fighting, indeed, for very life, hewed himself a way out of that terrible press, and contrived to join the other two of the three battles into which he had divided his army and which were press-ing forward now to the rescue. But they arrived too late. There was nothing left to rescue. The survivors of the flower of Boucicault's army had thrown down their arms and accepted quarter, and the reserves ran in to meet a solid enemy front, which drove wedges into their ranks, and mercilessly battered them, until Boucicault, routed beyond redemption, drew off with what was left.

"A swift action, which was a model of the harmonious col-laboration of the parts." Thus did Bellarion describe the battle of Novi which was to swell his ever-growing fame.

Boucicault, as Bellarion said, had sought to grasp more than he could hold when he had responded to Gian Maria's invita-tion, and at Novi he lost not only Milan, but Genoa as well. In ignominy he took the road to France, glad to escape with his life and some battered remnants of his army, and Italy knew him no more after that day.

In the Fregoso Palace at Genoa, overlooking the harbour, where Theodore of Montferrat had taken up his quarters, and where the incapacitated Facino was temporarily lodged, there was a great banquet on the following night to celebrate at once the overthrow of the French and the accession of Theodore as Prince of Genoa. It was attended by representatives of the twelve greatest families in the State as well as by Facino, hobbling painfully on a crutch, and his captains; and whilst the official hero of the hour was Theodore, the new Prince, the real hero was Bellarion.

He received without emotion, without any sign either of pride or of modesty, the tribute lavishly paid him by illustrious men and distinguished women, by the adulatory congratulatory speech of Theodore, or the almost malicious stress which Carmagnola laid on his good fortune.

"You are well named Bellarione 'Fortunato,'" that splendid soldier had said. "I am still wondering what would have happened if Boucicault had perceived the trick in time."

Bellarion was coldly amiable in his reply.

"It will provide you with healthy mental exercise. Consider at the same time what might have happened if Buonterzo had fathomed our intentions at Travo, or Vignate had guessed my real purpose at Alessandria."

Bellarion moved on, leaving Carmagnola to bite his lip and digest the laughter of his brother captains.

His interview later with Prince Theodore was more serious. From its outset he mistrusted the fawning suavity of the courtly Regent, so that, when at the end of compliments upon his prowess, the Regent proposed to take him and his company into the pay of Montferrat at a stipend vastly in excess of that which Florence had lately paid him, Bellarion was not at all surprised. Two things became immediately clear. First, that Theodore desired greatly to increase his strength, the only reason for which could be the shirking, now that all his aims were accomplished, of his engagements towards Facino. Second, that he took it for granted—as he had done before—that Bellarion was just a venal, self-seeking adventurer who would never permit considerations of honour to stand in the way of profit.

And the cupidity and calculation now revealed in Bellarion's countenance assured Theodore that his skill in reading men had not been at fault on this occasion.

"You offer me . . ." He broke off. Stealthily his glance swept the glittering groups that moved about the spacious white-and-gold room to Facino Cane where he sat at the far end in a great crimson chair. He lowered his voice a little. "The loggia is empty, my lord. We shall be more private there."

They sauntered forth to that covered balcony overlooking the great harbour where ranks of shipping drawn up against the mole were slumbering under the stars. A great towering galley was moving across the water with furled sails, her gigantic oar blades flashing silver in the moonlight.

With his glance upon that craft, his voice subdued, Bellarion spoke, and the close-set eyes of the tall, elegant Regent strained to pierce the shadows about the young condottiero's face.

"This is a very noble offer, Lord Prince . . ."

"I hope I shall never begrudge a man his worth." It was a speech true to the character he loved to assume. "You are a great soldier, Bellarion. That fact is now established and admitted."

Bellarion did not contradict him. "I do not perceive at present

your need for a great soldier, highness. True, your proposal seems to argue plans already formed. But unless I know something of them, unless I may judge for myself the likely extent of the service you require, these generous terms may in effect prove an illusion."

Theodore resumed his momentarily suspended breath. He even laughed a little, now that the venal reason for Bellarion's curiosity was supplied. But he deemed it wise to probe a little further.

"You are, as I understand, under no present engagement to the Count of Biandrate?"

Bellarion's answer was very prompt.

"Under none. In discharge of past favours I engaged to assist him in the campaign against the Marshal Boucicault. That campaign is now ended, and with it my engagement. I am in the market, as it were, my lord."

"That is what I assumed. Else, of course, I should not have come to you with my offer. I lose no time because soon you will be receiving other proposals. That is inevitable. For the same reason I name a stipend which I believe is higher than any condottiero has ever yet commanded."

"But you have not named a term. That was why I desired to know your plans so that for myself I might judge the term."

"I will make the engagement to endure for three years," said Theodore.

"The proposal becomes generous, indeed."

"Is it acceptable?"

Bellarion laughed softly. "I should be greedy if it were not."

"It will carry the usual condition that you engage for such

service as I may require and against any whom circumstances may make my enemy."

"Naturally," said Bellarion. But he seemed to falter a little. "Naturally," he repeated. "And yet . . ." He paused, and Theodore waited, craftily refraining from any word that should curb him in opening his mind. "And yet I should prefer that service against my Lord Facino be excepted."

"You would prefer it?" said Theodore. "But do you make it a condition?"

Bellarion's hesitation revealed him to the Regent for a man torn between interest and scruples. Weakly, at last, he said: "I would not willingly go in arms against him."

"Not willingly? That I can understand. But you do not answer my question. Do you make it a condition?"

Still Bellarion avoided answering.

"Would the condition make my employment impossible?"

And now it was Theodore who hesitated, or seemed to hesitate. "It would," he said at last. Very quickly he added: "Nothing is less likely than that Facino and I should be opposed to each other. Yet you'll understand that I could not possibly employ a condottiero who would have the right to desert me in such a contingency."

"Oh, yes. I understand that. I have understood it from the first. I am foolish, I suppose, to hesitate where the terms are so generous." He sighed, a man whose conscience was in labour. "My Lord Facino could hardly blame me . . ." He left the sentence unfinished. And Theodore to end the rogue's hesitation threw more weight into the scales.

"And there will be guarantees," he said.

"Guarantees? Ah!"

"The lands of Asti along the Tanaro from Revigliasco to Margaria to be made into a fief, and placed under your vicarship with the title of Count of Asti."

Bellarion caught his breath. He turned to face the Marquis, and in the moonlight his countenance looked very white.

"My lord, you promise something that is not yours to bestow."

"It is to make it mine that I require your service. I am frank, you see."

Bellarion saw more. He saw the infernal subtlety with which this tempter went to work. He made clear his intentions, which must amount to no less than the conquest and occupation of all those rich lands which lay between High and Low Montferrat. To accomplish this, Alessandria, Valenza, and a score of other cities now within the Duchy of Milan would pass under his dominion. Inevitably, then, must there be war with Facino, who to the end of his days would be in arms to preserve the integrity of the Duchy. And Theodore offered this condottiero, whose services he coveted, a dazzling reward to be gained only when those aims were fulfilled.

On that seducer's arm Bellarion placed a hand that shook with excitement.

"You mean this, my lord? It is a solemn undertaking."

With difficulty Theodore preserved his gravity. How shrewdly had he not taken the measure of this greedy rogue!

"Your patent shall be made out in anticipation, and signed at the same time as the contract."

Bellarion stared out to sea. "Count Bellarion of Asti!" he murmured, a man dazzled, dazed. Suddenly he laughed, and laughing surrendered his last scruple as Theodore was already confident that he would. "When do we sign, Lord Prince?"

"Tomorrow morning, Lord Count," Theodore answered with a tight-lipped smile, and on that, the matter satisfactorily concluded, they quitted the loggia and parted company.

They met again for the signing of the documents early on the following morning in the Regent's closet, in the presence of the notary who had drawn up the contract at Theodore's dictation, of two gentlemen of Montferrat, and of Werner von Stoffel, who accompanied Bellarion, and who, as Bellarion's lieutenant, was an interested party.

The notary read first the contract, which Bellarion pronounced correct in all particulars, and then the ennobling parchment whereby Theodore created him Count of Asti, anticipatorily detailing the lands which he was to hold in fief. This document already signed and sealed was delivered to Bellarion together with the contract which he was now invited to sign. The notary dipped a quill and proffered it. But Bellarion looked at the Regent.

"Documents," he said, "are perishable, and the matter contained in these is grave. For which reason I have brought with me a witness, who in case of need can hereafter testify to your undertaking, my lord."

The Marquis frowned. "Let Messer Stoffel examine them for himself then."

"Not Messer Stoffel. The witness I prefer waits in your antechamber, highness." He stepped quickly to the door, followed by the Regent's surprised glance. He pulled it open, and at once Facino was revealed to them, grave of countenance, leaning upon his crutch.

The Regent made a noise in his throat, as Facino hobbled in

to take the parchments which Bellarion proffered him. Thereafter there was a spell of dreadful silence broken at last by the
Lord Theodore who was unable longer to control himself.

"You miserable trickster! You low-born, swaggering Judas! I
should have known better than to trust you! I should have known
that you'd be true to your false, shifty nature. You dirty fox!"

"A trickster! A Judas! A fox!" Bellarion appealed mildly to the
company against the injustice of these epithets. "But why such
violence of terms? Could I in loyalty to my adoptive father put
my signature to this contract until it had received his approval?"

"You mock me, you vile son of a dog!"

Facino looked up. His face was stern, his eyes smouldered.

"Think of some fouler epithet, my lord, so that I may cast it
at you. So far no term that you have used will serve my need."

That gave Theodore pause in his reviling of another. But only
for a moment. Almost at once he was leaping furiously towards
Facino. The feral nature under his silken exterior was now displayed. He was a man of his hands, this Regent of Montferrat,
and, beggared of words to meet the present case, he was prepared
for deeds. Suddenly he found Bellarion in his way, the bold,
mocking eyes level with his own, and Bellarion's right hand was
behind his back, where the heavy dagger hung.

"Shall we be calm?" Bellarion was saying. "There are half a
dozen men of mine in the anteroom if you want violence."

He fell back, and for all that his eyes still glared he made an
obvious effort to regain his self-command. It was difficult in the
face of Facino's contemptuous laughter and the words Facino
was using.

"You treacherous slug! I place you in possession of Vercelli; I make you Prince of Genoa, before calling upon you to strike a single blow on my behalf, and you prepare to use this newfound power against me! You'll drive me from Alessandria! You'll seduce from me the best among my captains to turn his weapons against me in your service! If Bellarion had been an ingrate like yourself, if he had not been staunch and loyal, whom you dare to call a Judas, I might have known nothing of this until too late to guard myself. But I know you now, you dastardly usurper, and, by the Bones of God, your days are numbered. You'll prepare for war on Facino Cane, will you? Prepare, then, for, by the Passion, that war is coming to you."

Theodore stood there white to the lips, between his two dismayed gentlemen, and said no word in answer.

Facino, with curling lip, considered him.

"I'd never have believed it if I had not read these for myself," he added. Then proffered the documents to Bellarion again. "Give him back his parchments, and let us go. The sight of the creature nauseates me." And without more, he hobbled out.

Bellarion lingered to tear the parchments across and across. He cast them from him, bowed ironically, and was going out with Stoffel when the Regent found his voice at last.

"You kite-hearted trickster! What stipend have you wrung from Facino as the price of this betrayal?"

Bellarion paused on the threshold. "No stipend, my lord," he answered equably. "Merely a condition: that so soon as the affairs of Milan are settled, he will see justice done to your nephew, the Marquis Gian Giacomo, now of age to succeed, and put a definite end to your usurpation."

His sheer amazement betrayed from him the sudden ques-

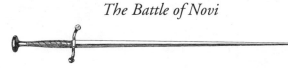

tion. "What is Gian Giacomo to you, villain?"

"Something he is, or else I should never have been at pains to make him safe from you by demanding him as a hostage. I have been labouring for him for longer than you think, highness."

"You have been labouring for him? You? In whose pay?"

Bellarion sighed. "You must be supposing me a tradesman, even when I am really that quite senseless thing, a knight-errant." And he went out with Stoffel.

Chapter III

Facino's Return

A strong party of men-at-arms rode out of Genoa that morning, their corselets flashing in the sunshine, and took the upland road by the valley of the Scrivia towards Novi and Facino's camp. In their midst went a mule litter wherein Facino brooded upon the baseness and ingratitude of men, and asked himself whether perhaps his ambitious Countess were not justified of her impatience with him because he laboured for purposes other than the aggrandisement of himself.

From Novi he despatched Carmagnola with a strong escort to Casale to bring the Countess Beatrice thence to Alessandria without loss of time. He had no mind to allow Theodore to hold her as a hostage to set against Gian Giacomo who remained with Facino.

Three days after leaving Novi, Facino's army, reduced by

Theodore's contingent of three thousand men which had been left behind, but still in great strength, reached Vigevano, and halted there to encamp again outside the town. Facino's vanity was the main reason. He would not cross the Ticino until he could sit a horse again, so that he might ride lance on thigh into Milan. Already his condition was greatly improved under the ministrations of a Genoese physician named Mombelli, renowned for his treatment of the podagric habit, who was now in Facino's train.

A week passed, and Facino now completely restored was only restrained from pushing on by the arguments of his physician. Meanwhile, however, if he did not go to Milan, many from Milan were coming to him.

Amongst the first to arrive was the firebrand Pusterla of Venegono, who out of his passionate vindictiveness came to urge Facino to hang Gian Maria and make himself Duke of Milan, assuring him of the support of all the Ghibelline faction. Facino heard him without emotion, and would commit himself to nothing.

Amongst the last to arrive was the Duke himself, in a rash trustfulness which revealed the desperate view he must take of his own case and of the helplessness to which his folly and faithlessness had reduced him. He came accompanied by his evil genius Antonio della Torre, the fop Lonate, the captain of his guard Bertino Mantegazza, and a paltry escort of a hundred lances.

With those three attending him he was received by Facino in the house of the Ducal Prefect of Vigevano.

"Your highness honours me by this proof of your trust in my integrity," said Facino, bending to kiss the jewelled ducal hand.

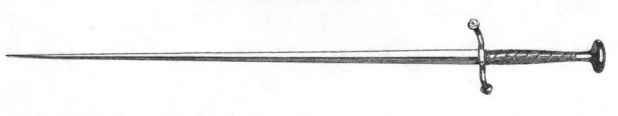

"Integrity!" The Duke's grotesque face was white, his red eyebrows drawn together in a scowl. "Is it integrity that brings you in arms against me, Facino?"

"Not against you, Lord Duke. Never yet have I stood in arms against your highness. It is upon your enemies that I make war. I have no aim but the restoration of peace to your dominions."

"Fine words on the lips of a mutinous traitor!" sneered the Duke. He flung himself petulantly into a chair.

"If your highness believed that, you would not dare to come here."

"Not dare? God's bones, man! Are these words for me? I am Duke of Milan."

"I study to remember it, highness," said Facino, and the rumblings of anger in his voice drove della Torre to pluck at his master's sleeve.

Thus warned, Gian Maria changed the subject but not the tone. "You know why I am here?"

"To permit me, I hope, to place myself at your potency's commands."

"Ah! Bah! You make me sick with your fair words." He grew sullen. "Come, man. What is your price?"

"My price, highness? What does your highness conceive I have to sell?"

"A little patience with his magnificence, my lord," della Torre begged.

"I thought I was displaying it," said Facino. "Otherwise it might be very bad for everybody." He was really growing angry.

And now the idiot Duke must needs go prodding him into fury.

"What's that? Do you threaten me? Why, here's an insolent dog!"

Facino turned livid with passion. A tall fellow among his captains, very noble-looking in cloth of silver under a blue houppelande, laughed aloud. The pale, bulging eyes of Gian Maria sought him out venomously.

"You laugh, knave?" he snarled, and came to his feet, outraged by the indignity. "What is here for laughter?"

Bellarion laughed again as he answered: "Yourself, Lord Duke, who in yourself are nothing. You are Duke of Milan at present by the grace of God and the favour of Facino Cane. Yet you do not hesitate to offend against both."

"Quiet, Bellarion," Facino growled. "I need no advocate."

"Bellarion!" the Duke echoed, glaring malevolently. "I remember you, and remember you I shall. You shall be taught . . ."

"By God, it is your highness shall be taught!" Facino crashed into the threatening speech roaring like a thunder-god. "Get you hence, back to your Milan until I come to give you the lesson that you need, and thank God that you are your father's son and I have grace enough to remember it, for otherwise you'd never go hence alive! Away with you, and get yourself schooled in manners before we meet again or as God's my life I'll birch you with these hands."

Terrified, cowering before that raging storm, the line of which had never yet broken about his ducal head, Gian Maria shrank back until his three companions were between himself and Facino. Della Torre, almost trembling, sought to pacify the angry condottiero.

"My lord! My lord! This is not worthy!"

"Not worthy! Is it worthy that I shall be called 'dog' by a cross-grained brat to whom I've played the foster-father? Out of my sight, sir! Out of my sight, all of you! The door, Bellarion! The Duke of Milan to the door!"

They went without another word, fearing, indeed, that another word might be their last. But they did not yet return to Milan. They remained in Vigevano, and that evening della Torre came seeking audience again of Facino to make the Duke's peace with him, and Facino, having swallowed his rage by then, consented to receive his highness once more.

The young man came, this time well schooled in prudence, to announce that he was prepared to give Facino peaceful entrance into Milan and to restore him to his office of ducal governor. In short, that he was prepared to accord all that which he had no power to refuse.

Facino's answer was brief and clear. He would accept the office again, provided that it was bestowed upon him for a term of three years, and the bestowal guaranteed by an oath of fealty to be sworn upon his hands by the Syndics of the Grand Council. Further, the Castle of Porta Giovia was to be delivered into his keeping absolutely, and not only the Guelphic Sanseverino, who now held the office of Podestà, but all other Guelphs holding offices of State must be dismissed. Lastly, Antonio della Torre, whom Facino accused of being at the root of most of the trouble which had distracted Milan, must go into banishment together with Lonate.

This last was the condition that Gian Maria would not swallow. He swore it was a vile attempt to deprive him of all his friends.

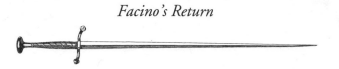

Thus the conference ended inconclusively, and it was not until three weeks later that the Duke finally yielded, and accepted Facino's terms in their entirety.

On the evening of Wednesday, the sixth of November of that year, attended by a large company, Facino Cane, Count of Biandrate, rode into Milan to resume his governorship, a governorship which he was resolved to render absolute this time. They entered the city in a downpour of rain, notwithstanding which the streets were thronged by the people who turned out to welcome the man in whom they beheld their saviour.

And in the Old Broletto, the young Duke, without a single friendly Guelph at hand to comfort him, sat listening to that uproar, gnawing his fingernails and shuddering with rage and spite.

It becomes necessary, however, to remember, lest we should be swept along by this stream of Viscontean history, that this present chronicle is concerned not with the fortunes of Milan, but with those of Bellarion, and that in these Facino Cane and Gian Maria Visconti are concerned only to the extent of the part they bore in moulding them.

In the confused pages of old Corio you may read in detail, though you may not always clearly understand, the events that followed upon Facino's triumphant return to Milan. You will gather that the strength in which he was known to be gave pause to Malatesta's plans to seize the Duchy; that in fact the arch-Guelph chose to content himself with his usurpation of the lordship of Brescia and Bergamo, and in Bergamo he remained until Facino went to seek him there some two years later. If he did not go before, it was because other more immediate and active enemies of Milan claimed his attention. Vignate was in arms again, as were also Estorre Visconti and his nephew Giovanni Carlo, and a host of lesser insurgents, chief of whom was the Duke's own brother, that Filippo Maria Visconti who was Count of Pavia. By the Ghibellines who had fled to him from Milan during the days of Malatesta and Boucicault's domination, Filippo Maria had been flattered into believing that he was that party's only hope in Northern Italy. His ambition thus aroused, he was ready to take advantage of the general distraction, and to appropriate for himself the ducal chlamys. To this purpose was he arming when Facino returned to Milan, and news of his preparations reached Facino whilst he was suppressing the various rebellious outbreaks in the Milanese, stamping out the embers of revolt in such places as Desio and Gorgonzola. Only when he had restored order, established a proper administration, and so brought back tranquillity to that harassed land, did be turn his attention to the menace of the enemies farther afield. And the first of these was Filippo Maria. He marched on Pavia, carried the city by assault and put it to sack, choosing of all nights in the year for that operation the night of Christmas.

That sack of Pavia is one of the most unsparing and terrible in the terrible history of sacks, and the deed remains a blot upon the fame of a soldier who, although rough and occasionally even brutal in his ways, was yet a leader of high principles and a high sense of duty.

Thereafter he dealt with Filippo Maria much as he had dealt with his ducal brother. He appointed himself governor of the young man's dominions, filled the offices of State with men in his own confidence and completely stripped the Count of authority.

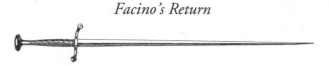

The fat, flabby young Prince submitted in a singularly apathetic fashion. He was of solitary, studious habits, a recluse, almost savagely shy, shunning the society of men because of his excessive consciousness of his own grotesque ugliness.

The spark of ambition that had been struck from him having been thus summarily quenched, he retired to his books again, and let Facino have his way with the State, nor complained so long as Facino left him in the enjoyment of the little that was really necessary to his eremitic ways.

Facino made now of Pavia his headquarters, coming to dwell in the great castle itself, and bringing thither from Alessandria his Countess. And with the Countess of Biandrate came also the Princess Valeria of Montferrat to rejoin at last her brother who had continued throughout in Facino's train. The Princess had left Casale with the Countess when Carmagnola appeared there as Facino's envoy with an escort. Her going had been in the nature of a flight, whose object had been first to rejoin her cherished brother, and second, to remove herself from the power of her uncle, which, in all the circumstances made clear by Carmagnola, seemed prudent. It is possible that she may also have hoped by her presence near Facino to stimulate him into the fulfilment of the threat against the Regent on which he had parted from him in Genoa.

But Facino had still more immediate matters to rectify before coming to the affair of the Lord Theodore. The Regent must wait his turn.

He moved against Canturio in the following May, and made short work of it. The campaign against Crema followed, and meanwhile Bellarion, with a condotta increased to fifteen hun-

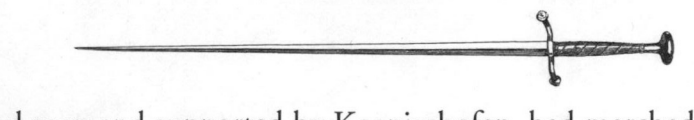

dred men and supported by Koenigshofen, had marched out of
Milan to deal with the rebellious Bignate, whom in the end he
finally and definitely defeated. That done he returned to Milan,
where, ever since Facino's descent upon Pavia, he had held the
position of Facino's deputy, and had earned respect and even
affection by the equable wisdom of his rule.

All this in greater detail you will find set forth by Corio and
Fra Serafino of Imola, and it is Fra Serafino who tells us that
Facino, determined that Bellarion should not suffer by the loyalty which had made him refuse the County of Asti, had constrained Gian Maria to create him Count of Gavi, and the
Commune of Milan to enlist the services of his condotta for two
years at a stipend of thirty thousand ducats monthly.

Chapter IV

The Count of Pavia

In the vast park of Pavia the trees stood leafless and black against the white shroud of snow that covered the chilled earth. The river Ticino gurgled and swirled about the hundred granite pillars which carried the great roofed bridge, five hundred feet in length, spanning its grey and turgid waters. Beyond this, Favia the Learned reared above white roofs her hundred snow-capped towers to the grey December sky, and beyond the city, isolated, within the girdle of a moat that was both wide and deep, stood the massive square castle, pink as coral, strong as iron, at once impregnable fortress and unrivalled palace, one of the great monuments of Viscontian power and splendour, described by Petrarch as the princeliest pile in Italy.

The pride of the place was the library, a spacious square chamber in one of the rectangular towers that rose at each of the four corners of the castle. The floor was of coloured mosaics, figuring birds and beasts, the ceiling of ultramarine star-flecked in gold, and along the walls was ranged a collection of some nine hundred manuscript parchment volumes bound in velvet and damask, or in gold and silver brocades. Their contents contained all that was known of theology, astrology, medicine, music, geometry, rhetoric, and the other sciences. This room was the favourite haunt of the lonely, morose, and studious boy, the great Gian Galeazzo's younger son, Filippo Maria Visconti, Count of Pavia.

He sat there now, by the log fire that hissed and spluttered and flamed on the cavernous hearth, diffusing warmth and a fragrance of pine throughout the chamber. And with him at chess sat the Lord Bellarion Cane, Count of Gavi, one of the newfound friends who had invaded his loneliness, and broken through the savage shyness which solitude and friendlessness had set about him like a shell.

The others, the dark and handsome Countess of Biandrate, the fair and now almost ethereal Princess of Montferrat, and that sturdier counterpart of herself, her brother, were in the background by one of the two-light windows with trefoil arches springing from slender monials.

The Princess was bending low over a frame, embroidering in red and gold and blue an altar cloth for San Pietro in Ciel d'Oro. The Countess was yawning over a beautifully illuminated copy of Petrarch's *Trionfo d'Amore*. The boy sat idle and listless between them, watching his sister's white tapering fingers as they flashed to and fro.

Presently he rose, sauntered across to the players, drew up a stool, and sat down to watch the game over which they brooded silently.

A crutch lay beside Bellarion, and his right leg was thrust out stiff and unbending, to explain why he sat here on this day of late December playing chess, whilst the campaign against Malatesta continued to rage in the hills of Bergamo. He was suffering the penalty of the pioneer. Having already demonstrated to his contemporaries that infantry, when properly organised and manœuvred, can hold its own in the field against cavalry, he had been turning his attention to artillery. Two months ago he had mounted a park of guns under the walls of Bergamo with the intention of breaching them. But at the outset of his operations a bombard had burst, killing two of his bombardiers and breaking his thigh, thus proving Facino's contention that artillery was a danger only to those who employed it.

The physician Mombelli, who still continued in Facino's train, had set the bone, whereafter Bellarion had been carefully packed into a mule litter, and by roads, which torrential rains had reduced to quagmires, he had been despatched to Pavia to get himself mended. His removal from the army was regretted by everybody with two exceptions: Carmagnola, glad to be relieved of a brother captain by comparison with whose military methods his own were constantly suffering in the general esteem; and Filippo Maria, when he discovered in Bellarion a chess-player who was not only his equal but his master, and who in other ways won the esteem of that very friendless boy. The Princess Valeria was dismayed that this man, who out of unconquerable prejudice she continued to scorn and mistrust, should become for a season her fellow inquiline. And it was in vain that Gian Giacomo, who in the course of his reformation had come to conceive a certain regard for Bellarion, sought to combat his sister's deep-rooted prejudice.

When he insisted that it was by Bellarion's contriving that he had been removed from his uncle's control, she had been moved to vehement scorn of his credulity.

"That is what the trickster would have us think. He no more than carried out the orders of the Count of Biandrate. His whole life bears witness to his false nature."

"Nay, now, Valeria, nay. You'll not deny that he is what all Italy now proclaims him: one of the greatest captains of his time."

"And how has he made himself that? Is it by knightly qualities, by soldierly virtues? All the world knows that he prevails by guile and trickery."

"You've been listening to Carmagnola," said her brother. "He would give an eye for Bellarion's skill."

"You're but a boy," she reminded him with some asperity.

"And Carmagnola, of course, is a handsome man."

She crimsoned at the sly tone. On odd visits to Pavia, Carmagnola had been very attentive to the Princess, employing all a peacock's arts of self-display to dazzle her.

"He is an honest gentleman," she countered hotly. "It is better to trust an upright, honest soldier than a sly schemer whose falsehood has been proven to us."

"If he schemes my ruin for my uncle's profit, he goes about it oddly, neglecting opportunities."

She looked at him with compassion. "Bellarion never aims where he looks. It is the world says that of him, not I."

"And at what do you suspect that he is aiming now?"

Her deep eyes grew thoughtful. "What if he serves our uncle to destroy us, only so that in the end he may destroy our uncle to his own advantage? What if he should aim at a throne?"

Gian Giacomo thought the notion fantastic, the fruit of too much ill-ordered brooding. He said so, laughing.

"If you had studied his methods, Giannino, you would not say that. See how he has wrought his own advancement. In four short years this son of nobody, without so much as a name of his own has become the Knight Bellarion, the Lord Bellarion of the Company of the White Dog, and now the Lord Count of Gavi holding the rich lands of Gavi in feud."

One there was who might have told her things which would have corrected her judgment, and that was Facino's Countess. For the Lady Beatrice knew the truth of those events in Montferrat which were at the root of the Princess Valeria's bitter prejudice, of which also she was aware.

"You hate him very bitterly," the Countess told her once when Bellarion had been the subject of their talk.

"Would not you, if you were in my place?"

And the Countess, looking at her with those long indolent eyes of hers, an inscrutable smile on her red lips, had answered with languorous slowness: "In your place it is possible that I should."

The tone and the smile had intrigued the Princess for many a day thereafter. But either she was too proud to ask what the Countess had meant, or else afraid.

When after some eight weeks abed, Bellarion had begun to hobble about the castle, and it was impossible for the Princess entirely to avoid him, she was careful never to be alone where he might so surprise her, using him when they met in the company of others with a distant, frigid courtesy, which is perhaps the most piercing of all hostility.

If it wounded Bellarion, he gave no sign. He was—and therein lay half the secret of his strength—a very patient man. He was content to wait for the day when by his contriving the reckoning should be presented to the Marquis Theodore, and she should know at last whose servant he really was. Meanwhile, he modelled his demeanour upon her own. He did not seek her company, nor indeed that of any in the castle save Filippo Maria, with whom he would spend long hours at chess or instructing him out of his own deep learning supported by one or another of the treatises in that fine library.

Until the coming of Bellarion, the Count of Pavia had believed himself a strong chess-player. Bellarion had made him realise that his knowledge of the game was elementary. Where against former opponents he had swept to easy triumphs, he now groaned and puffed and sweated over the board to lessen the ignominy of his inevitable defeats.

Today, however, he was groaning less than usual. He had piled up a well-supported attack on Bellarion's flank, and for the first time in weeks—for these games had begun whilst Bellarion was still abed—he saw victory ahead. With a broad smile he brought up a bishop further to strengthen the mass of his attack. He saw his way to give check in three and checkmate in four moves.

Although only in his twentieth year, he was of a hog-like bulk. Of no more than middle height, he looked tall when seated, for all the length of him was in his flabby, paunchy body. His limbs were short and shapeless. His face was as round as the full moon and as pale. A great dewlap spread beneath his chin, and his neck behind hung in loose fat folds upon his collar, so that the back of

his head, which was flat, seemed to slope inwards towards the crown. His short black hair was smooth and sleek as a velvet cap, and a fringe of it across his forehead descended almost to the heavy black eyebrows, thus masking the intellectual depth of the only noble feature of that ignoble countenance. Of his father all that he had inherited physically was the hooked, predatory nose. His mouth was coarsely shaped and its lines confirmed the impression of cruelty you gathered from the dark eyes which were small and lacklustre as a snake's. And the impression was a true one, for the soul of this shy, morose young Prince was not without its share of that sadic cruelty which marked all the men of his race.

To meet the bishop's move, Bellarion advanced a knight. The Prince's laugh rang through the silent room. It was a shrill almost womanish laugh, and it was seldom heard. High-pitched, too, was the voice that followed.

"You but delay the inevitable, Bellarion," he said, and took the knight.

But the move of the knight, which had appeared purely defensive to the Prince in his intentness upon his own attack, had served to uncover the file of Bellarion's queen. Supports had been previously and just as cunningly provided. Bellarion advanced his hand, a long beautiful hand upon which glowed a great carved sapphire set in brilliants—the blue and white that were his colours. Forth flashed his queen across the board.

"Checkmate, Lord Prince," said Bellarion quietly, and sank back smiling into the brocaded chair.

Filippo Maria stared unbelieving at the board. The lines of his mouth drooped, and his great pendulous cheeks trembled.

Almost he seemed on the point of tears.

"God rot you, Bellarion! Always, always is it the same! I plan and build and whilst you seem to do no more than defend, you are preparing a death-stroke in an unexpected quarter." Between jest and earnest he added: "You slippery rogue! Always you defeat me by a trick."

The Princess Valeria looked up from her embroidery on the word. Bellarion caught the movement and the glance in his direction. He knew the thought behind, and it was that thought he answered.

"In the field, my opponents use the same word to decry me. But those who are with me applaud my skill." He laughed. "Truth is an elusive thing, highness, as Pontius Pilate knew. The aspect of a fact depends upon the angle from which you view it."

Filippo Maria sat back, his great chin sunk to his breast, his podgy white hands gripping the arms of his chair, his humour sullen.

"I'll play no more today," he said.

The Countess rose and crossed the room with a rustle of stiff brocade of black and gold.

"Let me remove the board," she said. "A vile, dull game. I wonder that you can waste such hours upon it."

Filippo Maria raised his beady eyes. They kindled as they observed her, raking her generous yet supple lines from head to foot. It was not the first time that the watchful Bellarion had seen him look so at Facino's lady, nor the first time that he had seen her wantonly display herself to provoke that unmistakable regard. She bent now to the board, and Filippo's smouldering glance was upon the warm ivory beauty of her neck, and the swell of her breast revealed by the lowcut gown.

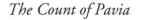

"It is human to despise what we do not understand," Bellarion was answering her.

"You would defend the game, of course, since you excel in it. That is what you love, Bellarion; to excel; to wield mastery."

"Do we not all? Do not you, yourself, madonna, glory in the power your beauty gives you?"

She looked at Filippo. Her heavy eyelids drooped. "Behold him turned courtier, my lord. He perceives beauty in me."

"He would be blind else," said the fat youth, greatly daring. And the next moment in a reaction of shyness a mottled flush was staining his unhealthy pallor.

Lower drooped the lady's eyelids, until a line of black lashes lay upon her cheek.

"The game," Gian Giacomo interposed, "is a very proper one for princes. Messer Bellarion told me so."

"He means, child," Filippo answered him, "that it teaches them a bitter moral: that whilst a State depends upon the Prince— the Prince himself is entirely dependent upon others, being capable in his own person of little more than his meanest pawn."

"To teach that lesson to a despot," said Bellarion, "was the game invented by an Eastern philosopher."

"And the most potent piece upon the board, as in the State, is the queen, symbolising woman." Thus Filippo Maria, his eyes full upon the Countess again.

Bellarion laughed. "Aye! He knew his world, that ancient Oriental!"

But he did not laugh as the days passed, and he observed the growing lechery in the beady eyes with which the Count of Pavia watched the Lady Beatrice's every movement, and the Lady

Beatrice's provocative complacency under that vigilance.

One day, at last, coming upon the Countess alone in that library, Bellarion unmasked the batteries he had been preparing.

He hobbled across to the arched window by which she was seated, and, leaning against its monial, looked out upon the desolate park. The snows had gone, washed away by rains, and since these had come a frost under which the ground lay now as grey and hard as iron.

"They will be feeling the rigours of the winter in the camp under Bergamo," he said, moving, as ever, obliquely to the attack.

"They will so. Facino should have gone into winter quarters."

"That would mean recommencing in the spring a job that is half done already."

"Yet with his gout and the infirmities of age, it might prove wiser in the end."

"Each age has its own penalties, madonna. It is not only the elderly among humanity who need compassion."

"Wisdom oozes from you like sweat from another." There was a tartness in her accents. "If I were your biographer, Bellarion, I should write of you as the soldier-sage, or the philosopher-at-arms."

Propped on his crutch and his one sound leg, Bellarion considered her, his head on one side, and fetched a sigh.

"You are very beautiful, madonna."

She was startled. "God save us!" she cried. "Does the soldier-sage contain a mere man, after all?"

"Your mouth, madonna, is too sweetly formed for acids."

"The choicest fruits, sir, have an alloy of sharpness. What else about me finds favour in your eyes?"

"In my eyes! My eyes, madonna, are circumspect. They do

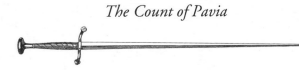

not prowl hungrily over another's pastures."

She looked at him between anger and apprehension, and slowly a wave of scarlet came to stain her face and bosom, to tell him that she understood. He lowered himself carefully to a chair, thrusting out his damaged leg, to the knee-joint of which articulation was only just beginning to return.

"I was saying, madonna, that they will be feeling the rigours of the winter in the camp under Bergamo. There was a hard frost last night, and after the frost there will be rains under which the hills thereabouts will melt in mud." He sighed again. "You would regret, madonna, to exchange for that the ease and comfort of Pavia."

"You have the fever again. I am not thinking of making that exchange."

"No. I am thinking of it for you."

"You! Saint Mary! And do you dispose of me?"

"It will be cold up there, madonna. But you need cooling. Coolness restores judgment. It will bring you back to a sense of duty to your lord."

She came to her feet beside him, quivering with anger. Almost he thought her intention was to strike him.

"Have you come here to spy upon me?"

"Of course. Now you know why I broke my leg."

She looked unutterable scorn. "The Princess Valeria is right in her opinion of you, in her disdain of you."

His eyes grew sad. "If you were generous, madonna—nay, if you were merely honest—you would not embrace her opinions; you would correct them; for you have the knowledge that would suffice to do so. But you are not honest. If you were, there would be no need for me to speak now in defence of the honour of your absent lord."

"Is it for you to say I am not honest?" There was now more of sorrow than indignation in her voice, and tears were gathering in her eyes, to deepen their sapphire hue. "God knows I have been honest with you, Bellarion. It is this very honesty you abuse in your present misjudgment of me. Oh! Me miserable!" It was the cry of a wounded soul. She sank down again into her chair. Self-pity welled in her to drown all else. "I am to be starved of everything. If ever woman was pitiable, I am that woman; and you, Bellarion, you of all living men that know my heart, can find for me only cruelty and reproach!"

It moved him not at all. The plea was too inconsequent and illogical, and the display of a lack of reason repelled him like a physical defect.

"Your plaint, madonna, is that Facino will not make you a duchess. He may do so yet if you are patient."

Her tears had suddenly ceased.

"You know something!" she exclaimed in a hushed voice.

The rogue fooled her with that illusion, whilst refraining from using words which might afterwards be turned against him.

"I know that you will lose the chance if meanwhile you should cease to be Facino's wife. If you were so mad as to become the leman of another, you know as well as I do that the Lord Facino would put you from him. What should you be then? That is why I am your friend when I think of the camp at Bergamo for you."

Slowly she dried her eyes. Carefully she removed all stains of tears. It consumed a little time. Then she rose and went to him, and took his hand.

"Thank you, Bellarion, my friend." Her voice was hushed and tender. "You need have no fear for me." She paused a moment. "What . . . what has my lord said to you of his intent?"

"Nay, nay," he laughed, "I betray no confidences." The trickster's tone was a confidence in itself. He swept on. "You bid me have no fear for you. But that is not enough. Princes are reckless folk. I'd not have you remain in jeopardy."

"Oh! But Bergamo!" she cried out. "To be encamped in winter!"

"You need not go so far, nor under canvas. In your place, madonna, I should retire to Melegnano. The castle is at your disposal. It is pleasanter than Pavia."

"Pleasanter! In that loneliness?"

"It is the company here that makes it prudent. And you may take the Princess Valeria and her brother with you. Come, come, madonna. Will you trifle with fate at such a time? Will you jeopardise a glorious destiny for the sake of an obese young lordling?"

She considered, her face fretful. "Tell me," she begged again, "what my lord has divulged to you of his intentions?"

"Have I not said enough already?"

The entrance of Filippo Maria at that moment saved him the need of further invention. It perturbed him not at all that the Prince's round white face should darken at the sight of them so close and fond. She was warned. Her greed of power and honour would curb her wantonness and ensure her withdrawal to Melegnano as he urged. Bellarion glowed with the satisfaction of a battle won, nor troubled about the deceit he had practised.

Chapter V

Justice

The Epiphany mummeries were long overpast, the iron hand of winter was withdrawn from the land, and in the great forest of Pavia, where Gian Galeazzo had loved to hunt, the trees were breaking into bud before Bellarion's condition permitted him to think of quitting the ease of Filippo Maria's castle. His leg had mended well, the knee-joint had recovered its suppleness, and only a slight limp remained.

He spoke of returning to Bergamo. "This lotus-eating has endured too long already," he told the Prince in answer to the latter's remonstrances; for Filippo Maria was reluctant to part with one who in many ways had beguiled for him the tedium of his lonely life, rendered lonelier than ever before by the withdrawal of the Countess of Biandrate, who had gone with the Montferrine Princess to Melegnano.

But it was not written that Filippo Maria should be left alone; for on the very eve of Bellarion's intended departure, Facino himself was borne into the Castle of Pavia, crippled by an attack of gout of a severity which had compelled him to leave his camp just as he was preparing to reap the fruits of his long and patient siege.

He had lost weight, and his face out of which the healthy tan had departed was grey and drawn. His hair from fulvid that it had been was almost white. But the spirit within remained unchanged, indomitable, and intolerant of this enforced inertia of the flesh.

He was put to bed immediately on his arrival, for he was in great pain and swore that the gout, which he called by all manner of evil names, had got into his stomach.

"Mombelli warned me there was danger of it."

"Where is Mombelli?" Bellarion asked. He stood with Filippo Maria by the canopied bed in a spacious chamber in the northern tower, adjacent to the Hall of Mirrors.

"Mombelli, devil take his soul, left me a month ago, when I seemed well, to go to Duke Gian Maria who desired to appoint him his physician. I've sent for him again to the Duke. Meanwhile some Pavese doctor will be required to give me ease." He groaned with pain. Then, recovering, rapped out his orders to Bellarion. "It's a mercy you are recovered, for you are needed at Bergamo. Meanwhile Carmagnola commands there, but he has my orders to surrender his authority to you on your arrival."

It was an order which Carmagnola did not relish, as he plainly showed when Bellarion reached the camp two days later. But he dared not disobey it.

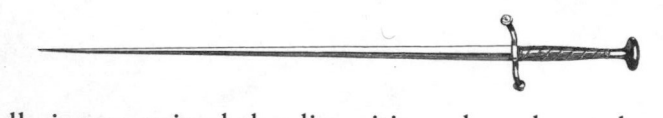

Bellarion examined the dispositions, but changed nothing. He carried forward the plans already made by Facino. The siege could be tightened no further, and, considering the straits to which Malatesta must be reduced, there could be little point in wasting lives on an assault.

A week after Bellarion's coming there rode into the great camp of green tents under the walls of Bergamo, a weary, excited fellow all splashed with mud from the fury of his riding.

Brought, by the guards who had checked his progress, to Facino's large and handsomely equipped pavilion, pitched beside the racing waters of the Serio, this slight, swarthy, fierce-eyed man proved to be that stormy petrel, Giovanni Pusterla of Venegono.

Bellarion rose from the couch, covered by a black bearskin on which he had been reclining, and closed the beautifully illuminated copy of Juvenal's *Satires*, which had been a parting gift from Filippo Maria. His gesture dismissed the Swiss halberdiers, who had ushered in this visitor. The very name of Venegono was of ill omen, and ill-omened was the man's haggard countenance now, and his own announcement.

"I bring evil tidings, Lord Count."

"You are consistent," said Bellarion. "A great quality."

Venegono stared at him. "Give me to drink," he begged. "God! How I thirst. I have ridden from Pavia without pause save to change horse at Caravaggio."

"From Pavia!" Bellarion's tone and manner changed; apprehension showed in both. But not on that account was he neglectful of the needs of his guest. On an ample square table in mid-tent stood a jug of wine and some beautiful drinking-cups, their bowls of beaten gold, their stems of choicely wrought silver, beside a dish of sweetmeats, bread, and a small loaf of cheese. Bellarion poured a cup of strong red Valtelline. Venegono drained it.

"Aye, I am consistent, as you say. And so is that hell-spawn Gian Maria Visconti. Of his consistency, mine. By your leave."

He flung himself wearily into the cushioned fald-stool by the table, and set down his cup. Bellanon nodded, and resumed his seat on the bearskin.

"What has happened in Pavia?"

"In Pavia nothing. Nothing yet. I rode there to warn Facino of what is happening in Milan, but Facino . . . The man is ill. He could do nothing if he would, so I come on to you." And now, leaning forward, and scarcely pausing to draw breath, he launched the news he had ridden so desperately to bring. "Della Torre is back in Milan, recalled by Gian Maria."

Bellarion waited, but nothing further came.

"Well, man?" he asked. "Is that all?"

"All? Does it mean so little to you that you ask that? Don't you know that this damned Guelph, whom Facino banished when he should have hanged him, has been throughout the inspirer of all the evil that has been wrought against Facino and against all the Ghibellines of Milan? Don't you understand that his return bodes ill?"

"What can he do? What can Gian Maria do? Their wings are clipped."

"They are growing fresh ones." Venegono came to his feet again, his weariness forgotten in his excitement. "Since della Torre's secret return a month ago, orators have been sent to Theodore of Montferrat, to the battered Vignati, to the Esti, and even to Estorre Visconti, to invite them into a league."

Bellarion laughed. "Let them league. If they are so mad as to do so, Facino will smash their league into shards when this Bergamo business is over. You forget that under his hand is the strongest army in Italy today. We muster over twelve thousand men."

"My God! I seem to be listening to Facino himself." Venegono slobbered in his excitement, his eyes wild. "It was thus he answered me."

"Why, then, have troubled to come to me?"

"In the hope that you would see what he will not. You talk as if the army were all. You forget that Gian Maria is a thing of venom, like the emblem of his accursed house. Where there is venom and the will to use it, beware the occasion. If anything should happen to Facino, what hope will remain for the Ghibellines of Milan?"

"What should happen to Facino? At what are you hinting, man?"

Venegono looked at him between rage and compassion. "Where is Mombelli?" he asked. "Why is he not with Facino now that Facino needs him? Do you know?"

"But is he not with Facino? Has he not yet arrived?"

"Arrived? Why was he ever withdrawn? To be made physician to the Duke. A pretext, my friend, to deprive Facino of his healing services. Do you know that since his coming to Milan he has not been seen? There are rumours that he is dead, that the Duke has murdered him."

Bellarion considered. Then he shrugged. "Your imagination fools you, Venegono. If Gian Maria proposed to strike Facino,

he would surely attempt something more active and effective."

"It may be little, I confess. But it is a straw that points the way of the wind."

"A straw, indeed," Bellarion agreed. "But in any case, what do you require of me? You have not told me that."

"That you take a strong detachment of your men and repair at once to Milan to curb the Duke's evil intentions and to deal with della Torre."

"For that my lord's orders would be necessary. My duty is here, Venegono, and I dare not neglect it. Nor is the matter so urgent. It can wait until Bergamo has been reduced, which will not be long."

"Too long, it may be."

But not all the passionate pleading with which he now distressed Bellarion could turn the latter from his clear duty, or communicate to him any of the vague alarms which agitated Venegono. And so, at last, he went his ways in despair, protesting that both Bellarion and Facino were beset with the blindness of those whom the gods wish to destroy.

Bellarion, however, saw in Venegono's warning no more than an attempt to use him for the execution of a private vengeance. Three days later he thought he had confirmation of this. It came in a letter bearing Facino's signature, but penned in the crabbed and pointed hand of the Countess, who had been summoned from Melegnano to minister to her lord. It informed Bellarion that the physician Mombelli had come at last in response to Facino's request, and that Facino hoped soon to be afoot again. Indeed, there was already a perceptible improvement in his condition.

"So much for Venegono's rumours that Mombelli has been murdered," said Bellarion to himself, and laughed at the scaremongering of that credulous hot-head.

But he thought differently when after another three days a second letter reached him signed by the Countess herself.

"My lord begs you to come to him at once," she wrote. "He is so ill that Messer Mombelli despairs of him. Do not lose a moment, or you may be too late."

He was more deeply stirred by that summons than by anything he could remember. If those who accounted him hard and remorselessly calculating could have seen him in that moment, the tears filming his eyes at the very thought of losing this man whom he loved, they must have formed a gentler opinion of his nature.

He sent at once for Carmagnola, and ordered a strong horse to be saddled and twenty lances to prepare to ride with him. Ride with him, however, they did not. They followed. For he rode like one possessed of devils. In three hours he covered the forty miles of difficult road that lay between Bergamo and Pavia, leaving one horse foundered and arriving on a second one that was spent by the time he reached Filippo Maria's stronghold. Down he flung from it in the great courtyard, and, staggering and bespattered, he mounted the main staircase so wide and of such shallow steps that it was possible to ascend it on horseback.

Without pausing to see the Prince, he had himself conducted straight to Facino's chamber, and there under the damask-hung canopy he found his adoptive father supine, inert, his countenance leaden-hued, looking as if he were laid out in death, save for his stertorous breathing and the fire that still glowed in the

eyes under their tufted, fulvid brows.

Bellarion went down on his knees beside the bed, and took, in both his own that were so warm and strong, the cold, heavy hand that lay upon the coverlet.

The grey head rolled a little on its pillow; the ghost of a smile irradiated the strong, rugged face; the fingers of the cold hand faintly pressed Bellarion's.

"Good lad, you have lost no time," he said, in a weak, rasping voice. "And there is no time to lose. I am sped. Indeed, my body's dead already. Mombelli says the gout is mounting to my heart."

Bellarion looked up. Beyond the bed stood the Countess, fretful and troubled. At the foot was Mombelli, and in the background a servant.

"Is this so?" he asked the physician. "Can your skill avail nothing here?"

"He is in God's hands," said Mombelli, mumbling indistinctly.

"Send them away," said Facino, and his eyes indicated Mombelli and the servant. "There is little time, and I have things to tell you. We must take order for what's to follow."

The orders did not amount to very much. He required of Bellarion that he should afford the Countess his protection, and he recommended to him also Filippo Maria.

"When Gian Galeazzo died, he left his sons in my care. I go to meet him with clean hands. I have discharged my trust, and dying I hand it on to you. Remember always that Gian Maria is Duke of Milan, and whatever the shortcomings he may show, for your own sake if not for his, practise loyalty to him, as you would have your own captains be loyal to you."

When at last, wearied, and announcing his desire to rest, Facino bade him go, Bellarion found Mombelli pacing in the Hall of Mirrors, and sent him to Facino.

"I shall remain here within call," he said, and oblivious of his own fatigue he paced in his turn that curious floor whereon birds and beasts were figured in mosaics under the gaudy flashing ceiling of coloured glass, whence the place derived its name.

There Mombelli found him a half-hour later, when he emerged.

"He sleeps now," he said. "The Countess is with him."

"It is not yet the end?" Bellarion asked.

"Not yet. The end is when God wills. He may linger for some days."

Bellarion looked sharply at the doctor, considered him, indeed, now for the first time since his arrival. This Mombelli was a man of little more than thirty-five. He had been vigorous of frame, inclining a little to portliness, rubicund if grave of countenance with strong white teeth and bright dark eyes. Bellarion beheld now an emaciated man upon whose shrunken frame a black velvet gown hung in loose folds. His face was pale, his eyes dull; but oddest of all the very shape of his face had changed; his jaw had fallen in, so that nose and chin were brought closer like those of an old man, and when he spoke he hissed and mumbled indistinctly over toothless gums.

"By the Host, man. What has happened to you?"

Mombelli shrank visibly from the questions and from the stern eyes that seemed to search his very soul.

"I . . . I . . . have been ill," he faltered. "Very ill. It is a miracle I am alive today."

"But your teeth, man?"

"I have lost them as you see. A consequence of my disease."

A horrible suspicion was sprouting in Bellarion's mind, nourished by the memory of the rumour of this man's death which Venegono had reported. He took the doctor by the sleeve of his velvet gown, and drew him towards one of the double windows. His shrinking, his obvious reluctance to undergo this closer inspection, were so much added food to Bellarion's suspicion.

"How do you call this disease?" he asked.

Clearly, from his hesitancy, Mombelli had been unprepared for the question. "It . . . it is a sort of podagric affection," he mumbled.

"And your thumb? Why is that bandaged?"

Terror leapt to Mombelli's eyes. His toothless jaws worked fearfully. "That? That is naught. An injury."

"Take off the bandage. Take it off, man. I desire to see this injury. Do you hear me?"

At last Mombelli with shaking fingers stripped the bandage from his left thumb, and displayed it naked.

Bellarion went white, and his eyes were dreadful. "You have been tortured, master doctor. Gian Maria has subjected you to his Lent."

This Lent of Gian Maria's invention was a torment lasting forty days, on each of which one or more teeth were torn from the patient's jaws, then day by day a finger nail, whereafter followed the eyes and finally the tongue, whereupon the sufferer being rendered dumb and unable to confess what was desired, he was shown at last the mercy of being put to death.

Mombelli's livid lips moved frantically, but no words came.

427

He reeled where he stood until he found the wall to steady him, and Bellarion watched him with those dreadful, searching eyes.

"To what end did he torture you? What did he desire of you?"

"I have not said he tortured me. It is not true."

"You have not said it. No. But your condition says it. You have not said it, because you dare not. Why did he do this? And why did he desist?" Bellarion gripped him by the shoulders. "Answer me. To what did the torments undergone suffice to constrain you? Will you answer me?"

"O God!" groaned the physician, sagging limply against the wall, and looking as if he would faint.

But there was no pity in Bellarion's face. "Come with me," he said, and it was almost by main force that he dragged the wretched doctor across that hall out to the gallery, and down the wide steps to the great court. Here under the arcade some men-at-arms of Facino's bodyguard were idling. Into their hands Bellarion delivered Mombelli.

"To the question chamber," he said shortly.

Mombelli, shattered in nerve and sapped of manhood by his sufferings, cried out, piteously inarticulate. Pitilessly Bellarion waved him away, and the soldiers bore him off, screaming, to the stone chamber under the northeastern tower. There, in the middle of the uneven stone floor, stood the dread framework of the rack.

Bellarion, who had followed, ordered them to strip him. The men were reluctant to do the office of executioners, but under the eyes of Bellarion, standing as implacable as the god of wrath, they set about it, nevertheless, and all the while the broken man's cries for mercy filled that vaulted place with an ever-mounting

horror. At the last, half-naked, he broke from the men's hands and flung himself at Bellarion's feet.

"In the name of the sweet Christ, my lord, take pity on me! I can bear no more. Hang me if you will, but do not let me be tortured again."

Bellarion looked down on the grovelling, slobbering wretch with an infinite compassion in his soul. But there was no sign of it on his countenance or in his voice.

"You have but to answer my question, sir, and you shall have your wish. You shall be hanged without further suffering. Why did the Duke torture you, and why did the torture cease when it did? To what importunities did you yield?"

"Already you have guessed it, my lord. That is why you use me so! But it is not just. As God's my witness, it is not just. What am I but a poor man caught in the toils of the evil desires of others? As long as God gave me the strength to resist, I resisted. But I could bear no more. There was no price at which I would not have purchased respite from that horror. Death I could have borne had that been all they threatened. But I had reached the end of my endurance of pain. Oh, my lord, if I were a villain there would have been no torture to endure. They offered me bribes, bribes great enough to dazzle a poor man, that would have left me rich for the remainder of my days. When I refused, they threatened me with death unless I did their infamous will. Those threats I defied. Then they subjected me to this protracted agony which the Duke impiously calls his Lent. They drew my teeth, brutally with unutterable violence, two each day until all were gone. Broken and most starved as I was, distracted by pain, which for a fortnight had been unceasing, they began upon my fingernails. But when they tore the nail from my left thumb, I could bear no more. I yielded to their infamy."

Bellarion made a sign to the men, and they pulled Mombelli to his feet. But his eyes dared not meet the terrible glance of Bellarion.

"You yielded to their demands that, under the pretence of curing him, you should poison my Lord Facino. That is the thing to which you yielded. But when you say 'they' whom do you mean?"

"The Duke Gian Maria and Antonio della Torre."

Bellarion remembered Venegono's warning —"He is a thing of venom, like the emblem of his house."

"Poor wretch!" said Bellarion. "You deserve some mercy, and you shall have it, provided you can undo what you have done."

"Alas, my lord!" Mombelli groaned, wringing his hands in a passion of despair. "Alas! There is no antidote to that poison. It works slowly gradually corroding the intestines. Hang me, my lord, and have done. Had I been less of a coward, I would have hanged myself before I did this thing. But the Duke threatened that if I failed him the torture should be resumed and continued until I died of sheer exhaustion. Also he swore that my refusal would not save my Lord Facino, whom he would find other means of despatching."

Bellarion stood between loathing and compassion. But there was no thought in his mind of hanging this poor wretch, who had been the victim of that malignant Duke.

He uttered an order in cold, level tones: "Restore him his garments and place him in confinement until I send for him again."

On that he departed from that underground chamber, and slowly, thoughtfully made his way above.

By the time he reached the courtyard his resolve was taken, though his neck should pay for it: Gian Maria should not escape. For the first and only time in those adventurous years of his did he swerve from the purpose by which he laid his course, and turn his hand to a task that was not more or less directly concerned with its ultimate fulfilment.

And so, without pausing for rest or food, you behold him once more in the saddle, riding hard for Milan on that Monday afternoon.

He conceived that he bore thither the first news of Facino's moribund condition.

But rumour had been ahead of him by a day and a half, and the rumour ran, not that Facino was dying, but that he was already dead.

In all the instances history affords of poetic justice to give pause to those who offend against God and Man, none is more arresting than that of the fate of Gian Maria Visconti. Already on the previous Friday word had reached the Duke, not only from Mombelli, but from at least one of the spies he had placed in his brother's household, that the work of poisoning was done and that Facino's hours were numbered. Gloating with della Torre and Lonate over the assurance that at last the ducal neck was delivered from that stern heel under which so long it had writhed like the serpent of evil under the heel of Saint Michael, Gian Maria had been unable to keep the knowledge to himself. About the court on that same Friday night he spoke unguardedly of Facino as dead or dying, and from the court the news filtered through to the city and was known to all by the morning of Saturday. And that news carried with it a dismay more utter and overwhelming than any that had yet descended upon Milan since Gian Maria had worn the ducal crown. Facino, when wielding the authority of ducal governor, had been the people's bulwark against the extortions, brutalities, and criminal follies of their Duke. When absent and deposed from power, he had still been their hope, and they had possessed their souls as best they could against the day of his return, which they knew must dawn. But Facino dead meant an unbridling of the Duke's bestiality, a free charter to his misrule, and for his people an outlook of utter hopelessness. It may be that they exaggerated in their own minds this calamity. It was for them the end of the world. Despair settled that morning upon the city. The Duke would have laughed if it had been reported to him, because he lacked the wit to perceive that when men are truly desperate catastrophes ensue.

And at once, whilst the great mass of the people were stricken by horror into a dull inertia, there were those who saw that the situation called for action. Of these were members of the leading Ghibelline families of Bagio, of del Maino, Trivulzi, Aliprandi, and others. There was that Bertino Mantegazza, captain of the ducal guard whose face the Duke had one day broken with his iron gauntlet, and fiercest and most zealous of all there was that Giovanni Pusterla of Venegono, whose family had suffered such deep and bitter wrongs at the Duke's hands.

There was no suspicion in the mind of any that the Duke himself was responsible for the death of Facino. It was simply that Facino's death created a situation only to be met by the destruction of the Duke. And this situation the Duke himself had

been at such hideous pains to bring about.

And so, briefly to recapitulate here a page of Visconti history, it came to pass that on the Monday morning, which was the first day of the Litany of May, as Gian Maria, gaily clad in his colours of red and white, was issuing from his bedroom to repair to Mass in the Church of Saint Gothard, he found in the antechamber a score of gentlemen not latterly seen about his court. Mantegazza, who had command of the entrance, was responsible for their presence.

Before the Duke could comment upon this unusual attendance, perhaps before he had well observed it, three of them were upon him.

"This from the Pusterla!" cried Venegono, and with his dagger clove the Duke's brow, slaying him instantly. Yet before he fell Andrea Bagio's blade was buried in his right thigh, so that presently that white-stockinged leg was as red as its fellow.

As a consequence, Bellarion reaching Milan at dusk that evening found entrance denied him at the Ticinese Gate, which was held by Paolo del Bagio with a strong following of men-at-arms. Not until he had disclosed himself for Facino's lieutenant was he admitted and informed of what had taken place.

The irony of the event provoked in him a terrible mirth.

"Poor purblind fool," was his comment. "He never guessed when he was torturing Mombelli that he was signing his own death-warrant." That, and the laugh with which he rode on into the city, left Bagio wondering whether his wits had turned.

He rode through streets in uproar, where almost every man he met was armed. Before the broken door of a half-shattered house hung some revolting bleeding rags, what once had been a

man. These were all that remained of Squarcia Giramo, the infamous kennel-master who had been torn into pieces that day by the mob, and finally hung there before his dwelling which on the morrow was to be razed to the ground.

He came to the Old Broletto and the Church of Saint Gothard, and paused there to survey the Duke's body where it lay under an apronful of roses which had been cast upon it by a harlot. Thence he repaired to the stables of the palace, and by making himself known procured a fresh horse. On this he made his way through the ever-increasing tumult of the streets, back to the Ticinese Gate, and he was away through the darkness to cover for the second time that day the twenty miles that lie between Milan and Pavia.

It was past midnight when, so jaded that he kept his feet by a sheer effort of the will, he staggered into Filippo Maria's bedchamber, ushered by the servant who had preceded him to rouse the Prince.

Filippo Maria sat up in bed, blinking in the candlelight, at that tall, swaying figure that was almost entirely clothed in mud.

"Is that you, Lord Bellarion? You will have heard that Facino is dead—God rest his soul!"

A harsh, croaking voice made him answer: "Aye, and avenged, Lord Duke."

A quiver crossed the pale fat face under its sleek black cap of hair. The coarse lips parted. "Lord . . . Lord Duke . . . you said?" The high-pitched voice was awe-stricken.

"Your brother Gian Maria is dead, my lord, and you are Duke of Milan."

"Duke of Milan? I am. . . ?" The grotesque young face showed bewilderment, confusion, fear. "And Gian Maria . . . Dead, do you say?"

Bellarion did not mince matters. "He was despatched to hell this morning by some gentlemen in Milan."

"Jesus-Mary!" croaked the Prince, and fell to trembling. "Murdered . . . And you. . . ?" He heaved himself higher in the bed with one arm, whilst he flung out the other in accusation. He did not love his brother. He profited greatly by his death. But a Visconti does not permit that others shall lay hands on a Visconti.

Bellarion laughed oddly. He had been forestalled. Perhaps it was as well. No need now to speak of his intentions.

"He was slain on his way to Mass this morning, at just about the hour that I arrived here from Bergamo."

The accusing arm fell heavily to the Prince's obese flank. The beady, lacklustre eyes still peered at the young condottiero.

"Almost I thought . . . And Giannino is dead . . . murdered! God rest him!" The phrase was mechanical. "Tell me about it."

Bellarion recited what he knew, then staggered out, on the arm of the servant who was to conduct him to the room prepared for him.

"What a world! What a dunghill!" he muttered as he went. "And how well the old abbot knows it. *Pax multa in cella, foris autem plurima bella!*"

Chapter VI

The Inheritance

Facino Cane, Count of Biandrate, Lord of Novara, Dertona, Varese, Rosate, Valsassina, and of all the lands on Lake Maggiore as far as Vogogna, was buried with great pomp in the Church of San Pietro in Ciel d'Oro.

His chief mourners were his captains summoned from Bergamo to do that last honour to their departed leader. At their head, as mourner in chief, walked Facino's adoptive son Bellarion Cane, Count of Gavi. The others included Francesco Busone of Carmagnola, Giorgio Valperga, Nicolino Marsalia, Werner von Stoffel, and Vaugeois the Burgundian.

Koenigshofen and the Piedmontese Giasone Trotta were absent, having remained at Bergamo with the army.

Thereafter the captains assembled in the Hall of Mirrors to hear the will and last instructions of Facino. To read them came

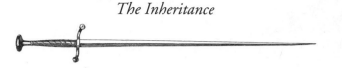

Facino's secretary, accompanied by the Pavese notary who had drawn up the testament three days ago. Thither also came the Countess robed entirely in black and heavily veiled.

The rich and important fief of Valsassina was now disclosed to have been left by Facino to his adoptive son Bellarion, "in earnest of my love and to recompense his loyalty and worth." Apart from that and a legacy in money for Carmagnola, the whole of his vast territorial possessions of cities, lands, and fortresses—mostly acquired since he had been deposed in favour of Malatesta—besides the enormous sum of four hundred thousand ducats, were all bequeathed to his widow. He expressed the wish that Bellarion should succeed him in the command of his condotta, and reminding his other captains that strength lies in unity he recommended them to remain united under Bellarion's leadership, at least until the task of restoring order to the duchy should be fulfilled. To his captains also he recommended his widow, putting it upon them to see her firmly established in the dominions he bequeathed to her.

When the reading was done, the captains rose in their places and turned to Madonna Beatrice where she sat like an ebony statue at the table's head. Carmagnola, ever theatrical, ever a man of attitudes, drew his sword with a flourish and laid it on the board.

"Madonna, to you I surrender the authority I held under my Lord Facino, and I leave it in your hands until such time as it shall please you to reinvest me in it."

The ceremonious gesture caught the fancy of the others. Valperga followed the example instantly, and presently five swords lay naked on the oak. To these, Bellarion, after a moment, a little scornful of this ritual, as he was of all unnecessary displays, added his own.

The Countess rose. She thanked them in a voice that shook with emotion, and one by one restored their weapons to them, naming each as she did so. Bellarion's, however, she left upon the board, wherefore Bellarion, wondering a little, remained when she dismissed the others.

Slowly then she resumed her seat. Slowly she raised and threw back her veil, disclosing a face, which beyond a deeper pallor resulting, perhaps, from contrast with her sable raiment, showed little trace of grief. Her feline eyes considered him, a little frown between their fine black brows.

"You were the last to offer me that homage, Bellarion." Her voice was slow and softly attuned. "Why did you hesitate? Are you reluctant?"

"It was a gesture, madonna, that becomes the Carmagnolas of this world. Sincerity requires no symbols, and it was only at the symbol that I boggled. My service and my life are unreservedly at your command."

There was a pause. Her eyes continued to ponder him. "Take up your sword," she said at last.

He moved to do so, and then checked. "Yourself you restored theirs to the others."

"The others are not as you. Upon you has fallen the mantle of Facino. How much of that mantle will you wear, Bellarion?"

"As much of it as my lord intended. You have heard his testament, madonna."

"But not your own interpretation of it."

"Have I not said that my life and services are at your command, as my lord, to whom I owe everything, enjoined upon me?"

"Your life and services," she said slowly. Her breast heaved as if in repressed agitation. "That is much to offer, Bellarion. Do you ask nothing in return?"

"I offer these in return for all that I have received already. It is I who make payment, madonna."

Again there was a baffled pause. She sighed heavily. "You make it hard for me, Bellarion." There was a pathetic break in her voice.

"What do I make hard?"

She rose, and in evident timidity came to stand before him. She set a white hand on the black velvet sleeve of his tunic. Her lovely face, with which time had dealt so mercifully, was up-turned to his, and there was now no arrogance in its lines or in her glance. She spoke quietly, wistfully.

"You may think, Bellarion, that with my lord scarce buried this is not the hour for . . . what I have to say. And yet, by the very fact of my lord's death and by the very terms of his testament, this is the hour, because it must be the hour of decision. Here and now we must determine what is to follow."

Tall and coldly stern he stood, looking down upon her who swayed a little there, so close to him that his nostrils were invaded by the subtle essences she used.

"I await your commands, madonna."

"My commands? My commands? Dear God! What commands have I for you?" She looked away for an instant, then brought her eyes back to his face and her other hand to his other sleeve, so that she held him completely captive now. A faint colour stirred in the pale cheeks. "My lord has left me great possessions.

They might serve as a footstool to help you mount to a great destiny."

A little smile hovered about his lips as he looked down upon her who waited so breathlessly, her breast now touching his own.

"You are offering me . . ." he said, and stopped.

"Can you be in doubt of what I am offering? It is the hour of great decisions, Bellarion, for me and for you." Closer she pressed, so that her weight was against him. She was deathly pale again, her eyes were veiled. "In unity is strength. That was Facino's last reminder to us. And in what unity could there be greater strength than in ours? Facino's army, the strongest that ever followed him, is solidly behind us so that we stand together. With that and my resources you need set no bounds to your ambition. You may be Duke of Milan if you will. You may even realise Galeazzo's dream and make yourself King of Italy."

His hovering smile settled and deepened. But the dark eyes grew sad.

"The world and you have never suspected," he said gently, "that I am not really ambitious. You have witnessed my rise in four short years from a poor nameless, starveling scholar to knighthood, lordships, wealth, and fame; and, therefore, you imagine that I am one who has striven for the bounties of Fortune. It is not so, madonna. I have laboured for ends that are nowise bound up with the hope of any of these rewards, which I hold cheap. They are hollow vanities, empty bubbles, gewgaws to delight the children of the world. Possessions come to me, titles, honours, which deceive me no more than I desired them."

She drew away from him a little, and looked at him almost in awe. "God! You talk like a monk!"

"It is possible that I think like one, and very natural remembering how I was nurtured. There is one task, one purpose which has detained me in this world of men. When that is accomplished, I think I shall go back to the cell where there is peace."

"You!" Her hands had fallen from his arms. She gasped now in her amazement. "With the world at your feet if you choose! To renounce all? To go back to the chill loneliness and joylessness of monkhood? Bellarion, you are mad."

"Or else sane, madonna. Who shall judge?"

"And love, Bellarion? Is there no love in the world? Does that not lend reality to all these things that you deem shams?"

"Does it heal the vanity of the world?" he cried. "It is a great power, as I perceive. For love men will go mad, they will become beasts: they will murder and betray."

"Heretic!"

That startled him a little. Once before he had been dubbed heretic for beliefs to which he clung with assurance; and experience had come to lay bare his heresy to his own eyes.

"Upon occasion, madonna, we have talked of love, you and I. Had I given heed, had your beauty beglamoured me, what a treacherous thing should I not have been in Facino's eyes! Do you wonder that I mistrust love as I mistrust all else the world can offer me?"

"While Facino lived, that . . ." She broke off. Her eyes were on the ground, her hands now folded in her lap. She had drawn away from him a little and leaned against the table's edge. "Now . . ." She parted her hands and held them out, leaving him to guess her mind.

"Now his behests are upon me, and they shall be obeyed as if he still lived."

"What is there in his behests against . . . against what I was offering? Am I not commended to you by his testament? Am I not a part of his legacy to you?"

"The service of you is; and your loyal servant, madonna, you shall ever find me." She turned aside with a little gesture of irritation, and remained silent, thoughtful.

A sleek secretary broke in upon them. The Count of Pavia commanded the Lord Bellarion's presence in the library. A courier had just arrived from Milan with grave news.

"Say to his highness that I come."

The secretary withdrew.

"You give me leave, madonna?"

She stood leaning sideways against the heavy table, her face averted. "Aye, you may go." Her voice rasped.

But he waited yet a moment. "The sword, madonna? Will you not arm me with your own hands for your service?"

She turned her head to look at him again, and there was now a curl of disdain on her pale lips.

"I thought you looked askance on symbols. Was not that your profession?" She paused, but, without waiting for his answer, added: "Take up your sword, yourself, you that are so fully master of your own destinies."

And on that she turned and went, trailing her funereal draperies over the gay mosaics of that patterned floor.

He remained where she left him until she had passed out of that great hall and the door had closed. Then, at last, he fetched a sigh and went to restore his blade to its scabbard.

His thoughts were on Facino hardly cold in the grave, on this

widow who had so shamelessly wooed him, yet in terms which demanded as a condition the satisfaction of her inordinate ambition; and lastly on that obese young Prince who waited for him. And in the mirror of his mind he saw a reflection of a scene now some months old. He saw again the glance of those beady, lecherous eyes lambent about Facino's Countess.

Inspiration came to him of how best he might gratify her vast ambition, her greed of greatness. Her suggestion to him had been that he should make her Duchess of Milan, and Duchess of Milan he would make her yet.

On that half-ironic thought he came to the library where the Prince waited. Filippo Maria was seated at a table near one of the windows. Spread before him were some parchments, writing-materials, and a horn of unicorn that was almost a yard long, of solid ivory, one of the library's most treasured possessions.

The Prince was more than usually pallid, his glance unsteady, his manner nervous and agitated. Perfunctorily he made the inquiries concerning the obsequies of Facino which courtesy demanded. He reiterated excuses already made for his own absence from the ceremony, an absence really based on resentment of the yoke which Facino had imposed upon him. That done, he picked up a parchment from the table.

"Here's news," he said, and his voice trembled. "Estorre Visconti has been created Duke of Milan." He paused, and the little dark eyes blinked up at the tall Bellarion standing composed at his side. "You knew already?"

"Not so, highness."

"And you show no surprise?"

"It is a bold step, and it may cost Messer Estorre his head.

But it was to be expected from what had gone before."

The beady eyes returned to the parchment, which shook in the podgy fingers.

"Fra Berto Caccia, the Bishop of Piacenza, preached a sermon to the people lauding the murder of my brother, and promising in Estorre's name a Golden Age for Milan, with immunity from taxation. Thereupon they laid at his bastard feet the keys of the city, the standard of the republic, and the ducal sceptre." He dropped the parchment, and sat back folding plump, white hands across his paunch. "This calls for action, speedily."

"We can provide action enough to surfeit Messer Estorre."

"Ha!" The great flabby face grew almost kindly, the little eyes beamed upon the condottiero. "Serve me well in this, Bellarion, and you shall know gratitude."

Bellarion's gesture seemed to wave the notion of reward aside. He came straight to facts. "We can withdraw eight thousand men from Bergamo. The place is at the point of surrender, and four thousand will well suffice to tighten the last grip upon the Malatesta vitals. Perhaps the Lord Estorre has not included that in his calculations. With eight thousand men we can sweep him out of Milan at our pleasure."

"And you'll give orders? You'll give orders at once? The army, they tell me, is now in your control. Facino's authority has descended to you, and has been accepted by your brother captains."

And now this arch-dissembler went to work.

"Hardly so much, highness. Facino's captains have sworn fealty, not to me, but to the Lady Beatrice."

"But . . . But you, then?" The news dismayed him a little. "What place is yours?"

"At your highness's side, if your highness commands me."

"Yes, yes. But whom do you command? Where, exactly, do you stand now?"

"At the head of the army in any enterprise into which the Countess sends her captains."

"The Countess?" The Prince shifted his bulk uneasily in his chair, slewing round so as to face the soldier more fully. "What then if . . . What if the Countess should not . . ." He waved his fat hands helplessly.

"It is not likely that the Countess should oppose your own wishes, highness."

"Not likely? But—Lord of Heaven!—it's possible." He heaved himself up, nervous, agitated. "I must know. I must . . . I'll send for her." He reached for a hand-bell on the table.

But Bellarion's hand closed over his own before he could ring.

"A moment, Lord Prince. Before you send for the Lady Beatrice, had you not best consider precisely what you will say to her?"

"What is to say beyond discovering her disposition towards me."

"Can you entertain a doubt upon that, Lord Prince?" Bellarion was smiling. Their hands came away together from the bell, and fell apart. "Her disposition towards your potency is, to my knowledge, of the very kindliest. Such, indeed, that—I'll be frank with you—I found it necessary once to remind her of her duty to her lord."

"Ah!" The fat pale face quivered into something akin to malevolence. The Prince remembered a sudden coolness in the Countess and her removal to Melegnano, and perceived in this meddler's confession the explanation of it. "By Saint Ambrose, that was bold of you!"

"I am accounted bold," Bellarion reminded him, deeming it necessary.

"Aye, aye!" The shifty eyes fell away uncomfortably under his glance. "But if she is kindly disposed, then . . ."

"I know that she was, highness, and may be rendered so again. Though perhaps less easily now than heretofore."

"Less easily? Why so?"

"As Facino's widow, she is in wealth and power the equal of many a prince in Italy. She has considerable dominions . . ."

"Torn by Facino from the great heritage left by the Duke my father." In that rare burst of indignation his whole bulk quivered like a great jelly.

"They might be restored to the ducal crown by peaceful arts."

"Peaceful arts? What arts? Will you be plain?"

But the time for direct answers was not yet. "And not only has the Countess lands, but the control of a vast fortune. Some four hundred thousand ducats. You will need money, highness, for the pay of this great army now under Bergamo, and your own treasury will hardly supply it. There is taxation. But your highness knows the ills that wait on that for a prince newly come into his own. And not only the lands and money of which your highness stands in need, but the men also does the Countess bring."

"You but repeat yourself."

Bellarion looked at him, and smiled. "Never, do I believe, did a Prince find a bride more richly dowered."

"A bride?" The youth was startled, terrified almost. "A bride?"

"Would less content your highness? Would you be satisfied

to receive the assistance of the Countess's possessions, when you may make them your own and wield them at your pleasure?"

The Prince stared, his jaw fallen. Then slowly he brought his lips together again, and licked them thoughtfully, screwing up his mean eyes.

"You are proposing that I should take to wife Facino's widow, who is twice my age?" He asked the question very slowly, as if pondering each word of it.

Bellarion laughed. "Not proposing it, highness. It is not for me to make such proposals. I do not even know what the lady will say. But if she is willing to become Duchess of Milan, she can provide the means to make you Duke."

Filippo Maria sat down suddenly. The sweat broke from his pale brow. He mopped it with his hand, disturbing the black fringe that disfigured it. Then, lost in thought, he stroked the loose folds of his enormous chin, and gradually his eyes kindled.

At long length he put forth his hand again to the bell. This time Bellarion did not interfere. He perceived in the act the young Prince's surrender to the forces of greed and lust which Bellarion himself had loosed against him.

He took his leave, and went out with the sad knowledge that greed and wantonness would make of the woman, too, a ready prey.

His work was done. She should have the thing she coveted, and find in it her punishment . . .

Chapter VII

Prince of Valsassina

As Bellarion had calculated and disposed, so things fell out, and Filippo Maria Visconti in the twenty-second year of his age led to the altar the widowed Countess of Biandrate who was thirty-nine. As a young girl, she had married, at the bidding of ambition, a man who was twenty years her senior; as a middle-aged woman now, and for the same reason, she married one who was almost as much her junior. She had not the foresight to perceive that the grievance on the score of disparity of years which she had nursed against Facino would be nursed against herself to her ultimate destruction by this sly, furtive, and cruel Prince to whom now she gave herself and her vast possessions. That, however, is no part of the story I have set myself to tell.

Estorre Visconti defended in vain his usurped dominion against Gian Maria's legitimate successor. Filippo Maria, with

Carmagnola in command of some seven thousand men, laid siege to Milan, whilst Bellarion went north to make an end of the Bergamo resistance. Because in haste to have done, he granted Malatesta easy terms of surrender, permitting him to ride out of the city with the honours of war, lance on thigh. Thereafter, having restored order in Bergamo and left there a strong garrison under an officer of trust, he marched with the main army to join Filippo Maria who was conducting operations from the mills on Monte Lupario, three miles from Milan. Some four weeks already had he spent there, with little progress made. Estorre had enrolled and constrained to the defence of the city almost every man of an age to bear arms. It was necessary to make an end, and Bellarion himself with a few followers entered the Castle of Porta Giovia which was being held against Estorre by Vimercati, the castellan. From its walls, having attracted the people by trumpet-blast, he published Filippo Maria's proclamation, wherein the Prince solemnly undertook that if the city were at once surrendered to him it should have nothing to fear; that there should be no pillage, executions, or other measures punitive of this resistance to the State's legitimate lord.

The news flew in every direction, with the result that before nightfall all those whom Estorre had constrained to follow him had fallen away, and he was left with only his mercenaries. With these, next morning, he hacked a way out through the Comasina Gate as the people were throwing open to the new Duke the gates of the city on the other side.

Filippo Maria entered with a comparatively small following and in the wake of a train of bread-carts sent ahead to relieve the famine which already was beginning to press upon the inhabitants. The acclamations of "Live the Duke!" quieted his natural timidity as he rode through the streets to shut himself up in the Castle of Porta Giovia, which remained ever afterwards his residence. Not for Filippo Maria the Palace of the Old Broletto or the gaiety of courts. His dark, scheming, yet pusillanimous nature craved the security of a stronghold.

For assisting him to the ducal throne, and no doubt to ensure their continued support, he rewarded his captains generously, and none more generously than Bellarion to whom he considered that he owed everything. Bellarion was not only confirmed in the lordship of Valsassina in feud, for himself and his heirs forever, but the Duke raised the fief into a principality.

Bellarion remained the Duke's marshal in chief and military adviser, and it was by the dispositions which he made during that summer and autumn of 1412 that the lands of the duchy were finally cleared of the insurgent brigands who had renewed their depredations.

Peace being restored at home, and industry being liberated at last from the trammels that had lain upon it since the death of Gian Galeazzo, prosperity flowed swiftly back to the State of Milan, and the people heaped blessings upon the shy, furtive ruler of whom they saw so little.

It is possible that Filippo Maria would have been content to rest for the present upon what was done, to leave the frontiers of the duchy as he found them, and to dismiss the greater part of the costly condottas in his employ. But Bellarion at his elbow goaded him to further enterprise, and met his sluggish reluctance with a culminating argument that shamed him into action.

"Will you leave, in tranquil possession, the brigands who have encroached upon the glorious patrimony built up by your illustrious father? Will you dishonour his memory and be false to your name, Lord Duke?"

Thus, and similarly, Bellarion, with a heat that was purely histrionic. He cared no more for the integrity of Gian Galeazzo's patrimony than he cared for that of the Kingdom of England. What he cared for was that the order to dispossess those tyrants would sound the knell of Theodore of Montferrat. Thus, at last, should he be enabled to complete the service, to which five years ago he had dedicated himself, and to which unfalteringly, if obscurely and tortuously, he had held. Very patiently had he waited for this hour, when, yielding at last to his bold importunities, the Duke summoned a council of the officers of State and the chief condottieri to determine the order in which action should be taken.

At once Bellarion urged that a beginning should be made by recovering Vercelli, than which few strongholds were of more importance to the safety of the duchy.

It provoked a protest from Beccaria, who was the Duke's Minister of State.

"An odd proposal this from you, Lord Bellarion, remembering that it was by your own action in concert with the Count of Biandrate that the Marquis Theodore was placed in possession of Vercelli."

Bellarion crushed him with his logic. "Not odd, sir, natural. Then I was on the other side. And if, being on the other side, I conceived it important that Theodore should hold Vercelli, now that I am opposed to him I conceive it equally important that he should be driven from it."

There was a pause. Filippo Maria, somnolent in his great chair, looked round the group. "What is the military view?" he asked. He had noticed that not one of the captains had voiced an opinion. He was answered now by the burly Koenigshofen.

"I have no views that are not Bellarion's. I have followed him long enough to know that he's a safe man to follow."

Giasone Trotta, uninvited, expressed the same sentiment. Filippo Maria turned to Carmagnola, who sat silent and thoughtful.

"And you, sir?" he asked.

Carmagnola reared his blond head, and Bellarion braced himself for battle. But to his amazement, for once—for the first time in their long association—Carmagnola was on his side.

"I am of Bellarion's mind, magnificent. We who were with my Lord Facino when he made alliance with Theodore of Montferrat know Theodore for a crafty, daring man of boundless ambition. His occupation of Vercelli is a menace to the peace of the duchy."

After that the other captains, Valperga and Marsilio, who had been wavering, threw in their votes, so that the military opinion was solidly unanimous.

Filippo Maria balanced the matter for a moment.

"You are not forgetting, sirs, that for Theodore's good behaviour I have in my hands a precious hostage, in the person of his nephew, the Marquis Gian Giacomo, in whose name Theodore rules. You laugh, Bellarion!"

"That hostage was procured to ensure, not the good faith of Theodore, but the safety of the real Prince of Montferrat. Carmagnola has told your magnificence that Theodore is crafty, daring, and ambitious. It is a part of his ambition to make him-

self absolute sovereign where at present he is no more than Regent. Let your magnificence judge if the thought of harm to the hostage you hold would be a deterrent to him."

A while still they debated. Then Filippo Maria announced that he would take thought and make known his decision when it was reached. On that he dismissed them.

As they went from the council chamber the captains witnessed the phenomenon of a yet closer unity between Bellarion and Carmagnola. The new Prince of Valsassina linked arms with Francesco Busone, and drew him away.

"You will do a service in this matter, Ser Francesco, if you send word to the Lady Valeria and her brother urging them to come at once to Milan and petition the Duke to place Gian Giacomo upon his throne. He is of full age, and only his absence from Montferrat enables Theodore to continue in the Regency."

Carmagnola looked at him suspiciously. "Why do you not send that message, yourself?"

Bellarion shrugged and spread his hands a little. "I have not the confidence of the Princess. A message from me might be mistrusted."

Carmagnola's fine blue eyes pondered him still with that suspicious glance. "What game do you play?" he asked.

"I see that you mistrust me, too."

"I ever have done."

"It's a compliment," said Bellarion.

"If it is, I don't perceive it."

"If you did, you wouldn't pay it. You are direct, Carmagnola; and for that I honour you. I am not direct, and yet you may come to honour me for that too when you understand it, if you ever do. You ask what game I play. A game which began long ago, in which this is the last move. The alliance I brought about between Facino and Theodore was a move in this game; the securing of the person of Gian Giacomo of Montferrat as a hostage was another; to make it possible for Theodore to occupy Vercelli and make himself Lord of Genoa, yet another. My only aim was to unbridle his greed so that he should become a menace to the duchy, against such a day as this, when on the Duke's side it is my duty to advise his definite destruction."

Carmagnola's eyes were wide; amazement overspread his florid handsome face.

"By the bones of Saint Ambrose, you play mighty deep!"

Bellarion smiled. "I am frank with you. I explain myself. It is tedious but necessary so as to conquer your mistrust and procure your cooperation."

"To make me a pawn in this game of yours?"

"That is to describe yourself unflatteringly. Francesco Busone of Carmagnola is no man's pawn."

"No, by God! I am glad you perceive that."

"Should I have explained myself if I did not?" said Bellarion to assure him of a fact of which clearly he was far from sure.

"Tell me why you so schemed and plotted."

Bellarion sighed. "To amuse myself, perhaps. It interests me. Facino said of me that I was a natural strategist. This broader strategy upon the great field of life gives scope to my inclinations." He was thoughtful, chin in hand. "I do not think there is more in it than that." And abruptly he asked: "You'll send that message?"

Carmagnola too considered. There was a dream that he had

dreamed, a game that he could play, making in his turn a pawn of this crafty brother captain who sought to make a pawn of him.

"I'll go to Melegnano in person," he announced.

He went, and there dispelled the fretful suspense in which the Princess Valeria waited for a justice of which she almost despaired.

He dealt in that directness which was the only thing Bellarion found to honour in him. But the directness now was in his manner only.

"Lady, I come to bid you take a hand in your own and your brother's reinstatement. Your petition to the Duke is all that is needed now to persuade him to the step which I have urged; to march against the usurper Theodore and cast him out."

It took her breath away. "You have urged this! You, my lord? Let me send for my brother that he may thank you, that he may know that he has at least one stout brave friend in the world."

"His friend and your servant, madonna." He bore her white hand to his lips, and there were tears in her eyes as she looked upon his bowed handsome head. "My hopes, my plans, my schemes for you are to bear fruit at last."

"Your schemes for me?"

Her brows were knit over her moist dark eyes. He laughed. A jovial, debonair, and laughter-loving gentleman, this Francesco Busone of Carmagnola.

"So as to provide a cause disposing the Duke of Milan to proceed against the Regent Theodore. The hour has come, madonna. It needs but your petition to Filippo Maria, and the army marches. So that I command it, I will see justice done to your brother."

"So that you command it? Who else should?"

Carmagnola's bright face was overcast. "There is Bellarion Cane."

"That knave!" She recoiled, her countenance troubled. "He is the Regent's man. It was he who helped the Regent to Vercelli and to the lordship of Genoa."

"Which he never could have done," Carmagnola assured her, "but that I abetted him. I saw that thus I should provide a reason for action against the Regent when later I should come to be on the Duke's side."

"Ah! That was shrewd! To feed his ambition until he over-reached himself."

Carmagnola strutted a little. "It was a deep game. But we are at the last move in it. If you mistrust this Bellarion . . ."

"Mistrust him!" She laughed a bitter little laugh, and she poured forth the tale of how once he had been a spy sent by Theodore to embroil her, and how thereafter he had murdered her one true and devoted friend Count Spigno.

Feeding her mistrust and bringing Gian Giacomo fully to share it, Carmagnola conducted them to Milan and procured audience for them with the Duke.

Filippo Maria received her in a small room in the very heart of the fortress, a room to which he had brought something of the atmosphere of his library at Pavia. Here were the choicely bound manuscripts, and the writing-table with its sheaves of parchment, and its horn of unicorn, which as all the world knows is a prophylactic against all manner of ills of the flesh and the spirit. Its double window looked out upon the court of San Donato where the October sunshine warmed the red brick to the colour of the rose.

He gave her a kindly welcome, then settled into the inscrutable inertia of an obese Eastern idol whilst she made her prayer to him.

When it was done he nodded slowly, and despatched his secretary in quest of the Prince of Valsassina. The name conveyed nothing to her, for she had not heard of Bellarion's latest dignity.

"You shall have my decision later, madonna. It is almost made already, and in the direction you desire. When I have conferred with the Prince of Valsassina upon the means at our command, I will send for you again. Meanwhile the Lord of Carmagnola will conduct you and your brother to my Duchess, whom it will delight to care for you." He cleared his throat. "You have leave to go," he added in his shrill voice.

They bowed, and were departing, when the returning secretary, opening the door, and holding up the arras that masked it, announced: "The Prince of Valsassina."

He came in erect and proud of bearing, for all that he still limped a little. His tunic was of black velvet edged with dark brown fur, a heavy gold chain hung upon his breast, a girdle of beaten gold gripped his loins and carried his stout dagger. His hose were in white and blue stripes.

From the threshold he bowed low to the Prince and then to Madonna Valeria, who was staring at him in sudden panic.

She curtsied to him almost despite herself, and then made haste to depart with Carmagnola and her brother. But there was a weight of lead in her breast. If action against Theodore depended upon this man's counsel, what hope remained? She put that question to Carmagnola. He quieted her fears.

"After all, he is not omnipotent. Our fealty is not to him, but to the Duchess Beatrice. Win her to your side, and things will shape the course you desire, especially if I command the enterprise."

And meanwhile this man whom she mistrusted was closeted with the Duke, and the Duke was informing him of this new factor in their plans against Montferrat.

"She desires us to break a lance in her brother's behalf. But Montferrat is loyal to Theodore. They have no opinion there of Gian Giacomo, and to impose by force of arms a prince upon a people is perhaps to render that people hostile to ourselves."

"If that were so, and I confess that I do not share your potency's apprehensions, it would still be the course I should presume to advise. In Theodore you have a neighbour whom ambition makes dangerous. In Gian Giacomo you have a mild and gentle youth, whose thoughts, since his conversion from debauchery, turn rather to religion than to deeds of arms. Place him upon the throne of his fathers, and you have in such a man not only a friendly neighbour but a grateful servant."

"Ha! You believe in gratitude, Bellarion?"

"I must, since I practise it."

There followed that night a council of the captains, and since they were still nominally regarded as in the service of Facino's widow, the Duchess herself attended it, and since the fortunes of the legitimate ruler of Montferrat was one of the issues, the Marquis Gian Giacomo and his sister were also invited to be present.

The Duke, at the head of the long table, with the Duchess on his right and Bellarion on his left, made known the intention to declare war immediately upon the Regent of Montferrat upon two grounds: his occupation of the Milanese stronghold and lands of Vercelli, and his usurpation of the regency beyond the Marquis Gian Giacomo's attainment of full age. Of his captains now he desired an account of the means at their disposal, and afterwards a decision of those to be employed in the undertaking.

Carmagnola came prepared with a computation of the probable forces which Theodore could levy; and they were considerable; not less than five thousand men. The necessary force to deal with him was next debated, having regard also to certain other enterprises to which Milan was elsewhere committed. At length this was fixed by Bellarion. It was to consist of the Germans under Koenigshofen, Stoffel's Swiss, Giasone Trotta's Italian mercenaries, and Marsilio's condotta, amounting in all to some seven thousand men. That would leave free for other eventualities the condottas of Valperga and of Carmagnola with whom were Ercole Belluno and Ugolino da Tenda.

Against this, and on the plea that the Duke might require the services of the Prince of Valsassina at home, Carmagnola begged that the enterprise against Montferrat should be confided to his leadership, his own condotta taking the place of Bellarion's, but all else remaining as Bellarion disposed.

The Duke, showing in his pale face no sign of his surprise at this request, looked from Carmagnola to Bellarion, appearing to ponder, what time the Princess Valeria held her breath.

At length the Duke spoke. "Have you anything to say to that, Valsassina?"

"Nothing if your highness is content. You will remember that Theodore of Montferrat is one of the most skilful captains of the day, and if this business is not to drag on unduly, indeed if it is to be brought to a successful issue, you would do well to send against

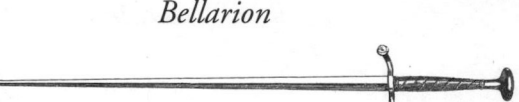

him of your best."

A sly smile broke upon that sinisterly placid countenance.

"By which you mean yourself."

"For my part," said Koenigshofen, "I do not willingly march under another."

"And for mine," said Stoffel, "whilst Bellarion lives I do not march under another at all."

The Duke looked at Carmagnola. "You hear, sir?"

Carmagnola flushed uncomfortably. "I had set my heart upon the enterprise, Lord Duke."

The Princess Valeria interposed. "By your leave, highness, does my vote count for anything in this matter?"

"Assuredly, madonna. Your own and your brother's."

"Then, Lord Duke, my vote, indeed my prayer, is that my Lord of Carmagnola be given the command."

The Duchess raised her long eyes to look at her in wonder.

Bellarion sat inscrutable.

The request wounded without surprising him. He knew her unconquerable mistrust of him. He had hoped in the end which was now approaching to prove to her its cruel injustice. But if occasion for that were denied him, it would be no great matter. What signified was that her own aims should be accomplished, and, after all, they were not beyond the strength and skill of Carmagnola, who had his talents as a leader when all was said.

The Duke's lacklustre eyes were steadily upon Valeria. He spoke after a pause.

"Almost you imply a doubt of the Prince of Valsassina's capacity."

"Not of his capacity. Oh, not of that!"

"Of what, then?"

The question troubled her. She looked at her brother, and her brother answered for her.

"My sister remembers that the Prince of Valsassina was once the Marquis Theodore's friend."

"Was he so? When was that?" The Duke looked at Bellarion, but it was Gian Giacomo who answered the question.

"When, in alliance with him, he placed him in possession of Vercelli and Genoa."

"The alliance was the Lord Facino's, not Valsassina's. Bellarion served under him. But so also did Carmagnola. Where is the difference between them?"

"My Lord of Carmagnola acted then with a view to my brother's ultimate service," the Princess answered. "If he was a party to the Marquis Theodore's occupation of Vercelli, it was only so that in that act the Marquis might provide a cause for the action that is now proposed against him by the Duke of Milan."

Bellarion laughed softly at the light he suddenly perceived.

"Do you mock that statement, sir?" Carmagnola challenged him. "Do you dare to say what was in my mind at the time?"

"I have honoured you for directness, Carmagnola. But it seems you can be subtle too."

"Subtle!" Carmagnola flushed indignantly. "In what have I been subtle?"

"In the spirit in which you favoured Theodore's occupation of Vercelli," said Bellarion, and so left him gaping foolishly. "What else did you think I had in mind?" He smiled almost ingenuously into the other's face.

The Duke rapped the table. "Sirs, sirs! We wander. And there

461

is this matter to resolve."

Bellarion answered him.

"Here, then, is a solution your highness may be disposed to adopt. Instead of Valperga and his troops, I take with me Carmagnola and his own condotta which is of a similar strength, and, like Valperga's, mainly horse. Thus we march together, and share the enterprise."

"But unless Bellarion commands it, Lord Duke, your highness will graciously consider sending another condotta in the place of mine," said Koenigshofen, and Stoffel was about to add his own voice to that, when the Duke losing patience broke in.

"Peace! Peace! I am Duke of Milan, and I give orders here. You are summoned to advise, not to browbeat me and say what you will and will not do. Let it be done as Valsassina says, since Carmagnola has set his heart upon being in the campaign. But Valsassina leads the enterprise. The matter is closed on that. You have leave to go."

Chapter VIII

Carmagnola's Bridges

Dissensions at the very outset between Carmagnola and Bellarion protracted by some days the preparations for the departure of the army. This enabled Theodore of Montferrat fully to make his dispositions for resistance, to pack the granaries of Vercelli and otherwise victual it for a siege, and to increase the strong body of troops already under his hand, with which he threw himself into the menaced city. Further, by working furiously during those October days, he was enabled to strengthen his bastions and throw up fresh earthworks, from which to shatter the onslaught when it should come.

Upon these very circumstances of which Bellarion and his captains were duly informed followed fresh dissensions. Carmagnola advocated that operations should be begun by the reduction of Mortara, which was being held for Theodore, and

which, if not seized before they marched upon Vercelli, would constitute, he argued, a menace upon their rear. Bellarion's view was that the menace was not sufficiently serious to merit attention; that whilst they were reducing it, Theodore would further be strengthening himself at Vercelli; and that, in short, they should march straight upon Vercelli, depending that, when they forced it to a capitulation, Mortara would thereby be scared into immediate surrender.

Of the captains some held one view, some the other. Koenigshofen, Stoffel, and Trotta took sides with Bellarion. Ercole Belluno, who commanded the foot in Carmagnola's condotta, took sides with his leader as did also Ugolino da Tenda who captained a thousand horse. Yet Bellarion would have overruled them but for the Princess Valeria who with her brother entered now into all their councils.

These were on the side of Carmagnola. Hence a compromise was effected. A detachment under Koenigshofen including Trotta's troops was to go against Mortara, to cover the rear of the main army proceeding to Vercelli.

To Vercelli that army, now not more than some four thousand strong, yet strong enough in Bellarion's view for the task in hand, made at last a speedy advance. But at Borgo Vercelli they were brought to a halt by the fact that Theodore had blown up the bridge over the Sesia, leaving that broad, deep, swift-flowing river between the enemy and the city which was their goal.

At Carpignano, twenty miles higher up, there was a bridge which Bellarion ascertained had been left standing. He announced that they must avail themselves of that.

"Twenty miles there, and twenty miles back!" snorted

Carmagnola. "It is too much. A weariness and a labour."

"I'll not dispute it. But the alternative is to go by way of Casale, which is even farther."

"The alternative," Carmagnola answered, "is to bridge the Sesia and the Cerva above their junction where the streams are narrower. Our lines of communication with the army at Mortara should be as short as possible."

"You begin to perceive one of the disadvantages of having left that army at Mortara."

"It is no disadvantage if we make proper provision."

"And you think that your bridges will afford that provision." Bellarion's manner was almost supercilious.

Carmagnola resented it. "Can you deny it?"

"I can do more. I can foresee what will happen. Sometimes, Francesco, you leave me wondering where you learnt the art of war, or how ever you came to engage in it."

They held their discussion in the kitchen of a peasant's house which for the Princess Valeria's sake they had invaded. And the Princess and her brother were its only witnesses. When Carmagnola now moved wrathfully in great strides about the dingy chamber, stamping upon the earthen floor and waving his arms as he began to storm, one of those witnesses became an actor to calm him. The Princess Valeria laid a hand upon one of those waving arms in its gorgeous sleeve of gold-embroidered scarlet.

"Do not heed his taunts, Messer Carmagnola. You have my utter trust and confidence. It is my wish that you should build your bridges."

Bellarion tilted his chin to look at her between anger and amusement.

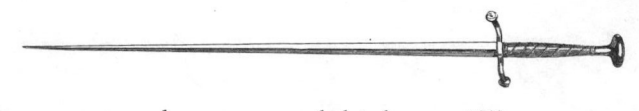

"If you are to take command, highness, I'll say no more." He bowed, and went out.

"One of these days I shall give that upstart dog a lesson in good manners," said Carmagnola between his teeth.

The Princess shook her head.

"It is not his manners, sir, that trouble me; but his possible aims. If I could trust him . . ."

"If you could trust his loyalty, you should still mistrust his skill."

"Yet he has won great repute as a soldier," put in Gian Giacomo, who instinctively mistrusted the thrasonical airs of the swaggering Carmagnola, and mistrusted still more his fawning manner towards Valeria.

"He has been fortunate," Carmagnola answered, "and his good fortune has gone to his head."

Meanwhile Bellarion went straight from that interview to despatch Werner von Stoffel with five hundred arbalesters and six hundred horse to Carpignano.

There was a fresh breeze with Carmagnola when the latter discovered this. He demanded to know why it should have been done without previous consultation with himself and the Princess, and Valeria was beside him when he asked the question.

Bellarion's answer was a very full one.

"You will be a week building your bridges. In that time it may occur to Theodore to do what he should have done already, to destroy the bridge at Carpignano."

"And what do I care about the bridge at Carpignano when I shall have bridges of my own here?"

"When you have bridges of your own here, you need not

care. But I have a notion that it will be longer than you think before you have these bridges, and that we may have to go by way of Carpignano in the end."

"I shall have my bridges in a week," said Carmagnola.

Bellarion smiled. "When you have them, and when you have put two thousand men across to hold them, I'll bid Stoffel return from Carpignano."

"But in the meantime . . ."

Bellarion interrupted him, and suddenly he was very stern.

"In the meantime you will remember that I command. Though I may choose to humour you and her highness, as the shortest way to convince you of error, yet I do not undertake to obey you against my better judgment."

"By God, Bellarion!" Carmagnola swore at him. "I'll not have you gay with me. You'll measure your words, or else you'll eat them."

Very coldly Bellarion looked at him, and observed Valeria's white restraining hand which again was upon Carmagnola's sleeve.

"At the moment I have a task in hand to which I belong entirely. While it is doing if you forget that I command, I shall remove you from the army."

He left the swaggerer fuming.

"Only my regard for you, madonna, restrains me," he assured the Princess. "He takes that tone when he should remember that, if it came to blows between us, the majority of the men here would be upon my side, now that he has sent nearly all his own away." He clenched his hands in anger. "Yet for your sake, lady, I must suffer it. There can be no quarrel between his men and mine until we have placed you and your brother in possession of Montferrat."

These and other such professions of staunch selfless loyalty touched her deeply; and in the days that followed, whilst the troopers, toiling like woodmen, were felling trees and building the bridges above the junction of the rivers, Carmagnola and Valeria were constantly together.

She was driven now to the discomfort of living under canvas, sharing the camp life of these rude men of war, and Carmagnola did all in his power to mitigate for her the hardships it entailed, hardships which she bore with a high gay courage. She would go with him daily to watch the half-naked labourers in the river, bundling together whole trees as if they were mere twigs, to serve as pontoons. And daily he gave her cause to admire his skill, his ingenuity, and his military capacity. That Bellarion should have sneered at this was but another proof of Bellarion's worthlessness. Either he could not understand it, or else of treacherous intent he desired to deprive her of its fruits.

Meanwhile Carmagnola beglamoured her with talk of actions past, in all of which he played ever the heroic part. The eyes of her mind were dazzled by the pictures his words drew for her. Now she beheld him leading a knightly charge that shattered an enemy host into shards; now she saw him at the head of an escalade, indomitably climbing enemy walls under a hail of stones and scalding pitch; now she saw him in council, wisely planning the means by which victory might be snatched from overwhelming opposition.

One day when he spoke of these things, as they sat alone watching the men who swarmed like ants about the building of his bridge, he touched a closer note.

"Yet of all the enterprises to which I have set these rude, soldier hands, none has so warmed me as this, for none has been worthier a man's endeavour. It will be a glorious day for me when we set you in your palace at Casale. A glorious day, and yet a bitter."

"A bitter?" Her great dark eyes turned on him in question.

His countenance clouded, his own glance fell away. "Will it not be bitter for me to know this service is at an end; to know that I must go my ways; resume a mercenary's life, and do for hire that which I now do out of . . . enthusiasm and love?"

She shifted her own glance, embarrassed a little.

"Surely you do yourself less than justice. There is great honour and fame in store for you, my lord."

"Honour and fame!" He laughed. "I would gladly leave those to tricksters like Bellarion, who rise to them so easily because no scruples ever deter them. Honour and fame! Let who will have those, so that I may serve where my heart bids me."

Boldly now his hand sought hers. She let it lie in his. Above those pensive, mysterious eyes her fine brows were knit.

"Aye," she breathed, "that is the great service of life! That is the only worthy service—as the heart bids."

His second hand came to recruit the first. Lying almost at her feet, he swung round on his side upon the green earth, looking up at her in a sort of ecstasy. "You think that, too! You help me to self-contempt, madonna."

"To self-contempt? It is the only contempt that you will ever know. But why should you know that?"

"Because all my life, until this moment, I have served for hire. Because, if this adventure had not come to me by God's grace, in such worthless endeavours would my life continue.

Now—now that I know the opinion in which you must hold such service—it is over and done for me. When I shall have served you to your goal, I shall have performed my last."

There fell a long pause between them. At last: "When my brother is crowned in Casale, he will need a servant such as you, Messer Carmagnola."

"Aye, but shall you, madonna? Shall you?"

She looked at him wistfully, smiling a little. He was very handsome, very splendid and very brave, a knight to win a lady's trust, and she was a very lonely, friendless lady in sore need of a stout arm and a gallant heart to help her through the trials of this life.

The tapering fingers of her disengaged hand descended gently upon his golden head.

"Shall I not?" she asked with a little tremulous laugh. "Shall I not?"

"Why, then, madonna, if you will accept my service, it shall be yours for as long as I endure. It shall never be another's. Valeria! My Valeria!"

That hand upon his head, overheating its very indifferent contents, drove him now to an excessive precipitancy.

He carried the hand he held almost fiercely to his lips.

It was withdrawn, gently but firmly as was its fellow. His kiss and the bold use of her name scared her a little.

"Carmagnola, my friend . . ."

"Your friend, and more than your friend, madonna."

"Why, how much more can there be than that?"

"All that a man may be to a woman, my Valeria. I am your knight. I ever have been since that day in the lists at Milan, when you bestowed the palm on me. I joy in this battle that is to be fought for you. I would joy in death for you if it were needed to prove my worship."

"How glibly you say these things! There will have been queens in other lists in which you have borne off the palm. Have you talked so to them?"

"O cruelty!" he cried out like a man in pain. "That you should say this to me! I am swooning at your feet, Valeria, you wonder of the world!"

"My nose, sir, is too long for that!" She mocked him, but with an underlying tenderness; and tenderness there was too in her moist eyes. "You are a whirlwind in your wooing as in the lists. You are reckless, sir."

"Is it a fault? A soldier's fault, then. But I'll be patient if you bid me. I'll be whatsoever you bid me, Valeria. But when we come to Casale . . ."

He paused for words, and she took advantage of that pause to check him.

"It is unlucky to plan upon something not yet achieved, sir. Wait . . . wait until that time arrives."

"And then?" he asked her breathlessly. "And then?"

"Have I not said that to plan is unlucky?"

Boldly he read the converse of that statement. "I'll not tempt fortune, then. I dare not. I will be patient, Valeria."

But he let it appear that his confidence was firm, and she added nothing now to shake it.

And so in ardent wooing whilst he waited for his bridge, Carmagnola spent most of the time that he was not engaged in directing the construction of it. Bellarion in those days sulked like Achilles in his tent, with a copy of Vegetius which he had

brought from Milan in his baggage.

The bridges took, not a week, but eleven days to build. At last, however, on the eve of All Saints', as Fra Serafino tells us, Carmagnola accompanied by Valeria and her brother bore word himself to Bellarion that the bridges were ready and that a party of fifty of his men were encamped on the peninsula between the rivers. He came to demand that Bellarion should so dispose that the army should begin to cross at dawn.

"That," said Bellarion, "assumes that your bridges endure until dawn."

He was standing, where he had risen to receive his visitors, in the middle of his roomy pavilion, which was lighted by a group of three lanterns hung at the height of his head on the tent-pole. The book in which he had been reading was closed upon his forefinger.

"Endure until dawn?" Carmagnola was annoyed by the suggestion. "What do you mean?"

Bellarion's remark had been imprudent. Still more imprudent was the laugh he now uttered.

"Ask yourself who should destroy them," he said. "In your place I should have asked myself that before I went to the trouble of building them."

"How should Theodore know of it, shut up as he is in Vercelli, eight miles away?"

Part of his question was answered on the instant by a demoniac uproar from the strip of land across the water. Cries of rage and terror, shouts of encouragement and command, the sound of blows, and all the unmistakable din of conflict, rose fiercely upon the deepening gloom.

"He knows, it seems," said Bellarion, and again he laughed.

Carmagnola stood a moment, clenching and unclenching his hands, his face white with rage. Then he span round where he stood and with an inarticulate cry dashed from the tent.

One withering glance Valeria flashed into Bellarion's sardonically amused countenance, then, summoning her brother, she followed Carmagnola.

Bellarion set down his book upon the table by the tent-pole, took up a cloak, and followed them at leisure, through the screen of bare trees behind which his pavilion had been pitched, and along the high bank of the swirling river towards the head of Carmagnola's bridge.

There, as he expected, he found them, scarcely visible in the gloom, and with them a knot of men-at-arms and a half-dozen stragglers, all that had escaped of the party that Carmagnola had sent across an hour ago. The others had been surrounded and captured. Last of all to win across, arriving just as Bellarion reached the spot, was Belluno, who had commanded them, an excitable Neapolitan who leapt up the bank from the bridge ranting by all the patrons of Naples that they had been betrayed.

Over the river came a sound of tramping feet. Dimly reflected in the water they could see the forms of men who otherwise moved invisible on the farther bank, and presently came a sound of axes on timber.

"There goes your bridge, Francesco," said Bellarion, and for the third time he laughed.

"Do you mock me, damn you!" Carmagnola raged at him, and then raised his voice to roar for arbalesters. Three or four of the men went off vociferously, at a run, to fetch them, whilst

Valeria turned suddenly upon Bellarion, whose tall cloaked figure stood beside her.

"Why do you laugh?" Her voice, sharp with disdain, resentment, and suspicion, silenced all there that they might hear his answer.

"I am human, I suppose, and, therefore, not entirely without malice."

"Is that all your reason? Is your malice so deep that you can laugh at an enemy advantage which may wreck the labour of days?" And then with increasing sharpness and increasing accusation: "You knew!" she cried. "You knew that the bridges would be destroyed tonight. Yourself, you said so. How did you know? How did you know?"

"What are you implying, madonna?" cried Carmagnola, aghast. For all his hostility towards Bellarion, he was very far from ready to believe that he played a double game.

"That I have no wits," said Bellarion, quietly scornful.

And now the impetuous Belluno, smarting under his own particular misadventure and near escape, must needs cut in.

"Madonna is implying more than that. She is implying that you've sold us to Theodore of Montferrat."

"Are you implying it, too, Belluno?" His tone had changed. There was now in his voice a note that the Princess had never heard, a note that made Belluno's blood run cold. "Speak out, man! Though I give licence for innuendo to a lady, I require clear speech from every man. So let us have this thing quite plainly."

Belluno was brave and obstinate. He conquered his fear of Bellarion sufficiently to make a show of standing his ground.

"It is clear," he answered sullenly, "that we have been betrayed."

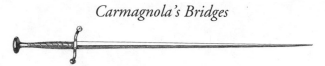

"How is it clear, you fool?" Bellarion shifted again from cold wrath with an insubordinate inferior to argument with a fellow man. "Are you so inept at the trade by which you live that you can conceive of a soldier in the Marquis Theodore's position neglecting to throw out scouts to watch the enemy and report his movements? Are you so much a fool as that? If so, I shall have to think of replacing you in your command."

Carmagnola interposed aggressively; and this partly to protect Belluno who was one of his own lieutenants, and partly because the sneer at the fellow's lack of military foresight was a reflection upon Carmagnola himself.

"Do you pretend that you foresaw this action of Theodore's?"

"I pretend that any but a fool must have foreseen it. It is precisely what any soldier in his place would do: allow you to waste time, material, and energy on building bridges, and then promptly destroy them for you."

"Why, then, did you not say this ten days ago?"

"Why?" Bellarion's voice sounded amused. His face they could not see. "Because I never spend myself in argument with those who learn only by experience."

Again the Princess intervened. "Is that the best reason you can give? You allowed time, material, and energy, and now even a detachment of men to be wasted, merely that you might prove his folly to my Lord of Carmagnola? Is that what you ask us to believe?"

"He thinks us credulous, by God!" swore Carmagnola.

Bellarion kept his patience. "I had another reason, a military one with which it seems that I must shame your wits. To move the whole army from here to Carpignano would have taken me at least two days, perhaps three. A mounted detachment from Vercelli to destroy the bridge could reach Carpignano in a few hours, and once it was seen that I moved my army thither that detachment would have been instantly despatched. It was a movement I feared in any case, until your bridge-building operations here deceived Theodore into believing that I had no thought of Carpignano. That is why I allowed them to continue. Though your bridges could never serve the purpose for which you built them, they could excellently serve to disguise my own intention of crossing at Carpignano. Tomorrow, when the army begins to move thither, that detachment of Theodore's will most certainly be sent to destroy the bridge. But it will find it held by a thousand men under Stoffel, and the probable capture of that detachment will compensate for the loss of men you have suffered tonight."

There was a moment's utter silence when he had done, a silence of defeat and confusion. Then came an applauding splutter of laughter from the group of men and officers who stood about.

It was cut short by a loud crash from across the stream, and, thereafter, with a groaning and rending of timbers, a gurgling of swelling, momentarily arrested waters, and finally a noise like a thunderclap, the wrecked bridge swinging out into the stream snapped from the logs that held it to the northern shore.

"There it goes, Carmagnola," said Bellarion. "But you no longer need bewail your labours. They have served my purpose."

He cast his cloak more tightly about him, wished them goodnight almost gaily, and went striding away towards his pavilion.

Carmagnola, crestfallen, swallowing his chagrin as best he could, stood there in silence beside the equally silenced Princess.

Belluno swore softly, and vented a laugh of some little bitterness.

"He's deep, always deep, by Saint Januarius! Never does he do the things he seems to do. Never does he aim where he looks."

Chapter IX

Vercelli

A letter survives which the Prince of Valsassina wrote some little time after these events to Duke Filippo Maria, in which occurs the following criticism of the captains of his day: "They are stout fellows and great fighters, but rude, unlettered, and lacking culture. Their minds are fertile, vigorous soil, but unbroken by the plough of learning, so that the seeds of knowledge with which they are all too sparsely sown find little root there."

At Carpignano, when they came there three days after breaking camp, they found that all had fallen out as Bellarion calculated. A detachment of horse one hundred strong had been sent in haste with the necessary implements to destroy the bridge. That detachment Stoffel had surrounded, captured, disarmed, and disbanded.

They crossed, and after another three days marching down the right bank of the Sesia they crossed the Cervo just above

Quinto, where Bellarion took up his quarters in the little castle owned there by the Lord Girolamo Prato, who was with Theodore in Vercelli.

Here, too, were housed the Princess and her brother and the Lord of Carmagnola, the latter by now recovered from his humiliation in the matter of his bridges to a state of normal self-complacency and arrogance.

An eighteenth-century French writer on tactics, M. Dévinequi, in his *L'Art Militaire au Moyen Age*, in the course of a lengthy comparison between the methods of Bellarion Cane and the almost equally famous Sir John Hawkwood, offers some strong adverse criticisms upon Bellarion's dispositions in the case of this siege of Vercelli. He considers that as a necessary measure of preparation Bellarion when at Quinto should have thrown bridges across the Sesia above and below the city, so as to maintain unbroken his lines of circumvallation, instead of contenting himself with ferrying a force across to guard the eastern approaches. This force, being cut off by the river, could, says M. Dévinequi, neither be supported at need nor afford support.

What the distinguished French writer has missed is the fact that, once engaged upon it, Bellarion was as little in earnest about the siege of Vercelli as he was about Carmagnola's bridges. The one as much as the other was no more than a strategic demonstration. From the outset—that is to say, from the time when arriving at Quinto he beheld the strong earthworks Theodore had thrown up—he realised that the place was not easily to be carried by assault, and it was within his knowledge that it was too well victualled to succumb to hunger save after a siege more protracted than he himself was prepared to impose upon it.

But there was Carmagnola, swaggering and thrasonical in spite of all that had gone, and there was the Princess Valeria supporting the handsome condottiero with her confidence. And Carmagnola, not content that Bellarion should girdle the city, arguing reasonably enough that months would be entailed in bringing Theodore to surrender from hunger, was loud and insistent in his demands that the place be assaulted. Once again, as in the case of the bridges, Bellarion yielded to the other's overbearing insistence, went even the length of inviting him to plan and conduct the assaults. Three of these were delivered, and all three repulsed with ease by an enemy that appeared to Bellarion to be uncannily prescient. After the third repulse, the same suspicion occurred to Carmagnola, and he expressed it; not, however, to Bellarion, as he should have done, but to the Princess.

"You mean," she said, "that someone on our side is conveying information to Theodore of our intentions?"

They were alone together in the armoury of the Castle of Quinto whose pointed windows overlooked the river. It was normally a bare room with stone walls and a vaulted white ceiling up which crawled a troop of the rampant lions of the Prati crudely frescoed in a dingy red. Bellarion had brought to it some furnishings that made it habitable, and so it became the room they chiefly used.

The Princess sat by the table in a great chair of painted leather, faded but comfortable. She was wrapped in a long blue gown that was lined with lynx fur against the chill weather which had set in. Carmagnola, big and gaudy in a suit of the colour of sulphur, his tunic reversed with black fur, his powerful yet shapely legs booted to the knee, strode to and fro across the room in his excitement.

"It is what I begin to fear," he answered her, and resumed his pacing.

A silence followed, and remained unbroken until he went to plant himself, his feet wide, his hands behind him, before the logs that blazed in the cavernous fireplace.

She looked up and met his glance. "You know what I am thinking," he said. "I am wondering whether you may not be right, after all, in your suspicions."

Gently she shook her head. "I dismissed them on that night when your bridges were destroyed. His vindication was so complete, what followed proved him so right, that I could suspect him no longer. He is just a mercenary fellow, fighting for the hand that pays. I trust him now because he must know that he can win more by loyalty than by treachery."

"Aye," he agreed, "you are right, my Princess. You are always right."

"I was not right in my suspicions of him. So think no more of those."

Standing as he did, he was completely screening the fire from her. She rose and crossed to it, holding out her hands to the blaze when he made room for her beside him.

"I am chilled," she said. "As much, I think, by our want of progress as by these November winds."

"Nay, but take heart, Valeria," he bade her. "The one will last no longer than the other. Spring will follow in the world and in your soul."

She looked up at him, and found him good to look upon, so big and strong, so handsome and so confident.

"It is heartening to have such a man as you for company in such days."

He took her in his arms, a masterful, irresistible fellow.

"With such a woman as you beside me, Valeria, I could conquer the world."

A dry voice broke in upon that rapture: "You might make a beginning by conquering Vercelli."

Starting guiltily apart, they met the mocking eyes of Bellarion who entered. He came forward easily, as handsome in his way as Carmagnola, but cast in a finer, statelier mould. "I should be grateful to you, Francesco, and so would her highness, if you would accomplish that. The world can wait until afterwards."

And Carmagnola, to cover his confusion and Valeria's, plunged headlong into contention.

"I'd reduce Vercelli tomorrow if I had my way."

"Who hinders you?"

"You do. There was that night attack . . ."

"Oh, that!" said Bellarion. "Do you bring that up again? Will you never take my word for anything, I wonder? It is foredoomed to failure."

"Not if conducted as I would have it." He came forward to the table, swaying from the hips in his swaggering walk. He put his finger on the map that was spread there. "If a false attack were made here, on the east, between the city and the river, so as to draw the besieged, a bold, simultaneous attack on the west might carry the walls."

"It might," said Bellarion slowly, and fell to considering. "This is a new thought of yours, this false attack. It has its merits."

"You approve me for once! What condescension!"

Bellarion ignored the interruption. "It also has its dangers. The party making the feint—and it will need to be a strong one or its real purpose will be guessed—might easily be thrust into the river by a determined sally."

"It will not come to that," Carmagnola answered quickly.

"You cannot say so much."

"Why not? The feint will draw the besieged in that direction, but before they can sally they will be recalled by the real attack striking on the other side."

Bellarion pondered again; but finally shook his head. "I have said that it has its merits, and it tempts me. But I will not take the risk."

"The risk of what?" Carmagnola was being exasperated by that quiet, determined opposition. "God's death! Take charge of the feint yourself, if you wish. I'll lead the storming party, and so that you do your part, I'll answer for it that I am inside the town before daybreak and that Theodore will be in my hands."

Valeria had remained with her shoulders to them facing the fire. Bellarion's entrance, discovering her in Carmagnola's arms, had covered her with confusion, filled her with a vexation not only against himself but against Carmagnola also. From this there was no recovery until Camagnola's words came now to promise a conclusion of their troubles far speedier than any she had dared to hope.

"You'll answer for it?" said Bellarion. "And if you fail?"

"I will not fail. You say yourself that it is soundly planned."

"Did I say so much? Surely not. To be frank, I am more

afraid of Theodore of Montferrat than of any captain I've yet opposed."

"Afraid!" said Carmagnola, and sneered.

"Afraid," Bellarion repeated quietly. "I don't charge like a bull. I like to know exactly where I am going."

"In this case, I have told you."

Valeria slowly crossed to them. "Make the endeavour, at least, Lord Prince," she begged him.

He looked from one to the other of them. "Between you, you distract me a little. And you do not learn, which is really sad. Well, have your way, Francesco. The adventure may succeed. But if it fails, do not again attempt to persuade me to any course through which I do not clearly see my way."

Valeria in her thanks was nearer to friendliness than he had ever known since that last night at Casale. Those thanks he received with a certain chill austerity.

It was to be Carmagnola's enterprise, and he left it to Carmagnola to make all the dispositions. The attempt was planned for the following night. It was to take place precisely at midnight, which at that time of year was the seventh hour, and the signal for launching the false attack was to be taken from the clock on San Vittore, one of the few clocks in Italy at that date to strike the hour. After an interval sufficient to allow the defenders to engage on that side, Carmagnola would open the real attack.

Empanoplied in his armour, and carrying his peaked helm in the crook of his arm, Carmagnola went to ask of the Princess a blessing on his enterprise. She broke into expressions of gratitude.

"Do not thank me yet," he said. "Before morning, God help-

ing me, I shall lay the State of Montferrat at your feet. Then I shall ask your thanks."

She flushed under his ardent gaze. "I shall pray for you," she promised him very fervently, and laid a hand upon his steel brassard. He bore it to his lips, bowed stiffly, and clanked out of the room.

Bellarion did not come to seek her. Lightly armed, with no more than back and breast and a steel cap on his head, he led out his men through the night, making a wide detour so that their movements should not be heard in Vercelli. Since mobility was of the first importance, he took with him only a body of some eight hundred horse. They filed along by the river to the east of the city, which loomed there a vast black shadow against the faintly irradiated sky. They took up their station, dismounted, unlimbered the scaling ladders which they had brought for the purposes of their demonstration, and waited.

They were, as Bellarion calculated, close upon the appointed hour when at one point of the line there was a sudden commotion. A man had been caught who had come prowling forward, and who, upon being seized, demanded to be taken at once before their leader.

Roughly they did as he required of them. And there in the dark, for they dared kindle no betraying light, Bellarion learnt that he was a loyal subject of the Duke of Milan who had slipped out of the city to inform them that the Marquis Theodore was advised of their attack and ready to meet it.

Bellarion swore profusely, a rare thing in him who seldom allowed himself to be mastered by his temper. But his fear of Theodore's craft drove him now like a fiery spur. If Theodore was forewarned, who could say what countermeasures Theodore had not prepared? This came of lending ear to that bellowing calf Carmagnola!

Fiercely he gave the order to mount. There was some delay in the dark, and whilst they were still being marshalled the bell of San Vittore tolled the seventh hour. Some moments after that were lost before they were spurring off to warn and withdraw Carmagnola. Even then it was necessary to go cautiously through the dark over ground now sodden by several days of rain.

Before they were halfway round the din of combat burst upon the air.

Theodore had permitted Carmagnola's men to reach and faggot the moat, and even to plant some ladders, before moving. Then he had thrown out his army, in two wings, one from the gate to the north, the other from a gate on the opposite side, and these two wings had swept round to charge Carmagnola in flank and to envelop him.

Two things only saved Carmagnola: in the first place, Theodore's counterattack was prematurely launched, before Carmagnola was sufficiently committed; in the second, Stoffel, taking matters into his own hands, and employing the infantry tactics advocated by Bellarion, drew off his men, and formed them up to receive the charge he heard advancing from the north. That charge cost Theodore a score of piked horses, and it failed to break through the bristling human wall that rose before it in the dark. Having flung the charge back, Stoffel formed his men quickly into the hedgehog, embracing within it all that he could compass of Carmagnola's other detachments, and in this formation proceeded to draw off, intent upon saving all that he could

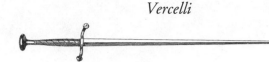

from the disaster that was upon them.

Meanwhile the other battle, issuing from the gate on the south and led by Theodore himself, had crashed into Carmagnola's own body, which Carmagnola and Belluno were vainly seeking to marshal. They might have made an end of that detachment, which comprised the best part of Bellarion's condotta, had not Bellarion with his eight hundred horse at last come up to charge the enemy rear. That was the saving stroke. Caught now between two masses, realising that his counter-surprise had failed, and unable in the dark to attempt a fresh manœuvre, Theodore ordered his trumpeters to sound the retreat.

Each side accounted itself fortunate in being able to retire in good order.

Chapter X

The Arrest

In the armoury of the castle of Quinto, Carmagnola paced like a caged panther, the half of his armour still hanging upon him, his blond head still encased in the close-fitting cap of blood-red velvet that served to protect it from the helmet. And as he paced, he ranted of treachery and other things to Valeria and Gian Giacomo of Montferrat, to the half-dozen captains who had returned to render with him the account of that galling failure.

The Princess occupied the big chair by the table, whilst her brother leaned upon the back of it. Beyond stood ranged Ugolino da Tenda, Ercole Belluno, Stoffel, and three others, their armour flashing in the golden light of the cluster of candles set upon the table. Over by the hearth in another high-backed chair sat Bellarion, still in his black corselet, his long legs in their mud-splashed boots stretched straight before him, his head cased in a

close-fitting cap of peach-coloured velvet, disdainfully listening to Carmagnola's furious tirade. He guessed the bitterness in the soul of the boaster who had promised so much to achieve so little. Therefore he was patient with him for a while. But to all things there must be an end, and an end there was to Bellarion's patience.

"Talking mends nothing, Francesco," he broke in at last.

"It may prevent a repetition."

"There can be no repetition, because there will be no second attempt. I should never have permitted this but that you plagued me with your insistence."

"And I should have succeeded had you done your part!" roared Carmagnola in fury, a vain, humiliated man reckless of where he cast the blame for his own failure. "By God's Life, that is why disaster overtook us. Had you delivered your own attack as was concerted between us, Theodore must have sent a force to meet it."

Bellarion remained calm under the accusation, and under the eyes of that company, all reproachful save Stoffel's. The Swiss, unable to contain himself, laughed aloud.

"If the Lord Bellarion had done that, sir, you might not now be alive. It was his change of plan, and the charge he delivered upon Theodore's rear, that enabled us to extricate ourselves, and so averted a disaster that might have been complete."

"And whilst you are noticing that fact," said Bellarion, "it may also be worthy of your attention that if Stoffel had not ranged his foot to receive the charge from Theodore's right wing, and afterwards formed a hedgehog to encircle and defend you, you would not now be ranting here. It occurs to me that an expression of gratitude and praise for Stoffel would be not so much gracious as proper."

Carmagnola glared. "Ah, yes! You support each other! We are to thank you now for a failure, which your own action helped to bring about, Bellarion."

Bellarion continued unruffled. "The accusation impugns only your own intelligence."

"Does it so? Does it so? Ha! Where is this man who came, you say, to tell you that Theodore was forewarned of the attack?"

Bellarion shrugged. "Do I know where he is? Do I care? Does it matter?"

"A man comes to you out of the night with such a message as that, and you don't know what has become of him!"

"I had other things to do than think of him. I had to think of you, and get you out of the trap that threatened you."

"And I say that you would have best done that by attacking on your own side, as we agreed."

"We never agreed that I should attack. But only that I should pretend to attack. I had not the means to push home an escalade." His suavity suddenly departed. "But it seems to me that I begin to defend myself." He reached for his steel cap, and stood up.

"It becomes necessary!" cried Carmagnola, who in two strides was at his side.

"Only that I should defend myself from a charge of rashness in having yielded to your insistence to attempt this night-attack. There was a chance, I thought, of success, and since the alternative of starving the place would entail a delay of months, I took that chance. It has missed, and so forces me to a course I've been considering from the outset. Tomorrow I shall raise the siege."

"You'll raise the siege!"

That ejaculation of amazement came in chorus.

"Not only of Vercelli, but also of Mortara."

"You'll raise the siege, sir?" It was Gian Giacomo who spoke now. "And what then?"

"That shall be decided tomorrow in council. It is almost day-break. I'll wish you a good repose, madonna, and you, sirs." He bowed to the company and moved to the door.

Carmagnola put himself in his way. "Ah, but wait, Bellarion . . ."

"Tomorrow," Bellarion's voice was hard and peremptory. "By then your wits may be cooler and clearer. If you will all gather here at noon, you shall learn my plans. Goodnight." And he went out.

They gathered there, not at noon on the morrow, but an hour before that time, summoned by messages from Carmagnola, who was the last to arrive and a prey to great excitement. Belluno, da Tenda, Stoffel, and three other officers awaited him with the Princess and the Marquis Gian Giacomo. Bellarion was not present. He had not been informed of the gathering, for reasons which Carmagnola's first words made clear to all.

When Bellarion did arrive, punctually at noon, for the council to which he had bidden the captains, he was surprised to find them already seated about the table in debate and conducting this with a vehemence which argued that matters had already gone some way. Their voices raised in altercation reached him as he mounted the short flight of stone steps, at the foot of which a half-dozen men of Belluno's company were lounging.

A silence fell when he entered, and all eyes at once were turned upon him. He smiled a greeting, and closed the door. But as he advanced, he began to realise that the sudden silence was un-natural and ominous.

He came to the foot of the table, where there was a vacant place. He looked at the faces on either side of it, and lastly at Carmagnola seated at its head, between Valeria and Gian Giacomo.

"What do you debate here?" he asked them.

Carmagnola answered him. His voice was hard and hostile; his blue eyes avoided the steady glance of Bellarion's.

"We were about to send for you. We have discovered the traitor who is communicating with Theodore of Montferrat, fore-warning him of our every measure, culminating in last night's business."

"That is something, although it comes at a time when it can no longer greatly matter. Who is your traitor?"

None answered him for a long moment. Saving Stoffel, who was flushed and smiling disdainfully, and the Princess whose eyes were lowered, they continued to stare at him, and he began to mislike their stare. At last, Carmagnola pushed towards him a folded square of parchment bearing a broken seal.

"Read that."

Bellarion took it, and turned it over. To his surprise he found it superscribed "To the Magnificent Lord Bellarion Cane, Prince of Valsassina." He frowned, and a little colour kindled in his cheeks. He threw up his head, stern-eyed. "How?" he asked. "Who breaks the seals of a letter addressed to me?"

"Read the letter," said Carmagnola, peremptorily.

Bellarion read:

DEAR LORD AND FRIEND, your fidelity to me and my concerns saved Vercelli last night from a blow that in its consequences might have led to our surrender, for without your forewarning we should assuredly have been taken by surprise. I desire you to know my recognition of my debt, and to assure you again of the highest reward that it lies in my power to bestow if you continue to serve me with the same loyal devotion.

THEODORE PALEOLOGO OF MONTFERRAT

Bellarion looked up from the letter with some anger in his face, but infinitely more contempt and even a shade of amusement.

"Where was this thing manufactured?" he asked.

Carmagnola's answer was prompt. "In Vercelli, by the Marquis Theodore. It is in his own hand, as madonna here has testified, and it is sealed with his own seal. Do you wonder that I broke it?"

Sheer amazement overspread Bellarion's face. He looked at the Princess, who fleetingly looked up to answer the question in his glance. "The hand is my uncle's, sir."

He turned the parchment over, and conned the seal with its stag device. Then the amazement passed out of his face, light broke on it, and he uttered a laugh. He turned, pulled up a stool, and sat down at the table's foot, whence he had them all under his eye.

"Let us proceed with method. How did this letter reach you, Carmagnola?"

Carmagnola waved to Belluno, and Belluno, hostile of tone and manner, answered the question. "A clown coming from the direction of the city blundered into my section of the lines this morning. He begged to be taken to you. My men naturally brought him to me. I questioned him as to what he desired with you. He answered that he bore a message. I asked him what message he could be bearing to you from Vercelli. He refused to answer further, whereupon I threatened him, and he produced this letter. Seeing its seal, I took both the fellow and the letter to my Lord Carmagnola."

Bellarion, himself, completed the tale. "And Carmagnola perceiving that seal took it upon himself to break it, and so discovered the contents to be what already he suspected."

"That is what occurred."

Bellarion, entirely at his ease, looked at them with amused contempt, and finally at Carmagnola in whose face he laughed.

"God save you, Carmagnola! I often wonder what will be the end of you."

"I am no longer wondering what will be the end of you," he was furiously answered, which only went to increase his amusement.

"And you others, you were equally deceived. The letter and Carmagnola's advocacy of my falseness and treachery were not to be resisted?"

"I have not been deceived," Stoffel protested.

"I was not classing you with those addled heads, Stoffel."

"It will need more than abuse to clear you," da Tenda warned him angrily.

"You, too, Ugolino! And you, madonna, and even you Lord Marquis! Well, well! It may need more than abuse to clear me; but surely not more than this letter. Falsehood is in every line of it, in the superscription, in the seal itself."

"How, sir?" the Princess asked him. "Do you insist that it is forged?"

"I have your word that it is not. But read the letter again."

He tossed it to them. "The Marquis Theodore pays your wits a poor compliment, Carmagnola, and the sequel has justified him. Ask yourselves this: If I were, indeed, Theodore's friend and ally, could he have taken a better way than this of putting it beyond my power to serve him further? It is plainly superscribed to me, so that there shall be no mistake as to the person for whom it is intended and it bears his full signature, so that there shall be no possible mistake on the score of whence it comes. In addition to that, he has sealed it with his arms, so that the first person into whose hands it falls shall be justified in ascertaining, as you did, what Theodore of Montferrat may have occasion to write to me."

"It was expected that the soldiers who caught the clown would bear him straight to you," Carmagnola countered.

"Was it? Is there no oddness in the fact that the clown should walk straight into your own men, Camagnola, on a section of the line that does not lie directly between Vercelli and Quinto? But why waste time even on such trifles of evidence. Read the letter itself. Is there a single word in that which it was important to convey to me, or which would not have been conveyed otherwise if it had been intended for any purpose other than to bring me under this suspicion? Almost has Theodore overreached himself in his guile. Out of his intentness to destroy me, he has revealed his true aims."

"The very arguments I used with them," said Stoffel.

Bellarion looked in amazement at his lieutenant. "And they failed?" he cried, incredulous.

"Of course they failed, you foul traitor!" Carmagnola bawled at him. "They are ingenious, but they are obvious to a man caught as you are."

"It is not I that am caught; but you that are in danger of it, Carmagnola, in danger of being caught in the web that Theodore has spun."

"To what end? To what end should he spin it? Answer that."

"Perhaps to set up dissensions amongst us, perhaps to remove the only one of the captains opposed to him whom he respects."

"You're modest, by God!" sneered Carmagnola.

"And you're a purblind fool, Carmagnola," cried Stoffel in heat.

"Then are we all fools," said Belluno. "For we are all of the same mind on this."

"Aye," said Bellarion sadly. "You're all of the same emptiness. That's clear. Well, let us have in this clown and question him."

"To what purpose?"

"That we may wring from him his precise instructions, since the letter does not suffice."

"You take too much for granted. The letter suffices fully. You forget that it is not all the evidence against you."

"What? Is there more?"

"There is your failure last night to make the false attack you undertook to make, and there is the intention you so rashly proclaimed here afterwards that you would raise the siege of Vercelli today. Why should you wish to do that if you are not Theodore's friend, if you are not the canker-hearted traitor we now know you to be?"

"If I were to tell you, you would not understand. I should merely give you another proof that I am Theodore's ally."

"That is very probable," said Carmagnola with a heavy sneer. "Fetch the guard, Ercole."

"What's this!" Bellarion was on his feet even as Belluno rose, and Stoffel came up with him, laying hands on his weapons. But Ugolino da Tenda and another captain between them overpowered him, whilst the other two ranged themselves swiftly on Bellarion's either hand. Bellarion looked at them, and from them again to Carmagnola. He was lost in amazement.

"Are you daring to place me under arrest?"

"Until we deliberate what shall be done with you. We shall not keep you waiting long."

"My God!" His wits worked swiftly, and he saw clearly that they might easily work their will with him. Of the four thousand men out there, only Stoffel's eight hundred Switzers would be on his side. The others would follow the lead of their respective captains. The leaders upon whom he could have depended in this pass—Koenigshofen and Giasone Trotta—were away at Mortara. Perceiving at last this danger, hitherto entirely unsuspected, he turned now to the Princess.

"Madonna," he said, "it is you whom I serve. Once before you suspected me, in the matter of Carmagnola's bridges, and the sequel proved you wrong."

Slowly she raised her eyes to look at him fully for the first time since he had joined that board. They were very sorrowful and her pallor was deathly.

"There are other matters, sir, besides that, which I remember. There is the death of Enzo Spigno, for one."

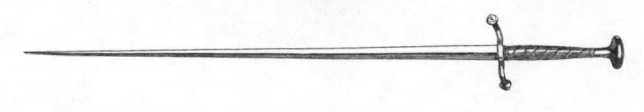

He recoiled as if she had struck him. "Spigno!" he echoed, and uttered a queer little laugh. "So it is Spigno who rises from his grave for vengeance?"

"Not for vengeance, sir. For justice. There would be that if there were not the matter that Messer Carmagnola has urged to convict you."

"To convict me! Am I then convicted without trial?"

None answered him, and in the pause that followed the men-at-arms summoned by Belluno clanked in, and at a sign from Carmagnola closed about Bellarion. There were four of them. One of the captains deprived him of his dagger, the only weapon upon him, and flung it on the table. At last Bellarion roused himself to some show of real heat.

"Oh, but this is madness! What do you intend by me?"

"That is to be deliberated. But be under no delusive hope, Bellarion."

"You are to decide my fate? You?" From Carmagnola, he looked at the others. He had paled a little; but amazement still rode above fear.

Stoffel, unable longer to contain himself, turned furiously upon Carmagnola. "You rash, vainglorious fool. If Bellarion is to be tried there is none under the Duke's magnificence before whom he may be arraigned."

"He has been arraigned already before us here. His guilt is clear, and he has said nothing to dispel a single hair of it. There remains only to decide his sentence."

"This is no proper arraignment. There has been no trial, nor have you power to hold one," Stoffel insisted.

"You are wrong, captain. There are military laws . . ."

"I say this is no trial. If Bellarion is to be tried, you'll send him before the Duke."

"And at the same time," put in Bellarion, "you'll send your single witness; this clown who brought that letter. Your refusal to produce him here before me now in itself shows the malice by which you're moved."

Carmagnola flushed under that charge, and scowlingly considered the prisoner. "If the form of trial you've received does not content you, and since you charge me with personal feeling, there is another I am ready to afford." He drew himself up, and flung back his handsome head. "Trial by battle, Lord Prince."

Over Bellarion's white face a sneer was spread.

"And what shall it prove if you ride me down? Shall it prove more than that you have the heavier weight of brawn, that you are more practised in the lists and have the stronger thews? Does it need trial by battle to prove that?"

"God will defend the right," said Carmagnola.

"Will he so?" Bellarion laughed. "I am glad to have your word for it. But you forget that the right to challenge lies with me, the accused. In your blundering stupidity you overlook essentials always. Your very dulness acquits you of hypocrisy. Shall I exercise that right upon the person in whose service I am carrying arms, upon the body of the Marquis Gian Giacomo of Montferrat?"

The frail boy named started, and looked up with dilating eyes. His sister cried out in very real alarm. But Carmagnola covered them with his answer.

"I am your accuser, sir; not he."

"You are his deputy, no more," Bellarion answered, and now the boy came to his feet, white and tense.

"He is in the right," he announced. "I cannot refuse him."

Smiling, Bellarion looked at Carmagnola, confused and awkward.

"Always you overreach yourself," he mocked him. He turned to Gian Giacomo. "You could not refuse me if I asked it. But I do not ask it. I only desired to show the value of Carmagnola's offer."

"You have some decency still," Carmagnola told him.

"Whilst you cannot lay claim even to that. God made you a fool, and that's the end of the matter."

"Take him away."

Already it seemed they had their orders. They laid hands upon him, and, submitting without further words, he suffered them to lead him out.

As the door closed upon him, Stoffel exploded. He raged and stormed. He pleaded, argued, and vituperated them, even the Princess herself, for fools and dolts, and finally threatened to raise the army against them, or at least to do his utmost with his Swiss to prevent them from carrying out their evil intentions.

"Listen!" Carmagnola commanded sternly, and in the silence they heard from the hall below a storm of angry outcries. "That is the voice of the army, answering you: the voice of those who were maimed last night as a result of his betrayal. Saving yourself, there is not a captain in the army, and saving your own Swiss, hardly a man who is not this morning clamouring for Bellarion's death."

"You are confessing that you published the matter even before Bellarion was examined here! My God, you villain, you hell-kite, you swaggering ape, who give a free rein to the base jealousy

in which you have ever held Bellarion. Your mean spite may drive you now to the lengths of murder. But look to yourself thereafter. You'll lose your empty head over this, Carmagnola!"

They silenced him and bore him out, whereafter they sat down to seal Bellarion's fate.

Chapter XI

The Pledge

Unanimously the captains voted for Bellarion's death. The
only dissentients were the Marquis and his sister. The latter was appalled by the swiftness with which this thing had come
upon them, and shrank from being in any sense a party to the
slaying of a man, however guilty. Also not only was she touched
by Bellarion's forbearance in the matter of trial by battle against
her brother, but his conduct in that connection sowed in her
mind the first real doubt of his guilt. Urgently she pleaded that
he should be sent for trial before the Duke.

Carmagnola, in refusing, conveyed the impression of a great
soul wrestling with circumstances, a noble knight placing duty
above inclination. It was a part that well became his splendid
person.

"Because you ask it, madonna, for one reason, because of the

imputations of malice against me for another, I would give years of my life to wash my hands of him and send him to Duke Filippo Maria. But out of other considerations, in which your own and your brother's future are concerned, I dare not. Saving perhaps Stoffel and his Swiss, the whole army demands his death. The matter has gone too far."

The captains one and all proved him right by their own present insistence.

"Yet I do not believe him guilty," the young Marquis startled them, "and I will be no party to the death of an innocent man."

"Would any of us?" Carmagnola asked him. "Is there any room for doubt? The letter . . ."

"The letter," the boy interrupted hotly, "is, as Bellarion says, a trick of my uncle's to remove the one enemy he fears."

That touched Carmagnola's vanity with wounding effect. He dissembled the hurt. But it served to strengthen his purpose.

"That vain boaster has seduced you with his argument, eh?"

"No; not with his argument, but with his conduct. He could have challenged me to trial by combat, as he showed. What am I to stand against him? A thing of straw. Yet he declined. Was that the action of a trickster?"

"It was," Carmagnola answered emphatically. "It was a trick to win you over. For he knew, as we all know, that a sovereign prince does not lie under that law of chivalry. He knew that if he had demanded it, you would have been within your right in appointing a deputy."

"Why, then, did you not say so at the time?" the Princess asked him.

"Because he did not press the matter. Oh, madonna, believe

me there is no man in Italy who less desires to have Bellarion's blood on his hands than I." He spoke sorrowfully, heavily. "But my duty is clear, and whether it were clear or not, I must be governed by the voice of these captains, all of whom demand, and rightly, this double-dealing traitor's death."

Emphatically the captains confirmed him in the assertion, as emphatically Gian Giacomo repeated that he would be no party to it.

"You are not required to be," Carmagnola assured him. "You may stand aside, my lord, and allow justice to take its course."

"Sirs," the Princess appealed to them, "let me implore you again, at least to send him to the Duke. Let the responsibility of his death lie with his master."

Carmagnola rose. "Madonna, what you ask would lead to a mutiny. Tomorrow either I send Bellarion's head to his ally in Vercelli, or the men will be out of hand and there will be an end to this campaign. Dismiss your doubts and your fears. His guilt is crystal clear. You need but remember his avowed intention of raising the siege, to see in whose interest he works."

Heavy-eyed and heavy-hearted she sat, tormented by doubt now that she was face to face with decision where hitherto no single doubt had been.

"You never asked him what alternative he proposed," she reminded him.

"To what end? That glib dissembler would have fooled us with fresh falsehoods."

Belluno got to his feet. He had been manifesting impatience for some moments. "Have we leave to go, my lord? This matter is at an end."

Ugolino da Tenda followed his example. "The men below are growing noisier. It is time we pacified them with our decision."

"Aye, in God's name." Carmagnola waved them away, and himself strode off from the table towards the hearth. He stirred the logs with his boot and sent an explosion of sparks flying up the chimney. "Bear him word of our decision, Belluno. Bid him prepare for death. He shall have until daybreak tomorrow to make his soul."

"O God! If we should be wrong!" groaned the Princess.

The captains clanked out, and the door closed. Slowly Carmagnola turned; reproachfully he regarded her.

"Have you no faith in me, Valeria? Should I do this thing if there were any room for doubt?"

"You may be mistaken. You have been mistaken before, remember."

He did not like to remember it. "And you? Have you been mistaken all these years? Are you mistaken on the death of your friend Count Spigno and what followed?"

"Ah! I was forgetting that," she confessed.

"Remember it. And remember what he said at that table, which may, after all, be the truth. That Count Spigno has risen from the grave at last for vengeance."

"Will you not send for this clown, at least?" cried Gian Giacomo.

"To what purpose now? What can he add to what we know? The matter, Lord Marquis, is finished."

And meanwhile Belluno was seeking Bellarion in the small chamber in which they had confined him on the ground floor of the castle.

With perfect composure Bellarion heard the words of doom. He did not believe them. This sudden thing was too monstrously impossible. It was incredible the gods should have raised him so swiftly to his pinnacle of fame, merely to cast him down again for their amusement. They might make sport with him, but they would hardly carry it to the lengths of quenching his life.

His only answer now was to proffer his pinioned wrists, and beg that the cord might be cut. Belluno shook his head to that in silence. Bellarion grew indignant.

"What purpose does it serve beyond a cruelty? The window is barred; the door is strong, and there is probably a guard beyond it. I could not escape if I would."

"You'll be less likely to attempt it with bound wrists."

"I'll pass you my parole of honour to remain a prisoner."

"You are convicted of treachery, and you know as well as I do that the parole of a convicted traitor is never taken."

"Go to the devil, then," said Bellarion, which so angered Belluno that he called in the guard, and ordered them to bind Bellarion's ankles as well.

So trussed that he could move only by hops, and then at the risk of falling, they left him. He sat down on one of the two stools which with a table made up all the furniture of that bare chill place. He wagged his head and even smiled over the thought of Belluno's refusal to accept his parole, or rather over the thought that in offering it he had no notion of keeping it.

"I'd break more than my pledged word to get out of this," said he to himself. "And only an idiot would blame me."

He looked round the bare stone walls, and lastly at the window. He rose, and hopped over to it. Leaning on the sill, which was at the height of his breast, he looked out. It opened upon the inner court, he found, so that wherever escape might lie, it lay not that way. The sill upon the rough edge of which he leaned was of granite. He studied it awhile attentively.

"The fools!" he said, and hopped back to his stool, where he gave himself up to quiet meditation until they brought him a hunch of bread and a jug of wine.

To the man-at-arms who acted as gaoler, he held out his pinioned wrists. "How am I to eat and drink?" he asked.

"You'll make shift as best you can."

He made shift, and by using his two hands as one contrived to eat and to drink. After that he spent some time at the sill, patiently drawing his wrists backwards and forwards along the edge of it, with long rests betweenwhiles to restore the blood which had flowed out of upheld arms. It was wearying toil, and kept him fully engaged for some hours.

Towards dusk he set up a shouting which at last brought the guard into his prison.

"You're in haste to die, my lord," the fellow insolently mocked him. "But quiet you. The stranglers are bidden for daybreak."

"And I am to perish like a dog?" Bellarion furiously asked him. With pinioned wrists and ankles he sat there by his table. "Am I never to have a priest to shrive me?"

"Oh! Ah! A priest?" The fellow went out. He went in quest of Carmagnola. But Carmagnola was absent, marshalling his men against a threatened attempt by Stoffel and the Swiss to rescue Bellarion. The captains were away about the same business, and there remained only the Princess and her brother.

"Messer Bellarion is asking for a priest," he told them.

"Has none been sent to him?" cried Gian Giacomo, scandalised.

"He'd not be sent until an hour before the stranglers."

Valeria shuddered, and sat numbed with horror. Gian Giacomo swore under his breath. "In God's name, let the poor fellow have a priest at once. Let one be sent for from Quinto."

It would be an hour later when a preaching friar from the convent of Saint Dominic was ushered into Bellarion's prison, a tall, frail man in a long black mantle over his white habit.

The guard placed a lantern on the table, glanced compassionately at the prisoner, who sat there as he had earlier seen him with pinioned wrists and ankles. But something had happened to the cords meanwhile, for no sooner had the guard passed out and closed the door than Bellarion stood up and his bonds fell from him like cobwebs, startling the good monk who came to shrive him. Infinitely more startled was the good monk to find himself suddenly seized by the throat in a pair of strong, nervous hands whose thumbs were so pressed into his windpipe that he could neither cry out nor breathe. He writhed in that unrelenting grip, until a fierce whisper quieted him.

"Be still if you would hope to live. If you undertake to make no sound, tap your foot twice upon the ground, and I'll release you."

Frantically the foot was tapped.

"But remember that at the first outcry, I shall kill you without mercy."

He removed his hands, and the priest almost choked himself in his sudden greed of air.

"Why? Why do you assault me?" he gasped. "I come to comfort and . . ."

"I know why you come better than you do, brother. You think you bring me the promise of eternal life. All that I require from you at present is the promise of temporal existence. So we'll leave the shriving for something more urgent."

It would be a half-hour later, when cowled as he had entered the tall, bowed figure of the priest emerged again from the room, bearing the lantern.

"I've brought the light, my son," he said almost in a whisper. "Your prisoner desires to be alone in the dark with his thoughts."

The man-at-arms took the lantern in one hand, whilst with the other he was driving home the bolt. Suddenly he swung the lantern to the level of the cowl. This priest did not seem quite the same as the one who had entered. The next moment, on his back, his throat gripped by the vigorous man who knelt upon him, the guard knew that his suspicions had been well-founded. Another moment and he knew nothing. For the hands that held him had hammered his head against the stone floor until consciousness was blotted out.

Bellarion extinguished the lantern, pushed the unconscious man-at-arms into the deepest shadow of that dimly lighted hall, adjusted his mantle and cowl, and went quickly out.

The soldiers in the courtyard saw in that cowled figure only the monk who had gone to shrive Bellarion. The postern was opened for him, and with a murmured "*Pax vobiscum,*" he passed out across the lesser bridge, and gained the open. Thereafter, under cover of the night, he went at speed, the monkish gown tucked high, for he knew not how soon the sentinel he had stunned might recover to give the alarm. In his haste he almost stumbled upon a strong picket, and in fleeing from that he was within an ace of blundering into another. Thereafter he proceeded with more caution over ground that was everywhere held by groups of soldiers, posted by Carmagnola against any attempt on the part of the Swiss.

As a result it was not until an hour or so before midnight that he came at last to Stoffel's quarters, away to the south of Vercelli, and found there everything in ferment. He was stopped by a party of men of Uri, to whom at once he made himself known, and even whilst they conducted him to their captain, the news of his presence ran like fire through the Swiss encampment.

Stoffel, who was in full armour when Bellarion entered his tent, gasped his questioning amazement whilst Bellarion threw off his mantle and white woollen habit, and stood forth in his own proper person and garments.

"We were on the point of coming for you," Stoffel told him.

"A fool's errand, Werner. What could you have done against three thousand men, who are ready and expecting you?" But he spoke with a warm hand firmly gripping Stoffel's shoulders and a heart warmed, indeed, by this proof of trust and loyalty.

"Something we might have done. There was a will on our side that must be lacking on the other."

"And the walls of Quinto? You'd have beaten your heads in vain against them, even had you succeeded in reaching them. It's as lucky for you as for me that I've saved you this trouble."

"And what now?" Stoffel asked him.

"Give the order to break camp at once. We march to Mortara to rejoin the Company of the White Dog from which I should never have separated. We'll show Carmagnola and those Montferrine princes what Bellarion can do."

Meanwhile they already had some notion of it. The alarm at his escape had spread through Quinto; and Carmagnola had been fetched from the lines to be informed of it in detail by a half-naked priest and a man-at-arms with a bandaged head. It had taken some time to find him. It took more for him to re-solve what should be done. At last, however, he decided that Bellarion would have fled to Stoffel; so he assembled his captains, and with the whole army marched on the Swiss encampment. But he came too late. At the last the Swiss had not waited to strike their camp, realising the danger of delay, but had de-parted leaving it standing.

Back to Quinto and the agitated Princess went Carmagnola with the news of failure. He found her waiting alone in the armoury, huddled in a great chair by the fire.

"That he will have gone to his own condotta at Mortara is certain," he declared. "But without knowing which road he took, how could I follow in the dark? And to follow meant fulfilling that traitor's intention of raising this siege."

He raged and swore, striding to and fro there in his wrath, bitterly upbraiding himself for not having taken better precau-tions knowing with what a trickster he had to deal, damning the priest and the sentry and the fools in the courtyard who had al-lowed Bellarion to walk undetected through their ranks.

She watched him, and found him less admirable than hith-erto in the wildness of his ravings. Unwillingly almost her mind contrasted his behaviour under stress with the calm she had observed in Bellarion. She fetched a weary sigh. If only Bellarion had been true and loyal, what a champion would he not have been.

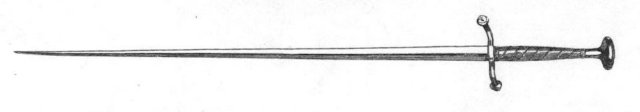

"Raging will not help you, Carmagnola," she said at last, the least asperity in her tone.

It brought him, pained, to a halt before her. "And whence, madonna, is my rage? Have I lost anything? Do I strive here for personal ends? Ha! I rage at the thought of the difficulties that will rise up for you."

"For me?"

"Can you doubt what will follow? Do you think that all that we have lost tonight is Bellarion, with perhaps his Swiss? The men at Mortara are mostly of his own company, the Company of the Dog. A well-named company, as God lives! And those who are not serve under captains who are loyal to him and who, knowing nothing of his discovered treachery here, will be beguiled by that seducer. In strength he will be our superior, with close upon four thousand men."

She looked up at him in alarm. "You are suggesting that we shall have him coming against us!"

"What else? Do we not know enough already of his aims? By all the Saints! Things could not have fallen out better to give him the pretext that he needed." He was raging again. "Had this sly devil contrived these circumstances himself, he could not have improved them. By these he can justify himself at need to the Duke. Oh, he's turned the tables on us. Now you see why I meant to give him no chance."

She kept her mind to the essence of the matter.

"Then if he comes against us, we are lost. We shall be caught between his army and my uncle's."

His overweening vanity would not permit him to admit, or even to think, so much. He laughed, confident and disdainful.

"Have you so little faith in me, Valeria? I am no apprentice in this art of war. And with the thought of you to spur me on, do you think that I will suffer defeat? I'll not lay down my arms while I have life to serve you. I will take measures tomorrow. And I will send letters to the Duke, informing him of Bellarion's defection and begging reenforcements. Can you doubt that they will come? Is Filippo Maria the man to let one of his captains mutiny and go unpunished?" He laughed again full of a confidence by which she was infected. And he looked so strong and masterful, so handsome in the half-armour he still wore, a very god of war.

She held out a hand to him. "My friend, forgive my doubt. You shall be dishonoured by no more fears of mine."

He caught her hand. He drew her out of the chair, and towards him until she brought up against his broad mailed breast. "That is the fine brave spirit that I love in you as I love all in you, Valeria. You are mine, Valeria! God made us for each other."

"Not yet," she said, smiling a little, her eyes downcast and veiled from his ardent glance.

"When then?" was his burning question.

"When Theodore has been whipped out of Montferrat."

His arms tightened about her until his armour hurt her. "It is a pledge, Valeria?

"A pledge?" she echoed on a questioning, exalted note. "The man who does that may claim me when he wants me. I swear it."

Chapter XII

Carmagnola's Duty

My Lord of Carmagnola had shut himself up in a small room on the ground floor of the castle of Quinto to indite a letter to the High and Most Potent Duke Filippo Maria of Milan. A heavy labour this of quill on parchment for one who had little scholarship. It was a labour that fell to him so rarely that he had never perceived until now the need to equip himself with a secretary.

The Princess and her brother newly returned from Mass on that Sunday morning, four days after Bellarion's escape, were together in the armoury discussing their situation, and differing a good deal in their views, for the mental eyes of the young Marquis were not dazzled by the effulgence of Carmagnola's male beauty, or deceived by his histrionic attitudes.

Into their presence, almost unheralded, were ushered two men. One of these was small and slight and active as a monkey, the

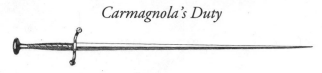

other a fellow of great girth with a big, red, boldly humorous face, blue eyes under black brows flanking a beak of a nose, and a sparse fringe of grey hair straggling about a gleaming bald head.

The sight of those two, who smirked and bowed, brought brother and sister very suddenly to their feet.

"Barbaresco!" she cried on a note of gladness, holding out both her hands. "And Casella!"

"And," said Barbaresco, as he rolled forward, "near upon another five hundred refugees from Montferrat, both Guelph and Ghibelline, whom we've been collecting in Piedmont and Lombardy to swell the army of the great Bellarion and settle accounts with Master Theodore."

They kissed her hands, and then her brother's. "My Lord Marquis!" cried the fire-eating Casella, his gimlet glance appraising the lad. "You're so well grown I should hardly have known you. We are your servants, my lord, as madonna here can tell you. For years have we laboured for you and suffered for you. But we touch the end of all that now, as do you. Theodore is brought to bay at last. We are hounds to help you pull him down."

At no season could their coming have been more welcome or uplifting than in this hour of dark depression, when recruits to the cause of the young Marquis were so urgently required. This she told them, announcing their arrival a good omen. Servants were summoned, and despatched for wine, and whilst the newcomers drank the hot spiced beverage provided they learnt the true meaning of her words.

It sobered their exultation. This defection of Bellarion and his powerful company amounting to more than half of the entire army altered their outlook completely.

Barbaresco blew out his great cheeks, frowning darkly.

"You say that Bellarion is the agent of Theodore?" he cried.

"We have proof of it," she sadly assured him, and told him of the letter. His amazement deepened. "Does it surprise you, then?" she asked. "Surely it should be no news to you!"

"Once it would not have been. For once I thought that I held proof of the same; that was on the night that Spigno died at his hands. Later, before that same night was out, I understood better why he killed Spigno."

"You understood? Why he killed him?" She was white to the lips. Gian Giacomo was leaning forward across the table, his face eager. She uttered a fretful laugh. "He killed him because he was my friend, mine and my brother's, the chief of all our friends."

Barbaresco shook his great head. "He killed him because this Spigno whom we all trusted so completely was a spy of Theodore's."

"What?"

Her world reeled about her; her senses battled in a mist. The thick, droning voice of Barbaresco came to deepen her confusion.

"It is all so simple; so very clear. The facts that Spigno was dressed as we found him and in the attic where we had imprisoned Bellarion should in themselves have explained everything. How came he there? Bellarion was all but convicted of being an agent of Theodore's. But for Spigno we should have dealt with him out of hand. Then at dead of night Spigno went to liberate him, and by that very act convicted himself in Bellarion's eyes. And for that Bellarion stabbed him. The only flaw is how one agent of Theodore's should have come to be under such a misapprehension about the other. Saving that, the thing would have been clear at once."

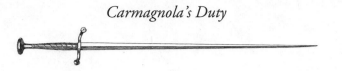

"That I can explain," said Valeria breathlessly, "if you have sound proof of Spigno's guilt, if it is not all based on rash assumption."

"Assumption!" laughed Casella, and he took up the tale. "That night, when we determined upon flight, we first repaired, because of our suspicions, to Spigno's lodging. We found there a letter superscribed to Theodore, to be delivered in the event of Spigno's death or disappearance. Within it we found a list of our names and of the part which each of us had had in the plot to kill the Regent, and the terms of that letter made it more than clear that throughout Spigno had been Theodore's agent for the destruction of the Marquis here."

"That letter," said Barbaresco, "was a safeguard the scoundrel had prepared in the event of discovery. The threat of its despatch to Theodore would have been used to compel us to hold our hands. Oh, a subtle villain, your best and most loyal friend Count Spigno, and but for Bellarion . . ." He spread his hands and laughed.

Then Casella interposed.

"You said, madonna, that you could supply the link that's missing in our chain."

But she was not listening. She sat with drooping head, her hands listlessly folded in her lap.

"It was all true. All true!" Her tone seemed the utterance of a broken heart. "And I have mistrusted him, and . . . Oh, God!" she cried out. "When I think that by now he might have been strangled and with my consent. And now . . ."

"And now," cut in her brother almost brutally considering the pain she was already bearing, "you and that swaggering fool Carmagnola have between you driven him out and perhaps set him against us."

The swaggering fool came in at that moment with inky fingers and disordered hair. The phrase that greeted him brought him to a halt on the threshold, his attitude magnificent.

"What's this?" he asked with immense dignity.

He was told, by Gian Giacomo, so fiercely and unsparingly that he went red and white by turns as he listened. Then, commanding himself and wrapped in his dignity as in a mantle, he came slowly forward. He even smiled, condescendingly.

"Of all this that you tell I know nothing. It may well be as you say. It is no concern of mine. What concerns me is what has happened here; the discovery that Bellarion was in correspondence with Theodore, and his avowed intention to raise this siege; add to this that he has slipped through our hands, and is now abroad to work your ruin, and consider if you are justified in using hard words to me but for whom your ruin would already have been encompassed."

His majestic air and his display of magnanimity under their reproach imposed upon all but Valeria.

It was she who answered him:

"You are forgetting that it was only my conviction that he had been Theodore's agent aforetime which disposed me to believe him Theodore's agent now."

"But the letter, then?" Carmagnola was showing signs of exasperation.

"In God's name, where is this letter?" growled the deep voice of Barbaresco.

"Who are you to question me now? I do not know your right, sir, or even your name."

The Princess presented him and at the same time Casella.

"They are old and esteemed friends, my lord, and they are here to serve me with all the men that they can muster. Let Messer Barbaresco see this letter."

Impatiently Carmagnola produced it from the scrip that hung beside his dagger from a gold-embossed girdle of crimson leather.

Slowly Barbaresco spelled it out, Casella reading over his shoulder. When he had done, he looked at Carmagnola, and from Carmagnola to the others, first in sheer amazement, then in scornful mirth.

"Lord of Heaven, Messer Carmagnola! You've the repute of a great fighter, and, to be sure, you're a fine figure of a man; also I must assume you honest. But I would sooner put my trust in your animal strength than in your wits."

"Sir!"

"Oh, aye, to be sure, you can throw out your chest and roar and strut. But use your brains for once, man." The boldly humorous red face was overspread by a sardonic grin. "Master Theodore took your measure shrewdly when he thought to impose upon you with this foxy piece of buffoonery, and, my faith, if Bellarion had been less nimble, this trick would have served its purpose. Nay, now don't puff and blow and swell! Read the letter again. Ask yourself if it would have borne that full signature and that superscription if it had been sincere, and considering that it imparts no useful information save that Bellarion was betraying you, ask yourself if it would have been written at all had anything it says been true."

"The very arguments that Bellarion used," cried the Marquis.

"To which we would not listen," said the Princess bitterly.

Carmagnola sniffed. "They are the arguments any man in his

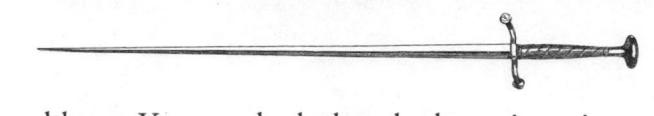

case would use. You overlook that the letter is an incentive, an undertaking to reward him suitably if he . . ."

Barbaresco broke in, exasperated by the man's grandiose stupidity.

"To the devil with that, numskull!"

"Numskull, sir? To me? By Heaven . . ."

"Sirs, sirs!" The Princess laid her hand on Barbaresco's great arm. "This is not seemly to my Lord Carmagnola . . ."

"I know it. I know it. I crave his pardon. But I was never taught to suffer fools gladly. I . . ."

"Sir, your every word is an offence. You . . ."

Valeria calmed them. "Don't you see, Messer Carmagnola, that he but uses you as a whipping boy instead of me? It is I who am the fool, the numskull in his eyes; for these deeds are more mine than any other's. But my old friend Barbaresco is too courteous to say so."

"Courteous?" snorted Carmagnola. "That is the last term I should apply to his boorishness. By what right does he come hectoring here?"

"By the right of his old affection for me and my brother. That is what makes him hot. For my sake, then, bear with him, sir."

The great man bowed, his hand upon his heart, signifying that for her sake there was no indignity he would not suffer.

Thereafter he defended himself with great dignity. If the letter had been all, he might have taken Barbaresco's views. But it was, he repeated, the traitor Bellarion's avowed intention to raise the siege. That, in itself, was a proof of his double-dealing.

"How did this letter come to you?" Barbaresco asked.

Gian Giacomo answered whilst Valeria added in bitter self-reproach, "And this messenger was never examined, although Bellarion demanded that he should be brought before us."

"Do you upbraid me with that, madonna?" Carmagnola cried. "He was a poor clown, who could have told us nothing. He was not examined because it would have been a waste of time."

"Let us waste it now," said Barbaresco.

"To what purpose, sir?"

"Why, to beguile our leisure. No other entertainment offers."

Carmagnola contained himself under that sardonic leer.

"Sir, you are resolved, it seems, to try my patience. It requires all my regard and devotion for her highness to teach me to endure it. The messenger shall be brought."

At Valeria's request not only the messenger, but the captains who had voted Bellarion's death were also summoned. Carmagnola demurred at first, but bowed in the end to her stern insistence.

They came, and when they were all assembled, they were told by the Princess why they had been summoned as well as what she had that morning learnt from Barbaresco. Then the messenger was brought in between the guards, and it was the Princess herself who questioned him.

"You have nothing to fear, boy," she assured him gently, as he cowered in terror before her. "You are required to answer truthfully. When you have done so, and unless I discover that you are lying, you shall be restored to liberty."

Carmagnola, who had come to take his stand at her side, bent over her.

"Is that prudent, madonna?"

"Prudent or not, it is promised." There was in her tone an asperity that dismayed him. She addressed herself to the clown.

"When you were given this letter you were given precise instructions for its delivery?"

"Yes, magnificent madonna."

"What were those instructions?"

"I was taken to the ramparts by a knight, to join some other knights and soldiers. They pointed to the lines straight ahead. I was to go in that direction with the letter. If taken I was to ask for the Lord Bellarion."

"Were you bidden to go cautiously? To conceal yourself?"

"No, madonna. On the contrary. My orders were to let myself be seen. I am answering truthfully, madonna."

"When you were told to go straight ahead into the lines that were pointed out to you, on which side of the ramparts were you standing?"

"On the south side, madonna. By the southern gate. That is truth, as God hears me."

The Princess leaned forward, and she was not the only one to move.

"Were you told or did you know what soldiers occupied the section of the lines to which you were bidden?"

"I just knew that they were soldiers of the besieging army, or the Lord Bellarion's army. I am telling you the truth, madonna. I was told to be careful to go straight, and not to wander into any other part of the line but that."

Ugolino da Tenda made a sharp forward movement. "What are you saying?"

"The truth! The truth!" cried the lad in terror. "May God

strike me dumb forever if I have uttered a lie."

"Quiet! Quiet!" the Princess admonished him. "Be sure we know when you speak the truth. Keep to it and fear nothing. Did you hear mention of any name in connection with that section of the line?"

"Did I?" He searched his mind, and his eyes brightened. "Aye, aye, I did. They spoke amongst them. They named one Calmaldola, or . . . Carmandola . . ."

"Or Carmagnola," da Tenda cut in, and laughed splutteringly in sheer contempt. "It's clear, I think, that Theodore's letter was intended for just the purpose that it's served."

"Clear? How is it clear?" Carmagnola's contempt was in the question.

"In everything, now that we have heard this clown. Why was he sent to the southern section? Do you suppose Theodore did not know that Valsassina himself and those directly under him, of whom I was one, were quartered in Quinto, on the western side?" Then his voice swelled up in anger. "Why was this messenger not examined sooner, or—" he checked and his eyes narrowed as they fixed themselves on Carmagnola's flushed and angry face "—or, was he?"

"Was he?" roared Carmagnola. "Now what the devil do you mean?"

"You know what I mean, Carmagnola. You led us all within an ace of doing murder. Did you lead us so because you're a fool, or a villain? Which?"

Carmagnola sprang for him, roaring like a bull. The other captains got between, and the Princess on her feet, commanding, imperious, added her voice sharply to theirs to restore order. They obeyed that slim, frail woman, scarcely more than a girl, as she stood there straight and tense in her wine-coloured mantle, her red-gold head so proudly held, her dark eyes burning in her white face.

"Captain Ugolino, that was ill said of you," she reproved him. "You forget that if this messenger was not examined before, the blame for that is upon all of us. We took too much for granted and too readily against the Prince of Valsassina."

"It is now that you take too much for granted," answered Carmagnola. "Why did Valsassina intend to raise this siege if he is honest? Answer me that!"

His challenge was to all. Ugolino da Tenda answered it.

"For some such reason as he had when he sent his men to hold the bridge at Carpignano while you were building bridges here. Bellarion's intentions are not clear to dull eyes like yours and mine, Carmagnola."

Carmagnola considered him malevolently. "You and I will discuss this matter further elsewhere," he promised him. "You have used expressions I am not the man to forget."

"It may be good for you to remember them," said the young captain, no whit intimidated. "Meanwhile, madonna, I take my leave. I march my condotta out of this camp within an hour."

She looked at him in sudden distress. He answered the look.

"I am grieved, madonna. But my duty is to the Prince of Valsassina. I was seduced from it by too hasty judgment. I return to it at once." He bowed low, gathered up his cloak, and went clanking out.

"Hold there!" Carmagnola thundered after him. "Before you go I've an account to settle with you."

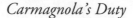

Ugolino turned on the threshold, drawn up to his full height.

"I'll afford you the opportunity," said he, "but only after I have the answer to my question, whether you are a villain or a fool, and only if I find that you're a fool."

The captains made a barrier which Carmagnola could not pass. Livid with anger and humiliation, his grand manner dissipated, he turned to the Princess.

"Will your highness suffer me to go after him? He must not be permitted to depart."

But she shook her red-gold head. "Nay, sir. I detain no man here against his inclinations. And Captain Ugolino seems justified of his."

"Justified! Dear God! Justified!" He apostrophised the groined ceiling, then swung to the other four captains standing there. "And you?" he demanded. "Do you also deem yourselves justified to mutiny?"

Belluno was prompt to answer. But then Belluno was his own lieutenant. "My lord, if there has been an error we are all in it, and have the honesty to admit it."

"I am glad there is still some honesty among you. And you?" His angry eyes swept over the others. One by one they answered as Belluno had done. But they were men of little account, and the defection of the four of them would not have reduced the army as did Ugolino's, whose condotta amounted to close upon a thousand men.

"We are forgetting this poor clown," said the Princess.

Carmagnola looked at him as if he would with joy have wrung his neck.

"You may go, boy," she told him. "You are free. See that he leaves unhindered."

He went with his guards. The captains, dismissed, went out next.

Carmagnola, his spirit badly bruised and battered, looked at the Princess, who had sunk back into her chair.

"However it has been achieved," she said, "Theodore's ends could not better have been served. What is left us now?"

"If I might venture to advise . . ." quoth Barbaresco, smooth as oil, "I should say that you could not do better than follow Ugolino da Tenda's example."

"What?"

"Return to your fealty to Bellarion."

"Return?" Carmagnola leaned towards him from his fine height, and his mouth gaped. "Return?" he repeated. "And leave Vercelli?"

"Why not? That would no more than fulfil Bellarion's intention to raise the siege. He will have an alternative."

"I care nothing for his alternatives, and let us be clear upon this: I owe him no fealty. My fealty was sworn not to him, but to the Duchess Beatrice. And my orders from Duke Filippo Maria are to assist in the reduction of Vercelli. I know where my duty lies."

"It is possible," said the Princess slowly, "that Bellarion had some other plan for bringing Theodore to his knees."

He stared at her. There was pain in his handsome eyes. His face was momentarily almost convulsed. And there was more than pain in his voice when he spoke.

"Oh, madonna! Into what irreparable error is your generous heart misleading you? How can you have come in a breath to place all your trust in this man whom for years you have known, as many know him, for a scheming villain?"

"Could I do less having discovered the cruelty of my error?"

"Are you sure—can you be sure upon such slight grounds— that you were in error? That you are not in error now? You heard what Belluno said of him on the night my bridges were destroyed—that Bellarion never looks where he aims."

"That, sir, is what has misled me, to my present shame."

"Is it not rather what is misleading you now?"

"You heard what Messer Barbaresco had to tell me."

"I do not need to hear Messer Barbaresco or any other. I know what I can see for myself, what my wits tell me."

She looked at him almost slyly, for one normally so wide-eyed, and her answer all considered was a little cruel.

"Are you still unshaken in your con*fidence in your wits? Do you still think that you can trust them?"

That was the death-blow to his passion for her, as it was the death-blow of the high hopes he is suspected of having centred in her, seeing himself, perhaps, as the husband of the Princess Valeria of Montferrat, supreme in Montferrine court and camp. It was a sword-thrust full into his vanity, which was the vital part of him.

He stepped back, white to the very lips, his countenance disordered. Then, commanding himself, he bowed, and steadied his voice to answer.

"Madonna, I see that you have made your choice. My prayer will be that you may not have occasion to repent it. No doubt the troops accompanying these gentlemen of Montferrat will be your sufficient escort to Mortara, or you may join forces with Ugolino da Tenda's condotta. Although I shall be left with not more than half the men the enterprise demands, with these I must make shift to reduce Vercelli, as my duty is. Thus, madonna,

you may yet owe your deliverance to me. May God be with you!" He bowed again.

Perhaps he hoped still for some word to arrest him, some retraction of the injustice with which she used him. But it did not come.

"I thank you for your good intentions, my lord," she said civilly. "God be with you, too."

He bit his lip, then turned, and threw high that handsome golden head which he was destined to leave, some few years later, between the pillars of the Piazzetta in Venice. Thus he stalked out. All considered, it was an orderly retreat; and that was the last she ever saw of him.

As the door banged, Barbaresco smacked his great thigh with his open palm and exploded into laughter.

Chapter XIII

The Occupation of Casale

When Bellarion proclaimed his intention of raising the siege of Vercelli, he had it in mind, in view of the hopelessness of being able to reduce the place reasonably soon, to draw Theodore into the open by means of that strategic movement which Thucydides had taught him, and to which he had so often already and so successfully had recourse.

His Swiss, being without baggage, travelled lightly and swiftly. They left their camp before Vercelli on the night of Wednesday, and on the evening of the following Friday, Bellarion brought them into the village of Pavone, where Koenigshofen had established himself in Facino's old quarters of three years ago. There they lay for the night. But whilst his weary followers rested, himself he spent the greater part of the night in the necessary dispositions for striking camp at dawn. And very early on that misty

November morning he was off again with Giasone Trotta, Koenigshofen, and all the horse, leaving Stoffel to follow more at leisure with the foot, the baggage, and the artillery.

Before nightfall he was at San Salvatore, where his army rested, and on the following Sunday morning at just about the time that Barbaresco was reaching Vercelli, Bellarion, Prince of Valsassina, was approaching the Lombard Gate into Casale, by the road along which he had fled thence years before, a nameless outcast waif whose only ambition was the study of Greek at Pavia.

He had travelled by many roads since then, and after long delays he had reached Pavia, no longer as a poor nameless scholar, but as a condottiero of renown, not to solicit at the University the alms of a little learning, but to command whatever he might crave of the place, holding even its Prince in subjection. Greek he had not learnt; but he had learnt much else instead, though nothing that made him love his fellow man or hold the world in high regard. Therefore, he was glad to think that here he touched the end of that long journey begun five years ago along this Lombard Road; the mission upon which he had set out blindly that day was, after many odd turns of Fortune, all but accomplished. When it was done, he would strip off this soldier's harness, abdicate his princely honours, and return on foot—humbler than when he had set out, and cured of his erstwhile heresy—to the benign and peaceful shelter of the convent at Cigliano.

There was no attempt to bar his entrance into the Montferrine capital. The officer commanding the place knew himself without the necessary means to oppose this force which so unexpectedly came to demand admittance. And so, the people of Casale, issuing from Mass on that Sunday morning, found the great square before Liutprand's Cathedral and the main streets leading from it blocked by outlandish men-at-arms—Italians, Gascons, Burgundians, Swabians, Saxons, and Swiss—whose leader proclaimed himself Captain-General of the army of the Marquis Gian Giacomo of Montferrat.

It was a proclamation that not at all reassured them of their dread at the presence of a rapacious and violent soldiery.

The Council of Ancients, summoned by Bellarion's heralds, assembled in the Communal Palace, to hear the terms of this brigand captain—as they conceived him—who had swooped upon their defenceless city.

He came attended by a group of officers. He was tall and soldierly of bearing, in full armour, save for his helm, which was borne after him by a page, and his escort, from the brawny, bearded Koenigshofen to the fierce-eyed, ferrety Giasone, was calculated to inspire dread in peaceful citizens. But his manner was gentle, and his words were fair.

"Sirs, your city of Casale has nothing to fear from this occupation, for it is not upon its citizens that we make war, and so that they give no provocation, they will find my followers orderly. We invite your alliance with ourselves in the cause of right and justice. But if you withhold this alliance we shall not visit it against you, provided that you do not go the length of actively opposing us.

"The High and Mighty Lord Filippo Maria Visconti, Duke of Milan, weary of the encroachments upon his dominions resulting from the turbulent ambition of your Prince-Regent, the Marquis Theodore, has resolved to make an end of a regency which in itself has already become an usurpation, and to place in the authority to which his majority entitles him your rightful

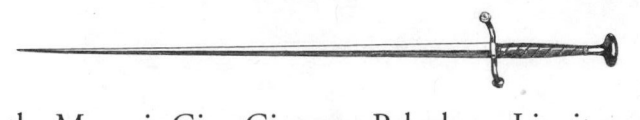

Prince, the Marquis Gian Giacomo Paleologo. I invite you, sirs, to perform your duty as representatives of the people by swearing upon my hands fealty to that same Marquis Gian Giacomo in the cathedral at the hour of vespers this evening."

That invitation was a command, and it was punctually obeyed by men who had not the strength to resist. Meanwhile a measure of reassurance had been afforded the city by Bellarion's proclamation enjoining order upon his troops. The proclamation was in no equivocal terms. It reminded the men that they were in occupation of a friendly city which they were sent to guard and defend, and that any act of pillage or violence would be punished by death. They were housed, some in the citadel, and the remainder in the fortress-palace of the Montferrine princes, where Bellarion himself took up his quarters.

In Theodore's own closet, occupying the very chair in which Theodore had sat and so contemptuously received the unknown Bellarion on that day when the young student had first entered those august walls, Bellarion that night penned a letter to the Princess Valeria, wherein he gave her news of the day's events. That letter, of a calligraphy so perfect that it might be mistaken for a page from some monkish manuscript of those days, is one of the few fragments that have survived from the hand of this remarkable man who was adventurer, statesman, soldier, and humanist.

"Most honoured and most dear lady," he addresses her— *Riveritissima et Carissima Madonna.* The exordium is all that need concern us now.

EVER SINCE AT YOUR OWN INVITATION I entered your service that evening in your garden here at Casale, where today I have again wandered reviving memories that are of the fairest in my life, that service has been my constant study. I have pursued it, by tortuous ways and by many actions appearing to have no bearing upon it, unsuspected by you when not actually mistrusted by you. That your mistrust has wounded me oftentimes and deeply, would have weighed lightly with me had I not perceived that by mistrusting you were deprived of that consolation and hope which you would have found in trusting. The facts afforded ever a justification of your mistrust. This I recognised; and that facts are stubborn things, not easily destroyed by words. Therefore I did not vainly wear myself in any endeavour to destroy them, but toiled on, so that, in the ultimate achievement of your selfless aims for your brother, the Marquis, I might prove to you without the need of words the true impulse of my every action in these past five years. The fame that came to me as a condottiero, the honours I won, and the increase of power they brought me I have never regarded as anything but weapons to be employed in this your service, as means to the achievement of your ends. But for that service accepted in this garden, my life would have been vastly different from all that it has been. No burden heavier than a scholar's would have been mine, and today I might well be back with the brethren at Cigliano, an obscure member of their great brotherhood. To serve you, I have employed trickery and double-dealing until men have dubbed me a rogue, and some besides yourself have come to mistrust me, and once I went the length of doing murder. But I take no shame in any of these things, nor, most dear lady, need you take shame in that your service should have entailed them. The murder I did was the execution of a rogue; the conspiracy I scattered was one that would have made a net in which to take you; the deceits I have put upon the Marquis Theodore, chiefly when I made him serve my dear Lord Facino's turn and seduced him into occupying Vercelli, so as subsequently to afford the Duke of Milan a sound reason for moving against him, were deceits employed against a deceiver, whom it would be idle to combat in honest fashion. In his eyes more than any other's—for he is not the only victim of the duplicity I have used to place you ultimately where you should be— I am a double-dealing Judas. And it is said of me, too, that in the field as in the council, I prevail by subterfuge and never by straightforward blows. But my conscience remains tranquil. It is not what a man does or says that counts; but what a man intends. I have embraced as a part of my guiding philosophy that teaching of Plato's which discriminates between the lie on the lips and the lie in the heart. On my lips and in my actions lies have been employed. I confess it frankly. But in my heart no lie has ever been. If I have employed at times dishonest means, at least the purpose for which they have been employed has been unfalteringly, unswervingly honest, and one in the final achievement of which there can be only pride and a sense of duty done.

To this if you believe it—and the facts will presently constrain you to do so, unless my fortune in the field should presently desert me—I need add no details of the many steps in your service. By the light of faith in me from what is written and what is presently to do, you will now read aright those details for yourself.

We touch now the goal whither all these efforts have been addressed.

Upon this follows his concise account of the events from the moment of his escape from Quinto, and upon that an injunction to her to come at once with her brother to Casale, depending upon the protection of his arm and the loyalty of a people which only awaited the sight of its rightful Prince to be increased to enthusiasm and active support.

That letter was despatched next day to Quinto, but it did not reach her until almost a week later between Alessandria and Casale.

Meanwhile early on the morrow the city was thrown into alarm by the approach of a strong body of horse. This was Ugolino da Tenda's condotta, and Ugolino himself rode in with a trumpeter to make renewed submission to the Lord Bellarion, and to give him news of what had happened in Quinto upon the coming of Barbaresco.

Bellarion racked him with questions, as to what was said, particularly as to what the Princess said and how she looked, and what passed between her and Carmagnola. And when all was done, far from the stern reproaches Ugolino had been expecting he found himself embraced by a Bellarion more joyous than he had ever yet known that sardonic soldier.

That gaiety of Bellarion's was observed by all in the days that followed. He was a man transformed. He displayed the light-heartedness of a boy, and moved about the many tasks claiming his attention with a song on his lips, a ready laugh upon the slightest occasion, and a sparkle in his great eyes that all had hitherto known so sombre.

And this notwithstanding that these were busy and even anxious days of preparation for the final trial of strength. He rode abroad during the day with two or three of his officers, one of whom was always Stoffel, surveying the ground of the peninsula

that lies between Sesia and Po to the north of Casale, and at night he would labour over maps which he was preparing from his daily notes. Meanwhile he kept himself day by day informed, by means of a line of scouts which he had thrown out, of what was happening at Vercelli.

With that clear prescience, which in all ages has been the gift of all great soldiers, he was able not merely to opine but quite definitely to state the course of action that Theodore would pursue. Because of this, on the Wednesday of that week, he moved Ugolino da Tenda and his condotta out of Casale, and transferred them bag and baggage—by night so that the movement might not be detected and reported to the enemy—to the woods about Trino, where they were ordered to encamp and to lie close until required.

On the morning of Friday arrived at last in Casale the Marquis Gian Giacomo and his sister, escorted by the band of Montferrine exiles under Barbaresco and Casella, and the people turned out to welcome not only the Princes, but in many cases their own relatives and friends. Bellarion, with his captains and a guard of honour of fifty lances, received the Princes at the Lombard Gate, and escorted them to the palace where their apartments had been prepared.

The acclamations of the people lining the streets brought tears to the eyes of the Princess and a flush to the cheeks of her brother, and there were tears in her eyes when she sought Bellarion in his room to abase herself in the admission of her grievous misjudgment and to sue pardon for it.

"Your letter, sir," she told him, "touched me more deeply than anything I can remember in all my life. Think me a fool if you must for what is past, but not an ingrate. My brother shall prove our gratitude so soon as ever it lies within his power."

"Madonna, I ask no proofs of it, nor need them. To serve you has not been a means, but an end, as you shall see."

"That vision at least does not lie in the future. I see now, and very clearly."

He smiled, a little wistfully, as he bowed to kiss her hand.

"You shall see more clearly still," he promised her.

That colloquy went no further. Stoffel broke in upon them to announce that his scouts had come galloping in from Vercelli with the news that the Lord Theodore had made a sally in force, shattering a way through Carmagnola's besiegers, and that he was advancing on Casale with a well-equipped army computed to be between four and five thousand strong.

The news had already spread about the city, and was causing amongst the people the gravest apprehension and unrest. The prospect of a siege and of the subsequent vengeance of the Lord Theodore upon the city for having harboured his enemies filled them with dread.

"Send out trumpeters," Bellarion ordered, "and let it be proclaimed in every quarter that there will be no siege, and that the army is marching out at once to meet the Marquis Theodore beyond the Po."

Chapter XIV

The Vanquished

Theodore's sally from Vercelli had been made at daybreak on that Friday morning. It had been shrewdly planned, for Theodore was no bungler, and, before he had brought more than half his men into action, Carmagnola, startled by the suddenness of the blow that fell upon him, was routed and in flight.

After that, this being no more than the preliminary of the task before him, Theodore marched out every man of his following to go against Bellarion at Casale. Thus, by that ancient plan of attacking a vital point that had been left undefended, had Bellarion succeeded in drawing his enemy from a point of less importance in which he was almost impregnably entrenched. Theodore had perceived, as Bellarion had calculated that he would, that it could serve little purpose for him to hold an outpost like Vercelli if in the meantime the whole of his dominions were to

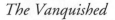

be wrenched from his grasp.

No sooner was he gone, however, than Carmagnola, informed of his departure, rallied his broken troops, and with drums beating, trumpets blaring, and flags flying, marched like a conqueror into the now undefended city of Vercelli. For the resistance it had made, he subjected it to a cruel sack, giving his men unbounded licence, and that same evening he wrote to Duke Filippo Maria in the following terms:

MOST POTENT DUKE AND MY GOOD LORD,—It is my joyous task to give your highness tidings that, informed of the reduction in our numbers resulting from the defection of the Prince of Valsassina and several other captains acting in concert with him, the Lord Theodore of Montferrat, greatly presumptuous, did today issue from Vercelli for wager of battle against us. A vigorous action was fought in the neighbourhood of Quinto, in which despite our inferior numbers we put the Marquis to flight. Lacking numbers sufficient to engage in pursuit, particularly as this would have led us into Monferrine territory, and since the reoccupation of Vercelli and its restoration to your duchy was the task with which your highness entrusted us, I marched into the city at once, and I now hold it in the name of your exalted potency. By this complete and speedy victory I hope to merit the approbation of your highness.

Meanwhile Theodore's march on Casale had anything but the aspect of a flight. The great siege train he dragged along with him over the sodden and too-yielding ground of that moist plain delayed his progress to such an extent that it was not until late on that November afternoon when he reached Villanova, here to receive news from his scouts that a considerable army, said to be commanded by the Prince of Valsassina, was circling northward from Terranova.

The news was unexpected and brought with it some alarm. He had gone confidently and rather carelessly forward fully expecting to find the enemy shut up in Casale. Hence all the ponderous siege train which had so hampered his progress. That Bellarion, forsaking the advantage of Casale's stout walls, should come out to meet him and engage him in the open was something beyond his dreams, and but for the unexpectedness of it, he would have rejoiced in such a decision on the part of his redoubtable opponent.

It was in that unexpectedness, as usual, that lay Bellarion's advantage. Theodore, compelled now to act in haste, not knowing at what moment the enemy might be upon him, made dispositions to which it was impossible to give that thought which the importance of the issues demanded. The first of these was to order the men, who were preparing to encamp for the night, to be up again and to push on and out of this village before they found themselves hemmed into it. That circling movement reported suggested this danger to Theodore.

They came out in rather straggling order to be marshalled even as they marched. Theodore's aim, and it was shrewd enough, was to reach the broad causeway of solid land between Corno and Popolo, where marshlands on either side would secure his flanks and compel the enemy to engage him on a narrow front. What was to follow he had not yet had time to consider. But if he could reach that objective, he would be secure for the present,

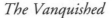

and he could rest his men in the two hamlets on the marshes.

But a mile beyond Villanova, Bellarion was upon his left flank and rear. He had little warning of it before the enemy was charging him. But it was warning enough. He threw out his line in a crescent formation, using his infantry in a manner which merited Bellarion's entire approval, and obviously intent upon fighting a rearguard battle whilst bringing his army to the coveted position.

But the infantry were not equal to their commander, and they were insufficiently trained in these tactics. Some horses were piked, but almost every horse piked meant an opening in the human wall that opposed the charge, and through these openings Giasone Trotta's heavy riders broke in, swinging their ponderous maces. From a rearguard action on Theodore's part, the thing grew rapidly to the proportions of a general engagement, and for this Theodore could not have been placed worse than he was with his left, now that he had swung about, upon the quaking boglands of Dalmazzo and his back to the broad waters of the Po. He swung his troops farther round, so as to bring his rear upon the only possible line of retreat, which was that broad firm land between Corno and Popolo. At last his skilful manœuvres achieved the desired result, and then, very gradually, fighting every inch of the ground, he began to fall back. At every yard now the front must grow narrower, and unless Bellarion's captains were very sure of their ground, some of them would presently be in trouble in the bogs on either side. If this did not happen, they would soon find it impossible, save at great cost and without perceptible progress, to continue the engagement, and with night approaching they would be constrained to draw off. Theodore smiled darkly to himself in satisfaction, and took heart, well pleased with his clever tactics by which he had extricated himself from a dangerous situation. He had won a breathing space that should enable him to marshal his men so as to deal with this rash enemy who came to seek him in the open.

And then suddenly, a quarter-mile away, from the direction of Corno, towards which they were so steadily falling back, came a pounding of hooves that swelled swiftly into a noise of thunder, and, before any measures could be taken to meet this new menace, Ugolino da Tenda's horse was upon Theodore's rear.

Ugolino had handled his condotta well, and strictly in accordance with his orders from Bellarion. From Balzola, whither he had been moved at noon so as to be in readiness, he had made a leisurely and cautious advance, filing his horse along the very edge of the bogland so that their hooves should give no warning of their approach. Thus until he had won within striking distance. And the blow he now struck, heavy and unexpected, crumpled up Theodore's rear, clove through, driving his men right and left to sink to their waists in the marshes, and scattered such fear and confusion in those ahead that their formation went to pieces, and gaped to Bellarion's renewed frontal attacks.

Less than three hours that engagement lasted, and of all those who had taken the field with Theodore, saving perhaps a thousand who fled helter-skelter towards Trino after Ugolino's passage, there was not a survivor who had not yielded. Stripped of their arms and deprived of their horses, they were turned adrift, to go whithersoever they listed so long as it was outside of Montferrat territory. The maimed and wounded of Theodore's army were conveyed by their fellows into the villages of Villanova,

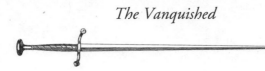

Terranova, and Grassi.

It was towards the third hour of that November night when the triumphant army, returning from that stricken field, reëntered Casale, lighted by the bonfires that blazed in the streets, whilst the bells of Liutprand's Cathedral crashed out their peals of victory. Deliriously did the populace acclaim Bellarion, Prince of Valsassina, in its enormous relief at being saved the hardships of a siege and delivered from the possible vengeance of Theodore for having opened its gates to Theodore's enemies.

Theodore, on foot, marched proudly at the head of a little band of captives of rank, who had been retained by their captors for the sake of the ransoms they could pay. The jostling, pushing crowd hooted and execrated and mocked him in his hour of humiliation. White-faced, his head held high, he passed on apparently unmoved by that expression of human baseness, knowing in his heart that, if he had proved master, the acclamations now raised for his conqueror would have been raised for him by the very lips that now execrated him.

He was conducted to the palace, to the very room whence for so many years he had ruled the State of Montferrat, and there he found his nephew and niece awaiting him when he was brought in between Ugolino da Tenda and Giasone Trotta.

Bareheaded, stripped of his armour, his tall figure bowed, he stood like a criminal before them whilst they remained seated on either side of the writing-table that once had been his own. From the seat whence he had dispensed justice was justice now to be dispensed to him by his nephew.

"You know your offence, my lord," Gian Giacomo greeted him; a cold, dignified, and virile Gian Giacomo, in whom it was

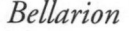

hardly possible to recognise the boy whom he had sought to ruin in body and in soul. "You know how you have been false to the trust reposed in you by my father, to whom God give peace. Have you anything to say in extenuation?"

He parted his lips, then stood there opening and closing his hands before he could sufficiently control himself to answer.

"In the hour of defeat, what can I do but cast myself upon your mercy?"

"Are we to pity you in defeat? Are we to forget in what you have been defeated?"

"I ask not that. I am in your hands, a captive, helpless. I do not claim mercy. I may not deserve it. I hope for it. That is all."

They considered him, and found him a broken man, indeed.

"It is not for me to judge you," said Gian Giacomo, "and I am glad to be relieved of that responsibility. For though you may have forgotten that I am of your blood, I cannot forget that you are of mine. Where is his highness of Valsassina?"

Theodore fell back a pace. "Will you set me at the mercy of that dastard?"

The Princess Valeria looked at him coldly. "He has won many titles since the day when to fight a villainy he pretended to become your spy. But the title you have just conferred upon him, coming from your lips, is the highest he has yet received. To be a dastard in the sight of a dastard is to be honourable in the sight of all upright men."

Theodore's white face writhed into a smile of malice. But he answered nothing in the little pause that followed before the door opened upon Bellarion.

He came in supported by two of his Swiss, and closely fol-

lowed by Stoffel. His armour had been removed, and the right sleeve of his leather haqueton, as of the silken tunic and shirt beneath, had been ripped up, and now hung empty at his side, whilst his breast bulged where his arm was strapped to his body. He was very pale and obviously weak and in pain.

Valeria came to her feet at sight of him thus, and her face was whiter than his own.

"You are wounded, my lord!"

He smiled, rather whimsically. "It sometimes happens when men go to battle. But I think my Lord Theodore here has taken the deeper hurt."

Stoffel pushed forward a chair, and the Swiss carefully lowered Bellarion to it. He sighed in relief, and leaned forward so as to avoid contact with the back.

"One of your knights, my lord, broke my shoulder in the last charge."

"I would he had broken your neck."

"That was the intention." Bellarion's pale lips smiled. "But I am known as Bellarion the Fortunate."

"Just now my lord had another name for you," said Valeria, and Bellarion, observing the set of her lips and the scorn in her glance as it flickered over Theodore, marvelled at the power of hate in one naturally so gracious. He had had a taste of it, himself, he remembered, and perhaps she was but passing on to Theodore what rightly had belonged to him throughout. "He is a rash man," she continued, "who will not trouble to conciliate the arbiter of his fate. My Lord Theodore has lost his guile, I think, together with the rest."

"Aye," said Bellarion, "we have stripped him of all save his

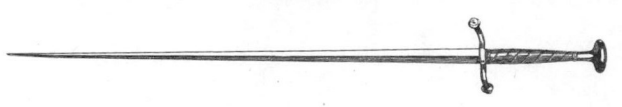

life. Even his mask of benignity is gone."

"You are noble!" said Theodore. "You gird at a captive! Am I to remain here to be mocked?"

"Not for me, faith," Bellarion answered him. "I have never contemplated you with any pleasure. Take him away, Ugolino. Place him securely under guard. He shall have judgment to-morrow."

"Dog!" said Theodore with venom, as he drew himself up to depart.

"That's my device, as yours is the stag. Appropriate, all things considered. I had you in my mind when I adopted it."

"I am punished for my weakness," said Theodore. "I should have left Justice to wring your neck when you were its prisoner here in Casale."

"I'll repay the debt," Bellarion answered him. "Your own neck shall remain unwrung so that you withdraw to your principality of Genoa and abide there. More of that tomorrow."

Peremptorily he waved him away and Ugolino hustled him out. As the door closed again, Bellarion, relaxing the reins of his will, sank forward in a swoon.

Chapter XV

The Last Fight

When he recovered, he was lying on his sound side on a couch under the window, across which the curtains of painted and gilded leather had been drawn.

An elderly, bearded man in black was observing him, and someone whom he could not see was bathing his brow with a cool aromatic liquid. As he fetched a sigh that filled his lungs and quickened his senses into full consciousness, the man smiled.

"There! It will be well with him now. But he should be put to bed."

"It shall be done," said the woman who was bathing his brow, and her voice, soft and subdued, was the voice of the Princess Valeria. "His servants will be below by now. Send them to me as you go."

The man bowed and went out. Slowly Bellarion turned his

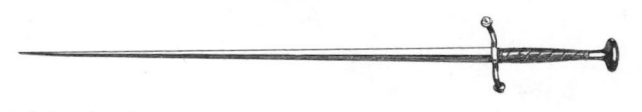

head, and looked up in wonder at the Princess with whom he was now alone. Her eyes, more liquid than their wont, smiled wistfully down upon him.

"Madonna!" he exclaimed. "Do you serve me as a handmaid? That is not . . ."

"You are thinking it an insufficient return for your service to me. But you must give me time, sir, this is only a beginning."

"I am not thinking that at all."

"Then you are not thinking as you should. You are weak. Your wits work slowly. Else you might remember that for five years, in which you have been my loyal, noble, unswerving friend, I, immured in my stupidity, have been your enemy."

"Ah!" he smiled. "I knew I should convince you in the end. Such knowledge gives us patience. A man may contain his soul for anything that is assured. It is the doubtful only that makes him fret and fume."

"And you never doubted?" she asked him, wondering.

"I am too sure of myself," he answered.

"And God knows you have cause to be, more cause than any man of whom ever I heard tell. Do you know, Lord Prince, that in these five years there is no evil I have not believed of you? I even deemed you a coward, on the word of that vain boaster Carmagnola."

"He was none so wrong, by his own lights. I am not a fighter of his pattern. I have ever been careful of myself."

"Your condition now proves that."

"Oh, this, today . . . That was different. Too much depended on the issue. It was the last throw. I had to take a hand, much though I dislike a rough-and-tumble. So that we won through, it

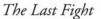

would not much have mattered if the vamplate of that fellow's lance had brought up against my throat. There are no more fights for me, so what matter if I left my life in the last one?"

"The last one, Lord Prince!"

"And that is not my title anymore. I am a prince no longer. I leave the rank behind with all the other vanities of the world."

"You leave it behind?" She found him obscure.

"When I go back to Cigliano, which will be as soon as I can move."

"What do you go to do at Cigliano?"

"What? Why, what the other brethren do. *Pax multa in cella.* The old abbot was right. There is yonder a peace for which I am craving now that my one task here is safely ended. In the world there is nothing for me."

"Nothing!" She was amazed. "And in five years you have won so much!"

"Nothing that I covet," he answered gently. "It is all vanity, all madness, greed, and bloodlust. I was not made for worldliness, and but for you I should never have known it. Now I have done."

"And your dominions, Gavi and Valsassina?"

"I'll bestow them upon you, madonna, if you will deign to accept a parting gift from these hands."

There was a long pause. She had drawn back a little. He could not see her face. "You have the fever, I think," she said presently in an odd voice. "It is your hurt."

He sighed. "Aye, you would think so. It is difficult for one reared in the world to understand that a man's eyes should remain undazzled by its glitter. Yet, believe me, I leave it with but one regret."

"And that?" The question came breathlessly upon a whisper.

"That the purpose for which I entered it remains unfulfilled. That I have learnt no Greek."

Again there was a pause. Then she moved forward, rustling a little, and came directly into his line of vision.

"I hear your servants, I think. I will leave you now."

"I thank you, madonna. God be with you."

But she did not go. She stood there between himself and the fireplace, slight and straight as on the first evening when he had seen her in her garden. She was dressed in a close-fitting gown of cloth of silver. He observed in particular now the tight sleeves which descended to the knuckles of her slim, tapering hands, and remembered that just such sleeves had she worn when first his eyes beheld her. Over this gown she wore a loose houppelande of sapphire velvet, reversed at throat and wide gaping sleeves with ermine. And there were sapphires in the silver caul that confined her abundant red-gold hair.

"Aye," he said wistfully, dreamily, "it was just so you looked, and just so will I remember you as long as I remember anything. It is good to have served you, lady mine. It has made me glorious in my own eyes."

"You have made yourself glorious, Lord Prince, in the eyes of all."

"What do they matter?"

Slowly she came back to him. She was very pale and a little frown was puckering her fine brows. Very wistful, and mysterious as deep pools, were those dark eyes of hers. She came back, drawn by the words he had used, and more than the words, by something odd in his gently musing tone.

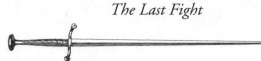

"Do I matter nothing, Bellarion?"

He smiled with an infinite sadness. "Must you ask that now? Does not the whole of my life in the world give you the answer, that never woman mattered more to a man? I have known no service but yours. And I have served you—*per fas et nefas.*"

She stood above him, and her lips quivered. What she said when at last she spoke had no apparent bearing upon the subject.

"I am wearing your colours, Bellarion."

Surprise flickered in his eyes, as they sought confirmation of her statement in the azure and argent of her wear.

"And I did not remark the chance," he cried.

"Not chance. It is design."

"It was sweetly and generously courteous so to honour me."

"It was not only to honour you that I assumed these colours. Have they no message for you, Bellarion?"

"Message?" For the first time in their acquaintance she saw fear in his bold eyes.

"Clearly they have not; no message that you look for. You have said that you covet nothing in this world."

"Nothing within my reach. To covet things beyond it is to taste the full bitterness of life."

"Is there anything in the world that is not within your reach, Bellarion?"

He looked at her as she smiled down upon him through her tears. He caught his breath gaspingly. With his sound left hand he clutched her left which hung at the level of his head.

"I am mad, of course," he choked.

"Not mad, Bellarion. Only stupid. Do you still covet nothing?"

"Aye, one thing!" His face glowed. "One thing that would

change into a living glory the tinsel glitter of the world, one thing that would make life . . . O God! What am I saying?"

"Why do you break off, Bellarion?"

"I am afraid!"

"Of me? Is there anything I could deny you, who have given all to serve me? Must I in return offer you all I have? Can you claim nothing for yourself?"

"Valeria!"

She stooped to kiss his lips. "My very hate of you in all these years was love dissembled. Because my spirit leapt to yours, almost from that first evening in the garden there, did it so wound and torture me to discover baseness in you. I should have trusted my own heart, rather than my erring senses, Bellarion. You warned me early that I am not good at inference. I have suffered as those suffer who are in rebellion against themselves."

He pondered her, very pale and sorrowful. "Yes," he said slowly, "I have the fever, as you said awhile ago. It must be that."

THE END

About the Author

RAFAEL SABATINI (1875-1950) was born in central Italy to an Italian father and an English mother. His birthplace, the medieval walled town of Jesi, was one of decaying palaces and ancient churches; it was this, perhaps, that inspired his lifelong passion for history. He studied in Switzerland and Portugal and traveled widely, settling in England as a young man. He mastered six languages, though he chose to write exclusively in English.

Sabatini's fictions, although not well-received by critics, proved immensely popular, and several of them were later made into films. Despite Sabatini's love of history, he had no more faith in the accuracy of historians than most historians had faith in the accuracy of *his* work. He cited such legends as William Tell, the Man in the Iron Mask, and some of the more outrageous claims made against the Borgias as examples of stories that had crept into history through bias and error.

In addition to *Bellarion, Scaramouche* and *Captain Blood*, all available in COMMON READER EDITIONS, Sabatini wrote over forty volumes of fiction (both novels and short stories) and non-fiction.